THEIRS TO PROTECT

A Marriage Raffle Novel

STASIA BLACK

AUTHOR'S NOTE

Full disclosure, I don't like post-apocalyptic and dystopian stories. They're usually depressing and so dark and *bleh*. There's enough depressing stuff in the world, ya know?! So when this story idea and these characters came to me, I was like, but! I don't like post-apocalyptic stories! I can't write one!

But these five guys came to me so *real* in my head. They were funny and tragic and beautiful and just...*so real*. They wouldn't leave me be. And I thought, well, what if I write a story where I cut out all the stuff I usually hate about post-apocalyptic stories? If I don't focus on the doom and gloom but instead I zoom in on the stuff I really care about —the relationships and family and love and, of course, let's not forget, the steamy bits, lol ;)

So that's what I did. And this book flew out in what's been the most thrilling creative experience of my entire life. All my ARC readers know, I sent them a 4am email squeeing when I got done with it and sent it off to them, lol. I was literally dancing around my house this morning, I'm so excited about this one (my 13yr old son was just giving me side-eye like, gah, Mom's a freak, LOL). Anyway, I love these guys *so* hard. Now I give them to you :)

In the not too distant future, a genetically engineered virus is released by an eco-terrorist in major metropolitan areas all over the globe. Within five years, almost 90% of the world's female population is decimated.

In an attempt to stop the spread of the virus and quarantine those left, a nuclear war was triggered. It's still unclear who began attacking who, but bombs were dropped on all major US cities, coordinated with massive EMP attacks.

These catastrophes and the end of life as people knew it were collectively known as *The Fall*.

MAP OF THE NEW REPUBLIC OF TEXAS

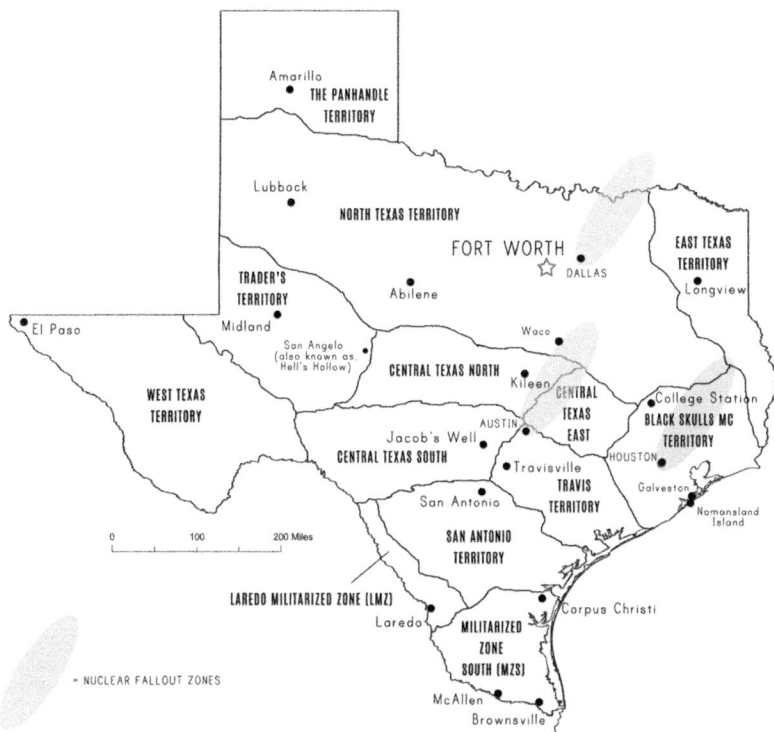

Amarillo
THE PANHANDLE
TERRITORY

Lubbock

NORTH TEXAS TERRITORY

FORT WORTH
☆
DALLAS

EAST TEXAS
TERRITORY

Longview

TRADER'S
TERRITORY

Abilene

El Paso

Midland

San Angelo
(also known as
Hell's Hollow)

Waco

CENTRAL TEXAS NORTH

Kileen

WEST TEXAS
TERRITORY

Jacob's Well

CENTRAL TEXAS SOUTH

AUSTIN

CENTRAL
TEXAS
EAST

College Station

BLACK SKULLS MC
TERRITORY

HOUSTON

Travisville

TRAVIS
TERRITORY

Galveston

San Antonio

Nomansland
Island

SAN ANTONIO
TERRITORY

0   100   200 Miles

LAREDO MILITARIZED ZONE (LMZ)

Laredo

MILITARIZED
ZONE
SOUTH (MZS)

Corpus Christi

= NUCLEAR FALLOUT ZONES

McAllen

Brownsville

PROLOGUE

AUDREY

"And do you, Audrey Dawson, accept the five men before you as your wedded husbands, for as long as you all shall live?"

Audrey's entire body shook as she looked around the front of the church at the men who had been strangers only three weeks before. She didn't know them much better now. God, was she really going through with this?

Yes. You already decided you would. No turning back now.

So she stood up straight and forced her voice not to waver as she said, "I do."

Nix, the biggest and scariest of all of them, leaned forward and kissed her knuckles before sliding a delicate gold band onto her fourth finger.

Oh God oh God oh God.

"Clan Hale is born today," the pastor announced triumphantly. "Six are united as one. What has been joined today let no man tear asunder!"

The crowd cheered and Audrey looked at the little church, packed mostly with men, women dotting the crowd only here and there.

"You may now kiss your bride."

Audrey felt her eyes pop wide open as she looked between her new husbands. Would they line up or something? Was this more of a ceremonial thing, like just a quick peck, or—

Clark, the handsomest of the five, stepped up, wrapped one arm around her waist and dug his other hand in the back of her hair.

And then he kissed the living daylights out of her.

His tongue wasn't forceful. It was teasing. Coaxing even. She gasped in surprise when he grabbed her and he'd used the opportunity to sneak his tongue in her mouth. It wasn't thrusting, though.

No, he teased just the very tip of it against hers in a way that had her gasping in shock. Because holy *crap*. She'd never known that her tongue was a direct conduit to— to— Down *there*.

By the time Clark pulled back, he had to steady her on her feet. He'd literally kissed her wobbly. She was gasping for breath and immediately lifted her hand to her mouth, blinking in confusion.

Well. That answered her question about whether the kiss was ceremonial or not.

Next stepped up husband number two, Graham. His cheeks were pink and his gaze was slightly off to the left, like usual, not quite meeting her gaze. Unlike Clark, he just dropped a quick kiss to her lips before pulling back. Okay, good. She didn't think her heart could take another Clark style kiss at the moment.

Then came Danny. Sweet, teddy bear Danny. Her eyes widened as he approached, though. His face was full of excitement, but he was coming at her with his tongue already half out of his mouth. Like a hungry dog panting for a meal. She was about to pull back in alarm but Clark grabbed Danny's arm and pulled him away before he could reach her. "Nope."

"Wait, what?" Danny exclaimed. "You can't do that. It's not official till I kiss her!"

"Not until I've sat you down and explained a little more bit about the birds and the bees, my boy. And how the hell to kiss a woman."

"But—" Danny whined.

"It's all right," Audrey laughed nervously. Okay, so she wasn't the only one who had no idea what the hell she was doing. She stepped forward impulsively and landed a quick peck on Danny's lips. When she pulled back he looked totally dumbstruck. Like she'd just revealed she'd cured him of an incurable disease, not given him a brief little peck on the lips.

Then was Mateo. He looked as pale and scared as Audrey felt and her heart melted. Mateo had been special from the beginning. Where Nix was constantly demanding, Mateo only wanted to give. To serve. To see to her every comfort and desire.

She felt a kinship with him she couldn't explain. Maybe because she could tell he'd experienced loss too. Not in the same way, perhaps, but he'd suffered. Deeply.

And in spite of her circumstances, Audrey couldn't help but want to give back to him. So when he stepped up to her, body trembling even more than hers had been throughout the wedding ceremony, she was the one who reached for him.

She lifted her head and pressed her lips to his. Tentatively at first. But then she remembered the way Clark had moved his tongue and so she experimented. She ran her tongue along the seam of his lips and he inhaled sharply. Feeling a little bolder, she cupped his face and deepened the kiss.

And it was sweet. Very sweet. Mateo's body melted against hers. He pulled her closer and she could feel his racing heartbeat through his chest. His tongue moved and started to dance with hers and it wasn't long before again, she was breathless and dizzy with the sensations being awakened in her body.

When she finally pulled away, the warmth pulsing out from her center was so shocking, for a moment she just stood there, frozen.

Not for long though, because Nix was apparently impatient for his turn.

He grasped her around her waist and all but dragged her up and into him. And his lips weren't gentle or teasing or coaxing.

They were demanding.

Devouring.

She gasped for air and it was his breath she was breathing in. He seemed determined to imprint his lips on hers.

Oh— *oh*—

He sucked her tongue into his mouth and it—

Her entire body shuddered against him. Oh God, was it possible to have an orgasm just from a *kiss*?

How was he doing that— She didn't even like him, so why was she — Oh, oh *God*—

She groaned into his mouth and he kissed her even deeper, though she wouldn't have thought that was possible. He swallowed her gasp, his hard body pressing into her soft one. He reached up and dug his fingers into her hair, ignoring the pins and cradling the back of her head so he could kiss her even more deeply still.

And she abandoned herself to it. She didn't mean to. God knew she didn't mean to. But he was— It was—

When he finally dragged his mouth away, she barely stopped herself from whimpering in disappointment.

It took her several moments to realize there were whistles and catcalls coming from all around them.

Because they were standing at the front of a church.

Oh God.

Embarrassment hit hot and blinding.

How had she lost control of herself so completely? She felt her cheeks flame.

"Time to take our wife home," Nix declared.

Then Nix was all but dragging her out the back of the church, the rest of her husbands—oh God, her *husbands, plural*—following on their heels.

But apparently she wasn't moving fast enough for Nix's liking because the next thing she knew, he'd hoisted her up and over his shoulder like he was a damn caveman and she was his most recent kill.

"Nix!" she called out, smacking at his back. It wasn't her fault she couldn't walk at his breakneck speed. Unless she literally wanted to break her neck. Whoever had invented high heels back before The Fall needed to die. Maybe with a high heel impaled in his neck. Those things were death traps. Why did women used to subject themselves to them?

On the other hand, maybe this was better. After several jarring steps, she closed her eyes and clung to Nix's back. Just go loose, go along with what the guys had planned.

She would not hyperventilate. She would not hyperventilate.

So she was about to lose her virginity.

In a fivesome.

No big deal.

She just had to lay there. Right?

...

Who the fuck was she kidding?

It was a big deal. It was a huge, giant fucking deal. But she'd told herself she was doing it tonight and it was a promise she meant to keep.

Before she knew it, and far before she was ready—because who was she kidding, she wasn't sure she'd ever be ready for this—she was being deposited on the bed.

Five men.

Her.

And one very large bed.

Apparently there wouldn't be any waiting to consummate this marriage.

CHAPTER ONE

AUDREY

Three Weeks Earlier

"Water!" Audrey yelled at her brother, Charlie. "See, I told you it would lead to water!" She threw off her backpack and ran the last few feet to the small stream of water trickling out from the rocks.

They'd been trekking uphill for what felt like hours, following a muddy culvert. And finally, *finally*, they'd found its source.

And God was she thirsty. She hadn't had a drink in a day and a half and the Texas heat was punishing—but she still threw her exhausted hands up in the air and did an exuberant little dance.

Charlie rolled his eyes at her. Only two years older than her twenty-two, he liked to pretend he was sooooo superior. Didn't stop him from grabbing his tin cup from their pack and dropping to his knees unceremoniously in front of the rocks. He put his hand underneath the cup, licking the water off his fingers that didn't make it in.

As soon as the tiniest bit of water gathered in the bottom, he held it out to Audrey. "Drink."

She shook her head. "*You* drink." Her throat felt raw from being so dry but she croaked out anyway, "Saw you slip the last of your water in my flask yesterday. Don't need you always taking care of me. I do just fine."

"Less talking, more drinking, baby sis." He held out the cup to her again.

She crossed her arms and glared. "I can out-stubborn you any day," she rasped. "Remember the green beans?"

He rolled his eyes again but swigged the water from the cup.

She grinned, knowing they were both remembering what had become Dawson family legend—the time she'd once sat at the dinner table all weekend when she was seven because Dad said she couldn't leave the table until she ate her green beans.

So she sat. And sat. And slept with her head on the table. And sat some more until it was time to go to school on Monday.

She grinned at Charlie but he just shook his head as he refilled the cup. "Figured if I drank I'd get the water in you quicker." He handed it over once a small pool of water settled at the bottom. "Here you go, Miss Self-Sufficient."

She gave him a saccharine smile and, point made, she snatched the cup and swallowed every drop down. Before upturning the cup and all but licking it clean.

Cause *damn*, she was thirsty. If they hadn't found the spring, she'd been about to face plant into the mud and start sucking on it.

She and Charlie each took several more mouthfuls, exchanging the cup back and forth. Then he leaned back against a rock and shut his eyes.

He looked tired.

Bone tired.

And skinnier than when they'd left Uncle Dale's just a week ago.

They should have been to the coast by now. But just their luck, the motorcycle popped a tire only two hours into the journey. They'd been traveling at night because it was safer and must have run over some debris on the road. It had slashed the tire wall to shreds.

Audrey had wanted to walk back to Uncle Dale's. It was only forty miles back. But two *hundred* to get to the coast.

It would be so much safer for Charlie if they just went back. But Charlie wouldn't hear of it.

Uncle Dale made his choice, was all he'd say about it. So they'd kept going on foot.

"Dad was so pissed," Charlie chuckled.

"What?"

"About you and those damn green beans." Charlie shook his head, a tired smile still on his face. "I heard him and mom fighting." He lowered his voice to imitate Dad's, *"It's not about the green beans, Martha. It's about respect."*

Audrey huffed out a small laugh. "Na, it was mainly just the beans. I really hated them."

Then she looked out at the uninviting scrub brush, stumpy trees, and cacti that made up the landscape all around them.

Growing up, she remembered thinking the Texas Hill Country was beautiful. Now it just looked like a really tough place to take a two-hundred-mile walk.

"Pretty sure I'd kill for a plate of green beans now," she said, pulling off her hat and letting her long red hair free of its confines, something she rarely did. *"Literally.* It's the apocalypse, right? I bet someone's set up some gladiatorial combat somewhere—winner gets the plate of beans."

Ooo," she smacked Charlie's leg, "if they haven't, we could do it. Claim a high school football stadium. We wouldn't even have to do fight to the death. Just first blood. We'd make a fortune. All the beans we could eat and—"

"Aud—" Charlie cut her off.

"What?"

"Look at the cup."

Audrey glanced down at the cup Charlie had been holding to the rock. It was half full with water, more than either of them had had the patience to let fill yet.

He was smiling. The freckles across his nose had gotten darker than ever with all the sun they'd been getting and Audrey knew hers must be the same. They both had identical coloring, from freckles to their bright red-orange hair.

"Drink up so you can tell me more about this amazing new idea of yours. You know, how we'll be up to our eyeballs in beans."

She narrowed her eyes at him but took the cup. She drank *half* and handed him the rest. "Remember what I said about not taking care of me?"

He sighed, looking tired again. "It's not a bad thing that I want to look out for you, baby sis. You're precious cargo."

Her mouth tightened and she looked away. "Don't remind me."

"Hey," he said, reaching out and nudging her on the arm. "I didn't mean because of Xterminate."

Her whole body tightened at even hearing the name of the bioengineered genetic virus that had decimated almost ninety percent of the world's female population starting a decade ago.

"I mean because you're my sister," he went on. "It's sort of what big brothers do. We watch out for our annoying turd little sisters."

She let out a huff but didn't say anything back. She knew he felt that way. But when was he going to understand? She wasn't some precious vase he had to constantly worry about protecting. She wasn't just *cargo*.

She'd spent the last eight years in Uncle Dale's bunker learning and working out. She'd practiced martial arts with Uncle Dale, read all his field manuals about which indigenous Central Texas plants and berries were edible fifty times cover to cover, and become a true connoisseur of cooking canned foods over a Bunsen burner.

All so that when and if the day finally came that they had to leave the bunker, she wouldn't be some useless damsel in distress.

But here Charlie was, treating her just like Dad always did.

And look what that got Dad. A chill ran down her spine.

"I'm going to go scout a little," Charlie said after finishing the water in the cup. "You stay here and fill up our flasks."

"Be careful," she said, her throat suddenly tight. Shit, the last thing she needed to be doing right now was thinking about Dad.

"Always am." He flashed his dimpled smile as he stood and started toward the trees off to their left.

She took a deep breath and let it out. She started to rebraid her hair again to put it back up under the cap. She shouldn't have taken it down in the first place but the pins had been yanking and driving her crazy for hours.

Her boobs were wrapped too. With the cap on, she should look like Charlie—just a skinny redheaded guy, trying to make it in this brave new world.

She needed to focus on the positives. It was enough that they'd survived another day. And found water. She could sit here drinking swallowful by swallowful all damn *day*.

The thing was... no matter how much she thought she'd prepared, she hadn't had any idea how *hard* it would be on the outside.

She regretted ever whining about being bored in Uncle Dale's fallout shelter. *You don't know what you got till it's gone,* wasn't that the saying? Or a song? Something.

Well the grass was *not* greener on the other side of the fence... or ya know, outside the bunker.

"Never thought I'd miss those ugly ass concrete walls," she muttered, about to take another swallow of water. She finished braiding her hair. Now for the hair tie—

"Run!" Charlie's panicked shout split the air. "Audrey, run!"

Audrey spilled the cup of water as she jumped to her feet and spun around.

Just in time to see a giant, terrifying man covered in tattoos swinging a bat right at Charlie's head.

CHAPTER TWO

AUDREY

"No!" she screamed, hand out, as Charlie's body crumpled to the ground.

She froze with horror as Charlie's eyes went lifeless. Blood pooled on the ground by his head.

No. *No*, it couldn't be.

Charlie wasn't—

He couldn't be—

Just five minutes ago they'd been talking and joking and... This was all a bad dream. A really, really bad dream.

Wake up. Wake *up*.

She slapped herself in the face but the scene in front of her didn't change.

"Well look what we have here."

Two other men stepped out from behind the monster who'd killed her brother.

Killed.

Oh God. Charlie was dead. He was *dead*.

She bent over and threw up.

"Looks like we got ourselves another filly for the stables, boss."

Audrey's head jerked up at that. Oh God. This was *real*. Charlie was dead and these men wanted to—

She shut the thought off before she could finish it. Her eyes flicked down. Shit. The backpack was more than five feet away. She'd dropped it in her excitement over finding the stream.

Her gun was in the backpack.

And if they could best Charlie, what hope in hell did she have? There were three of them. And they were *massive*.

"I call dibs," said the greasy man to the left of Charlie's murderer.

"Fuck you do," said the man on his other side. "You know boss always likes to break 'em in."

"So we just take turns fuckin' her ass before we bring her back," said the giant in the middle, cracking his knuckles in anticipation. "We'll just say we found her that way."

Well that cleared up that decision.

No way she was going down without a goddamned fight. The gun was in the front pocket of the backpack. She didn't even have to unzip anything. Just reach inside.

One. Two—

She dove for it, slamming hard into the ground and snatching the gun out before the three bastards even realized what she was doing.

But the element of surprise didn't last long. The toadie on the left lunged for her. She barely managed to get the safety off and cock the gun before he landed right on top of her.

Bang.

She'd pulled the trigger without even fully thinking through what she was doing. The guy immediately started screaming his head off and pulling a bloody stump to his chest.

Shit, shit! She just blew half his hand off!

She scrambled backwards and got to her feet, swinging her gun towards the other men.

"Back!" she screamed, her whole body shaking. "Get back or I'll shoot you too!"

Except shit, they had their guns trained on her. One was a rifle—a fancy one, like a sniper rifle—the other a machine gun.

She was going to die.

Charlie was dead and now she was going to die and it was all her fault.

If not for her, Charlie could have stayed at Uncle Dale's and been safe.

"Drop the gun, girlie," said the giant man.

"Never," she screamed. "You think you're real men? Murdering a man in cold blood by attacking him from behind and then kidnapping a girl? You're cowards." She spit on the ground.

"You just gonna let her sit here and talk to us like—"

The big man ignored his comrade and suddenly looked down the sight of his rifle right at her.

Oh God. Here it was. The end of everything. All those years in the bunker preparing. Preparing for what? One week and she'd gotten both her and her brother killed. Oh God.

Her eyes squeezed shut and her whole body went tense as she waited for it. To die. Right now. Any second—

Her gun exploded out of her hand. She screamed and looked down. It took her a second to realize what had happened—the big man had shot the gun out of her hand, only making her hand smart.

Because they wanted her alive. How had she forgotten, even for a second?

So we just take turns fuckin' her ass.

She turned and ran.

The big, ugly man's laugh echoed behind her. "I haven't had good hunting in a while, little rabbit. Just know, I consider this foreplay."

She jumped over a log and kept sprinting. She was heading uphill. Which was stupid. It took more effort and she had no clue where she was going. At least downhill, the way they'd come, she had a *little* more idea of the landscape.

But she was a good runner, she knew that. And while it wasn't exactly the same, she could go for hours on Uncle Dale's mechanical stationary bike in the bunker on its hardest setting.

So in *theory*, she should be able to keep running for a good long while.

Problem was, this was the real world. And out here there were things like pesky logs to get in her way. And bushes and thorny green-briers and cacti— Jesus, did every plant in Texas have to have burs or thorns attached to it? Each step she took her jeans and flannel shirt were getting torn at by the damn wildlife.

Which was nothing compared to what the two men crashing through the woods behind her wanted to do to her.

But goddammit, if she didn't get free of these bushes, she was never going to get anywhere. She ripped her arm away from the thorn bush that had hold of her, tearing her sleeve off and heading toward an area that looked clearer.

Only to realize once she ran out into an open field that—*duh*, it was a fucking *open field* and she'd just made herself a sitting duck.

The man with the rifle was obviously a crack shot. How stupid could she get? Making decisions under this kind of pressure was screwing with her.

Charlie was usually the one who— She didn't— She couldn't—

"*Shit!*" she whispered frantically, spinning around and trying to judge which was the best way to go before realizing she was only wasting more time.

There. The field was narrowest to her left. She started sprinting in that direction. If she could just make it to the woods on the other side, then maybe she could find a place to hide, or just keep one step ahead of—

The ground exploded beside her.

"Shit!" she screamed. Bastard was shooting at her. Guess he'd gotten tired of playing chase.

Cover. She needed cover. She looked frantically around for any trees big enough to shield her, but the field only had a few thin, reedy saplings. None she could hide behind.

And the grass was so high she could barely see where she was step-ping. If her ankle turned on a rock, she'd be shit out of lu—

"Ooaf—" she cried, tripping and going down like a stone.

Only to land on a big, warm body.

Her eyes shot open wide and she was about to screech and jerk away, but a huge hand clapped over her mouth.

They had her. Was it the big bastard who'd killed her brother? They must have circled around, one of them shooting at her to distract her while the other—

But when she twisted in the man's grip, she saw it wasn't any of the three men she'd seen at the spring with her brother.

No, lying beside and half on top of her was a man even more terrifying. He was easily equal to the other man in size and stature. But this one had a ragged beard, a horrific scar running down the side of his face, and he smelled strongly.

She twisted and fought to get away from him but he just shook her and held his hand over her mouth even more forcefully. He pulled her to him, bearhugging her from behind to hold her still.

"Shhh," he hissed in her ear.

"Just let me kill the fuckers."

Audrey's head jerked to the left at hearing yet another voice. Sure enough, there was a second man crouched down beside them, eyes locked in the direction she'd just come from.

"Commander'd have your ass," said Scarface. "No unprovoked attacks between us and Travis. You know Article 48 of the new Constitution just as well as I do."

The other man's jaw went rigid. "He was chasing an unarmed woman and you know what he would have done if he'd caught her. You call that *unprovoked?*"

"Enough, Finn," Scarface snapped. "Move out." He moved his hand in a sharp, slashing downward motion.

The other man—Finn, apparently—nodded even though he didn't seem happy about it. He looked one last time at the way Audrey had come before army crawling through the grass.

Scarface finally let his hand off Audrey's mouth and she scrambled back from him. He grabbed her arm before she could get far. "Listen, if you don't want to get raped, mutilated, and murdered, not necessarily in that order, you come with us."

"Let go of me," she hissed.

His eyes narrowed. "You can't get out of here on your own. They'll be on top of us in three minutes. Maybe less. We've got a truck. We can get you someplace safe."

She scoffed at that. Safe didn't exist anymore. Not when there was only one woman to every twelve or so men.

Still, sitting still in this field would only get her dead. Or captured. Or worse.

One threat at a time.

So she followed Finn's example and started army crawling through the grass as fast as she could. She gritted her teeth against the burrs and ground thorns tearing at her arm where her sleeve had gotten ripped off.

The New Republic of Texas might be a proud new country but it was a land determined to make you bleed, one way or another. Still, she scrambled as fast as she could. Her life depended on it.

And then before she even knew what was happening, she was suddenly being lifted to her feet. She looked around. They were at a dense copse of trees at the other end of the field.

"Whoa, who's this gorgeous creature?"

She jerked back from a third stranger who rubbed her red hair back and forth between his fingers.

"Jeffries," Scarface snapped at the man who'd touched her hair. "You're scaring her."

Ha. Ironic coming from Scarface. He looked like the posterchild for brutality. She held her hands up and backed away from all of them.

"Look," she whispered. "Thanks for helping out, but I'm all good now. I'll just be going."

"We don't have time for this," Finn said. "Those fuckers are almost on top of us and you can be sure they won't give a shit about Article 48."

Scarface nodded and held out his hand.

Audrey was confused.

Until Finn tossed something to him.

A *gun*.

Shit! Out of the frying pan and into the damn fire.

Audrey turned and again started sprinting like her life depended on it.

But she barely got four steps before she felt a sharp prick in the back of her butt. Just another thorn. No big deal.

She just... had... to... get to...

She collapsed to the ground.

Her last thought was of Charlie's face before everything went black.

CHAPTER THREE

PHOENIX 'NIX'

Well shit. Tranquing her wasn't going to go down well with the Commander. But Finn was right. They needed to get the fuck out of here.

While they were technically in the neutral zone between Travis Territory and Central Texas Sector South, they were closer to Travis's boundary line than theirs. And Arnold Travis's bastards would look for any excuse to kill them some Centrals.

Still, Nix took his time when he lifted her from where she'd fallen. He brushed leaves from her hair and some dirt from her cheek.

Fuck but she was beautiful. He didn't even think it was just because she was the first female he'd touched in more than five years.

Her round face, soft cheekbones, full lips—she'd be beautiful by anyone's standards. His cock hardened at the warmth of her in his arms as he carried her back to the truck.

Maybe he'd even put his name in for the lottery this time around.

Then he laughed at himself. *Going soft now, Nix?* More like *hard*.

Jesus, was he finally getting as pussy-starved as every other dumb fuck around?

"Careful," Finn said, flipping the front seat down and climbing up into the narrow space behind it. Finn flipped down one of the jump seats and reached for the woman. Nix felt oddly reluctant to give her up.

Fucking stupid. He shook his head at himself and handed her off to Finn so he could settle her in.

He turned his attention back to the field behind them and lifted his rifle, eye to the scope.

"You expecting trouble?" Jeffries asked.

"Any second now."

"Shit." Jeffries ran around the front of the truck and jumped in the driver's seat. Only once he was in did Nix drop the rifle and get in the passenger seat.

He barely had the door shut before gunfire came from the trees that had been shielding them from the field.

"Get her down, Finn," Nix shouted. "And fucking drive!"

"I'm driving," Jeffries said, jamming the truck in drive and kicking up a cloud of dirt behind him as they took off.

The back window of the cab shattered and Nix ducked. Fuckers. He shoved his rifle through the now empty space and started firing back. He wouldn't hit anyone like this, but some return fire might slow them down.

Soon they'd outdistanced the bastards. Nix swung to look in the backseat. "Is she okay?"

Finn nodded, his face pale. The woman was slumped over, still totally out of it. Finn's hand trembled when he lifted it to run through his hair.

"They could've killed her. Just like *that*." He looked up at Nix wide-eyed. "She's one of the last one's left and she could've just died right in front of me."

Sometimes Nix forgot just how young Finn actually was. He was what, eighteen? Nineteen? He'd seen so much action, he usually seemed twice that old. Everyone did. Then again, Finn usually just went out on scrapper runs. He hadn't gone on any of the rescue raids

Nix arranged every few months.

Female slavery was officially illegal in the New Republic but the Constitution was only three years old. There were plenty folks who chose to ignore the fact that there was a government back in power at all. Anarchy suited them just fine.

Nix liked the new President of Texas, James Goddard—formerly Colonel Goddard of Fort Worth's 10th Air Base. After D-Day, everything was fucked.

No one really knew who started nuking who—Xterminate had gone global at that point and women were dying off in millions, billions even. But maybe Russia thought they could contain it in America if they took us off the map? Or vice versa? Who the hell knew?

But the bombs started falling in all the major cities. Three in Texas. Dallas. Austin. Houston. There happened to be a northeasterly wind that week. So Central Texas and Fort Worth were fine. Not even any radiation poisoning from fallout. Just the luck of the damn draw.

But folks in Pflugerville and all the suburbs north of Austin, Houston, and Dallas got fucked. Not to mention the hundreds of thousands in the cities themselves.

And the electrical grid? Hasta la vista.

Simultaneous EMP carpet attacks took care of the rest. The Electromagnetic Pulses fried everything with a circuit board from cell phones to smart cars. Basically, every single modern convenience people relied on for daily life—gone in one stroke.

Fucking technology.

Took them all back to the stone ages.

"How long you think before the lottery?" Jeffries asked, glancing over his shoulder to look back at the woman.

"Eyes on the fucking road," Nix snapped. "Besides, don't you already have a woman?"

"Jesus," Jeffries eyes slid toward him before focusing back ahead of him as the truck finally bounced onto a dirt path that let back to a local highway. "A guy can't even take a peek at the merchandise? Sheesh. Ain't like you aren't thinkin' about it."

Nix wasn't going to dignify that with a response.

But then he remembered Roxy's scream. His sister's tiny hand reaching for him as she was ripped out of his arms.

"Actually I wasn't thinking with my dick because we aren't the same as them." Nix jerked a thumb over his shoulder. "We aren't fucking animals."

"Whoa," Jeffries said, eyebrows up as he looked over at Nix. "I was just saying it's only natural if you were looking to get your thrill drill down there some greasin' if you know what I mean. We ain't had a new girl in over two months. Everyone's getting restless."

Nix jaw went hard. "You'll want to stop talking now. You're just digging yourself fucking deeper."

Fact was, if the fucker wasn't driving, Nix might be tempted to introduce his face to a wall. Jeffries was his second in command on the Security Squadron, sure—and at the Commander's personal request, no less—but that didn't mean Nix thought the guy wasn't a weaselly son of a bitch.

Nix took a long breath in and let it out. Jeffries did his job. And really, that was all Nix cared about.

It's not like you want to date the motherfucker.

No, Nix ate, drank, and slept the job. Keep the Jacob's Well Township and all the souls who lived there safe—that was it. Full stop. He didn't do shit like whining about not liking his second in command.

Jeffries rolled his eyes and held his hands up, letting go of the steering wheel.

"Jesus," Nix shouted, grabbing for the wheel.

Jeffries just laughed and took the wheel, swerving the truck back into their lane from where they'd started drifting onto the shoulder, almost into the ditch.

"Relax, man. You always got a stick up your ass. Ain't like you're better'n everyone else."

Fucker was getting on Nix's nerves. He pinched the tip of his nose and looked out the window. It was barely noon and already he felt one fuck of a headache coming on.

Should have known he was in for one as soon as he saw he was teamed up with Jeffries on the Scraper team today. The Security rotation—now that one Nix himself scheduled.

And he conveniently gave Jeffries opposite shifts to himself. The fact that these were mostly night shifts was just a *tiny* little added bonus.

He smirked, thinking how tired Jeffries had looked coming in this morning off a shift. And hey, at least finding the woman meant they could head back early.

Nix glanced over his shoulder again at her. Now that they were out of the range of fire, Finn had settled her in the narrow jump seat opposite his.

Her head was tipped back, mouth slack. Her shocking red hair was tangled all to hell and dirt streaked her face, but goddamn she was beautiful. It struck him all over again. Those soft apple cheeks, her plump, inviting lips...

Fuck. His jeans were starting to get tight again. He jerked back around front and ground his teeth. She was nothing to him.

As soon as he got her back to town, he'd barely ever see her again. And that was the way it was meant to fuckin' be.

CHAPTER FOUR

AUDREY

Her mouth was dry.

That was Audrey's first thought when she tried to blink her heavy eyes open. Her mouth was so dry it felt like she hadn't drunk anything in days. Her tongue felt swollen.

She squinted and looked around.

Walls. A ceiling.

"Water," she squawked, hand reaching for her throat. "Please."

"Here you go, honey."

Her head jerked at that.

It was a *woman's* voice.

Okay, so this had to be a dream. Audrey hadn't heard another woman's voice in person in over *eight* years.

The cool glass cup that was pressed against Audrey's lips felt real enough, though. So did the water that dribbled over her lips and down her throat. She choked on it at first, and then wanted to cry, because *no!* It was spilling out of her mouth. She was wasting it!

The woman, whoever she was, seemed to sense her anxiety because a light touch landed on her shoulder. "Shh, it's okay, just slow down. There's plenty. You don't have to rush."

Plenty? Of water?

Now she knew it was a dream.

But it was such a *lovely* dream. She let her eyes drift closed as she reached up and took the cup, drinking swallow after swallow of the most sinfully delicious water she'd ever drunk. It didn't even have the sharp aftertaste of bleach or that mud taste from the homemade filtration system Uncle Dale used.

Fresh like from a *spring*.

A spring.

Oh God.

Charlie.

She dropped the cup and her eyes shot open.

A young woman who looked barely older than a teenager was sitting on the bed beside her. A bed. In a strange room. Strange woman in a strange room.

The woman held out her hands. "It's okay. You're safe here."

"Back up, Sophia," said *another* woman from the doorway of—what the hell? Had Audrey entered the Twilight zone or something? "Let her catch her breath for a second."

Audrey looked left and right, but the bedroom covered head to toe in pink girly crap like the last apocalyptic decade had never happened was still there.

God, it could have been Audrey's room when she was a kid. Before the bombs. Before Xterminate. Even before Mom got cancer—back when the most stressful thing Audrey had to worry about was whether Jimmy Redmond in her fourth-grade class liked her back. Check the box, yes or no.

And then she remembered again. *Charlie.*

"Where am I?" She jumped to her feet. "What did you do with my brother—" She grabbed her head as she stumbled forward on jelly legs.

"Whoa there." The woman by the door jumped forward and caught Audrey right before she faceplanted.

"Let's take it easy, how about that?"

Audrey blinked in confusion as the woman helped her back to the bed.

Audrey rubbed her temples. Everything was so fuzzy. Nothing made sense. She and Charlie found the spring. They'd been so happy. Then he was yelling for her to run and there'd been those terrible men...

She squeezed her eyes shut, trying to remember what happened after that.

"The other men!" she shouted, eyes popping back open. Her hand shot to her ass. "They shot me."

Both women winced.

"I can't believe they used a tranq on you," Sophia said, blue eyes wide. "That's not what we're like here. The situation must have been extremely dangerous. It was for your own safety. I promise you," she shook her head emphatically. "women are safe here. It's not like other places."

Sophia spoke so passionately, Audrey wasn't sure if she was naïve or just really young. But Audrey wasn't about to start drinking the cool aid. They'd freaking *tranqued* her. Then kidnapped her.

"What exactly *is* this place?" she asked carefully. These women were being nice to her right now. Okay. She could play along. Until she could find a way to get the *hell* out of here.

Sophia smiled wide. "Let me be the first to welcome you to Central Texas South."

"Specifically, this is Jacob's Well Township," the brown-haired woman added. "It's the regional seat."

"One of the first townships to be formed after D-Day. And we've been going strong ever since." Sophia beamed with pride.

Central Texas South? Audrey wanted to drop her face into her hands. That was a day's walk *backwards*. Uncle Dale *had* said this territory was rumored to be safer than where she and Charlie had been heading next, but they'd been aiming for the coast.

What did any of it matter now?

Charlie was gone.

"My dad's the Commander here," Sophia said, smile still wide, eyes bright.

Aha. Well, that answered *that* question. No surprise that daddy's little girl had such a rosy outlook on the place.

"I'm Camila, by the way," said the brown-haired woman. "Good to meet you, too."

Audrey hesitated for a second in holding out her hand, but then she remembered—play nice. "Audrey."

Camila nodded. "Like I said. Nice to meet you."

"You too."

The woman's smile went wry, like she could tell Audrey was bull-shitting her.

"Me and Sophia will give you a little space. And go get you some food. See if we can take care of those sea legs of yours." She gave a head nod and then headed for the door.

Sophia looked reluctant to go but eventually followed. She paused at the doorway, all but bouncing on her feet. "It's so exciting to have a new girl. We haven't had anyone new for *ages*. I can't wait for you to get to meet everyone."

Her smile widened even further, though Audrey didn't know how that was possible. "I know they're all *so* excited to get to meet *you*."

Why did that sound ominous as hell?

"Sophia," came Camila's voice in a sharp, warning tone.

Sophia closed the door before Audrey could ask any questions. Alrighty then.

Fuck.

This.

Shit.

Audrey wasn't about to wait around to see whatever the hell these people had planned for her. There was a reason Uncle Dale, Charlie, and she had agreed there was only one place that was safe for her— there was an all-woman colony in south Texas somewhere near the coast called Nomansland. Get it? NoMan...

It wasn't an open secret, either. Uncle Dale only knew because he'd been part of the dark web conspiracy community forever. Even he didn't know exactly where it was. She and Charlie only had coordinates for a rendezvous spot to meet with a representative. Like an interview for both of them to feel each other out so they could see they were the real deal. Then they'd take her in to their colony.

Audrey scrubbed her hand down her face. But now she had to get there on her own.

But could she? Make it all the way to the coast? By herself?

Oh Charlie, Charlie, *Charlie.*

Her chest squeezed so tight, she could barely breathe.

No. No thinking about him right now. If she did, she'd curl up into a ball right here and maybe never get up again. She'd quit.

And she was a lot of things, but Dad hadn't raised a quitter.

She took a deep breath in and forced thoughts of Charlie deep down with it. She squared her jaw, put one hand on the nightstand table, the other on the bedframe, and hauled herself to her feet.

Her fingers went white knuckled on the bedframe because goddammit, she was *so* dizzy for a moment she was sure she was gonna throw up again. But she closed her eyes, breathed in slowly, and after a couple minutes, it passed.

She started walking, one hand to the wall to steady herself. She reached for the doorknob. "All right, let's see just how friendly this place really is."

As she'd suspected, the knob didn't turn. She was locked in.

"Safe place my ass," she whispered under her breath.

She blinked and shook her head against the lingering fog in her brain. One of the many lessons she'd mastered early on in her years in the bunker was picking locks.

She pulled a bobby pin out of the side of her worn sneakers.

This one was almost laughably easy. It was a simple flip lock on a hollow bedroom door. She could have kicked the thing down if she wanted. Okay, she was a little weak at the moment, but she probably still could have done it.

Either way, the lock clicked and the next second, she had the door open. She slipped out into a hallway.

It was still startling to see sunlight after being underground for years. It made her breath catch. That and just how *normal* everything looked.

She could be standing in any pre-D-day house, anywhere in a US suburb. It was an upstairs hallway and light poured in from huge arched windows by the staircase.

Staircase. Bingo.

She glanced left and right and then hurried toward the stairway. She felt a little sturdier with every step—*shit*. She barely managed to recover from stumbling face first down the stairs by grabbing the rail at the last second.

Really fucking genius, Aud. Cause you tumbling head over ass won't attract *any* attention whatsoever. Or end with a broken neck.

She bit her cheek to try to help her focus putting one foot in front of the other as she headed down stairs. And she kept a death-grip on the rail.

Her vision started going topsy-turvy but she managed to make it to the bottom.

Which was when she heard voices. Female voices.

God, that was still trippy.

She still had her bobby pin clutched in hand as she padded to the front door, but it opened without problem. It must have recently been oiled too because it swung in without so much as a squeak. Thank you, Jesus.

And right there on a rack right by the door—*hello*—a baseball cap. She snatched it and slipped out the door. She even *mostly* managed not to trip as she ran down the front stairs and onto the perfectly mani-cured lawn.

She didn't stop moving until she got to the side bushes. But there she let herself fall to her knees and look around because. What. The. Fuck.

It wasn't Maybury exactly. The houses weren't cookie cutter.

But it was a neighborhood that didn't look like it had suffered the same Apocalypse everywhere else had. Sure, she and Charlie had stuck to the map Uncle Dale gave them of areas that would be less inhabited, but they'd still seen plenty.

Neighborhoods that were burnt to shit. *Every* store no matter where it was had broken windows and was looted all to hell. Cars overturned.

Bodies. Some were years old, some were new. Women, so many

women. But men too. Old, young, it didn't matter. People just stopped caring enough to bury them.

But here—Audrey shook her head. It was like none of it ever happened. It didn't make any sense.

She swallowed hard and wished she'd had the sense to look for more water before she'd fled. Oh well. This place was so perfect it was fucking creepy.

Any situation that seemed too good to be true usually was—God, even Uncle Dale's in the end.

Audrey looked up. The sun was setting. She turned around and oriented herself. Okay, so *that* way was south. She glanced down the road and felt her belly go tight. Maybe she should have waited around for them to feed her first after all.

So they could drug you? Great plan, dumbass.

Right. No time like the present.

She rolled her hair into a bun on the top of her head, pinned it using her escape bobby pin, and shoved the hat on her head.

Then she hurried low to the ground to the next house over. She slipped around to the back and hopped the fence, then the next, and the next.

Pulling herself up and over the fifth fence was grueling and she basically tumbled over the other side. All right, that was putting it nice. She fell. She fell over the other side of the fence.

Oof. Her breath was knocked out of her and she struggled to gasp for air and sit up. It didn't work. She fell back and let out a small whimper.

Keep moving. Keep fucking moving.

But all she could do was gasp for air that wouldn't come.

Is this what Charlie died for? So you could give up after making the most lame ass escape attempt in fucking history?

She clenched her teeth and sat up in spite of the searing pain in her lungs. She gulped and forced air in.

And she dragged herself back to her feet. So what if she stumbled? She was moving. One foot in front of the other.

"Just one foot in front of the other," she wheezed to herself. She only had to take one more step. And then another. Then one more.

She seemed to have made it to the front of the neighborhood because the last backyard opened up to a sidewalk. She looked behind her but there wasn't anyone chasing her. Camila and Cultist Barbie hadn't sounded the alarm. Yet.

Then she heard noise up ahead. Like voices. A lot of voices. Maybe even a crowd.

And for the first time since she'd woken up and remembered Charlie was gone, she felt—not hope, she wasn't sure she'd ever feel that again—but maybe a little less active despair.

Because she could just disappear into the crowd. She could blend. Her breasts were still bound and with the hat, Charlie said she totally passed as a boy.

She'd just slip into the crowd and discretely find her way out of this happy little 'township.'

She headed toward the noise. The closer she got, the more casually she walked.

She'd studied Charlie's gait and put everything she had into the performance now. An easy, confident stride, feet turned slightly out. Basically, the trick to pretending you were a guy was to lead with your dick—even if you didn't have one.

And it worked. Audrey's heart pounded a thousand beats per minute as she crossed a little cobbled bridge onto main street. If she stopped and stared a little longer than necessary at the clean, fresh looking river water rushing underneath the bridge, well, maybe that wasn't too odd.

She wasn't the only one walking toward the town center. Other men passed her without giving her a second look.

Ahead there appeared to be a mass of people—okay, a mass of *men* —gathered around a town square that was so quaint it looked like something out of a Norman Rockwell painting. With a courthouse in the center and everything.

It was the sort of place Audrey's grandma would love to drag her along to go *antiquing* when she was a kid. Quaint wooden facades to buildings that advertised names like, *Pete's Hardware* and *Scents and Soaps*.

If there were women other than Sophia and Camila anywhere in town, Audrey wasn't seeing them. Just men, men, and more men.

So many men the street was packed and Audrey was getting pressed in from all sides. So maybe this hadn't been her *best* plan ever...

If any *one* of these guys realized she was a woman. Shit. It would be a riot. And she'd be ripped apart.

Okaaaaaaaaaay. Time to exit stage left. Right now. She'd just slip out the other side of the square and keep moving south. No harm no foul.

"All right, all right, settle down," came a voice over a bullhorn.

Everyone's faces turned up and to the right. Audrey followed their gaze even as she tried to move to the edge of the crowd. She didn't dare say anything or try to excuse herself. Even if she deepened her voice, it was far too risky.

"If you're here then you've qualified for one of the lottery pools," the booming voice continued.

Audrey finally saw who they were all looking at. In the center of the square a man in Army fatigues stood on a second-floor balcony, bullhorn to his mouth. A tall man stood beside him holding a large box.

"Thank you for your hard work and dedication to the Jacob's Well Township. All right, enough with the bullshit. Let's get to the reason you're all here."

Shouts and hoots went through the crowd, along with several ear-piercing whistles. For a second, Audrey could only stare.

"And the first to become one of the new woman's five husband's is..." The man beside him reached blindly into a cardboard box but Audrey had already taken several stumbling steps back.

Five?

Husbands!

Holy shit. She had to get the fuck out of here. Now.

"Phoenix Dunn."

The crowd roared as the name was announced and Audrey couldn't help looking the same way everyone else did even as she kept moving backwards, trying to maneuver her way to the edge of the crowd.

That was when her eyes landed on *him*. The one everyone was looking at.

Phoenix.

Scarface.

And he was looking right back at her, recognition and fury clear on his face.

CHAPTER FIVE

NIX

What the fucking *fuck* was she doing here?

Nix shoved man after man out of his way as he headed her direction. When he'd dropped her off with the Commander earlier, he'd been trusting the bastard to take care of her. Not to fucking drop the goddamned ball and let her loose to wander out in this pack of wild fucking dogs.

Any second these cunt-starved fuckheads were going to realize exactly what she was, but he swore, if any of them so much as fucking laid a *finger* on her, he'd—

"Out of my fucking way," he snarled, pushing another dumb asshole aside.

"I said out of my fucking way!" he roared when the crowd shifted, blocking his view of her.

Fuck being polite. He turned sideways and stomped forward, using his shoulder as a battering ram. Too bad if someone got in his way. He'd fucking warned them.

Curses and shouts came from all sides as he rammed his way forward through the packed bodies. But then he heard something else being murmured in excited whispers throughout the crowd. Something that had his heart jackhammering in his chest.

It's her.

The new girl.

She's here.

Right over there.

Bastards were in his way again and he couldn't fucking see—

Then he finally broke through the crowd. There she was. Frozen like a startled fucking rabbit. Her hands were out in front of her defensively. Her eyes darted back and forth as men created an empty circle around her.

For once they were behaving themselves. Probably because the Commander had only announced one name so far. They were all still hoping their name would be chosen. No one would dare fucking up their chances by jumping the gun.

Nix had thought this whole lottery idea was fucking nuts when the Commander first came up with it, but maybe there was something to it after all. And thank Christ for that, if it was keeping Audrey safe right now.

Speaking of... her eyes went even wider with terror when she saw him.

Yeah, that didn't make him feel awesome.

"You shot me," she whispered, eyes narrowing.

He winced. He'd been hoping she'd forget that part.

He held out his hand, trying to get her to calm down. "You were in danger. Travis's men were maybe a minute behind us. We couldn't fuck around trying the nice way to get your ass in the truck."

"So you could bring me here to be a sister-wife to five men?" she spat.

"Technically, in this situation, we're the brother husbands."

What the fuck? Nix swung his head to the right. Who'd said that—?

He all but groaned when he saw Clark. If he thought Jeffries was annoying, that guy had nothing on Clark when it came to ego and self-importance.

"Hi there, wifey," Clark said, smiling in a way that flashed his dimples.

Aw, come the fuck *on*. Clark? Nix had been so concerned with getting to Audrey, he hadn't even heard the Commander announce a second name. But Clark, out of all people?

"You can just think of me as the sexy one in this little entourage." Clark winked at her and under other circumstances, Nix would have laughed at the corresponding look of horror that came over her face. Except for the fact that she looked at Nix the same way.

"Help me get her out of here," Nix snapped at Clark. This might have been something Nix never expected for himself—he didn't know *who* the hell had put his name in for the lottery tonight—but it was now his primary duty to protect and care for Audrey. Along with Clark, apparently.

"Keep those fuckers back," Nix growled, stepping in front of Audrey and facing the crowd, crossing his arms over his chest.

"Anyone who wants to fuck with her has to come through me," he announced loudly.

"And me," Clark said, puffing up his chest.

Audrey let out an annoyed huff. "How about all of you big, dumb oafs get the hell out of my way? I can take care of myself."

Where was a damn dart gun when you needed one? Apparently he'd need to keep it handy with this one, if she was going to keep running head long into situations that could get her killed.

Nix turned to face her and her eyes went wide again as she tipped her head up to look at him. Fuck but she was tiny. She couldn't be more than what, five-six, five-seven, to his six-three?

"Enough," Nix said. "Watch our six," he called out to Clark, who nodded. And then he easily scooped Audrey up and flopped her over his shoulder, fireman carry style.

She didn't seem especially happy about the situation if her constant high-pitched screaming, kicking, and punching were any indication.

He hooked an arm around her legs to lever them in place. He only barely stopped himself from smacking her sweet ass.

He couldn't believe anyone in the square had been fooled for one hot second that she was anything but female. She had hips and ass for days.

And damn, having so much contact with all that warm, squirming woman was already fucking with his head. Even if she was screaming enough curses at him to impress a sailor.

"She's got a mouth on her, that's for sure," Clark said approvingly as he came up behind them.

"You're supposed to be on the lookout for trouble." Nix winced as Audrey pulled up his shirt and dug her fingernails into his lower back.

Some of the men in the crowd starting hooting and laughing as they went past. Nix rolled his eyes.

"Thank you, thank you," Clark shouted. "Glad to entertain. We'll be here every Wednesday and Saturday. Matinees on Sundays. Bring the kiddies."

It would be bad to start off this relationship by punching Clark in the face, right? They were supposed to work so closely together as a unit that they became family. A clan.

Nix scoffed and— *Goddammit*. Sharp pain sliced through his shoulder. Well, she had good teeth, nice to know.

This time he did spank her ass. "Bite me again and just see what you'll get."

She seemed to lose some of her fight and went limp over his shoulder.

Family.

Ha.

They were getting off to a bang-up start. Then again, he'd always been shit as family.

Which was why he'd never put his name in for the damn lottery.

But as he finally walked down the familiar streets to the Commander's house and handed Audrey off to Sophia and Camila, the way his chest went tight at the sight of Audrey's obvious distress—he knew it was already too late.

Maybe it'd been too late the moment he heard gunshots back at the field, and after going to investigate, saw the most beautiful woman he'd ever laid eyes on running for her life.

He'd only been that afraid once before.

And look how that had turned out.

But no.

This time he'd protect her.

This time, everything would be different.

CHAPTER SIX

AUDREY

Sophia was nothing but apologetic when Phoenix—or *Nix*, as Sophia said everyone called him—deposited Audrey back to her pink prison.

Camila, on the other hand, watched Audrey warily. That woman had seen some shit, Audrey was sure.

"I'm so sorry everything got out of hand," Sophia said, deep distress lines carved in her forehead. "If you would've just given us a little bit of time, we could have explained everything and—"

"How many days does it usually take before you spring the whole five husbands on a girl?" Audrey asked, carefully eyeing both Sophia and then Camila.

She'd decided to take the path of least resistance—at least for the moment. She would gather information, learn all she could, and escape when her chances were better.

"Daddy would have explained it all tonight," Sophia said, sitting down on the bed beside Audrey and taking her hand. Audrey wanted to yank it back but she just took a long breath in through her teeth instead and looked to Camila.

Sophia, Audrey understood. The Commander was her dad. Who knew how long she'd been brainwashed by all this shit?

But Camila? She didn't seem naïve. So what was her deal?

"You'll be so happy here," Sophia gushed. "Just look at Camila. She came to us a year and a half ago and now she and her husbands are as happy as can be. Isn't that right, Camila?"

Sophie's beaming faced turned to the other woman. Camila couldn't be much older than thirty but compared to Sophia's exuberant youth, even Audrey felt ancient and world-weary. And Camila was in one of these insane so-called *marriages*?

"And when exactly is this, *happy occasion*," Audrey let sarcasm positively drip from her voice, "supposed to happen?" Aka, how quick did she need to make sure to get the *hell* out of here?

"Usually within the first few weeks," Sophia said, then hurriedly added, "but you have three months to consummate the union." Her cheeks went pink at the word consummate and she looked down to her lap.

A virginal tell if Audrey'd ever seen one. Was it just because she was the Commander's daughter that she'd been left unmolested by the scores of men in the town? According to Uncle Dale, there were only a handful of places in the world still safe for women. Nomansland being the only one he knew of anywhere nearby.

Audrey frowned and looked to Camila

"Even though you get married pretty quick, nothing is forced. We're not like that here. Look," Camila held up her hands. "It's not my place to tell you all this stuff. The Commander will be here right after the lottery celebrations finish and—"

"And you're okay with that?" Audrey exploded. "The fact that they're just raffling us off like we're, we're—" she sputtered, "—cattle or something."

Camila sighed and Sophia looked wounded. "I told you it's better for the Commander to explain things," Camila said.

Screw this crap. "Oh, so he can start doing whatever brainwash voodoo he's obviously done on you and Sophia?"

Camila leveled her eyes on Audrey, but Audrey didn't back down.

Sure her last comment had come out bitchy, but she stood by it. She was just calling a spade a spade.

"You been out in the world lately, little girl?" Camila's jaw worked as she took a step toward Audrey. "Maybe what we have here isn't perfect, but it's a helluva a lot better than what's out there." She shook her head and turned to Sophia. "I'm sorry, Soph, I know I said I'd help out, but I gotta go."

She brushed past Sophia and out the door.

Sophia looked even more upset, head swinging back and forth between Audrey and Camila, like she was torn about whether to stay or go after her friend. Audrey was about to tell her to go, by all means, go, but then a knock came at the door.

And the Commander himself stepped in. He seemed even taller up close. He was still in his military fatigues.

Audrey couldn't help but to swallow when staring down the tall, stern-faced man. She stood up from the bed. He was maybe in his early forties? He'd almost be handsome if it wasn't for those hard, gray eyes and too sharp jaw. The guy was all edges.

"What was all that about?" he asked Sophia, looking out the door and down the hall. "Cam looked upset."

"Oh, just a misunderstanding," Sophia tried to wave it off, but her distress was still clear on her face. Then she shook her head and smiled. "Hi Daddy." She stood up and gave him a brief hug.

"I was just telling Audrey you'd be here any minute to tell her about all the wonderful things you've done with Jacob's Well Township." She turned back to Audrey, her easy-going smile back in place.

The Commander's hard face softened for just the briefest moment. "Do you mind giving me and Miss Audrey a few moments alone? Thank you for all your help today."

He pressed a kiss to Sophia's forehead. She smiled worshipfully up at him and then, with a smile and one last quick wave at Audrey, left her alone in the lion's den.

The resounding noise of the door shutting behind her struck an ominous note to Audrey.

Shit. She was alone with the Commander. What the hell happened now? Was this the part where he initiated her into his harem or something? Because if he thought for one *second* she was going to—

"Take a seat." He gestured to two wing-backed chairs by the bay window opposite the bed.

"No thanks, I'll stand." Audrey crossed her arms over her chest.

One edge of his mouth quirked up. "Sophia said you were spirited. That will serve you well here."

Audrey's hands tightened into fists. This fucking guy. "Having your daughter work as your spy, huh? Real classy."

He didn't take the bait or react to her tone. "Sophia's hardly a spy. She's just worried about you. She gets like that about all our newcomers."

"Newcomer. That's a nice misnomer for kidnapping and enslavement."

He scoffed at that, like she'd said something outrageous.

"Cut the bullshit," she said. "When are my *husbands* going to come to drag me off and rape me? If you think I'm going down without a fight, you've got another fucking thing com—"

"No one's going to rape you." The Commander all but spat the words.

Well, looked like she'd finally managed to ruffle his calm demeanor. She huffed out a humorous laugh. "Oh, so you're one of those people who think if it's done under the umbrella of this 'marriage' bullshit," she used air quotes, "then it doesn't count as rape? Well let me tell you, buddy, no always means no."

Those piercing gray eyes of his went even harder. "I would never condone violence against any woman, married or not, in the Jacob's Well township or the Central Texas South territory for that matter. It is our most strictly enforced law. If a man raises a hand to a woman in violence, he loses the hand and then is banished from the community."

Audrey paused, momentarily startled. Surely he didn't mean that *literally*. Did he? She narrowed her eyes at the Commander.

"The world's population has been decimated by war, disease, and famine. Healthy female survivors like you are the only hope for the human race."

Okay, wait. What? This stuff was the last thing she'd expected him to be spouting.

"With you coming, we now have one hundred and forty-seven women in Jacob's Well, and I treat that as an awesome responsibility."

"So I don't get it. If you revere women so much, why won't you just help me get where I'm trying to go?"

His hard stare met hers and his jaw worked. "I've seen the slums in San Antonio. The slave markets in Mexico and Louisiana. We give you three months to get to know your partners and to consummate your marriage. I assure you, that's a far more generous offer than you'll find anywhere else in the territories."

Audrey huffed out a breath and shook her head. It always came down to the same thing when it came to men, didn't it? Even if this guy wanted to dress it up and pretend it was something nicer.

"You really think it's not still rape? What about your daughter, huh? When does she get raffled off to be gang-raped by five guys?"

The next second the Commander was right in front of her, finger in her face. His voice was ice cold. "You'll want to keep a civil tongue when it comes to my daughter."

Okaaaaaay. So, it probably wasn't the best idea to piss off the guy in charge of her immediate future. Still, it wasn't in her to apologize to this asshole.

She just jutted her chin out and started heading toward the door. "I'll take my chances out there."

He stepped in front of her, easily blocking her path with his large body.

She stopped, chest going tight. In spite of her bravado, every second she spent in this place made her feel more and more claustrophobic.

This guy was talking about consummating a marriage with *five* men. Did he mean one after the other, all at once? Or like, did they each take different nights? What the hell, this entire thing was insane!

"So I'm a prisoner here," she spat.

"If you leave, you'll die." His voice was perfectly calm again.

Which just fucking enraged Audrey. "Are you threatening me? So all that was bullshit about raising a hand to a woman—"

"I'm simply stating a fact. Unlike you, I know *exactly* what dangers lie outside the boundaries of my territory."

For a second, he got a distant look on his face. But then his attention snapped back to her. "And that's simply an unacceptable waste of resources."

Resources. Was he calling her a fucking *resource*? Why not be blunt about it? There was only one part of her that was the resource—her cunt.

"If you think I'm having sex with you, you can fuck—"

His burst of laughter cut her off.

"Not me. I'm not one of your five."

"What?" Okay, now she was really confused. Wasn't that how these things worked? This guy was the cult leader or whatever, so he got to have all the women?

"The lottery is a win win for everyone. It helps keep the men in line. We only rescue a new woman—"

Audrey's eyes narrowed at the term *rescue*.

"—four or five times a month. Well," he waved a hand, "last year we came across that slave shipment headed for Fort Worth and got fifteen at once. But nothing like that since. And when you're talking a ratio of one woman to every twelve men on earth, well," he shook his head, "I never said peace didn't come at a price. Believe me, there were plenty who wanted to make it ten men to a marriage instead of five. But I fought for it."

She gave him a saccharine smile. "What a saint. How convenient that the price for peace is one you don't have to personally pay."

Just like before, the easy-going guy disappeared and he slammed the wall beside him, eyes going icy. "Everyone has paid in this war. You're no better or worse than anyone else. And you're right, when my daughter turns nineteen, she'll be old enough for the lottery. Which is why I've made damn sure to build in protections every step of the way so the women are safe."

He started listing things off on his fingers. "A man has to live in the township for a year before he's eligible for the lottery. Even then, he goes through a vetting process."

"When he applies, I put one of my agents on him to learn everything possible about his habits, his vices, whether or not he's prone to violence, what kind of porn he likes to jack off to—"

The Commander ignored Audrey jerking back from him in distaste and continued, "and there are different tiers to the lottery so that out of every five chosen, there's always one man I've known long enough to trust with my own life. It's his job to ensure the physical safety and emotional well-being of the women put in his charge and to keep the other men in line."

His gaze skewered hers. "I don't know a single person whose family wasn't torn to shreds by everything that's happened the last decade."

"What we're trying to do here is give people new family units, *clans*, and then build a community on those bonds. Is it a new kind of family? Sure it is. And maybe it's one we're not so comfortable with at first. But it's a new world now. We have to change with it if we're going to survive."

Audrey didn't know what to say in response to that little speech. Except to know that with every word that came out of his mouth, a certainty grew more and more deep in her stomach—she had to get outta here the first chance she got.

"Now," the Commander took in a deep breath and released it, like he was intentionally calming himself down, "this conversation is over. Your fiancés will begin their courtship duties tomorrow."

Audrey's eyes shot wide open. Courtship *what*?

The Commander strode toward the door but just as he opened it and made to leave, he paused and turned back to her.

"And Audrey? I've posted sentries at the front and back of the house. If you try to leave again, you'll only be escorted back to the house. It's your first night here and I'd hate for it to be filled with unpleasantness. Why not rest, clean up, and enjoy your new life here?"

He closed the door before she could shout all the obscenities she had stored up.

CHAPTER SEVEN

AUDREY

Turned out the Commander wasn't bluffing about those sentries. Three escape attempts later, when Audrey finally climbed into bed, bleary-eyed at five a.m., she gave into sleep the second her head hit the pillow.

Which meant she was less than delighted when Sophia came bounding in at eight a.m. asking her how she could sleep so late, and didn't she want to wake up and get a start on the day?

The silver lining?

Sophia brought breakfast in bed. And while it wasn't super exciting —it was largely a sprouted bean and cornmeal mix, there was one precious fresh egg.

That wasn't what had Audrey sitting up in bed and almost hugging Sophia, though. No, that was due to the steaming mug full of black liquid that was the equivalent of gold these days.

"Coffee!" Audrey exclaimed, cupping the mug to her chest like it was the most precious thing she'd ever held.

Sophia grinned as Audrey brought it to her lips and sipped. It was hot and bitter and absolutely fucking perfect.

"We bring it out for special occasions. I can add some milk if you'd like. Margie's our milk cow. She makes the sweetest, freshest tasting—"

"No." Audrey shook her head. "I don't want anything to ruin this perfection." She closed her eyes and breathed in the aroma, then took another sip. Sweet baby Jesus that was divine.

"I'm so glad you like it." Sophia sounded genuinely pleased. "I'll let you eat and then you can shower and get cleaned up. I thought we could show you around town today."

Audrey perked up and opened her eyes, focusing on Sophia. Getting a look around town sounded fabulous to her.

Then maybe she could make a plan more sophisticated than try to sneak out the front door or climb out the window down the trellis in the middle of the night—both obviously flawed plans since the sentries picked her up within five minutes of hitting the yard every time.

After breakfast and all but licking every drop from the coffee mug, Audrey headed for the shower.

An actual shower.

The Commander's house had its own well. And the solar panels installed on the roof gave enough power for the pump to pipe water into the house—at least on special occasions. Apparently Audrey showing up qualified.

They had so much water here they could just throw it away down the drain. Miracle of miracles.

The water was cold, but Audrey wasn't going to look a gift horse in the mouth. There'd only been sponge baths in the bunker and washing her hair twice a month in the water bucket Uncle Dale brought down.

She couldn't help but luxuriate as she scrubbed her hair clean with the shampoo—real *shampoo*. It smelled like lilacs.

Charlie's dead and you're letting your captors bribe you with a shower? What the hell, Audrey?

She squeezed her eyes shut as the lilac scented shampoo ran down her face.

No, it wasn't like that. She just had to regroup. Take a few days. Get cleaned up. Eat their food. Drink their water. And then get the hell out of here.

She couldn't just keep going off half-cocked. Getting out of here and down to the coast was going to require planning and patience.

If the Commander wasn't bullshitting her and it was as dangerous out there as he said—something her limited experience didn't exactly contradict, her heart squeezed remembering Charlie's body hitting the ground—then she'd need supplies. She pushed the image of Charlie away.

Guns. She'd need guns. At least one. And a vehicle. Making it there on foot by herself just wasn't realistic.

And whatever she did, she couldn't allow any room for distractions.

She rinsed her hair and then quickly finished with the shower. Sophia had left her clothes to wear and just like the shower, it felt unspeakably good to slide into a fresh, clean pair of jeans and a t-shirt.

A knock came at the bedroom door, and then Sophia's sunny voice. "You decent? I heard the shower turn off a while ago and I want to get a start on our day."

Audrey glared at the sound of Sophia's voice. "Catch more flies with honey," she whispered to herself. Her mom used to always say that.

Then she smirked, cause once she'd said it in front of Uncle Dale and he'd just gotten this confused look on his face. "You'd catch a helluva lot more flies with some Die Fly. Sprinkle a little of that around and you can kill a thousand flies, easy. After The Fall, all those dead bodies piling up, we were up to our eyeballs in flies, lemme tell you. Don't know what we woulda done without our barrel a' Die Fly."

But that was Uncle Dale for ya, always with a tale of how to best mix lye in order to dissolve decomposing bodies the quickest, or how his militia helped secure the western border in the bloodiest battle of the Texas War for Independence against the Southern States Alliance, or how he'd pooped into a plastic bag for two weeks while he dug out his outhouse.

Audrey shook her head to rid herself of the memories and called back, "I'm dressed."

Sophia burst in the door, wide smile on her face. Did she just smile so much her face got stuck that way, or what? Seriously, it was not natural to flash that many teeth so often.

"Come on, your tour of town awaits!"

"Oh goody."

Sophia was also apparently immune to sarcasm. She just laughed and grasped Audrey's elbow, pulling her forward out of the room.

"Oh hi, Nix," Sophia said as soon as they stepped out the front door. Audrey had been watching Sophia as she slipped the door key back in her pocket but her head whipped up at the name.

And there stood the too large, overly muscled, overly tattooed man with his bulging arms crossed over his chest. The menacing scar running diagonally down his face. He leaned against the porch rail like he'd been waiting on them.

He dipped his head. "Morning, Sophia." Then his eyes moved to Audrey. Dark gray eyes that were too attentive, too intense. She pulled back, ignoring Sophia's grip on her arm.

"Audrey," was all he said to her, a smirk curling up one side of his lips.

"What's he doing here?" She turned to Sophia.

"He's our bodyguard. Well," Sophia smiled. "*Your* bodyguard anyway. All the married women have one. One of their husbands." Her eyes went a little dreamy.

Audrey glanced at the scarred giant. Of course all the women had one of their 'husbands' watching them twenty-four hours a day. More like prison guards. Audrey huffed out in disbelief.

"Next year I turn nineteen, you know," Sophia said conversationally. "And then I'll get my own lottery. I can't wait, I'm so excited."

Audrey eyed her in disbelief. Surely she wasn't *that* innocent to want to invite this bullshit, was she?

"Don't get ahead of your britches, girl," Nix said, brows lowering at Sophia. "There's plenty of time before then."

For the first time since Audrey'd known her, Sophia finally got some fire in her eyes. "You all think I'm still a child. But I'm not. I'm ready to take my place in the community. To have a clan of my own."

Yep. She'd definitely been drinking the cool aid.

"So where to first, trusty tour guide?" Audrey asked, taking Sophia's arm again. Time to get her lay of the land so she could get the hell out of here.

———

Audrey thought Sophia would make more of a show of everything as they walked the couple blocks into town, but they passed most buildings without a single explanation, even when they came to the picturesque town square, complete with a stately courthouse in the center of a wide greenspace.

The streets were full of people. Mostly men, but Audrey glimpsed a few women here and there. Just walking around free as could be. No one mobbing or harassing them.

Horses clattered down the pavement and a line of people curved around the block outside a building with a rudimentary sign proclaiming Food Pantry. Out of an open front window, a woman served man after man steaming bowls of food.

Audrey had a hundred questions but Sophia just kept marching forward like she had a particular destination in mind. Nix followed several paces behind them, dark eyes watchful.

On the far side of the square was a long strip of buildings. Sophia headed for one several doors down. *City Hall*, the sign overhead proclaimed in peeling gold paint. Though old and weathered, the sign looked original to the building—or at least pre-D Day.

The visitor area was sparse but well kept. A man in a sharp pinstriped suit sat behind a desk with several books open, making small notations in a ledger. Light from the large front window bathed the room in light.

"Hi Henry," Sophia said brightly.

The man's head lifted and his eyes locked on Sophia. "Sophia." He said her name like a caress. He had to be close to Sophia's dad's age. The way he was looking at her was anything but fatherly though.

Audrey flicked her eyes back and forth between them. And the plot thickened...

"Oh," Sophia blushed and moved to the side. "This is Audrey. She's new."

"Yes," Henry smiled, eyes never moving from Sophia. "I gathered that."

But finally he turned to Audrey. "Lovely to meet you, Miss...?"

"Just Audrey's fine." She narrowed her eyes at him. This guy was entirely too smooth. And he was perving over a girl half his age. Okay so Sophia might be eighteen already, but *still*.

"I wanted her to meet Graham," Sophia said.

"He's in the back, excelling at being a hermit as always." Henry waved to the hallway that led further back into the building.

Sophia said goodbye to Henry and then led the way. There weren't any windows so it was dark until they came to the end of the hallway where it opened to another large office.

Where a young guy with heavy black glasses sat at a desk typing furiously away on a laptop.

A working laptop.

He looked up at Audrey's gasp.

"Oh. You're here." He pushed his glasses up his nose and blinked owlishly at them.

"Graham," Sophia laughed. "Get up. Come say hi."

"Oh. Right." He laughed self-deprecatingly, pushed his glasses up again and then got to his feet. He was tall and lanky, with thick brown hair that hadn't been cut recently and curled at the back of his neck.

He had on a gray t-shirt that said in faded lettering, *My Password is the Last Seven Digits of Pi*. He held his hand out to Audrey. His eyes slid slightly to the left when he looked at her, like he couldn't quite handle eye contact.

Her attention was quickly drawn back to the laptop though. Talk about precious commodities.

Audrey looked at the ceiling. She remembered what Sophia had said about where the electricity came from for the water pump back at the house. "Solar panels on this building too?"

Both Sophia and Graham nodded but it was Graham who spoke up. "Twenty-one buildings in town have panels."

Audrey felt her eyebrows go up at that. "So many?"

"There was a company in town who installed them before... well, before," Sophia said.

Graham nodded. "After the Commander took over and established Jacob's Well as a township, the first thing he did was start prioritizing energy needs."

"Lemme guess," Audrey couldn't keep the snark out of her voice, "the Commander decides who gets the electricity?"

Graham looked confused. "Uh... no. Community members submit requests and the council votes on them."

Oh. Well. That wasn't what Audrey had expected.

"Every request goes into a category of need," he explained. "Shelter, food, and security requests come first. Then on down the list to things like entertainment."

"When we can manage, we have movie night over at the old theater," Sophia added.

"And the laptop," Audrey said, hoping her eagerness wasn't showing too much, "You're online?"

Graham looked surprised at her question. He nodded. "Most people don't even know there is an internet anymore."

Audrey shrugged. "My Uncle was well prepared." That was one word for it. Uncle Dale had taken the term *Prepper* to the extreme, way before The Fall. He inherited the fallout shelter from his dad along with a healthy paranoia that one day the world was gonna go to hell in a handbasket. And then... when it did, he was one of the few with all the supplies and know how to survive. Including EMP-proof computers that stayed linked to satellite backups of the basic internet infrastructure.

Graham nodded, letting out a low, impressed whistle. "It took us awhile to find a laptop that wasn't fried by the EMP attacks but we finally managed. Satellites stored back up images of big portions of the internet and once President Goddard got us access keys, we've started rebuilding. It's still pretty basic stuff, but we've got global communications, satellite imagery, commerce and trade. It's a start."

Audrey eyed the laptop and she fought the impulse to bite her lip. She still had three weeks to make it to the coast in time for the meetup with the Nomansland representative. But if for some reason she missed that window?

She'd need to contact them again for a new set of coordinates.

Just one problem.

No matter how many hours she spent with Uncle Dale at the computer, she was total crap at programming and learning to follow the million rabbit trails on the dark web it took to contact Nomansland in the first place. She just never had a head for math. Charlie, he'd been the mathlete.

Sophia must have mistaken her intense stare of concentration at the laptop.

"I know, just looking at it makes you want to check your email, doesn't it?" Sophia joked. "I was glued to screens when I was a kid."

Audrey jerked her eyes away from the laptop and smiled at Sophia and shook her head. "Me too. But God, that feels like a hundred years ago."

"It wasn't healthy anyway," Sophia said. "The kids in our community are growing up knowing the important things."

Audrey stopped herself midway through rolling her eyes but she apparently wasn't fast enough because she caught Nix smirking at her reaction. When had he even come in?

She took a step closer to Sophia and turned her back on him.

"Well, you guys should get going," Sophia said, looking from Audrey to Graham, toothy smile showing. "The town won't show itself." She gestured toward the door.

What? Wasn't Sophia going to—

"Oh. Yeah, um, I mean. Yes." Graham pushed his glasses up his nose and tugged on the bottom of his t-shirt. "I'll be your tour guide today." He smiled at Audrey, his eyes quickly shifting slightly to the side of her gaze.

"Well, I'm off," Sophia said enthusiastically. "Great to see you, Graham. Y'all have fun. Ta ta!"

Then Sophia was off, fairly prancing down the hall. Audrey tilted her head watching her go. Yep. Prancing was the only word for that.

"Why's she in such a good mood all the damn time?" she muttered.

"I don't know, but maybe you should take notes."

Audrey glared at Nix, her mouth dropping open. Had he really just insinuated—?

"Come on," Graham said, completely ignoring Nix. "There's so much to show you. Santiago is the town's premier engineer and he's been doing some really amazing things this year."

While no one could stand up to Sophia's bubbly cheer, Graham did sound excited. A pretty obvious ploy, if you asked her. Use the town's two least offensive, most cheerful members to try to sell the place.

Flash some running water, electricity, and technology at a girl and the shine of it all was supposed to make her forget the fact that they'd raffled her off like the prize pig at a fair last night? Fat chance.

Graham waved to Henry as they passed him in the front office and then it was back out into the sunshine of the morning on the town square.

"What did Sophia show you already?" Graham asked, holding a hand up to shade his eyes as he looked around.

"Nothing really. She pretty much just made a beeline to your office."

He nodded and dropped his hand, pushing his glasses up his nose as he did. "Okay, well, this is the town."

He gestured awkwardly with both his hands. "There's the Food Pantry. Everyone who comes into town is given a ration card. Two square meals a day. Now," his face scrunched, "it's not the most *amazing* food. There's a lot of sprouted beans and grains. But they do make sure everyone gets a daily amount of Vitamin C so no one gets scurvy and Michelle—she's the town's nutritionist works with the Commander and Henry in there to coordinate imports and exports—"

"Imports and exports?" Audrey raised her eyebrows.

"Bartering," Nix growled from behind them, making Audrey jump. How did he keep sneaking up on her? "He means bartering."

Graham turned to Nix. "It's thinking like that that's keeping the economy in the dark ages. While yes," he waved a hand, "we still do mostly exchange goods and services, and within Central Texas South we use credits, the Army pays their soldiers in paper script. It won't be too long before we're back to a currency-based economy."

"Don't see the problem with sticking to silver and gold," Nix muttered.

Graham narrowed his eyes in Nix's direction. "Is that sarcasm? You know I'm not good with sarcasm."

Nix's face cracked into a grin. "No champ. No sarcasm here." He clapped Graham on the back and Graham jumped forward out of his grasp like Nix had just jolted him with a hot poker.

"I don't like nicknames either," Graham mumbled.

Audrey understood the feeling. Nix was enough to ruin anyone's mood.

"So what's first on the list?" Audrey asked. "Are we checking out the Food Pantry?"

"Aw God, please say no," Nix grumbled. "That place stinks. They're always sprouting something or other. Don't know why the food that's already grown has to grow extra right before you eat it."

"Didn't you hear what I was just saying?" Graham said. "Sprouting beans and seeds prevents scurvy. For centuries the Chinese stopped scurvy by eating sprouted beans during long winters in the north. Captain James Cook kept his sailors from getting it during a three-year—"

"*That* was sarcasm." Then Nix tilted his head. "Okay, more of a rhetorical statement. But still, same idea."

Graham just shook his head in annoyance and then turned back to Audrey. "I thought I'd just show you around the square. Then if you want, we can go down to the river. And maybe take a drive over to the well the township's named after."

"A drive?"

"Sure," Graham smiled. "The water truck goes out there twice a week and today's a fill up day. We can hop on for a ride there and back."

"Sounds great," Audrey said and for once her smile was even genuine. Then she felt Nix's calculating gaze on her. Dammit. Maybe if she was lucky there wouldn't be enough space on the truck and they could ditch the guard dog.

In the meantime, Audrey kept her eyes peeled and she made mental notes as Graham led her around the square.

First, he showed her the communal laundry—they might have more access to water than most but that didn't mean they squandered it.

Next were the stables. Horse breeding had become a new boom business and Audrey couldn't help fawning over a couple of new colts.

Sentries stood guard all over the stable, though. If she was going to take a horse instead of a vehicle, she'd have to be careful about it.

Next stop was an unexpected one—the library. A young woman who couldn't be more than a year or two older than Audrey herself stood behind the check in counter. A tall man sat in a chair off to the right, observing Audrey and her entourage as they filed in the library.

The woman, Gina, smiled broadly as they came in. "I was hoping you'd stop by." She came out from behind the desk and Audrey's eyes widened, taking in her large, pregnant belly.

"Oh," Audrey gasped.

Gina laughed. "I know, right? It still startles me whenever I look in a mirror." Her hands dropped lovingly to her belly.

Audrey felt like there were things she was supposed to say. Small talk that happened when someone was having a baby. But she really hadn't been around women in such a long time, and even back then, she'd just been a teenager.

"So, um," Audrey fumbled, "when are you due. Do you know if it's a boy or girl?" Then she winced internally. It wasn't like they could just plug into an ultrasound machine or—

"It's a *girl*," Gina said, giggling. "The whole town celebrated when we found out. Every one of us counts, you know?"

"Hah." Audrey blinked. So was this woman like, excited that in nineteen or so years her baby girl would get her own lottery? She couldn't forget even for a second—beneath all the niceties, this place was seriously screwed up.

Gina must have mistaken whatever look was on her face because she hurried to fill in, "We have two doctors in town and a couple years ago one of the salvage teams managed to find an ultrasound machine that wasn't fried by the EMPs. One of the doctors is even a surgeon. He specialized in podiatry."

Her nose crinkled slightly before she continued brightly, "But a surgeon's a surgeon, you know? He had a residency at John's Hopkins and everything." She said all this like Audrey should be impressed so Audrey nodded and made an appropriately awed noise.

"John and I can't wait to meet our little Johanna. Isn't that right?" Gina reached out a hand to the man sitting off to the side and he came over. He stood at Gina's back and wrapped his arms around her stomach from behind.

Okay, where was the barf bag on this ride? This was a little too much indoctrination for one morning. Audrey was more than glad when Graham made their excuses and they moved on to the salvage yard and the smithy at the edge of town.

"Scrapper teams are always going out and bringing salvage back."

Audrey's interest perked as they walked through what was essentially a large yard that looked several acres wide. All around her men sorted and separated junk, using crow bars and hammers to take apart everything from old computers to cars.

"Your basic salvage operation falls into three categories," Nix said. "Luxury items, metals, and fuel. Pre-D-Day luxuries are getting harder and harder to find. You can make a mint on toilet paper and tampons these days."

Audrey spun and gave him a *wtf* look but he just kept looking out at the salvage yard and talking like he was discussing the daily catch of fish.

"Other high value items are anything you can melt down," Nix said. "Copper. Aluminum. Nickel. Steel. Then of course there's your fuels. Most diesel and natural gas sources have been locked down, but every once in a while, you run across a real find."

Audrey glanced around her at all the people so dutifully going about their tasks, morning light falling on the pristine little town like something out of a fucking Norman Rockwell painting.

And she couldn't help thinking that this whole day felt like the first thirty minutes of a horror movie. She'd loved watching them when she was a kid. For the first half hour of the movie, everything was always hunky dory.

The crew of the space ship got along perfect. The family moved into the old fixer upper that just needed a little tender loving care. The community appeared to be a well-oiled machine of friendly neighbors and PTA meetings.

Until night fell and then shit started getting real.

So if Jacob's Well Township looked so picture perfect on the outside, just how rotted would the underbelly be once the sun went down?

CHAPTER EIGHT

NIX

She was trying not to let on but Nix could see the way Audrey's body was stringing tighter and tighter with every hour that passed.

He could also tell she was less than pleased when he told the driver of the water hauler truck to take a hike and took his place behind the wheel. With Audrey in the center seat of the narrow front bench between him and Graham. Nix had the pleasure of watching her squirm the entire drive out to Jacob's Well.

It was probably wrong to get so much amusement out of the situation. But she was safe. And she was scrappy. She had spirit.

He'd been trying to put his finger on it all day, and that was what it was.

Too many of the women they rescued were just... *broken*. Not beyond repair. But damaged bad.

Nix looked out at the fading sun while Graham nattered Audrey's ear off about Jacob's Well, the large natural spring that had a nine-foot circular opening at the top. It did indeed make it look like a well. Nature made.

It went down about thirty feet before breaking off into a series of underground caverns. A couple of the Commander's men had tried diving it but no one got very far before having to come up for air.

Nix had seen the well a hundred times, anyway. He was far more interested in watching Audrey. Her red hair flashed in the setting sun. A thousand little golden starbursts.

Then there were her eyes. And the way she seemed to soak up every little thing Graham told her about the town.

No doubt she was planning her next escape attempt. He'd talked to Holder and Crawford about her multiple attempts last night. It had him smiling all through his morning calisthenics.

Scrappy.

It would serve her well.

The few times he'd even considered putting his name in for the lottery, it was the thought of those world-weary, wounded women that had him pulling back. Not because they were broken. Lord knew he was no one to judge. But a woman like that, and the way he liked what he liked in the bedroom? No, it'd never work. He'd only terrify some poor girl even more.

A woman like Audrey though? Scrappy? Full of spirit? Ready to give back as good as you gave?

It just might.

As long as you keep her safe.

His gut went tight as Audrey turned his way, her hand going over her eyes. She wasn't looking at him. Or at least she was pretending not to even see him.

That was okay. She could pretend all she wanted. All day, the awareness between them had been as thick as the air before a storm.

"So how far beyond the well does the border of the township go?" Audrey asked.

Nix covered his smirk. *Come on, baby, you can do better than that.* Her pretenses of subtlety had dropped off as the day wore on.

When they'd walked through the corn and grain fields, she'd eyed everything from the storage granaries to the horses the farmers rode to the hoes and spades they used to till the fields. It was like he could see her ticking off boxes in her head.

Food. Transportation. Weapons.

The question was when she was going to make a run for it again.

Tonight, if she was impatient.

Nix cocked his head and narrowed his eyes at her. This was the woman who had tried *three* times last night to escape. Patience probably wasn't her strong suit.

"Alrighty," Danny said as he came back to where they were standing. He'd stripped off his shirt and Nix shook his head.

Showing off his muscles might have worked for Danny back in the day but five minutes in Audrey's presence and Nix knew that was the totally wrong approach to take with her. If he could have smacked Danny up the back of the head he would have.

"Got the tanker all filled up." Danny grinned at Audrey, oblivious to her rigid posture. And then the dumb bastard just kept on staring after she nodded politely back at him.

Danny was no master of subtlety either. "I'm really looking forward to getting to know you, Audrey. Can't tell you how long I waited for..." He wiped his hands on the sides of his jeans and all but bounced where he stood. "You know." He gestured her way. "To meet someone like you."

Audrey's eyebrows dropped in confusion though she kept smiling vaguely. "Someone like me?"

Danny just kept that goofy grin on his face. "You're real pretty."

Audrey's smile dropped and Danny stepped back, his face going ashen. "Sorry, was I not supposed to say that?" Danny looked to Nix and Graham. "Till like, the official courtship stuff starts tonight?"

"Tonight?" Audrey's voice sounded about an octave higher than normal. "You're one of the..."

She whipped around and looked toward Graham like he'd betrayed her. "Did you bring me out here so you could— You think you can just gang up on me like this?"

"What?" Graham squeaked, hand pushing his glasses up over and over like he did when he was upset about something. "No, it's not like tha—"

"Get back," Audrey said, stepping back so she could see all three of them, her hands up like she was ready for an attack.

Nix sighed. He knew he should have brought the dart gun. "You got us. This was all a big conspiracy. We showed you around town today as an elaborate ruse just to get you out here alone so we could have our wicked, wicked way with you."

If looks could kill, Nix would be sliced into ribbons on the ground by Audrey's glare.

"No we didn't!" Graham exclaimed. "I swear, Audrey, that's not true at all—"

"Sorry I forgot my sarcasm sign to flash at you," Nix pushed Graham aside and stepped up in front of Audrey. She didn't back up but her fists clenched and her fighting stance went even more rigid.

"You're gonna pull a muscle standing like that. Fighting's all about being loose." He reached out to readjust her stance and she swung at him. He barely ducked out of the way in time.

Feisty. He'd have to add feisty to the list of things he liked about her.

She swung again and he grabbed her hand midair. "Now look, woman, you gotta fight smarter."

She growled and swung with her free hand. He captured it in his other hand and continued shaking his head at her. "If you'd landed that hit, all you would have gotten out of it was a broken hand," he chided.

Well that just seemed to piss her off more.

"Oh yeah?" she asked, eyebrows lowered and eyes wide. "Please do tell me more, oh wise master."

The next thing Nix knew, she was yanking and rolling backwards—and he was flying through the air.

He landed hard on his back, all the air knocked out of him.

What the— How had she managed to fucking *flip* him?

She stood over him, dusting her hands off, a satisfied smile on her face. "You were saying?"

He tried to sit up but she was quicker. Her booted foot landed on his hand.

"Ah ah ah," she said, steel in her voice now. "Just remember, if you try to touch me with this hand tonight during whatever this courtship bullshit is, I'll personally ensure that every single one of these fingers ends up broken before morning. You got it, *pal?*"

It would probably piss her off if he grinned right now.

So with as straight a face as he could manage, all he said was, "Got it."

CHAPTER NINE

AUDREY

For all her bravado, Audrey was scared shitless as the four of them road back to town. Yes, *four*. There was no space in the cab so Danny climbed onto a narrow ledge on the back of the tanker and was apparently just *holding on*.

Maybe he'd fall off on the way back. She should be so lucky.

God, his muscles had been even bigger than Nix's. This morning she wouldn't have even thought that was possible. He wasn't as tall as Nix, but he could probably choke her to death without even breaking a sweat.

Remember your training.

It didn't matter how big her opponent was. You just had to use their own strength against them. She'd fought men off before who wanted what these men would eventually try to take. Okay, just *one* man, but still.

Her back went ramrod straight at the memory. She'd been asleep when the spineless little shit attacked. She'd woken up to hands squeezing her breasts and yanking at her jeans.

She'd screamed and screamed but no one was around to help. Charlie was off with Uncle Dale hunting.

He knew that. He'd waited for them to go.

Her own *cousin*.

Uncle Dale's son, Rodney.

He was just eighteen but he was plenty big. He took after Uncle Dale—brawny with big, broad shoulders—and he was always eating more than his share to stay that way. Charlie hadn't liked the way he'd looked at her for a while by that point but Audrey always told him not to be ridiculous. Rodney was *related* to her, for God's sake.

She'd never be so naïve again.

When she started fighting back, Rodney had dragged her off the cot and slammed her on the floor.

But he was the one who'd been in for the rude awakening.

He never had the patience for Uncle Dale's jujitsu lessons. He relied on his size and brute force.

One broken nose, dislocated shoulder, and bitten off pinky finger later, he'd learned better.

That's right, she'd bitten his damn finger completely off. He was the one left crying on the floor in a crumpled ball while she locked him in the bunker and scrambled up the tunnel to the backyard. It was the first time she'd been outside in eight years.

And she couldn't even enjoy it. She'd raced across the yard and into the house, hiding in the closet until Uncle Dale and Charlie got back.

Uncle Dale didn't want to believe it of his son. Audrey could see it broke something in him to hear it.

Didn't stop him from choosing his son over her. Charlie was welcome to stay, but she had to go.

His excuse?

Rodney was becoming a man and with there being no women around, well, Audrey was just 'too much temptation for the boy.'

Rodney was still down in the bunker during all this. Charlie wanted to go down there and kill him. When Uncle Dale got in his way, Charlie punched him.

She and Charlie left the next day, never speaking another word to their uncle.

And Audrey would always have to live with the knowledge that if not for her, Charlie would never have had to leave Uncle Dale's.

He'd still be alive.

The truck bounced when it hit a pothole and her thigh glanced off of Nix's. She jerked it back. Nix didn't look her way but she still saw a smirk tip the edge of his lips.

She looked back and forth between him and Graham. So they hadn't attacked her at the spring like she'd first thought.

Apparently they were committed to this veneer of civility. But if she was 'too much temptation' for her own *cousin*, how did she think these sex-starved men who'd been promised a wife would behave?

She could play their game.

Sure, one bitten off finger didn't make her a cold-hearted killer, exactly, but she liked to think she could take care of herself.

Just not Charlie. Or Dad.

Well, she was the only one left, so what did it matter anymore?

Only minutes later, they were back in town.

"All right," Graham said as he climbed down from the truck. "Clark told me he'd have dinner ready at the residence tonight. Mateo will be there too. So we can just head over th—"

"What? Who's Clark? And R— R whatever?" Audrey ignored Nix's hand to help her down from the cab and got out Graham's side.

"Um." Graham pushed his glasses up his nose. For Christ's sake, why didn't he just get some better fitting glasses? They sat crooked on his face too.

"They're the fourth and fifth," Nix said, coming around the front of the truck as Danny strolled up from the back.

Audrey swallowed. It felt like they were closing in on her. "Who's the third?" she asked, her voice going much higher pitched than she would have preferred.

"Um," Graham said, again with his finger on those damn glasses.

"You?" she asked, stepping away from him and feeling like she'd just been punched in the stomach.

Sure there'd been that moment at the well spring where she thought he'd led her out for them to fuck with her, but other than that, she'd considered Graham an ally. A non-threatening ally.

Stupid. So fucking stupid that she felt betrayed.

Or that she'd let herself feel for even a moment that he could be a friend in this place.

No wonder Sophia had been so eager to drop her off with him this morning.

"So you think I'll fuck you because you were nice to me for a few hours?"

Graham's brow furrowed and he'd looked genuinely upset. Well too fucking bad.

"You can all go fuck yourselves. Enjoy dinner without me."

She spun on her heel and started stomping away. Back to Sophia's house since she didn't have anywhere better to go.

Within a few feet, though, she heard heavy clomping footsteps behind her. She looked over her shoulder and glared at Nix.

A big, dramatic exit felt far less satisfying when one of the people you were storming away from followed you.

At least Graham was still standing where she'd left him, looking appropriately devastated.

So why did she feel a twinge of regret at her harsh words? He looked like a kicked puppy.

She shook her head at herself.

Graham was a grown up and *they* were the ones with the fucked-up system. She was the victim here.

Then she grimaced. No. Fuck that. She wasn't a victim. She was the one stalking off. Controlling her own damn destiny. Not going along like some stupid sheep to that dinner to meet the rest of her *fiancés*.

Ugh.

She got to Sophia's house—or rather, the Commander's house— and was glad the front door was unlocked. And if slamming it behind her once she got inside was a little childish, well, considering the circumstances, fuck it.

She ran up the stairs to her room and slammed that door too. She'd forgotten how ridiculously good slamming doors felt.

Until she was all alone in her room. No. Not her room. She looked around the overly pink, girly room.

Hundred to one odds, Sophia had decorated this place.

Audrey flopped backwards on the bed dramatically. She was starving but she ignored the growling of her stomach. There were plenty nights she'd gone without in the bunker during lean times when Uncle Dale got extreme with the rations. Going hungry one more night wouldn't kill her.

Her eyelids were soooooo heavy. She'd just close them for a second. Just a few... seconds...

CHAPTER TEN

CLARK

Damn, they weren't kidding. She was gorgeous. Clark stood at the entrance to the bedroom where she was sleeping.

The last rays of sunset washed over her graceful form as she slowly inhaled and exhaled, her softly rounded face empty of any of the world's concerns.

When Graham had come in earlier bumbling about how pretty and nice their wife was, Clark had just rolled his eyes.

Clark put his name in the lottery for the same reason every other man in town did. He hadn't had a good fuck in almost seven goddamned years.

Some nights he thought he'd die if he didn't have a wet, inviting female body to sink his cock into.

Before The Fall, women had thrown themselves at him. He was twenty-five when Xterminate first hit. An up and coming lawyer at a big-shot law firm in Austin, he was the *shit*. He'd been fucking chicks for almost a decade. And going from having a hot, willing woman in his bed every other night to... nothing. *Christ*.

But he was no animal. He'd never, *ever* force what a woman wasn't willing to give.

He'd fought in the Texas War for Independence more because it seemed something to do when everything else was suddenly gone.

He'd just happened to be on a weekend trip out to Big Bend when D-Day hit and Austin was blasted off the damn map. Mom, Dad, everyone and everything was just... *blam-o*. Gone.

So why the fuck not join up?

He managed to survive that shitshow somehow but life after, well, it was pretty much just as fucking ugly and shitty as before. He no longer had any illusions about basic human decency. There was no such thing.

But he heard about Jacob's Well—finally one place that sounded like it wouldn't make him want to blow his damn brains out every day, he'd moved here and settled in.

And there, on the bed in front of him, was the woman who would be his.

Well, his and four other guys, but hey, times they were a changin'. He could go with the flow. Especially now that he'd literally won the jackpot.

She stirred on the bed, doing this fucking adorable thing where she scrunched up her nose and batted at the air with her hand.

Then she blinked and screeched, shooting up in bed and glaring daggers at him. "Who the fuck are you?" she shouted.

"Morning kitten," he said, striding into the room holding his pot of roast beef stew aloft. "Have a good cat nap?"

He smiled his most charming smile. In the old days a smile like that would have had the panties melting off even the most frigid coed.

But his Audrey didn't look even remotely melted by it.

"Get the fuck out of here." She reached for the closest thing she could, the heavy antique candelabra by the bed. She swung it toward them, dumping the unlit candles as she went.

"How nice," Nix said, walking in with Graham on his heels. "I see you're already getting acquainted. Danny's on his way up and Mateo is—"

"You can't be in here!" Audrey scrambled off the other end of the bed, still brandishing the candelabra. "This is *my* room."

Nix and Clark looked at each other. Then they laughed.

"As soon as a betrothal is announced," Graham hurried to explain, "everything becomes communal. Property, wealth, status and standing in the township. What's ours is yours and yours is ours." He shoved his glasses up his nose and looked at the floor like he was afraid of being chastised.

Clark just put the stew pot on the nightstand where she'd grabbed the candlestick from and sat on the edge of the bed, one leg crossed over the other.

"Yes, Kitten, so if this *were* your room, it would be ours as well. But this is the Commander's house and therefore, the Commander's room. Your room is in the house that was bequeathed to us as the newest betrothed family. About five houses down—" He glanced out the window to get his bearings and then pointed, "—*thataway*."

Audrey just glared back at him. "And I suppose you think my body belongs to you too? So you're all here to take what's yours, is that it?"

"You haven't started eating yet, have you?" came Danny's baritone as he barreled into the room. He looked around at everyone then his eyes paused on Audrey, candelabra still raised over her head.

"What'd I miss?"

Clark rolled his eyes but then he settled his gaze on Audrey. Like she could feel his eyes on her, she looked back at him.

"I'm sure you've been informed that no one here will take anything you aren't willing to give. But baby, I assure you I'll make it my mission in life to make you *crave* what we can offer you." He didn't bother hiding the husky drawl at the end of that sentence. Neither did he miss the way his kitten swallowed as her eyes darted momentarily to his lips.

Then her eyes widened like she was appalled at herself and she took another step back.

"No use cornering yourself over there, gorgeous," Clark said. "Come. Dine with us." He lifted the lid off the pot. "Venison stew. When was the last time you had fresh meat?"

Her face jerked toward the pot of stew and he'd have sworn he saw her nostrils flare. Jesus, if she was that voracious for some stew, what other hungers could he awaken in her?

The lottery was, well, what it was—a total crapshoot. The women who were brought back were usually at least in their thirties if not middle-aged. Or at least they all looked that way, life had been so hard the last decade.

To be fair, Clark would have enjoyed any of them. He'd realized over the last handful of years that there was beauty to be found in any woman. It was the shape of them—whatever form that shape came in. The rounding of the hips. That softness of the breasts and stomach. Soft where men were all hard. So, so soft...

Shit, he was staring. And getting hard. Fuck, he hadn't realized how difficult it would be just being in the same room as her and knowing that one day, one day soon if he had anything to do with it, he'd have his hands on all that softness. He'd hear her womanly moans of pleasure as he—

Nix smacked him upside the back of his head and he was roughly jerked back to the present.

Right. Fuck. Focus.

If there was one thing all his playboy days had taught him, it was that—contrary to popular belief—the way into a woman's panties wasn't through charm and wit alone. That helped, sure.

But the way to win more than a one-night pass into the gates of heaven? Build trust.

"Some stew?"

"So you can drug me and make it easier on yourselves?" she spat. "No fucking way."

"Audrey, we would never—" Graham sputtered but Clark held up a hand to cut him off.

"You're right to be wary," Clark said. "I have no idea what it's like to be coming into this situation like you are. To have been through what you have. What any woman has in the last decade."

"Danny, if you would," Clark gestured the big bronze-skinned man forward. Clark had never had much to do with him before. The Assistant Trade Secretary and a general laborer didn't have much in common.

Except now, they had Audrey, so he supposed he'd get to know him fairly intimately. Maybe a few years ago, the thought of sharing his wife would have disturbed Clark, but, considering the new circumstances, *only* having to share her with four men seemed like a luxury.

He took a bowl and spoon from the tray Danny had carried upstairs. With the ladle, he poured himself a generous helping of stew. For once, there should be enough to go around.

The town made all sorts of concessions for a newly betrothed family. As if a woman wasn't enough incentive.

The Commander was a smart bastard. The hope of winning the lottery was enough to keep even the most unruly townsfolk in line. Guys would do anything not to fuck up their chances at getting their name on the ballot.

Clark took a loaded spoonful and popped it in his mouth. Fuck, it was still hot but he didn't care. The flavor of the meat exploded on his tongue and he didn't conceal his groan of pleasure. Because while trust was the main way to connect to a woman, good old-fashioned lust had gotten plenty of men most of the way there too.

He glanced at Audrey over the rim of the bowl and saw her eyes locked on his mouth. Her eyes were dark with hunger and he didn't know if it was his lips or the stew she was eyeing. He'd go out on a limb and say it was both.

Back before The Fall, it had been popular belief that men needed sex more than women, but his extensive experience had shown just the opposite. He knew some women who were all but starved for it. Who could barely wait to get him out of the club or to his car or even to the back alley of the bar before they were yanking up their miniskirts and tugging on his belt.

"See," he said, licking the spoon lazily, eyes still on Audrey. "Perfectly safe."

Her eyes narrowed, but then glanced back to the stew longingly before finally snapping back to his. "Leave the bowl on the bed and back up." She shook the candlestick in a circle. "All of you. Back up."

Nix nodded at them and they all shuffled back until they were lined up against the wall with the window to the outside. The setting sun caused the light in the room to dim gradually as the minutes passed.

Audrey crawled back over the bed, awkward with the heavy candelabra in her hand, and sat against the headboard. She snatched the bowl of soup up and began to all but shovel it into her mouth.

She was voracious.

Fuck but Clark's cock was aching. He shifted on his feet, glad he'd opted for formal wear. He slipped off his suit jacket and folded it over one arm in front of his body to cover up the hard-on tenting the front of his slacks.

All in good time, buddy. All in good time.

"So sorry I'm late, so, so sorry," said Mateo as he walked into the room holding a tray of—

"Holy shit, is that chocolate?" Danny yelled, jogging over to Mateo, eyes glued to what he held.

Mateo jerked back so violently he almost dropped the tray.

Everyone in the room gasped at the thought of the chocolate truffles spilling—even Audrey, Clark was gratified to see.

"Step back," Nix ordered Danny. He yanked Danny back by his elbow.

"Hey man," Danny jerked his arm back. "I just wanted to see. Chill out."

Mateo glared at Danny. "They're for our wife."

Audrey's whole demeanor went cold at that. "You think I'll whore myself out just because you scrounged up some chocolate?"

Mateo was a tall, rail thin Hispanic guy. He had the perfect, smooth, symmetrical features that would have made him perfect for modelling back in the day.

He didn't flinch at Audrey's harsh words. He just walked around the foot of the bed.

Which Clark could admit took balls considering the heavy brass candelabra she'd grabbed up again.

Mateo stopped several feet away and dropped down to his knees, head bent toward her. He set the tray down on the ground.

"I'm your servant. I vow to protect you with my body and to give you all that I own. I vow to see to your food, shelter, and safety for as long as we both shall live. I vow to—"

"Stop it," Audrey snapped, stepping back from Mateo's bowed form. "Get up."

Mateo nodded and got to his feet. He lifted the tray toward her again. Clark had no idea how the hell he'd pulled that off, getting his hands on some chocolate.

Mateo was a mechanic and tinkerer—he worked at the shop in town fixing old shit that Clark and Henry then bartered.

It was a good job.

But still. Fucking *chocolate*? It was the one thing that was prized almost as much as gold.

"I assure you these aren't drugged," Mateo said. "I'll take a bite of any one of them to prove they're safe."

Danny brightened. "Hey, I can do that too. I'll show her how safe they are."

"Shut up," Clark and Nix said at the same time.

Audrey just glared at all of them in turn. "I told you I can't be fucking bought with fucking chocolate."

Mateo just nodded his head. "I didn't mean to insinuate that you could. I should have been more sensitive to the situation. Is there anything else I can bring you to help your comfort as you settle in?"

Audrey's eyes narrowed in on Mateo shrewdly. "You said you'll do anything I want you to?"

Mateo nodded eagerly. "Yes. Anything that's within my power."

Audrey leaned in, never breaking eye contact with Mateo. For a second Clark was almost jealous of the skinny bastard. He was standing closer than any of them had gotten to her all night.

"Then get me a truck and help get me the *hell* out of here and back on my way down to the coast where I was trying to get when that fucknut," she jabbed a finger in Nix's direction, "shot me in the ass with a tranq gun!"

For a second it looked like Mateo was almost considering it. Clark was about to go knock some sense into the man when his head suddenly dropped and his face knit in pain.

"I am sorry. I vowed to protect you. I can't in good conscience do something I know would put your life in danger."

Audrey huffed out in frustration then clenched the candelabra tighter. "Get out of here," she yelled, taking a swing that Mateo only managed to dodge at the last second. "All of you! I can't stand to look at your faces for one more second."

Nix nodded his head toward the door and one by one, they headed out.

It was probably the right move. They weren't going to get anywhere with her tonight. But Clark couldn't help stealing one last lingering glance her direction.

Standing there like an avenging angel, eyes flashing and red hair glinting in the last rays of the setting sun like a halo of fire, she was the most magnificent thing he'd ever seen.

CHAPTER ELEVEN

AUDREY

One week later and Audrey was no closer to getting the hell out of there. But, true to their word, none of her *fiancés* had laid a hand on her.

They had, however, continued to barrel their way into her room every night for dinner. Nothing as extravagant as that first night. But Mateo always managed to bring a little something extra.

Yesterday it had been cornbread sweetened with honey. The day before, two whole oranges, just for her. She'd stopped resisting the gifts of food. God knew she could use the nutrition and variety in her diet.

And so what if they were eventually expecting something in return for the supposed 'generosity'? She'd be long gone before they came to collect, she'd make damn sure of that.

Because during the long days, she'd been scouting and making plans. Under the guise of wanting to be useful—or, as she'd put it to Nix, wanting to earn her share so they couldn't say she owed them anything—she'd been strategically taking on odd jobs here and there throughout town.

Like helping out at the soup kitchen line and conveniently noting where the surplus grain and jerky was kept. That kind of thing. She couldn't get out of wasting a couple afternoons volunteering at the library and helping with candle-making. Both Sophia's ideas, and Audrey hadn't known how to beg off without looking suspicious.

But today she was getting back to some meaningful scheming. She was volunteering at the stables and trying to butter up some of the horses again. Get them familiar with her scent. Get them to like her.

That was the idea anyway.

Too bad it had been a total clusterfuck. Turned out horses could sense when you were nervous or uneasy. Damn things were friggin' lie detectors.

She'd barely get near one before the damn thing bolted on her. Instead of bonding with a potential means of escape, she'd spent her afternoon relegated to shoveling manure and sweating her ass off.

All she had to show for the day were some wicked blisters and the image lodged forever in her brain of Nix's amused face as he smirked at her every chance he got. Ugh!

Whose bright idea was it anyway to fling themselves on the back of a giant animal that weighed to a ton, and then hurtle themselves down the road at speeds of up to twenty-five miles per hour?

Nope. It was back to looking for a vehicle and some gas.

Which was a problem. The whole reason she'd come back to the damn stables was because she had no freaking idea how to get her hands on a car or truck.

Even if she did manage to find one that hadn't been fried in the EMP bombings, she also needed one that was gassed up. And considering gas was one of the premium bartering currencies... Yeah, cars and gas were some of the most guarded things in town.

With a car or truck and clear roads, she could make it down to the coast in as little as five hours. Granted all the highways were congested with abandoned cars so it would take her longer still.

She was just five to ten *hours* from freedom. When they'd left Uncle

Dale's, Charlie had made her *swear* that if anything happened to him, she'd go on without him and start over...

She glanced down at her lap as she pulled the towel off her wet hair and swallowed hard.

Once she got to the coast, she could finally just *stop*. Stop fighting so hard. Stop running breakneck toward the finish line and never taking a breath. She might even finally give herself a moment to grieve Charlie.

Her jaw went rigid. But until then, *no*.

She had to go harder.

Get more cunning.

Outthink and outsmart.

So the horses wouldn't work out. Fine. Back to Plan A. She'd wanted to leave inconspicuously but if she gave up on subtlety, maybe just stealing one of the town's larger vehicles would work. But that would mean she'd have to—

A knock came at her bedroom door. "Are you decent?" called a male voice. Clark's, she thought. "I sure hope not, cause we're coming in." Yep, definitely Clark.

She scrambled to yank a t-shirt on over her head. Thank God she already had her jeans on.

The door slammed shut instead of pushing further open. Audrey heard multiple muffled voices through the door yelling at each other.

"Audrey?" Graham asked with a knock. "Are you ready for us?"

Audrey blew out a long breath and tipped her head back to face the ceiling. "No," she whispered. "Definitely not."

But louder, she called, "Yes, you can come in."

"Excellent," Clark said, pushing through the door, a wide, charming smile across his face like always.

Danny eagerly pushed in behind him, followed by Nix and then Graham, and finally, Mateo. She made eye contact with Mateo for only a second before his eyes dropped and he clasped his hands behind his back.

She couldn't focus on him for long, though, because Danny was busy putting himself on display with all the subtlety of a peacock. He pulled his shirt off over his head.

"Whew, is it hot in here? The sun was roasting us out there while we worked on Clan McKinley's roof." He wadded his t-shirt up into a ball and tossed it near the wall, then grinned at Audrey.

She didn't know whether to laugh at him or go snatch his shirt up from where he'd thrown it and tell him *no shirt no shoes no service*.

Except... well... Okay so a *little* part of her *might* admire the way his abs were cut and just so damn well defined. Seriously, back before The Fall, he could have been an underwear model. Hands down. His face was nice too, his features blunt and boyish, but that body... *whew*.

While she'd been intimidated by Danny that first day, after spending a week with him, the idea of being afraid of him seemed laughable now. He was like a big, sweet, goofy puppy. And when she wasn't afraid all those muscles were going to be used to attack her, well... she couldn't say he wasn't nice to look at.

"Do you want to know what we're having for dinner tonight?" Clark asked, "or should we just leave you alone with Danny's abs?"

"What?" she shouted, jerking her eyes away from Danny's happy trail at the same time, Danny said, "Awesome!"

Audrey crossed her arms over her chair and glared at Clark. "You're not as funny as you think you are."

Clark held up a hand in a so-so gesture. "I don't know. I think I *might* be."

Audrey rolled her eyes and threw her hands up in the air but thankfully conversation moved on. Too bad she didn't like the next topic any better than the last.

"Let's get going," Nix said in his characteristic rumbling bass. "It's moving day. Food's ready at the house and we don't want it getting cold."

Audrey was the one who went cold. "Moving day?"

"Didn't someone tell you?" Graham asked, pushing his glasses up his nose. "After a week, you move into the residence with your clan."

Audrey's mouth dropped open. "No, I was *not* informed." Her eyes darted from one face to another. Goddammit. She wanted to lose her shit on them.

She wanted to scream and throw a fit and grab the candelabra like she had the first time they'd barged into her room. Except this time, she'd throw it. At Clark's head. Or Nix. Ooo, it'd feel good to clock Nix right in the forehead.

But dammit, she had a strategy.

Outthink. Outsmart.

Play it cool, Aud. Play it fucking cool.

They hadn't attacked her.

Her virtue was intact.

So far at least.

It wasn't that she didn't catch their eyes wandering. She did. Clark and Danny were especially bad about it.

But it didn't the feel the same as when she'd catch Rodney staring at her back at Uncle Dale's. When these guys looked at her, she didn't feel that... unnerving sense of menace behind it. At the time she'd thought Rodney was resentful of her costing him extra rations. Till she learned better.

And maybe it was just because these guys expected her to put out soon. If she continued denying them, would all the good easy banter disappear? Would they turn into monsters just like her cousin had?

Either way, just because they'd managed to play nice for a week, she was still outta here. If only she was closer to being ready. Every avenue she looked into, she only had more doors close in her face. She still had no weapons or transportation leads.

And now they thought she was moving in with them?

She took a deep breath in and out and leveled her glare at each man in turn. "There's still no sex. Got it?"

"Got it," said everyone.

Fine. She wouldn't balk because she still needed to play a certain role if she was going to make what she needed to happen. But that didn't mean she was going to be Mary fucking Poppins about it.

"Fuck right, you got it," she muttered, snatching up another pair of jeans and a couple shirts Sophia had provided that she'd come to think of as hers.

Then she stomped down the stairs and out of the Commander's house, all her fiancés on her heels like a trail of ducklings.

CHAPTER TWELVE

NIX

Audrey was up to something.

Nix stared at her shapely ass as she stormed down the sidewalk to their new house. All the other guys' eyes were glued the same place.

Well, except for Mateo, but who the hell knew what was up with that guy? Nix hadn't thought much about him before, but if anyone had asked, he would've guessed he was gay. Guess not if he'd put in for the lottery.

But Nix was getting off track.

Audrey hadn't tried to escape since that first night. But no way a woman like her would have just given up. No way in hell.

So this little act she'd been putting on all week? Going along with them, if not gracefully, at least without kicking and screaming? He didn't buy it for a second.

She was buttering them up. Trying to get them to let down their guard.

Well, he wasn't the town Security Squadron Captain for nothing. The Commander had given him the position because he was a damn good fighter and he had a nose for sniffing out security threats. Both from without and within. And Audrey was a flight risk if he'd ever seen one.

Which was a problem.

Because she was theirs.

Theirs to protect.

Theirs to pleasure.

Theirs to create a clan with. A family.

The more time he spent with her, the more attached he got to the idea. *Him.* If he wasn't so busy blowing off work and shadowing her every step to make sure she was safe, he might take a second to be disturbed at the sudden swing his priorities had taken.

But then, fuck that. Because the world was full of bitter and if you were lucky enough to get a taste of sweet, he was gonna hold onto it as hard as he fucking could.

"Come on." Graham waved Audrey up the drive to their house. "Mateo made spicy black beans and rice. I had a taste earlier and it's amazing."

Audrey smiled at him. And then her eyes darted around the yard. Like she was sizing it up and checking for escape routes.

At the same time, when Graham put his hand on her back to guide her through the front door, she didn't jerk back from his touch.

Nix smiled. She was getting used to them. Little by little, they were burrowing their way in. The Commander knew what he was doing by setting a three month get-to-know-you period.

Time and patience brought down barriers more effectively than force ever could. It was your run of the mill siege tactic.

Nix followed everyone in the house. Like others in the neighborhood, it was a basic two-story design, with a big open living room and kitchen area downstairs and bedrooms upstairs. It was built about eighty years ago and remodeled maybe a decade before The Fall. It was extravagant to have a house all to themselves for just six people.

Moving in here after years spent living four men to a room, sharing 'sanitation buckets' with all the other guys in the apartment complex... yeah, Nix had only been out of there for five days and already he felt so damn pampered by this place he never wanted to leave.

Each of the houses in this little neighborhood had its own septic tank, so if you were willing to go pump the water from the well a couple houses down and haul it, you could even keep using the damn *toilet*. You just had to pour a bucket of water in the bowl and you could flush. That simple.

He'd forgotten what a luxury it was to shit like a civilized man.

"Here, sit down, take a load off." Danny pulled out the chair at the head of the dining room table.

Clark rolled his eyes and shoved Danny out of the way. "Go put a damn shirt on," he said. "You're embarrassing yourself."

Danny was undeterred. "What? You jealous you don't have the brass to compete in this gun show, old man?" He lifted his arms and proceeded to flex one bicep and then the other.

"Old *man*? I'm only—" Clark sputtered. "I mean, I can't be that much older than—" Then his eyes narrowed. "Just how old are you?"

"Twenty-three years young," Danny proclaimed proudly. "What about you? Forty? Forty-five?"

A vein stood out on the side of Clark's neck. "I'm thirty-six," he said through clenched teeth. "And I don't look a day over thirty-three."

"Yeah, old man, you keep telling yourself that." Danny clapped him on the shoulder, before pulling back. "Oh, my bad. I should take it easy on you. Be kind to your elders and all that."

Nix was keeping out of this one. At thirty-eight, he was pretty sure he was the oldest one of the group. Fuckin' last thing he needed was anyone making Dad jokes.

Audrey had her hand over her mouth but she wasn't doing a good job of stifling her giggles. Clark pretended to glare at her.

"This is not funny, young lady." Then he frowned. "How old are you, darlin'?"

Audrey sobered. "Twenty-two."

Suddenly she looked small and vulnerable, standing there surrounded by the five of them. Christ, Nix had never felt more like the big bad wolf.

"All this talking is making me hungry." Nix grabbed a chair and hefted himself down.

Everyone else murmured agreement and sat too. Well, except

Mateo. He put the rice and beans in the center of the table so everyone could serve themselves and then went around filling up everyone's glasses with water.

The last time Nix had been waited on like this was pre-Fall at an Olive Garden his sister had dragged him to for his birthday.

She'd been so pretty that day. Black bows in her hair and that black lipstick that made mom so fucking nuts. But that was Roxy. If there was a way to express herself and piss Mom off while doing it, she was all for it.

"How was your day?" Graham asked Audrey as everyone tucked into their rice and beans. "Were you making candles again? I saw you there yesterday with Camila when I was walking by to the Pantry."

"No, I was helping out with the horses today."

Nix snickered and Audrey shot him a glare before looking back to Graham.

Still Nix couldn't help adding, "More like you were on sanitation duty for the horses."

Audrey's lips pursed and she pointedly ignored looking his direction. "Mucking out stalls was invigorating exercise. It really made me appreciate the effort that goes into working with the animals that are so crucial to the town. And seeing the composting system the town has set up is really remarkable."

"That was Graham's idea," Mateo said.

Audrey's eyebrows lifted. "Really? It's really impressive."

Graham's cheeks went pink and he shoved his glasses up his nose. "It's no big deal. It was just the logical solution. Two birds with one stone. That's the saying."

Audrey tilted her head, eyes questioning. "How so?"

"Well," Graham shifted in his chair. "We use horses so much now but there was all the shit that kept piling— Sorry, I mean," he adjusted his glasses again, "there was all the manure piling up. Then we have the crops and we can't run down to the Lowe's to get fertilizer anymore. So it just made sense to compost the manure. I knew about the basic principles of what was necessary for the oxygenation process, so it wasn't hard to set it up."

Audrey just shook her head, eyes wide. "You're kind of awesome, you know that?"

Graham shoved his glasses up his nose so violently Nix thought the things would fly off his damn head.

Alright. Nix called bullshit.

You didn't go from four escape attempts to suddenly laughing with and admiring your supposed captors just one week later.

He narrowed his eyes at Audrey.

But she looked genuine as she smiled and laughed along with everyone as Clark told a story about the delegation from the West Texas Coalition trying to pass off a wagonload of solar batteries.

"Really? Solar batteries?" Audrey asked.

Clark scoffed. "Maybe if they were real. It was so obvious they'd basically raided an auto shop and gotten a load of car batteries and then jerry-rigged some shitty little half-baked solar panels on to them. One of those tiny solar panels might be enough to generate the power for an electric toothbrush. For about a minute at a time. But they certainly wouldn't be enough to charge a battery that size, even if those *had* been solar batteries."

"Oh no," Audrey said, taking a bite of beans. "So what'd you do?"

Nix tuned out as Clark rambled on about riding the swindlers out of town.

"What about you, Mateo?" Audrey asked when Clark finished his story. "How was your day?"

Mateo's cheeks pinkened, eyes lowering like he was embarrassed to be the center of attention. "Oh, well. Not much. Just tinkering with things. Working on a few long-term projects."

"What kind of projects?"

Mateo shrugged. "Odds and ends. Sometimes an engine when we get one in, but mostly other machinery. Stuff that wasn't killed by the EMP blasts."

Clark clapped Mateo on the back and Mateo about jumped a foot out of his chair. Clark either didn't notice or didn't care. "Mateo here is our resident Mr. Fix It."

Graham nodded. "He can fix almost anything."

"Oh?" Audrey's eyebrows went up and she looked interested. Almost *too* interested.

Nix studied her as she leaned in to listen as Mateo described a microwave he'd just restored. She seemed very engaged, just like she had when Clark was talking. She laughed at the right moments. *Oooed* and *ahhed* when she was supposed to. Smiled and nodded as she cleaned her plate.

It was a good performance. But where was the fiery candlestick-wielding vixen from six days ago?

"So, are you excited about the wedding?" Nix interrupted, taking a leisurely bite of rice. "Just two weeks away now."

Ah, *there* it was. Audrey's blue eyes flashed with rebellion—a clear *over my dead body, pal* expression if Nix had ever seen it.

The next second, though, she took a deep breath and looked down at her plate. To her credit, she didn't paste on some bullshit smile.

She met his gaze dead on.

"Am I happy about the situation? No. Is this how I pictured my life?" She looked around the table. She shook her head and let out a long, drawn out breath. "God, none of us did. And yes, I'll admit, part of me hopes that getting to know me will make you change your minds." Her eyes came back to Nix. "That you'll choose to help me get to the coast and to Nomansland instead of forcing me into a marriage I never chose."

Her gaze dropped to her plate and her voice got quieter. "But I'm starting to realize that might be more and more of a pipedream."

"Audrey, we'd help you in a second if we didn't think it was a death sentence," Mateo said, his face more pained than ever. "We'd do anything to protect you. Give our own lives—"

Her jaw tightened and she glared at Mateo. "Other people have made it. The broadcasts on the dark web are real." She turned to Graham. "Tell them."

Graham looked around uncomfortably and of course, his forefinger went to the bridge of his glasses. "I *have* heard rumors of an all-female colony. But that's all they are. Rumors."

Nix put a hand to his temple. Jesus Christ. Didn't the idiot know that any kind of support or validation for her idea would only make her ten times more stubborn?

"They're more than rumors," Audrey said, chin jutting out. "My Uncle was a programmer too and he communicated with them. So did I. They're real. I video-chatted with the woman who leads the colony."

Nix sat up straighter in his chair. Shit. This was more than just a pipe-dream to her. Most people these days had one of those—some place or time they fantasized about where the hell would end. And if they could just survive long enough to make it there, then everything would be okay. It was the biology of hope—it kept people alive sometimes when the going was so tough you'd just lay down and die otherwise.

But Audrey... She truly believed the fantasy place was real. That there was a magical island utopia where women were free and safe and there were no men around to dominate and abuse them.

Nix had seen enough of the world to know better.

Violence was like a virus—when there was an outbreak, it spread as far and wide as it could, multiplying and replicating to the furthest reaches of the earth. And the coast she was talking about was between them and Mexico, one of the most fought over boundaries of the entire war after The Fall.

Even now, President Goddard was still barely managing to hold the line. Hardly the ideal spot for a matriarchal paradise.

"It's just not safe," Danny said, eyebrows drawn. "You gotta forget about it. You're safe *here*. Where we can protect you."

Her eyes might be demurely downcast as she said, "I don't need protecting," but there was steel in her voice.

Shit, Nix was going to have to make sure one of them was with her 24/7, wasn't he? He looked at Graham who was watching her with a similar look of dismay and worry as all the others.

With the hissy fit she'd thrown about the dart gun, wanting to surgically implant a GPS tracker in her arm *probably* wouldn't go over well.

"You just need to settle in," Clark said, moving to stand behind Audrey so he could massage her shoulders. Her entire body went tense at the initial contact, but as Clark started working his magic, bit by bit, Nix watched her eventually relax.

"Life is good here," Clark went on, kneading her shoulders. Sneaky bastard. Finding a way to get his hands on her before any of the rest of them. "Wow, you've really got a lot of tension in here. Working with the horses must have been some hard labor."

He massaged her for several moments in silence before he went on. "We'll make sure you're safe and comfortable here. You won't want for anything. Not anything," Clark said, leaning over and whispering seductively in her ear.

Even from across the table, Nix could see the small quiver than ran through her body.

Shit. Were the rest of the guys at the table fighting a monster stiffy like he was? Seeing her react to Clark like that, just, *damn*. She was so goddamned responsive, it was driving him crazy.

Nix hadn't had a woman in five years and even then, it had only been one of the prostitutes at a San Antonio brothel. The joint seemed like one of the less sordid establishments and she was nice enough. She'd given him a quick suck and fuck. He'd paid the extra twenty grams of gold for a condom—only a year out of date, too.

You were always taking your life in your hands when you went to a place like that. STD meds were one of the highest value items in a post-Fall world. Ironically, it was the same gene-splicing technology that allowed scientists to find the cure to Herpes as it was for the madman who created Xterminate. With universal healthcare in most developed countries, indiscriminate sex was fairly safe... until there were barely any women left to have sex with.

But that was part of the thrill of going to a brothel, right? Taking your life in your hands? There was even a name for it—*whore roulette*.

At the end, Nix had measured out the gold and felt so goddamned empty he'd sworn he'd never do it again, no matter how tired of his own damn hand he got.

Audrey let out a small moan as Clark dug his thumbs into her shoulder blades. Mateo had gotten on his hands and knees, massaging one of her feet as well.

"Just give us time," Clark whispered in a low, rasping voice. "Let us show you what life could be like here. We'll give you everything if you let us."

Audrey's eyes dropped closed and she seemed to give herself over to the pleasure and release Clark and Mateo were bringing her.

"Well, the women here do seem happy," she said in a breathy little voice. With those cherubic cheeks and her pink little mouth, she looked like a beautiful, filthy, filthy angel.

Goddamn.

Well Nix's hand would sure as shit be getting a helluva workout tonight.

CHAPTER THIRTEEN

AUDREY

Every morning that dawned, Audrey heard the timer ticking down. She'd been here for two and a half weeks now.

There were only eight days left until the window for the rendezvous with the Nomansland contact was lost, maybe forever.

Six days until the supposed *wedding*.

And she still didn't have any weapons other than the stupid bread knife she'd been eyeing from their kitchen. It wouldn't be any use against a gun. Not to mention that if she was close enough to be able to use the damn thing then she was probably already screwed.

But there was no use in thinking about that because she had a much bigger problem. She still didn't have a vehicle.

"Don't overthink shit," she whispered to herself as she pulled a fresh t-shirt on and glanced at her hair. Sophia had a homemade dry shampoo made out of arrowroot and cornstarch that worked surprisingly well.

For the first time in years, Audrey didn't feel like an oily, bedraggled mess.

She'd asked Mateo if she could spend the day helping out at the shop. At this point she could only desperately hope she'd find something valuable enough to steal so she could barter it down the road for gas.

Because it wasn't strictly true she hadn't found *any* cars. There were some old pre-electric cars from around town. All the trucks had been co-opted by the city and were held in a heavily guarded lot by the central gas dispensary.

But Audrey took long walks through town sometimes and had made note of an abandoned white Toyota Corolla. Yes, the windows were broken and she didn't want to think about what it smelled like inside after being abandoned for who knew how many years, but if she could find a working battery and gas and if the engine was still in working order...

Her head slumped.

Those were a lot of *ifs*.

The other option was to steal one of the township vehicles. She'd seen Danny driving a communal construction truck around town carrying materials. It probably wouldn't be too hard to manipulate him into taking her on a drive. Then she could incapacitate him—maybe poison him?—and steal the truck.

Just the thought gave her a sour feeling in her stomach, though. Danny was a bit of a goof, but he was a *sweet* goof.

Maybe it wouldn't come down to that, anyway. She wasn't completely out of options yet. She gave herself one more glance in the mirror, took a deep breath, and headed for her bedroom door.

Who better to help her than Mateo—*Mr. Fix It*, that's what Clark called him, right? She might discover all sorts of delightful weaponizable little items in the shop.

Not to mention, out of the five, he was definitely the one most sympathetic to her cause. Yes, he was adamantly opposed to her leaving, but with him, she genuinely believed it was out of concern for her safety. With Clark and Nix, it was likely nothing more than lip service. A handy excuse for them to keep her there.

But Mateo. He wore his heart on his sleeve. She was surprised such a sensitive guy had made it in this world, but hey, all the better for her.

She opened her bedroom door.

And yelped in fright at the figure looming in the hall.

"Jesus, Nix," she shouted. "You scared the crap out of me." She smacked him on the chest. "What are you doing lurking outside my room?"

He just lifted a mocking eyebrow and held out his arm. "I'm your faithful escort for the day, me lady."

She glared at him. "You mean you're still on guard dog duty. Will it still be like this after we're married? I won't be able to go to the outhouse without tripping over you?"

Nix shrugged. "I wouldn't worry. Mateo seems up for the role of lapdog. I bet if you ask him, he'll lug all the water you want up the stairs so you can keep using the toilet like the princess you are."

Audrey's teeth ground together. She swore she'd never wanted to punch anybody as much as she wanted to punch the man standing right in front of her. Okay, that wasn't strictly true, but Nix was a close second.

She still vowed to someday get him back for the whole dart-in-her-ass incident the day they met. And, you know, the kidnapping her and forcing her to marry him thing too.

"If you'll excuse me," she pushed roughly past him. He didn't budge, which meant far more of their bodies came into contact than she would have liked. Jerk. He did that on purpose.

When she got downstairs, it was quiet. It galled her to even talk to him, but she asked anyway. "Where's Mateo? I told him I'd help out at his shop today."

"He always gets an early start. He left some bread and prickly pear jam for you in the kitchen, though."

She glared at Nix. "At least *some* people know what it means to be a gentleman."

Nix smirked. "Darlin', I'll bet you ten pounds of gold that that supposed gentleman you're so impressed with did the same thing we all did when we climbed into bed last night. Grabbed his cock and choked the chicken until he was screaming your damn name into his pillow."

"You're a pig," she spat, pushing past him again and heading for the kitchen.

He didn't follow her, but his laughter echoed around the sparsely decorated house.

She put a hand to her cheek as soon as she got out of sight. She couldn't believe he'd just said that to her face! And how he'd put it. *Did the same thing we all did in bed last night.* So that meant Nix had— While thinking about her—

The thing was, when Clark and Mateo had their hands on her last night, she'd gotten so relaxed, and there'd been that buzz of electricity zooming all throughout her body. She'd felt it before and sure, when she'd been the only one in the shelter, she'd explored herself *down there* sometimes. Figured out just how to touch herself so she'd—

She poured herself a glass of water from the pitcher and took several long swallows, then grabbed the jam covered bread.

Enough of all that. She was on a mission.

She shoved a large bite of bread in her mouth. The bread was stale and a bit tasteless, and the jam was too tart without much sugar to balance it out. But it wasn't porridge, which meant it was a damn treat.

She swept back through the living room and out the front door without giving Nix another glance. Nix's deep chuckle sounded behind her as he followed behind her.

———

"So you've fixed all of these things?" Audrey couldn't keep the awe out of her voice. She didn't know what she'd expected when Mateo talked about where he worked but it hadn't been *this*. She supposed she thought it would be in one of the small shops along main street.

But nope, Nix had led her about a mile and a half down the road to an old grocery store that had been cleared out—on the front there were faded letters proclaiming it had once been an HEB.

They'd entered from the back where big loading dock doors were all open. Audrey's mouth dropped open when she saw the vast array of engines—some inside cars, some not—and farm equipment and shelves full of trinkets and children's toys and kitchen appliances.

Her heart started beating a mile a minute as she took it all in.

She'd hit the friggin' *jackpot*.

She didn't know where to look first. Cars. There were cars here! If any of them were close to working, that meant— And if there were cars, then surely there was gas too. Holy shit, the answer to all her problems was right here.

"Well, most of them are in progress," Mateo said, wiping his temple with his forearm. "And as you can see," he gestured out at the men working at stations all over the open floor. In the far corner sparks flew as men did welding. "I'm just one of many worker bees."

"But still," Audrey said, walking forward and trying to take everything in. There had to be something she could use as a weapon amid all this stuff. Maybe there was even a cordless chainsaw or something. Anyone came near her and waaa-chaa! She'd slice them in two.

"This is so awesome," she said, turning back to Mateo. She didn't try to hide her enthusiasm. She didn't know anyone alive today who wouldn't find this place amazing.

The buzzing noise of electronics came from all around her—after living with only the noise of nature for almost a decade, the sound made her want to cry.

"What did I tell you about taking breaks?" said a balding, middle-aged man striding up to Mateo, "Get back to your rathole n—" He cut off midsentence, eyes widening when he saw Audrey.

His countenance did a complete one-eighty. Suddenly he was all charm. "Oh, ma'am. I'm sorry. I didn't see you there." He puffed up his chest. "I'm Shawn Rawlings. The manager of the Jacob's Well Township Machine Shop here. Everything you see here is my brainchild." He smiled wide, showing off yellowed teeth.

Ugh, and to think, if a different slip of paper had been drawn, *this* man could have ended up one of her betrotheds.

She didn't respond to the pompous ass. She simply turned her back in his face and looked to Mateo. "So," she smiled. "Show me to your workstation."

Mateo had been standing stiffly, eyes to the floor, but they flashed up at this. And they were full of... gratitude? Adoration? Something more? It almost took Audrey aback.

She was leaving. It wasn't good for him to get so attached. She was about to take a step back when his annoying boss said, "You heard her, rat, take her to your workstation."

"Maybe you have work of your own you're supposed to be attending to," Nix said, stepping out from the shadows behind them. "I'd hate to have to tell The Commander his chief tinkerer was too busy getting involved in petty bullshit power plays to do his job."

That had Shawn going so pale Audrey thought he might pass out. But it served him right.

He just lifted his chin, stared down Mateo and then nodded toward Audrey. "Lovely to meet you."

And then he turned on his heel and ran away with his tail between his legs.

"You didn't need to do that," Mateo said, eyes flashing up at Nix. "I can take care of myself."

"Good." Nix shrugged. "Then do it next time."

A cord stood out in Mateo's neck but he didn't say anything else.

"Will you show me around?" Audrey held out an arm to Mateo. A peace offering.

"Oh sure," she heard Nix mutter behind her, "*his* arm you can't wait to take."

She rolled her eyes and then turned a mega-watt smile on Mateo. "So, tell me everything. Where'd did you learn to *do* all this? What are you working on today? Can I help?"

Mateo finally seemed to relax. He chuckled and it was a nice sound. When he looked her way, his brown eyes were full of warmth. "You know I'd never deny you anything. Come on."

He led her on a tour of the huge shop, pausing at each station to introduce her to his fellow workers and to give a little bit of background on who they were and what they were working on.

She was impressed with how much he knew about each individual as much as what their projects were. Some were much older than Mateo and others young, maybe even Sophia's age. And to a one, they all treated Mateo with the utmost respect, several asking his guidance on problems they were stuck with. He always seemed ready with an answer or a fix.

After the fourth time that happened, Audrey turned to him. "Why aren't *you* running the shop? You seem to know more than anyone here."

"Don't be ridiculous," Mateo brushed her words off with a wave of his hands.

Audrey pursed her lips. Then asked her other burning questions. "Well where'd you learn all this stuff? And just how old *are* you exactly?"

Mateo laughed. "I get asked that all the time. I'm twenty-eight. People mistake me for a decade younger. As for how I learned it all—" Another shrug. "I grew up in foster care and I don't know, stuff just didn't get done unless I did it."

"I'm sorry." Audrey took a small step closer, only just barely tamping down the impulse to put a hand on his arm. "Was that after Xterminate? Did you lose your mother?"

He shook his head, a sad smile on his face. "No, I never knew her. She left right after I was born. My Dad was in and out of jail so," he shrugged, "foster care."

Wow. Audrey's eyebrows furrowed and again she had to fight the urge to reach out to him. She both wanted to and didn't. In the end, she stopped herself. Because she didn't know if she would be doing it out of genuine empathy or because she was trying to manipulate Mateo into helping her and that just felt...well, wrong.

She was used to everyone having a sad story—most of the population lost their mother or sisters when Xterminate hit. Charlie used to say she was too soft. *You gotta be hard, Aud. No matter what, you keep going. Surviving is all that matters.*

"So I was always tinkering with something or other," Mateo continued, oblivious to her internal debate. "One of my foster dads was into restoring old cars. I learned a lot about working on engines that year and then I just kept up with it everywhere I went after that."

Be hard. Surviving is all that matters.

"So you work on a lot of cars?" Audrey forced herself to ask.

"Sure," he said. "Come on, I'll show you some."

And he did. Just like that, with no more coaxing or prompting. He showed her a couple trucks whose engines he and a team were rebuilding. Something called a dune buggy that was in pieces all over the floor.

Which was unfortunate, because it looked like the perfect light little vehicle to take on any terrain.

But any of the trucks would do just fine too.

"What about gas?" she asked, hoping the question came off as casual.

"Well, we're lucky here in Texas. First thing President Goddard did was get the oil derricks and a small refinery back up and running. Clark knows more about it since he's assistant to the Trade Secretary but we export water, troops, some crops, working cars," he gestured out at the floor, "anything and everything else we can."

"And that?" Audrey stopped and looked at the bigger engine set up in the center of the warehouse. Three men in coveralls were working on it at the same time.

"Is that a—" Nix started saying from behind them. He'd been following them around the whole time but so far Audrey had been successfully ignoring him. Mostly, anyway.

"Yep." Mateo smiled broadly like a proud papa. "This one will put us on the map if we can get her running."

What?" Audrey looked at the big hunk of metal. It looked just like all other complex machines or engines or whatever they'd been walking past the last fifteen minutes. "What is it?"

"It's a helo engine," Nix said.

Audrey felt her eyebrows scrunch. "A *what?*"

"A helicopter engine," Mateo explained. "Or as good of one as we can jerry-rig. The Scrapper team found an old helicopter—the kind they used back in some war a hundred years ago—in some guy's back yard."

"No way," Nix said. "His back yard?"

Mateo shook his head. "Guy must have been a real eccentric. Rich too. He had a whole dinosaur skeleton set up in his living room, decorated with lights like he was using it as a Christmas tree."

"Anyway, he was long gone. Some of the Scrappers stayed with the find and sent for the big hauler to bring her back to town. Most of the engine was useless after all this time, but we're seeing if we can't rebuild something that will get her up in the air again."

Audrey could only shake her head, eyes wide, as she walked around the huge, complex engine. "Holy crap. You're going to have a helicopter."

With a helicopter, she could get to the coast in two hours.

Mateo made a pained face. "Maybe one day. It seems like every time we fix one problem, another crops up. Trying to build a helicopter engine from scratch when you can't just call in and order parts you need," he let out a little whistle as he reached out a hand to run it over a valve going down the side of the engine.

"She's giving us a run for our money that's for sure. I've been rigging whatever I can from other engines. Then we're welding some things we can't find."

He laughed. "We're throwing everything but the kitchen sink at it to see if we can't get her running. I like to be optimistic. Maybe she'll fly sometime in the next six months, if we're lucky."

Six months. All right, so cross off the helicopter. It wasn't like she could fly it anyway. She wanted to ask Mateo how close the trucks were to being ready, but she could feel Nix's eyes on her.

While Mateo didn't seem suspicious about any of the questions she'd asked so far, Nix's attention was entirely too focused for her comfort.

"Okay, so what are you working on today? This engine? How can I help?" Audrey looked around and laughed.

"Not sure what I could do... but," she grabbed a wrench off a nearby table, "I'm an excellent tool-hander. You're the engine doctor and I'll be your nurse." She teased the wrench in front of Mateo's face and he laughed.

"I was planning to work on some smaller projects and yes, I can always use the help."

Audrey smiled back and it didn't feel forced or manipulative. She genuinely liked Mateo. He led the way to the back corner that was sectioned off by dividers so it felt secluded and quiet.

Mateo entered and right before Audrey could follow, she spun on her heel and confronted Nix head on.

"You stay out here," she said, eyes hard.

He looked surprised but then crossed his arms over his chest. "I go where you go."

She rolled her eyes. Infuriating man. "I'll be all of ten feet away right behind this partition. Could you just let up for ten minutes so I have some room to relax without you breathing down my damn neck."

"Careful Princess," Nix whispered, leaning in. He lifted her hair off her shoulder and then exhaled a long breath on the side of her neck and up along her ear. "You don't have to play hard to get. If you want me, all you have to do is ask."

For a moment she was frozen. His words and the moist heat of his breath against her neck seemed connected to a line tied straight to her clit. Her sex clenched and she felt achingly empty.

Then she jerked back. "Pig," she hissed.

"You love it."

She made an offended, scoffing noise. "I do not."

"Then why are your pupils blown and your nostrils flaring like you can't get enough of the way I smell?"

Damn him, she *had* been inhaling him. But only because he smelled so damn scrumptious.

Her formative years were spent with only her brother and Uncle for company. This was the first time she'd been around humans of the opposite sex for any extended period of time since before she'd gone through puberty.

And her body, damn, she didn't know what was going on with it. Except that it seemed to have a mind of its own—especially where Nix was concerned.

Last night after dinner, he'd walked straight up to her and put his hands around her waist. She'd been like a deer caught in headlights as his mouth lowered to hers.

His mouth had been so close, *so close* to hers.

And then at the last second, he'd veered ever so slightly to the side until he was kissing her cheek, right at the outermost edge of her mouth.

She'd almost screamed, the need inside her had built so high with every moment his lips lingered against her skin.

Even worse, all the other guys had followed his example. One by one, they'd lined up and given her a kiss goodnight. Mouth after mouth, dropping close and brushing just to the side of her lips.

Each of them pulling her close and then releasing her. Even shy Graham pulled her close with surprising intensity.

But none of it meant anything, she reminded herself harshly.

She was *leaving*.

"You stay out here," she snapped at Nix and then turned to follow Mateo into his workshop area.

As soon as she passed the cubicle barrier, she froze. She didn't know what she'd expected to find him working on back here.

But it wasn't big colorful posters of basic electric circuits and children's toys and board books and a hundred other odds and ends that looked like they'd come straight out of a pre-Fall schoolroom.

"I'm teaching later," Mateo said, the easy confidence he'd had out on the floor with his coworkers absent. His eyes lowered to the floor. "I wondered... well, I hoped maybe you would join me in the classroom and help me with some experiments we're running this afternoon."

"You teach? Kids?" Audrey couldn't help blinking several times. This man was full of surprises.

Mateo nodded, his lips curving up even though he still didn't look at her. "I like kids a lot."

Audrey stepped further into the small space. She ran a forefinger over a spool of copper wire. "What do you teach them? Science?"

He nodded. "Physical Science mostly."

Audrey tilted her head sideways. "But there's barely any electricity. Shouldn't they be learning, I don't know," she shrugged, "how to plant crops?"

"They learn that too," he said, still smiling. "But they're the future. They'll be the ones putting the world back together. We can't let all the knowledge die off with us. They're our hope."

Mateo was actually managing to hold her gaze and Audrey felt the strangest fluttering in her chest.

Followed by the most insane thought:

What if she didn't leave?

What if what the guys said *wasn't* bullshit? What if her best chance at survival was staying right here? With them.

Staying and being their wife.

She swallowed and wrapped her arms across her stomach,

completely wigged out. Because the thing was, when she thought about having five husbands, she didn't have the knee jerk response of: *hell no, that's fucked up!* anymore.

She'd gotten to know them all a little. Two and a half weeks was hardly enough to know if you wanted to make a lifetime commitment —she still thought the whole thing was insane... but at the same time, maybe the Commander was right.

It was a new world. The old rules didn't apply here. They were all making them up as they went.

But Charlie, she'd promised Charlie she wouldn't stop until she got to—

Charlie was dead.

She swallowed hard and bit her tongue even harder against the tears that threatened.

Charlie was dead and what if she could make her new start here? What if life could be about more than survival? Was what the guys promised actually possible? Love? A home? A *family*?

What was the smart thing to do here? The right thing? If she screwed up, there was little chance she'd ever get another shot at Nomansland. She simply didn't have the computer skills.

It was now or never.

Please, Charlie, give me a sign. I don't know what to do. Give me a sign. Something. Anything.

She squeezed her eyes shut and waited.

Nothing.

There was nothing.

She was only more confused than ever.

"Audrey?" Mateo sounded concerned. "Is everything okay?"

"I'm sorry," she said, backing up and almost knocking over a stack of books on the counter behind her. "I— I told Sophia I'd help her with something this morning. Sorry, I have to go."

She didn't wait for a response before she turned and sped out of the cubicle.

Nix was waiting right outside. He'd probably eavesdropped on every word they'd said.

"Out of my way." Audrey pushed past him.

"What's wrong?" Nix asked. "Do I need to kick Mateo's ass? Did he do something?"

He sounded murderous and she just stared at him with her mouth open. "No he didn't *do* anything. Just leave me alone. God, can't I have a second without you breathing down my freaking neck?"

She started jogging through the maze of stations set up around the workshop. And damn Nix, of course he was following her. She heard his heavy footsteps right on her heels.

"I need the bathroom," she called over her shoulder. "I'm having female problems."

There. That was usually enough to make Charlie and Uncle Dale leave her alone when she got into what her brother used to call her 'moods.'

But thinking about Charlie only made the tightness in her chest worse. And no matter what, she would *not* cry in front of Nix of all people.

"Audrey," Mateo called out from behind her. He sounded upset but she couldn't so much as look back.

She ran toward the front of the store, opposite the entrance they'd come in. She was heading for the area marked off "Bathroom" with a big hanging sign. She knew it wouldn't be anything more than a sanitation bucket, but she just had to get away from everyone.

Right as she was about to jerk the bathroom door open, though, she saw something that had her stopping in her tracks.

There, to the right of the bathroom, was a motorcycle. She didn't know the model. Charlie would have. He was crazy about bikes. Always had been. But it wasn't too big and it wasn't too small.

And unlike all the other cars and vehicles in the shop, parts weren't laying all around it. It looked completed. Perfect. Ready to drive off of the workshop floor.

Exactly what she needed to get herself to the coast.

She wouldn't have to rely on roads that might be blocked. Motorcycles had great gas mileage. She should be able to make it to the coast just on one tank.

She'd asked for a sign.

And here it was.

CHAPTER FOURTEEN

MATEO

Mateo was sure he was sweating through his fancy suit as he stood at the front of the church, side by side with the rest of Audrey's soon-to-be husbands.

He'd wanted everything to be perfect. But now as he stood here, the church as full as it was for every wedding, he knew he'd been kidding himself.

Putting his name in for the lottery was always supposed to be his secret. Just a dumb little indulgence. A flight of fancy he allowed himself.

But that's all it was *ever* supposed to be.

The night of the drawing, when the Commander had called his name, Mateo was so shocked, he'd frozen where he stood. It was a mistake. It had to be a mistake.

He'd meant to go clear it up right then and there.

But then he'd seen her face.

She was beautiful, sure. That wasn't what stopped him where he stood. She was terrified. It was so clear on her face. She thought she was surrounded by enemies. That she was all alone.

He knew what that felt like.

In that instant, he pledged his life to her. It wasn't even a conscious thought. He just knew throughout his entire *being* that whatever it took, he would protect her. He'd never felt anything with such soul-deep certainty before.

And the best way to protect her was to go through with the farce. To become her husband. *Him*.

He was a filthy, disgusting, foul, shit blister of a human being.

The idea of him as her husband nauseated him. She was so beautiful and perfect and he was... he swallowed back bile at the thought of all that he was.

At what he'd become after The Fall.

For years and years and *years*.

People thought the slave markets in Mexico were bad. They had no idea how depraved some trading posts in the outer Texas territory only three hours away were.

Mateo had been picked up fleeing Fort Worth just a few days after the D-Day nukes. Fort Worth hadn't been bombed directly, but Dallas had, and everyone was running, terrified of the fallout.

He was on a Ducati he'd been fixing up at the garage where he worked. He figured he deserved it more than the rich bastard who'd dropped it off, ignoring his latest arm candy and screaming at his kid whenever he started crying that he was hungry.

Mateo was able to zoom past the traffic that had quickly gotten congested on the I20.

He was just a terrified kid, barely nineteen, fleeing for his life. But eventually he ran out of gas.

And he was the dumb fuck who had the bright idea to try hitch-hiking.

When the big, Army barricaded truck came to a stop, he thought it was salvation. He was quick to find out that getting into the back of that truck was the first step on a one-way trip to hell.

It turned out, in a world short on women, a lanky, skinny boy was a perfectly adequate substitute for lawless men who were murderous, raping bastards. They set in on him almost immediately.

When they got where they were going—a criminal trading post that had sprouted up outside San Angelo in the years after D-Day called Hell's Hollow, though he wouldn't find that out for years—they threw him in a cage, brought out only to be *used* before being tossed back in.

It was total anarchy for a while before President Goddard brought back some form of law and order. No one cared about a skinny kid in the slums of the most dangerous trading posts in Texas, though.

So he did what he had to to get by.

Mateo swallowed hard against the bile that rose again at the thought of those filthy, hideous years when he'd been more of an animal than anything else.

And you think you can stand up here now and pretend to be a man for her? You think you can protect her from anything when you couldn't even protect yourself?

He looked around him. Nix, Clark, Danny, even Graham—they were real men. If anyone was worthy of a woman like Audrey, and the more he got to know her, the less he thought anyone was—but still. If anyone was worthy, it was them.

Nix was the man who'd led the raid on Hell's Hollow. Nix himself who'd freed Mateo.

But it was too late by then. Years and years too late.

He'd already been used and defiled in every way imaginable. Beyond the imaginable.

He should leave.

Right now.

Make his excuses and run out the back of the church.

Run and keep running.

He wasn't worthy to touch a hair on Audrey's head, much less—

Piano music started and Mateo's head jerked up. All the breath swept out of his lungs in one great heave.

There she stood, at the opposite end of the aisle.

She was gorgeous. Even more than usual.

Her long, fire red hair had been set into curls that framed her face.

She was in a wedding dress—a real one. Sometimes women just wore whatever was on hand for these ceremonies but Audrey was in a bona fide wedding dress.

Mateo had talked to Sophia about it but she hadn't told him she'd been able to track one down. Mateo dragged his eyes away from Audrey only long enough to search out Sophia in the crowd. She was beaming at Audrey, but, like she could feel his eyes on hers, she looked Mateo's way and gave him a conspiratorial wink. She *had* been the one to find it.

Like a magnet, Mateo's eyes quickly dragged back to Audrey. The Commander stood beside her in full military regalia.

Mateo's eyes hungrily devoured every detail. Her tiny waist. Her full bosom and the hint of cleavage revealed by the dress.

He swallowed but his mouth was so dry he barely managed it.

And he knew in that moment that come hell or high water, he was going to stay exactly where he was and marry the most beautiful, strong, and kind woman he'd ever met in his life.

Fuck his past.

Fuck right and wrong.

It would be the most selfish act of his life and maybe he'd never forgive himself for it, but he would take her to have and to hold, till death did them part.

CHAPTER FIFTEEN

NIX

Nix was stunned as Audrey walked down the aisle toward them. And not just because of her beauty. He'd been so sure she would bolt. Hundred to one odds.

He hadn't slept a wink last night. She wouldn't go out her bedroom door, he'd known that. No, she'd have thought of a more ingenious way to escape.

But whatever plan she'd been concocting over the last few weeks, last night was the night. It had to be.

Waiting until the last possible second was ballsy, he'd give her that. But he wasn't going to let her go on some insane suicide mission looking for a place that didn't exist.

Yes, she'd hate him when he caught her and foiled her plans, but she'd get over it. If he had his way, she'd have a very long and healthy life to hate him for it and that was all that mattered.

She thought *she* was stubborn? Well Phoenix Alonzo Hale was born an ass and it was a reputation he'd worked hard to live up to over the years.

Not to mention, he had the other guys on his side.

In only three and a half weeks, they'd already broken down so many of Audrey's barriers. They just had to get this whole running-off-to-some-coastal-all-woman-paradise idea out of her head once and for all.

After that, well, she'd be their wife.

Which was a good thing, because then he'd be able to keep an even closer eye on her. He wondered if the Commander would agree to let him put a GPS tracker under her skin. Just so he could know where she was at all times when he was at work.

He'd been blowing off his duties far too often. Though Jeffries had been far more understanding than he would have expected in picking up the slack. Maybe he was just happy to be finally off nights.

He'd tried to get the Commander to go for chipping all the women in town a couple years ago. The Commander had been *this* close to cracking and giving in before his daughter talked him out of it.

Sophia was a nice enough kid, but sometimes she could be a royal pain in his ass.

He'd tried slipping a tracker into Audrey's jeans pocket last night but it had stopped moving around seven-thirty. She must have had an early bath before bed.

So he'd spent last night hovering on a ladder by the trellis that ran up the wall near her bedroom window. He'd been positive she was planning to try to climb down it and make yet another ridiculously stupid escape attempt.

But... her window never opened. Her curtain never so much as twitched. At four am, he was sure he'd fucked up royally and she'd found some way to sneak past the guard he'd posted outside her door.

But when he climbed down from the ladder, legs and arms so cramped he about fell and cracked his head open, he went in the house and inched her bedroom door open.

And found her fast asleep.

Oh she was good, he'd give her that.

Maybe she knew about the ladder and the guards he'd posted. She was smart.

But he wasn't wrong about her escape plans. He knew he wasn't.

She wasn't as good a liar as she thought she was. She had

several glaring tells. Like how she ran her fingers through her hair when she was nervous. Or how her eyes always shifted slightly to the right when she was telling something patently untrue.

And he'd been watching her carefully the past few weeks.

Her body language screamed that she couldn't get out of this place fast enough.

But then a day would pass. And then another. And another.

Until finally it was the night before the wedding and Nix figured it been her strategy all along.

Play nice to pacify them and distract everyone with wedding preparations.

Especially when she sat them down last night and told them she intended to consummate their wedding night.

Consummate, his *ass*.

She was gonna run.

That confirmed it. She'd wait till they were all asleep and slip off in the wee early hours of morning.

Except—she stayed put *all night long*.

And all this morning.

And throughout the afternoon pre-wedding ladies' brunch.

His team sent a runner to update him every half hour and they'd reported that Audrey was doing... normal, wedding-y things with Sophia and Camila and the other women.

Brunch was on the sun porch. Scones with jam and cream. Fucking scones. Paul reported that she'd looked happy and relaxed.

Nix had been two seconds away from showing the fucker *happy and relaxed*.

Who the hell had come up with the idea of a 'sunset wedding' anyway? The town had done it this way forever but it was just fucking torture waiting all day. Especially with that bullshit about it being 'bad luck' to see the bride before the nuptials. He wanted to fucking hand-cuff her to him.

But no, he'd been forced to rely on reports from his men all day long—topped off by ten minutes of sheer hell standing up here at the altar, tense as fuck, sure at any second one of his guys was going to come running in saying they'd lost her. That somehow she'd slipped away from them.

But then there she was. Standing in that white gown like fucking Cinderella, smiling shyly at all of them in turn.

She wasn't running.

This was actually happening.

Nix blinked, stunned, as the music began and she came down the aisle, step by step, the Commander on her arm.

In what felt like no time, she was suddenly in front of them and the Commander was giving her a kiss on the cheek. Then he presented her to the five of them and the pastor.

Well, *former* pastor, but Jonas was the best the township had.

Jonas held a bound copy of the Texas Constitution in his hand. "We gather here today to celebrate the wedding of Audrey, Clark, Daniel, Graham, Mateo, and Phoenix. A new family clan—Clan Hale— is born today, six become one."

Warmth washed through Nix's chest at hearing Jonas speak his new clan's name—which was Nix's own last name. As the highest-ranking member of the clan, everyone in the family would now take his surname as their own.

Jonas smiled out at the church. It was full to the brim. Mostly with the other clan families, groups of men peppered with the occasional woman. The back of the church, though, it was crowded with other single men, standing room only. All wishing like hell it was them in Nix's or one of the other guys' spot and dreaming of the one day they might be.

You have come here to share in this commitment they make to each other," Jonah continued, "to offer your love and support to this union, and to allow Clan Hale to start their married life together surrounded by the people who support them."

Audrey sucked her bottom lip into her mouth, biting it for a second nervously before releasing it.

God she was brave, standing up here in front of all these strangers, giving herself to men she'd only known a few weeks.

But *why*?

What was the trick?

He blinked hard several times. Maybe there was no trick and he'd just been imagining things that weren't there. Sure, he was bad at letting people close. But that was for the best.

He did his job better when he stayed a step removed from the action. It let him observe things with a clear head.

Aka, the opposite of everything he'd done with Audrey starting day one. She just got under his skin. So recklessly putting herself in danger in the field that day— He still didn't know how she'd gotten there. It wasn't like she'd ever exactly opened up to any of them.

But still, when they finally got her somewhere safe and sound, for her to keep trying to run away when there were so many fucking lunatics out there, he—

He'd never met anyone so frustrating in his life. If she would just *listen*—

He breathed out in a rush. Yeah, so he'd given her a hard time. Pressed her at every turn, then pushed and prodded at the tension between them. It was sexual but it was more than that too.

He'd been going along just fine in his life before she showed up. Doing his job. Keeping the town safe. It was all he cared about.

His eyes traced the soft curve of her cheek. The little cupid's bow of her upper lip. The way her eyelashes flipped nervously and her mouth scrunched in that adorable way it did when she gnawed on her bottom lip.

She was so clearly a distraction he didn't need in his life.

"Marriage is a permanent union," Jonas went on, his voice lower, like he was speaking more to just them instead of the congregation at large. "The six of you will no longer live for yourselves alone. You will belong to one another. An unbroken circle. You must trust, love, and respect one another. This you will vow, and it is a vow you can never break."

Audrey's eyes immediately dropped to the floor.

Another tell. Nix knew he hadn't been imagining it all. He swallowed and his hands briefly clenched into a fist.

What was it she objected to? The love part? Or the trust and respect? Which did she not think she could ever bring herself to give them?

And had he really expected her to?

No matter what *he* knew about the town—that it was the best of many, many worse options in a merciless world—it was all new to her. And they were strangers.

Big, intimidating strangers who were demanding things of her she might not feel ready to give.

The former preacher looked at each of them in turn. "In this community, marriage provides a stabilizing unit to begin building a new world. Marriage establishes rights and obligations between all spouses."

Nix swallowed. Now this part he could get on board with. This was why he hadn't objected when his name had been called even though he hadn't put it in for consideration.

Rights and obligations.

He wanted her obligated to them. If they could get her knocked up, then she'd be forced to give up the ridiculous notion of ever leaving.

If there had only been a place like this when he and his sister were on the run, all those years ago... It was true, he didn't know if she would have been one of the lucky ten percent to survive Xterminate, but anything would have been better than—

"But more than that," Jonas's voice softened again and Audrey looked up from the floor, blue eyes wide and vulnerable. Christ, she really was the most beautiful woman Nix had ever seen. "—marriage is meant to be a safe haven. Both for you and your husbands. *Be ye not afraid, for I am with you*, the Bible says."

"In these recent days, many of us might wonder where God has gone." Jonas's voice went momentarily strained. "Whether there is a God at all. But I do believe that the fact that good can still exist in the face of such ugliness means that not all grace is lost. And that's what marriage is meant to be in this community. A place of grace. The one safe haven where you can still find the face of God in the loving-kindness of your new family."

Audrey's eyebrows furrowed and her lip began to tremble. Her eyes moved from the pastor around the semi-circle of her soon to be husbands. First to Graham, then Mateo. Onto Danny and Clark, and then finally, finally, to Nix.

Nix had been to these things before and never paid any attention to Jonas's pastor mumbo jumbo, but suddenly it made perfect sense.

Because regardless of how they'd gotten here, what he felt in this moment, it *was* holy. There was no other word to describe it. The ritual of binding his life to Audrey and to their new clan. Watching the raw emotion in her eyes as she felt it too.

It was like finally he was seeing beneath all the bravado she'd shielded herself behind ever since she'd stepped into the town square the night of the lottery.

But here, finally, was the real Audrey. She wasn't running anymore. She was standing still. With him. With them. And together, if they would let it, they could create something new and beautiful.

"Now to the vows," Jonah said. "Clark Hale, do you take this woman, Audrey Hale, to be your wedded wife, in sickness and in health, for richer or for poorer..."

As Clark recited the vows, Jonah took Clark's hand in one hand and Audrey's in the other. After Clark finished his vows, Jonas moved Clark's hand to Audrey's. She slid Clark's ring onto his finger and then took his hand.

Then the pastor repeated the steps with Danny. Clark put Danny's ring on and held his hand, continuing the circle. And then Graham repeated the vows and Danny gave him his ring. And so on with Mateo.

Finally it came Nix's turn. He knew Jonas was just going around in alphabetical order, but it felt significant somehow that he was last.

His mouth was dry and his voice more gritty than usual as he repeated the vows after Jonas.

"For as long as we both shall live," he finished. Nix kept his composure fine as Mateo slid the ring on his finger. It wasn't until he lifted Audrey's ring to her finger that his hand started trembling. When he saw hers shaking just as hard, though, he relaxed.

It was his job now to be strong when she was scared. To care for her so she never had to be afraid again. Not a day in her life. He would protect her. Always.

"And do you, Audrey Dawson, accept the men before you as your wedded husbands, for as long as you all shall live?"

Her entire body shook but her voice was strong and sure as she said the words: "I do."

Nix didn't expect the satisfaction that roared through his chest. Or the way his entire body was felt lit with electricity as he leaned over and kissed her knuckles, sliding the delicate gold band onto her fourth finger.

Completing the circle.

"Clan Hale is born today," Jonas shouted triumphantly. "Six are united as one. What has been joined today let no man tear asunder!"

The crowd cheered and Nix felt a grin split his face. Audrey looked a little shell-shocked but then Jonas was shouting over the crowd. "You may now kiss your bride."

Nix and the guys had discussed it before-hand. Which was good because otherwise Nix was pretty sure he would have shoved the rest of them out of the way to claim his new wife.

Instead, he stood by, exhibiting what he thought was inhuman restraint while one by one, starting with Clark, they kissed their wife. No one was pulling any punches either.

Clark grabbed her and kissed her so deep Nix was pretty sure he'd explored her damn tonsils by the time he was done. Graham's cheeks colored and he just deposited a quick, perfunctory kiss on her lips.

And Danny, Jesus Christ. He started toward Audrey with eyes so bright and excited they were about to pop out of his damn head, his tongue already half out. The bastard would have licked her if Clark hadn't intervened.

"Nope," Clark said, grabbing his arm and veering him away at the last second.

"Wait, what?" Danny exclaimed. "You can't do that. It's not official till I kiss her!"

"Not until I've sat you down and explained a little more bit about the birds and the bees, my boy. And how the hell to kiss a woman."

"But—" Danny whined.

"It's all right," Audrey laughed, stepping forward and landing a quick peck on Danny's lips. He looked so stunned and in love Nix would have laughed if he wasn't shoving Mateo forward so it'd be his own turn quicker.

Audrey had seemed good-natured about all the kissing but she suddenly looked little shy when it came to Mateo.

And Mateo, Christ, he was so deathly pale it was more like he was facing a firing squad than his new wife. His arms were locked by his side and Nix guessed he was about three point two seconds from passing the fuck out.

Again, Audrey was the first to move. But it wasn't just a quick peck like she'd given Graham and Danny. She lingered, first with her lips just barely pressing against Mateo's.

And then, fuck him, Nix watched her tiny little tongue peek out and begin to explore the seam of Mateo's lips. Mateo inhaled sharply and Audrey took his face in her hands, deepening the kiss.

Nix went hard as a rock. She was the most fucking glorious thing he'd ever seen. He wanted to yell at every damn person to get the fuck out so he could rip that wedding dress off over her head and he and the guys could get to work exploring her perfect little body right this fucking instant.

Because as much as he liked to pretend he only wanted to be her husband so he could keep an eye on her and protect her... it was a damn lie.

He wanted to fuck her brains out. He wanted to claim her body in a way that she'd never forget, never recover from, and never be able to live without.

She and Mateo kissed for what felt like a goddamned eternity. When she finally pulled back, she continued holding Mateo's face. She leaned her forehead to his, eyes closed, some kind of unspoken communion passing between them.

Nix was jealous and impatient. But he'd let them have their moment. If only because if anyone tried to interrupt *him* when he got his turn, he'd murder them.

Audrey finally broke away from Mateo, giving him the sweetest damn smile Nix had ever seen. And Mateo, he looked like his whole damn universe had just been blown away. The guy already worshipped Audrey, but Nix was pretty sure she'd just cemented Mateo's loyalty all through this world and into the afterlife. And fuck, probably through reincarnation and into the next.

But screw all that. She'd let Mateo go.

Which meant it was Nix's turn. Thank fuck.

He took a step forward and put his hands on her waist, dragging her up and into him. She let out a surprised little gasp and then his lips were on hers. Devouring her. This wasn't a polite ask and answer. Fuck that. He was claiming her.

She was his wife. Their wife.

Let what had been joined today never be fucking torn asunder.

He sucked her tongue into his mouth, swallowing every breathy gasp and reveling in the way her body shook against him. He reached up and dug his fingers into her hair, ignoring the pins and cradling the back of her head so he could kiss her even harder.

He needed more.

He needed fucking everything.

And she gave it. Fuck him, but she gave. Everything he asked for and more.

His little spitfire was just as hungry for it as he was. Her lips were a little awkward. Untrained. Like this was the first time she'd really been kissed by a man.

The thought made Nix's cock harden to fucking stone.

He dragged his mouth away from hers, only vaguely taking in the whistles and catcalls coming from the church pews behind them.

He couldn't even think in complete sentences. He needed her too much. There was only one thought pinging through the desire clogging his every pore.

Audrey.

Bed.

Now.

There wouldn't be any waiting to consummate this marriage.

CHAPTER SIXTEEN

AUDREY

"Nix," Audrey exclaimed as he all but dragged her out the back of the church, the other men—her *husbands*, oh God, oh God, she almost hyperventilated at the thought—right on his heels. "The feast!" she said. "Sophia and Camila and all the other women spent all week putting together the most beautiful—"

"No one expects us there," Nix growled, turning and picking her up over his shoulder because apparently, she wasn't moving fast enough for his liking.

"Nix!" she shouted again, smacking at his back. It wasn't her fault she couldn't walk at his breakneck speed. Unless she literally wanted to break her neck. Whoever had invented high heels back before The Fall needed to die. Maybe with a high heel impaled in his neck. Those things were death traps. Why did women used to subject themselves to the damn things?

On the other hand, maybe this was better. After several jarring steps, she closed her eyes and clung to Nix's back. Just go loose, go along with what the guys had planned.

She would not hyperventilate. She would not hyperventilate.

So she was about to lose her virginity.

In a fivesome.

No big deal.

She just had to lay there. Right?

...

...

Who the fuck was she kidding?

It was a big deal. It was a huge, giant fucking deal. But she'd told herself she was doing it tonight and it was a promise she meant to keep.

Her eyes popped open again and she lifted her head to see they were almost to the house.

"Set me down!" She smacked again at Nix's back with her fists.

"All right, all right, feisty little wife," Nix said, and then her world was going topsy turvy again until the next thing she knew, she was wobbling on the ridiculous heels again. She almost lost her footing and went down but Clark and Mateo were immediately at her side, steadying her.

"It's tradition to carry the bride over the threshold," Clark grinned at her.

"Let me," Danny grinned wide as he stepped forward and swept Audrey off her feet again like she weighed no more than a feather.

She let out a high-pitched yelp as he pulled her close to his massive, muscled chest, his other arm under her knees.

He didn't waste any time getting her inside. And he didn't stop there. Nope, he went straight up the stairs to the master bedroom.

Mateo went ahead of them to open the door and Danny swept inside, almost knocking Audrey's feet into the doorframe in his excitement.

"Careful!" Mateo and Nix yelled. Audrey had pulled her feet back just in time and Danny looked back at them, obviously confused at what they were talking about.

Clark rolled his eyes. "Just get her to the bed without inflicting any bodily damage please."

Danny hefted Audrey in his arms and she had to admit, being manhandled by all that big, strong male was doing something to her.

As was seeing how Clark and Nix were looking at her. Mateo and Graham were staying in the background, eyes downcast, but Clark and Nix hid nothing. They didn't even try to hide the lust burning in their eyes.

Audrey's breath hitched.

God. Had she made the right decision? Was she doing the right thing?

Or was it beyond insane to be here, in this room, giving herself to these men?

All right, yes, it was definitely insane. But that didn't necessarily mean it was the wrong move.

She expected Danny to just toss her on the bed. No matter how hot he was, he didn't seem to have much going on in the finesse department.

But he was surprisingly tender as he put one knee on the bed and laid her down in the center of the mattress.

"You're the prettiest thing I've ever seen," he whispered, his voice low and growly in a way she'd never heard it before.

And then, before she could even register it, the huge mattress squeaked more as the men climbed on from all sides, surrounding her in a circle.

Caging her in.

If she screamed for them all to get back, to stop, would they? Or would they take what they now thought was theirs by right? Suddenly she couldn't breathe.

"Stop," she said, holding up a hand.

Danny jerked back and everyone went still, all around her.

One by one, she met each of their gazes.

Graham.

Danny.

Clark.

Mateo.

Nix.

"What if I can't do it?" she whispered, bracing for a fight even though she thought she'd made peace with doing this—going through with her wedding night and consummating it in every sense of the word. But giving herself willingly and them taking were two entirely different things.

And she had to know. "What if I say no?" Her voice barely came out as more than a whisper.

Nix's eyebrow furrowed and he reached out a hand like he was going to cup her face. He stopped at the last moment, before he made contact.

"Then we stop," he said. "Any time. You say stop, we stop. No matter what. No matter when. No matter where."

Her breath caught at his words.

Damn him. Why did he have to say the perfect thing? Why couldn't he be the asshole he was the rest of the time?

But he wasn't. His eyes were gentle, his face softer than she'd ever seen it.

You can do this, she whispered internally.

There was nothing to do but take the plunge. She moved from her back onto her knees.

And then she turned, leaned forward, and kissed Graham, her eyes on Nix.

CHAPTER SEVENTEEN

NIX

Fucking vixen. Nix didn't know if she was taunting him by kissing Graham first or what, but he'd show her exactly who was going to be in charge of this little show.

He'd undone the buttons of his dress shirt on the way upstairs while Danny carried Audrey and he whipped his off, then yanked his undershirt over his head.

Clark did the same and Danny too. Mateo stripped down to his undershirt but left it on.

Mateo was moving around light what had to be fifty candles as the room dimmed now that the sun had set. An extravagant waste but Nix could have kissed him because he wanted to didn't want to miss seeing a moment of what was about to happen.

And Graham, well, Graham was too busy lost in fucking heaven, having Audrey all to himself.

Enough of that. Nix moved up the bed until he was positioned behind Audrey's back. Clark joined him and while Clark pulled the zipper down on Audrey's gown, Nix nipped at the back of her neck, his nose brushing against her, soft, lavender scented hair.

She gasped and pulled back from Graham but he made a discontented sound.

"Ten more seconds," Graham said, a line forming between his furrowed brows. "We need to kiss for ten more seconds. It has to be for the full sixty."

Audrey stopped and frowned in confusion. Oh right, she'd only spent that one afternoon with Graham and he'd been surprisingly not —well, whatever it was that made Graham *Graham-like*. The obsession with numbers and details and how he freaked out at loud noises.

"Graham's detail oriented. He likes numbers to come in sets," Nix said, rubbing a hand down her spine as Mateo exposed more and more, unzipping the gown tiny bit by tiny bit. "It helps relax him." Nix leaned in from behind her ear. "One perk? He never leaves a job unfinished—if you know what I mean."

He slid his hand inside her sagging gown and around to the front of her waist, dipping ever so slightly into the top of what felt like lacy underwear before retreating again.

The way Audrey trembled in his arms in response was beyond satisfying.

Clark cupped Audrey's face and then slowly guided her back to Graham's lips so that they began kissing again.

Fuck, why was that so hot? Clark apparently thought so too because his eyes went dark as he leaned in and started kissing down Audrey's exposed shoulder.

When he was done, he and Danny and Mateo moved so they could get hands on Audrey's body as well. Mateo slipped between her and Graham so he could suck her nipple into his mouth through the lacy white bra she still wore.

She gasped into Graham's mouth and he murmured, "Another sixty," before grabbing her face in his hands and deepening the kiss.

Nix didn't mind.

If he had his way, they'd pleasure Audrey so well that she'd be begging for more all-night long.

Her wedding gown pooled at her waist. Christ, seeing her and remembering her so pristine in the church compared to now with five men kissing, licking and sucking at her—*fuck*. Nix pressed a hand to try to calm his raging erection.

He couldn't stand even a second not touching her though, so the very next moment, he had to be touching her again.

He slid his hand back around her and down her stomach. But this time when he got to the top of her panty line, he found another hand already there. He glanced around her and traced the hand back to Clark.

Clark's eyes were locked on the spot where he thumbed over Audrey's clit through her underwear.

A trembling shiver rocked her body in response and she groaned into Graham's mouth.

Shit. She was so goddamn sexy. Nix was gonna lose it if he wasn't careful. He'd meant to jack off this morning or afternoon, but well, he'd just been too preoccupied. So sure she'd try to run.

But she hadn't. She was here. Half-naked. Her hot skin on his.

His cock pulsed in his pants and he reached down to pop his button and yank his zipper down.

Jesus, that was better. He pulled his shaft out and ran his hand up and down it once. Then again. But then he yanked away, because if he stroked himself even one more time he might spill in his goddamned hand.

"Oh shit," Danny said, face going tight, hand on his cock too. "I'm gonna— Can I—?"

Graham had just broken away from Audrey, their second minute apparently up.

Right in time too, because Audrey had barely turned to Danny and let him pull her into his arms. He shoved her bra down and latched onto her nipple. With one hand he shoved her panties down and dipped his finger inside her.

Jets of cum shot from Danny's cock almost immediately upon contact.

"Oh *Jesus*," Danny heaved like he'd just run a marathon. "Oh my fucking God." He slumped against Audrey's breasts, for just a second before dipping down to lick around her areola and suck her nipple back into his mouth.

Danny kept stroking himself and sucking on Audrey's breast long after he was spent.

When he finally unlatched and looked up, his eyes were wide but also suddenly worried. "Was that okay?" Then he looked down and the back of his neck went red. "I'm sorry for the mess. I just— You're so pretty and I've never—"

Audrey looked like she was barely containing a smile, but she put a hand on Danny's shoulder. "It's just fine," she said reassuringly. "You're fine."

Fuck she was sweet.

Clark apparently thought so too because he took advantage of the moment, swooping in to kiss Audrey's pink, kiss-plumped lips.

That was fine. Clark could have her mouth. For now.

Nix was more interested in another part of her body. And how she would sound when he made her scream in pleasure.

She was still up on her knees while she kissed Clark so it was easy to put his thumbs in the sides of her underwear and slip it down her thighs. Mateo's hands joined his, and together they exposed the most perfect ass on God's green earth.

Nix's hand trembled as gently cupped one of her ass cheeks. It was so sweetly rounded. And her hips. Utterly feminine. He squeezed her ass and she wriggled beneath his touch.

Had he ever been with a woman as responsive as she was? Even before The Fall?

He couldn't remember. He couldn't think of anything except her hot, yielding flesh underneath his hand.

His brain exploded with sensory input of all things Audrey. Her skin was so, so fucking *soft*. The lavender scent of her soap or shampoo or whatever was driving him crazy. Then there were the sounds of her breathy, needy gasps.

And her body, *Christ*, seeing the sweetly curved hourglass figure revealed as Mateo and Clark helped her climb out of the wedding dress and toss it to the side, along with her bra, was enough to bring any man to his knees.

There was only one thing left to do. When she resettled on the bed, Nix urged her onto her back. And then he climbed between her legs and completed his sensory investigation with the one he'd been missing.

Taste.

He licked up the seam of Audrey's pussy and if he thought she was shuddering before, it was nothing to the way her entire body quaked when he tongued back and forth across her clitoris.

Her hands balled into the sheets and her eyes squeezed shut.

The other guys immediately joined in, kissing and tasting every inch of her body they could reach. Looking up her body, the image reminded Nix of animals feasting on a recent kill.

And while Audrey was no one's prey, Nix couldn't say he didn't feel predatory. He sucked and devoured her pussy. She was so fuckin' wet.

Every time her body spasmed and she let out those little escalating cries of pleasure, he felt like a fucking king.

Her eyes were still shut, chest thrust outwards where Graham and Clark both sucked mercilessly on her breasts.

Mateo had moved behind her head and was massaging her shoulders and dropping small kisses all along her temple.

She was a fucking miracle.

"Open your eyes," Nix demanded.

Her eyes popped open wide. He wasn't sure if it was at the command in his voice or all the things that were happening to her body.

She looked bewildered and simultaneously lost in a haze of pleasure.

"Watch me while I make you cum," Nix said, dropping his head so he could lick her bud with his long tongue but never taking his eyes off her.

She blinked and her chest pumped up and down with heaving breaths, but she did as he said. She kept her eyes on him.

Goddamn, his cock was so hard, if he wasn't careful, he'd come just from grinding against the bed while he ate her out. She tasted so fucking amazing. Everything about her was just—

Audrey's needy whining gave way to a high-pitched scream as her face scrunched in pleasure. Her entire body went stiff for a second, then she started shuddering with her orgasm.

It lasted at least three seconds, and Nix was torn. He wanted to be up at her face, memorizing her every micro-expression so he could replay it over and over in his head.

But sucking her sweet cunt and bringing her to the peak a second time was just as good, maybe even better—knowing he was the one giving it to her. Shaking the foundations of her whole goddamned world. Giving her the first glimpse of how good it would be with them.

She collapsed back against the mattress, limbs limp when the second orgasm finally subsided.

She lay there, that dazed look still on her face, eyes soft with replete desire.

Nix crawled over her, kissing up her stomach, then to her breasts, and finally to her mouth. "Do you taste yourself on my tongue?" he whispered after kissing her deep. The way her breasts arched up and into him at the question, he took it that his wife liked dirty talk.

"Do you love tasting your honey on me and knowing I was just sucking on your hot little clit, devouring your juices while you came all over my face?"

Audrey made little whimpering noises and wiggled restlessly beneath him. He laughed softly.

"That's right, gorgeous. This is just the beginning. We're only getting started."

Nix glanced up and Clark was already pinning him with his gaze. Nix smirked. He could tell the fucker was about three seconds from yanking him off their wife and decking him. They'd made certain agreements before walking into this room and Nix had every intention of sticking to them.

At the same time, he wasn't above stealing what extra moments he could here and there. So Nix didn't rush as he dropped and kissed Audrey deep again, pulling his heavy cock out of his pants and thrusting his shaft along the wet folds of her sex. He didn't penetrate but he got his shaft good and wet with her honey. Reaching down, he used the tip of his cock to tease at her clit until she was gasping with need again.

"Alright, Prince Charming," Clark finally growled. "Stop hogging Cinderella."

"Yeah, yeah," Nix muttered, biting Audrey's bottom lip ever so softly as he finally dragged himself away from her.

Clark was happy to immediately take his place.

But Mateo put a hand out to stop him. "On her knees, remember?"

Clark made what Nix could only describe as a pouting face, but he nodded and reached down for Audrey's hand. "Up on your knees, sexy."

Audrey's eyes flicked back and forth between Mateo and Clark, and then over to Nix. Like she was checking if it was something he thought was okay.

And that just hit Nix straight in the fucking gut. He wasn't sure how he managed the smile and weak nod, but he did.

She trusted him. Even if she wasn't fully conscious of it yet. She was relying on him to protect her.

He got off the bed and staggered a step backward as Mateo laid down between her legs, propping himself up just enough so that his mouth was right at her center. Clark lined himself up on the bed behind her, hands skimming down her back and settling at her hips. His cock was long and full, bobbing against her ass.

Nix blinked, still flabbergasted.

Audrey trusted him. She was his goddamned *wife*. He'd made vows today. Sacred vows.

And what if he failed Audrey just like he had Roxy?

She'd trusted him completely and he'd failed her.

In the blink of an eye, he was back there with Roxy eating breakfast around the campfire. Almost eight years ago, before the bombs had dropped, when they all still thought Xterminate was something the world could recover from.

Roxy flashed her megawatt smile as she finished her eggs. Then she threw her arms around Nix. She was always doing that. She knew he didn't like getting touchy-feely but she would just hug him randomly throughout the day. More and more often since they'd lost Mom to Xterminate six months before.

She'd been on a business trip to Atlanta and never come home. Dad had never been around much and that didn't change with mom's death.

It was just him and Roxy. She was sixteen and he was terrified of losing her. People talked about a cure for Xterminate being just around the corner. Any day now. That's what everyone said on the TV and radio.

So Nix was taking Roxy to hide in the hills away from anyone who could infect her. They'd just make camp and wait it out until a cure became available.

They'd been hiking the hill country for about three days by that point. Nix figured they'd make camp somewhere close enough to the Pedernales River to have access to fresh water but not so close anyone would come across their camp.

"Hey, watch it, you're gonna break a rib if you don't let up," he'd joked, but she'd just squeezed him tighter.

"You know why I'm not afraid no matter what happens? How I manage to make it through the days?" she'd whispered into his chest. He'd barely heard her, her voice was so muffled by his shirt.

But then she'd pulled back and looked up at him, her bright blue eyes full of trust.

"Because I'm with you," she said. "And I know you'll never let anything bad happen to me."

It was later that same day when a so-called militia *caught them trying to sneak through the woods around the cluster of cabins they'd claimed as their* base.

Stupid. Nix had seen the grouping of cabins listed on his map as resort cabins, never dreaming what they had become. But he should have. Everything had gone to hell in a handbasket over the past year. Apocalyptic motherfuckers were going to ground everywhere.

Nix fought. He fought like a demon. One man slashed a dagger down his face and even though he couldn't see through the flood of blood, he kept fighting.

But in the end, there were just too damn many. The last thing he saw before they knocked him unconscious was three men dragging a crying Roxy away.

When he woke up, even from where they had him chained up clear across camp, he heard Roxy's screams. For hours.

Fucking hours.

She never stopped fighting them. Until finally all her fight was gone.

Nix looked up again at the bed. At the four men poised around Audrey. And he saw fucking red.

"Enough," he shouted, stomping back to the bed and shoving Clark to the side.

"Hey, what the fuck?"

But Nix was already scooping Audrey up.

She squeaked in surprise and threw her arms around his neck.

"What the hell do you think you're doing?" Clark asked, getting in his way.

Danny joined his side, thick arms crossed over his chest. Mateo and Graham were still on the bed but Nix could feel the tension coming off them too.

"This isn't happening like this," Nix growled, holding Audrey closer to his chest. "Not today. It's too soon. I'm taking her back to her bedroom."

Clark's jaw flexed. "This is her bedroom. She belongs with us now."

This son of a bitch wanted a fight, fine with him. Nix's nostrils flared. But first he had to get Audrey out of here, away from these horny fucks who only wanted to—

"Nix."

Nix was so startled by Audrey's gentle voice and the soft hand on his face that he almost lost his grip on her.

She was frowning but there was something else in her eyes. They searched his back and forth. Like she was trying to make up her mind about something and was searching for the answers there. They said the eyes were the windows to the soul. He didn't want to think about how black his was, so he dropped his gaze.

Unfortunately, that meant he was staring directly at her perky, hardened nipples. His cock, which had gone soft, immediately started hardening again. Fuck, that was the last thing he needed.

He clenched his jaw. He would protect Audrey no matter what. Even if it was from himself.

Still, nothing could have prepared him for the words that next came out of Audrey's mouth. "It's okay, Nix. I— I— " She swallowed hard, eyes flicking down and then back up again, cheeks going pink.

"I want this. I need to..." Her voice broke off like she was looking for the right words and failing to find them.

Finally she shook her head and met his gaze, her bright blue eyes shining with an intensity Nix had never seen in them before. "I need to *know*." She took a deep breath. "I want to do this. Tonight." She reached a hand out for Clark. "With all of you."

Nix's breath caught as his shaft went fully hard again.

Well, fuck him.

It looked like they were going to have their wedding night after all.

CHAPTER EIGHTEEN

CLARK

He'd be her first. No matter how many times they shared her for the rest of their lives, Clark would always have this first.

He hadn't expected the sense of satisfaction that gave him to be so intense.

She was on her knees in front of him on the bed, spread-eagled over Mateo's face. But it was Clark's cock she'd be taking. He rubbed the tip through the lips of Audrey's sex from behind and threw his head back.

Jesus *fuck* that was the best thing he'd felt in seven years. Seven shitty, hard-up years dreaming of a sweet little pussy like this and finally here he was, about to stick his cock back where it was always meant to be.

He gripped her luscious, round hips in his fingers and couldn't help giving her sweet little ass a light smack.

"Hey," Nix snapped at him from where he sat beside Audrey on the bed, holding her hand. Dude wasn't even touching her anywhere else. Just holding her hand.

And Clark wasn't sure if he was jealous of that or not.

Which made him frown.

Because he was just in this for the pussy. Right?

Yeah, sure, Audrey was great. The little bit of time he'd spent with her anyway. Trade negotiations had taken him out of town twice the past three weeks.

And it was true, Clark only wanted *willing* pussy. Hence his seven-year dry spell.

But still. That was all there was too it.

So why did he feel like punching Nix for his big caveman show of concern a few moments ago, almost dragging Audrey off like that?

Clark had been hard all week waiting for this, but he'd waited seven years. A little longer wouldn't kill him if Audrey wasn't ready yet.

Clark would have been the first to hand her her robe and tell her it was okay, they didn't have to do anything.

All right, well, *maybe* he would have left off the robe part. She was just sooooo fuckin' hot. He was a man, after all.

Maybe it was the world they lived in. It stripped everything back to its most basic. And Clark hated Nix trying to claim Audrey like that— as if he was the only one who cared about her wellbeing.

That was bullshit. She was *theirs*. Not Nix's.

And for the next twenty minutes, her sweet, virgin little pussy would be all *Clark's*.

"You ready, baby?" Clark asked, gripping the bottom of his shaft and rubbing his tip more ardently against her wet, slippery clit.

He held her hips and felt her trembling. His cock jerked against her hot flesh at the response. But was it excitement or fear? Or just plain old nerves?

"Baby?" Clark asked, leaning over her back and drawing her face around so he could look her in the eye.

And when their eyes met, Jesus fuck but she took his breath away. He swallowed hard, finding his throat suddenly dry.

She was an innocent. Somehow in this fucked up world, she was still an innocent. And he didn't just mean that she was a virgin. Vulnerability shone from her eyes. A look that said, *please*. And *don't hurt me* and yet at the same time, if Clark wasn't wrong, *I want this*.

"Are you sure?" Clark whispered.

"Stop asking so many questions," she said, then dropped her head to lay on Mateo's stomach where he was laying underneath her again, head returning between her legs.

"Mateo, put him in me."

Mateo's gulp was audible but the next second, a surprisingly firm hand grasped Clark's shaft and slowly, so achingly slowly, brought the head of his cock back to Audrey's drenched pussy lips.

"Christ," Clark hissed. It was so close now. He was almost there. Almost to the promised land.

But then he told himself to stop it.

There was no way this could live up to all the hype he'd built in his mind. She was a virgin. This wasn't about him. They needed to take care of her. Introduce her to bed play without scaring the bejesus out of her.

It was the reason he'd been chosen to go first.

Apparently he had the Goldilocks of cocks. Not too big, not too small. It was *juuuuuuust* right. Well, a little longer than most, but the width was very manageable. Which was what would be important for this first time. He wouldn't go balls deep or anything.

But he'd get his cock plenty wet. The head of his cock was already drenched. So naturally lubricated that when he shifted his hips ever so slightly forward, he slid between her outer lips.

And then he felt the resistance of her hymen.

Jesus fuck, was it wrong that his dick got even harder at feeling the proof of her innocence?

He was the first man to ever plow this sweet, sweet pussy. The *first*. It was something no one could ever take away from him, no matter what.

"Mateo, you taking care of our girl?" Clark asked, rocking back and forth ever so slightly against Audrey's barrier, stretching what he could.

Mateo's response was muffled, his face buried in Audrey's sex. Clark smirked. The guys had all gotten together yesterday and discussed the extent of their sexual experiences so they could plan tonight.

Mateo had apparently only eaten pussy a couple times before, but he immediately volunteered for the job of official pussy eater tonight. There was some back and forth, until Mateo said he'd give up actually having his turn at penetration if only he could be the one who ate her out for most of the night.

Clark gripped Audrey's hips as he pushed in further. He winced when he felt her tense up underneath him but just kept pushing, knowing it was more merciful to get the pain over with as quickly as possible.

He pushed halfway in, breaking through her barrier and then freezing.

And it was like the air in the whole room had gone still.

Shit. What was he thinking? It was fucking barbaric that women's first times had to hurt. They should have gotten her shitfaced on some vodka so she wouldn't have felt it. Or weed. He was always moving a ton of that shit. It was like currency. There was gold, silver, and pot. He should've—

"Audrey," Nix anxious voice broke into his thoughts. "Are you okay? Because I'll—"

"I'm fine." Audrey blew out a big breath. Nix, still clutching her hand, leaned in so that he was looking right in her face where she laid it sideways on Mateo's stomach.

"Are you sure?"

She glared at Nix and lifted a little so she could look down at Mateo. "Do I need to get myself off?"

She dropped her hand down like she was going to start rubbing her own clit but Mateo got there first, his mouth slurping loudly at her clit. She clenched around Clark and Jesus fuck, how was he supposed to hold back when she did shit like that?

"Move," she growled, glaring over her shoulder at Clark.

His balls tingled and he thought he might fucking die if he didn't get some friction. But it was only when she shouted, "Move, goddammit," that he pulled out and then pushed in again.

Another long hiss slipped out of her mouth, and her head dropped to Mateo's stomach again.

Danny and Graham had just been watching from the other side of the bed opposite Nix, but now they both reached for Audrey. Graham ran his hands down Audrey's flank all the way to her feet and back up again.

Clark pushed back in, this time with just a tad more force. "Fucking Christ," he said, throwing his head back and clenching his teeth.

Keep it together. Keep it to-fucking-*gether*. Are you gonna let her first be a quick wham-bam-thank-you-ma'am?

No. He brought himself back under control right at the last second.

Turned out to be right in time, too, because even though he was fucking Audrey in slow, measured thrusts, she clenched her slick walls all around him and cried out. One of her arms extended to Nix, the other to Danny, and Graham stroked her calf lovingly.

They'd made her cum. All of them this time—all of them together. Surrounding her. Worshipping her. And it looked and sounded and felt like she'd come ten times harder this time than before.

And it was *his* cock inside her making her cum. Or at least significantly helping her along, that was for damn sure.

He knew he hadn't lost it. What did years matter when you were a sex god incarnate? Not a damn thing, that was what.

"What's she feel like?" Nix asked, leaning over to kiss Audrey. He pulled back just long enough to demand. "Tell us. Tell us every goddamned detail of what she feels like around your cock."

Audrey shuddered at Nix's words. Or maybe it was Mateo's mouth. Or the way Danny was pinching at her nipples and watching in awe at how they pebbled up between his thumb and forefinger.

Or from Clark's cock. Because as her body went more and more relaxed, Clark stopped holding back.

And Jesus fucking *Christ*. The more he thrust the more he felt like he *was* a god. He'd never been more alive, or fucking here, or just— Jesus, listen to the way his balls slapped her ass every time he thrust—

His ass clenched against the need threatening to burst through his spine and out through his cock. Not yet. Not fucking yet.

He wanted more. He wanted to fuck Audrey all night and then all tomorrow and then all tomorrow night.

Had sex always been this good?

No. No way it had been this good.

He never would have left his apartment during college if it had been this good. He would have married some girl just so he could have twenty-four-hour access to her body.

And the noises she was making.

Unless she was faking, it seemed like she was over the pain and back to enjoying herself.

But suddenly that wasn't enough. She'd had some clitoral orgasms and that was all well and good.

But Clark's specialty was hitting the G-spot. His long dick was perfect for it and this position helped too.

Oh fuck yeah. He was going to make her come and come.

He reached his arm around her hips and waist to hold her in place so he could make sure he was really hitting the spot he was aiming for.

"You have no idea how fucking tight she is," Clark said through heaving breaths, finally answering Nix. And only because he thought it might get Audrey hotter.

"Her sweet little virgin cunt is like a vise on my cock." Clark thrust faster and he knew when he found her spot because she screamed in a way she hadn't all night.

"That's right, baby. That's your fucking G-spot. That's my cock hitting you so deep inside. So fucking good. Scream for me, baby. Scream for your fucking husband because you can't get enough of my cock."

"I can't get enough of your cock!" she yelled and a long shudder rolled through her body. Her hand was buried in Nix's hair and Clark could see she was almost yanking it out by the roots she was coming so fucking hard.

That was the last straw. No matter how much he wanted to keep fucking her forever, it was too much. She was too much. She clenched so hard on his cock when she came.

"CHRIST!" he roared as he pumped cum deep into her pussy. So fucking deep. He stilled, but only for a second, because fucking Christ, he wanted more, he wanted it back, he fucking needed it. He thrust again and again, but it was already fading.

He thrust several more times anyway.

He slumped over Audrey's back, kissing her spine and then it was like he'd been unplugged. All the electricity blasting through his body only moments before was just... gone.

But fuck, the memory of it.

As soon as he could, he was getting back in that beautiful, beautiful pussy.

Graham made space for him as he slid off to the side.

Clark reached out to take over where Graham had been stroking Audrey's leg. No matter how suddenly exhausted he was, he couldn't bear losing contact with her. Not after that life-altering fuck.

Audrey was panting hard too. There was a sheen of sweat over her back and at her temple, darkening the red curls at her hairline.

But her words were crystal clear.

"Who's next?"

CHAPTER NINETEEN

NIX

Several hours later, Audrey had never looked more beautiful.

Or more exhausted.

Not surprising considering she'd just taken three men into her body one after the other. First Clark, then Graham, then Danny.

The sun had long set and the room was lit by what seemed like fifty glittering candles. A wild extravagance and all Mateo's doing.

Now Nix sat behind Audrey on the couch, her back to his chest, ass nestled between his legs. He was hard, but ignoring it.

He'd lost count of how many times Audrey had come. He'd only vaguely remembered that being a thing before The Fall—that women could come more than men. A lot more. Or maybe it was just his previous, long past lackluster experience in bed talking.

But Audrey came along and kept astounding him at every turn. The amount of passion she had pent up in that tiny little body of hers. And how generous she'd been with each and every one of them.

Mateo let them all know last night that he wasn't going to have intercourse with her tonight—it was why he got to have the job as pussy-eater in chief.

And damn could the man *eat*. Start to finish, they'd been fucking for at least a couple hours now and once Mateo had taken over, he hadn't let up once.

Watching Clark take Audrey's virginity had been one of the best and worst moments of Nix's life. Getting to be there, to hold her hand and kiss her while she experienced it—to swallow her cries of pleasure and hold her through the shaking orgasm Clark brought her to— goddamn, he'd never forget it.

But fuck if Nix hadn't wished it was him. Jealousy was an emotion he didn't have much experience with.

To be jealous, you had to care about something.

Which, as a rule, he didn't.

But it was too damn late.

Audrey had wormed her way in, and he didn't see how there was any way to get her out now.

After Clark took her virginity, they'd flipped her over on her back for Graham's turn. Methodically. While counting to sixty. Six times. He came on that sixth sixtieth thrust.

Meanwhile, Mateo kept finding acrobatic ways to get at her clit, managing to make her come twice more.

Then they'd moved to the couch. Nix had pulled Audrey into his lap and played with her breasts while Danny finally managed to get his cock inside her.

He pumped away for a whole thirty seconds before coming this time.

And was damn proud of himself for it too.

"Look, I did it right this time!" he'd exclaimed as he jumped up, cock still slick and bobbing around half-hard. Then he'd collapsed on the bed beside a napping Clark while Mateo headed downstairs getting snacks.

That was about five minutes ago and ever since, Nix had been staring over Audrey's shoulder, down her body, to her pussy. He couldn't look away.

Cum still dripped out of her.

The combined cum of three men.

Nix didn't know why that idea was so fucking hot, but it was. Filthy dirty and sexy as *fuck*.

And having her ass nestled right over his cock? Yeah, he was harder than he'd been all night, and that was saying something.

Audrey shifted and glanced over her shoulder, eyelids heavy. "Your turn," she said with a yawn.

And, no matter how much he wanted to flip her on the couch and fuck her right then, right there, he just smiled and brushed her damp curls back from her face.

"Shh, you can barely keep your eyes open."

He kissed the side of her temple. Then he'd lifted her into his arms. He was heading to take her to the bathroom so he could get her cleaned up.

Danny jumped off the bed, running over and throwing his arms around Audrey and Nix.

"Oh," Nix said, just managing to keep Audrey aloft in spite of Danny's vigorous hugging. Danny was grinning when he finally pulled back, his eyes shining. The dude looked drunk with happiness.

"Audrey." Danny's voice burst with enthusiasm as he took her hand. "I want you to know that I love you. You're the *best* thing that's ever happened to me. I'm the luckiest man in the world to be your husband. I love you and I'll do *anything* for you."

His eyes searched her face, features going even more earnest. "I'd die for you, that's how much I love you. We all would."

But Nix was more concerned with the way Audrey had suddenly gone tense in his arms.

"Don't say that." Her voice was thin and reedy. "Don't ever say you'd die for me."

Danny looked befuddled. "But I would. Of course I would. That's what you do when you're in love."

Audrey turned away from Danny, burying her face in Nix's chest. Nix got the message. He started toward the bathroom again.

He didn't know what had gotten her so upset, but it had obviously been Danny flapping his big, stupid mouth.

"Ignore Danny," Nix said, giving her a squeeze as they got to the master bathroom and he kicked the door shut behind them.

Two candles were burning in here, so even though she squirmed to be let down and turned away from him, he could still see her unhappy expression in the mirror.

"Just think of him like a big, adorable puppy. He's always bumbling around and running into shit, but we give him a break because well," Nix shrugged and tried a smile, "he's great with a pickax."

Audrey didn't return his smile. "I'm fine," she said, still not looking his way. Which was a lie. She was clearly *not* fine.

She dipped a cloth in the water bucket on the counter and started swiping at her sex. She winced and Nix couldn't stand it. Couldn't stand seeing her there, obviously hurting, and not do anything.

"You're sore and exhausted." He moved close. "Here. Lean on me." He pulled her into a one-armed hug and while she resisted at first, eventually she rested her weight against him.

Nix considered it a true victory when he got her to hand over the rag.

He wiped down her pussy in long, slow, gentle strokes.

When she started shaking against him a few moments later, he thought it was from the cold water.

"I'm sorry, beautiful. I'll get you back under the covers in just a moment here. I want you to be clean so you don't—"

But her shuddering just got harder the more he talked.

Which was when he looked down and saw she was crying.

"What the fuck? Audrey?" Shit. "Did I do something wrong? Did we hurt you?" His gaze went to the doorway. If one of those bastards had pushed too hard or—

"No, no," Audrey said, waving a hand and then swiping at her cheeks. "God, it's not anything like that. It's just—"

But she broke off before she could tell him what was upsetting her and Nix wanted to punch something. To put his fist through someone's face. To pull the guts out of anyone who even looked at her sideways—

"It's just today," she said, shaking her head at herself and wiping her eyes. "It was all so *much*. The wedding and then tonight."

She swallowed hard and squeezed her eyes shut. She pressed her palms into her eyes and then dropped them, taking a deep breath and looking toward the ceiling like she was praying for strength.

Nix's guts twisted with every action. Finally, her gaze fell back on him. "I'm sorry, can we just ignore that ever happened?"

She tried for a smile but it was watery. She tried harder, holding up her hands. "God, I swear I'm not this weak person."

Always the fighter. Even against what she thought of as her own weaknesses.

He pulled her into his chest again.

He remembered how much his sister Roxy said hugs helped when she was upset. He always just wanted to get down to fixing whatever her problem was but she got mad at him. *No, just* listen *to me. And then give me a hug,* she'd always say.

If only every problem could be solved so easily.

But with the way Audrey burrowed into his chest, he thought it might have been the right move after all.

They stood together for a long time like that. Audrey in his arms, face buried against his bare chest.

He knew he should tell her they ought to go back to the bedroom. She needed rest. She thought today was tiresome. Tomorrow was the reception and the receiving of gifts from everyone in town. He knew it could be an overwhelming prospect, even for people who'd lived here a long time.

"What Danny said out there," she said, surprising him after the long silence. "Do you feel the same way?"

Suddenly Nix was the one going tense. Was she asking him if he lo — He wasn't sure if... It was complicated.

The gut-twisting feeling came back. He wasn't sure if he could ever — Not after losing Roxy. Yeah she was his sister, not his lover, but it had still broken something basic in him that couldn't be fixed and—

"Would you die for me?"

Nix immediately relaxed at her clarification. That was an easy one. "Yes," he said simply.

She nodded and her hold around his waist tightened. But only for a moment. Because the next second, her wide sea-blue eyes were focused on him.

"Nix," she lifted a hand to cradle his face and he couldn't help sinking against her gentle touch.

"Let's just forget the rest of the world for a little while, okay? Let's play pretend. We'll pretend it's before The Fall. And you're just a normal man and I'm a normal woman."

She licked her lips and her gaze dropped to his mouth. "And this is our wedding night." Her whisper was barely audible. She moved so that they were chest to chest and her pelvis was flush with his. His cock went immediately back to full mast.

"Audrey," Nix frowned. "You're sore. And exhausted."

But when he tried to pull back, her fingernails dug into his hips.

"It's our wedding night," she repeated. Then she went up on her tiptoes, rubbing her breasts against his chest as she went.

She kissed up his neck, teasing her tongue against his earlobe.

"*Fuck*, woman," he growled.

"That's the idea." Her words and hungry kiss broke the last of his restraint.

He shoved the bucket of water off the counter and landed her ass there instead. He didn't care that the damn water spilled everywhere or that it was another bucket he'd have to haul up from the well.

He kissed Audrey deep. Taking everything she was offering.

Her legs went around his waist and his cock bobbed against her sex.

Yes. Fuck. Yes. *Finally*.

She was the one who reached down and guided him inside her.

Nix didn't know if it was still remnants of all the other guys' cum or if she was just that wet for him, but he slid right in.

Her body went stiff for a moment and she hissed in a breath.

Nix stilled immediately. "Shit, I'm sorry gorgeous. Are you okay?"

A devouring kiss was her response. Nix groaned against her lips.

Fuck. So hot. So *tight*. His cock surged in her pussy. And Jesus, she squeezed around him like a damn vice. Then she relaxed. Then squeezed again.

It felt like his heart was going to explode out his cock. That was how fucking insane and amazing being buried inside her felt.

"You're bigger than they are," she gasped into his mouth.

And fuck if that didn't make his giant cock even harder.

"There's a reason I didn't take you first," he growled, lifting her ass slightly off the counter so he could shift to get a deeper angle.

She groaned and her legs wrapped around him even tighter.

"But you're ready for me now, aren't you? They stretched your little virgin pussy just enough so you can take all of me."

Her high-pitched cry of pleasure was the only response he got as he ground down against her clit with his next thrust.

She cried out again, arching her back and thrusting her breasts upwards.

She wrapped her arms around his neck and clung to him. "Let's go out there," she whimpered, restlessly grinding on his cock. "I want to be with them while you fuck me. I want it to be together. It should be together."

That was fine with Nix. As long as he got to stay buried inside her, he didn't care if he did it parading down the center of main street.

She was so light, he could carry her and still keep fucking her as they went, lifting and dropping her body up and down on his pole.

As soon as they came back in the other room, Mateo and Graham looked their way. Graham's hand immediately dropped to his dick. He'd put sweatpants on, but he shoved them down so he could jack himself better.

Clark stirred and sat up groggily, immediately coming to attention when he saw Nix and Audrey.

"Against the wall," she said in between kisses, digging her fingers in Nix's hair and scraping down his scalp in a way that drove him fucking crazy. "And don't be gentle. I'm not a goddamned vase that needs to be handled with kid gloves."

So Nix slammed her up against the wall. And for once, he didn't apologize about it. The action only seemed to excite her more.

He held her up by her ass and she rode him, flexing up against the wall and back down, her ankles locked around his back.

Aww *fuck*. She was squeezing on him again. Squeezing. Releasing. Squeezing again.

"Jesus, Aud. Do you know what you're doing to me?"

"Less talking," she muttered between biting kisses. "More fucking."

Daaaaaamn. What was a man supposed to do with that? Other than give a lady exactly what she asked for?

They fucked. Nix lost track of time. Of everything.

There was only Audrey's pussy.

His cock.

Her tits.

Her tongue and nipping teeth.

She sucked his bottom lip into her mouth, dragging her teeth along it as she released it and then fuck—she was squeezing on him tighter than she ever had yet.

She was coming.

Her face scrunched in agonized ecstasy as she came and Nix lost it. He came with her, shouting her name as he pumped cum into her hot, tight as hell little cunt.

And after they were spent, he stumbled over to the bed, managing to carry her with the last little bit of his strength. He shoved Clark over, only briefly noticing Mateo cleaning cum off his own stomach and smirking. He could just bet that was one hell of a show he and Audrey had put on.

Audrey.

His wife.

Their wife.

As he looked down at her settling into his side, little spoon to his big, his chest expanded in a way he hadn't felt in a very, very long time.

And it had him wondering if maybe it was time to rethink the whole never-letting-anyone-in promise he'd made to himself after losing Roxy.

Maybe there was room in his life for love after all.

CHAPTER TWENTY

AUDREY

They were all sleeping.

Audrey wasn't.

She'd been pretending to sleep.

It was a trick she'd learned when practicing meditation with Uncle Dale. You had to figure out some way not to go nuts with all the quiet, alone time. Some people got real religious. Other's went the hedonism route.

Audrey had never been much into religion and she was in a bunker in the middle of nowhere, so a life of reckless pleasure wasn't exactly an option for her. So meditation turned out to be her ticket to keeping herself free of the looney bin.

You counted your breaths and relaxed every one of your muscles and practiced letting go. Letting go.

Let go, she whispered silently to herself. *Let go of all of it.*

She'd been faking sleep for twenty minutes now. Just to be sure.

Deep manly snores came from all around the room. She counted the distinct patterns. Three on the bed with her. One on the couch where Danny had passed out. And Mateo on the floor right beside the bed.

She'd have to be careful not to step on him when she got up.

It was time.

Move, she ordered herself.

And then stayed exactly where she was.

Nix's arms were so warm around her. So strong and safe.

Ha. Safe.

Her father thought he could keep her safe. She'd just been thirteen when Xterminate hit their town, a suburb of San Antonio. Her mom had died several years before of breast cancer, so it was just her, her dad, and Charlie.

Then, about eight months after reports of Xterminate first appeared, all the girls and women in town got sick.

All except Audrey.

When the women started dying in droves, it was like the men left lost their minds. The police abandoned the department the second day fighting and looting broke out. Fires burned all over town. It was all out anarchy.

Charlie and dad tried to keep Audrey hidden.

But then one of their neighbors who—a man who'd had four daughters, girls Audrey had played with all growing up—came to the door, grief-stricken over his daughters' deaths. He demanded to see Audrey's body. Everyone else had been taking their daughters and wives to the center of the neighborhood to burn them. So where was Audrey?

When Dad told him he needed to leave, it attracted an audience. A crowd started gathering and apparently Dad gave Charlie some sort of prearranged signal. Then he stepped out the front door, locking it behind him.

Charlie grabbed her hand and they ran for the back door. They'd cut her hair short and been dressing her like a boy for weeks in case anyone glimpsed her through a window and Dad had the motorcycle gassed up and ready to go out back.

There was no chance to say stop or even ask what was going on. Charlie all but tossed her on the bike, climbed on behind her, and they sped off.

Uncle Dale had a couple of his friends go back to check on Dad—planning bring him up to the bunker to reunite with them.

But he was dead. He'd died that day he tried distracting the crowd on the front porch.

The crowd had apparently torn him apart when someone reported they'd recognized Audrey driving off with her brother, healthy and whole. People she'd known her whole life, turned into animals by their grief and some kind of madness Audrey still didn't understand.

I'd die for you, that's how much I love you.

Fucking idiots.

Her anger was finally enough to get her moving. Slowly. She couldn't ruin it now by rushing. She'd come this far. She bit her lip as she lifted Nix's heavy arm and slipped out from underneath it.

His snoring stopped and he shifted in bed. He squeezed his arm tighter for a moment and Audrey had to act fast.

She slid out from his grasp and shoved a pillow underneath his arm instead. He squeezed the pillow close and settled back to snoring.

Audrey breathed out in relief.

One obstacle down.

She looked down at the floor where Mateo was sprawled. He'd put out most of the candles earlier and one was still burning. And it was minutes from going out. Every few seconds it flickered and sputtered, flickered and sputtered.

Audrey held her breath as she stepped in the small clear bit of floor between Mateo's outstretched arm and his head.

Right as she did, the candle flamed out.

Shit.

She looked down, heart in her throat. Dammit. Was his other arm by his side or was it closer to his head? How far out did she need to step to avoid landing on him?

She closed her eye and tried to remember, but it was no use. Too much adrenaline was pumping through her veins.

The wedding had been hard enough to get through but then getting back to the room with the guys...

She'd told herself it would be no big deal.

So she'd have some sex.

Then they'd finally let down their guard and then she could escape.

She'd always been curious about sex and this seemed like as good a place to lose her V-card as any. It wasn't like there would be any dudes around in Nomansland. The name of the place was kind of a giveaway —it wasn't somewhere a girl could find a lot of action.

Plus, after getting to know the guys over the past month, she couldn't really imagine doing it with anyone else.

So yeah, she figured, she'd sleep with them. Then sneak out.

But she was such an idiot. She'd been in no way prepared for what had happened tonight.

She'd touched herself before. Uh, hello? Locked in an underground bunker for eight years. Whenever Uncle Dale and Charlie left, fantasizing and getting herself off were high on her agenda.

So she thought she knew what sex would be like. At least a little bit.

But having a man's *mouth* on her sex? Sucking on her clit?

And then their cocks. Oh God, the *cocks*.

Her cheeks flushed even remembering it. Her pussy throbbed. She'd be sore for days but it was worth it. Every sordid, amazing, filthy moment of it.

Midway through sex with Clark, she decided that if all she'd walk out of here with was memories, she was damn well gonna make some spectacular ones.

But now that was over.

It was over and now it was time to go.

She lifted her leg, closed her eyes, and took a giant step in the direction she hoped wouldn't end up on Mateo's bicep.

And her foot landed on wood.

She didn't even give herself a moment to breathe out in relief. Because any of them could wake up at any second. And if they realized she was gone and she was still in town, she'd be *fucked*.

And not in the fun way she had been all evening.

She held her breath while she slowly tiptoed across the rest of the room in the direction she thought the door was.

Annnnnnnnd ran headfirst into a wall. *Owwww.*

She managed not to stumble backwards and fall on her ass, but only barely. She rubbed at her head with one hand while feeling around for the doorknob with the other.

She searched for way too long and almost knocked a damn picture frame off the wall before finally finding the damn thing.

Then, of *course*, the door squeaked on its hinges so loud she was sure it would wake the whole room. But after a several seconds of tense silence, everyone's snores continued on as normal.

She hurried as quickly as she dared down the stairs. *Ha*. Wouldn't that be just her luck. Dad and Charlie died to protect her and then she goes and does herself in by being stupid enough to run down a pitch-black staircase.

She clutched the rail and forced herself to slow down. But only until she got to the bottom of the stairs. Then she ran to the kitchen and pulled out a pair of clothes she'd stowed in the back of a rarely used cabinet, along with a small backpack with a flashlight and some worst-case-scenario supplies—on the motorcycle she should make it to the coast in a day, but if she'd learned anything, it was to prepare for the unexpected.

She'd packed some food and a change of clothes. Along with Nix's dart gun. There was a night guard she'd need to sneak up on and tranq.

Her heart sped up just thinking about. But not nearly as much as when she pulled out the last item in the backpack...

The *real* gun she'd stolen from the Commander's house this morning when she was there to get ready for the wedding.

She pulled it out and looked at it. There was just enough moonlight coming in from the windows to see it's outline in the dark.

Audrey had been about to take a shower at Sophia's this morning but the well pump had been acting up, something it did from time to time, apparently. Sophia went out to fiddle with it and Audrey took a chance.

There was always one door was locked when she'd stayed there, but she'd never dared trying to pick it when the Commander was home. He was gone this morning, though. So Audrey, heart in her throat, ran over and used a couple bobby pins to pop the lock.

And it opened to the motherload.

It was the Commander's personal armory. There were guns of every shape, size, and model. Antique guns and ones that looked so sophisticated they must have been manufactured the year the bombs dropped.

Audrey wasn't ambitious. She picked one of the small ones that was out of the way in the corner. She made sure it was loaded. And then she got the hell out of there. She'd barely buried it in her pile of clothes and pulled on a bathrobe when Sophia came back in, smiling and saying the pump was all fixed.

Audrey blew out a breath at remembering the close call. Then she pulled her clothes and shoes on as fast as humanly possible, checked the safety on the gun, and shoved it in the back of her jeans. She yanked her shirt over it and pulled on the backpack, then jogged over to the back door. She slipped out as quietly as she could, pulling the door shut behind her.

She was breathing hard as she looked out at the still, quiet back yard. Well, it was far from quiet, actually. The locusts were making a damn racket.

But that was good. She could use all the noise cover she could get.

Not that she should be standing around wasting any time. Right. *The plan.* Stick to the plan. She hurried across the back lawn to the fence, pressing her hand to her jeans pocket as she went. Good, Mateo's key was still there.

She'd stolen it off him last night after he got home. It was too easy. He was so sweet. He always wore his keys on a carabiner attached to his belt. All she had to do was sit down with him on the couch when he was reading last night. She curled up beside him and asked him to read to her.

Her tummy clenched a little at how she'd deceived him.

But then she gave a mirthless laugh. Pretty sure realizing she'd stolen his key was nothing to what they'd all feel tomorrow morning when they woke up to find her gone.

It seemed so glaringly obvious now, but she really hadn't thought about how her leaving like this after their night together would be a—

She swallowed hard and clenched her jaw. Why the hell was she second-guessing herself now? She was so close.

She shook her head and hopped up to grab the top of the wooden fence at the corner. Climbing it was more awkward than she'd imagined. But she finally managed to shimmy over. And toppled less than gracefully over the other side.

She immediately got up and dusted herself off.

No time to stop and think. Just keep moving. Stick to the plan.

After double-checking the gun was still in place, she started moving. She stuck to the fence line because the land dropped off pretty steeply behind the neighborhood to a gulch.

Thankfully it was just shy of a full moon, so she could see fairly well in spite of a little bit of tree cover.

She only paused when she came to the last of the continuous fences. There was a small open area she'd have to cross before she got to the woods beside the road she could follow all the way to Mateo's workshop.

Okay. She took a deep breath in and out. She could do this. Almost there.

From sneaking into Nix's home office, she'd seen the guard schedule and knew there was a shift change of the perimeter guards after midnight.

According to her calculations, there was an abandoned road out of town that no one would be watching between 12:10 and 12:25. She glanced down at her watch—ironically, a wedding present from Sophia.

She ignored her twisting stomach. In less than half an hour and she'd be speeding out of town.

All of this would be behind her.

Suddenly she felt short of breath. She'd never see any of them again. Ever. She spun around and looked back the way she'd come.

Betrayal.

The word landed like a heavy weight right in her gut. That's what her leaving after their night together was.

It was betrayal.

She squeezed her eyes shut against the flood of feelings she'd been trying to suppress ever since she'd pulled away from Nix's sleeping embrace.

There was just no other way.

She didn't know it would feel so— She pressed her fist against her stomach, feeling like she was going to throw up. Nix watched her like a hawk. If she could have escaped earlier, done it *any* other way, she would have. But after one week, then two, it was obvious that even if she could have found a vehicle earlier, Nix never let his guard down. Not for a second.

So she'd come up with this plan. She'd give him what he wanted. And do the only thing she could think of to finally get him to let his guard down—convince him he'd won. She'd marry them. Sleep with them. And then—

But she hadn't known what it would be like.

In the church... she'd made *vows*.

And then consecrated those vows with their bodies.

She was betraying them.

Maybe she hadn't realized it when she made the plan. But now? She knew now.

She dragged a hand through her hair and looked back down the fence line again. And had a thought so insane she immediately started shaking head to toe.

What if she didn't leave?

What if...

What if she *stayed?*

She bent over, hands on her knees. God, what was she even thinking? This had always been the plan. Earn their trust, do whatever it took so they'd get complacent and then she'd run...

She had three days till the window closed on the Nomansland rendezvous. With the motorcycle from Mateo's shop, she could make it there in time.

It was a no-brainer.

But then Mateo's face flashed through her mind. He'd looked so terrified and at the same time full of awe when he repeated the vows after the pastor. Like he didn't believe he deserved to be so lucky.

And for all Clark's bravado, he was so *gentle* with her as he took her virginity. All of them were tender, going as slow as she needed, doing everything they could to bring her as much pleasure as possible.

And Danny's boyish enthusiasm. God, she couldn't help but smile remembering the look on his face when he'd managed to have sex with her on the second try. Like it was his life's crowning achievement.

And Graham and...

... and Nix.

Her chest clenched at the thought of Nix.

Their lovemaking had been hard and raw and he was the reason she'd been moving so stiff. But there had been something in his eyes as he took her. An emotion so intense she didn't even know how to describe it. She'd felt it too. And it scared the living shit out of her.

She squeezed her eyes shut and leaned her forehead against the last fence of the neighborhood.

Was she running because it was the right thing to do?

Or because she was afraid?

The last time she'd asked for a sign, she thought it was so clear. The motorcycle had been right there. It meant Charlie wanted her to go, right?

Or was she just grasping at straws? Charlie was dead. A motorcycle was just a motorcycle. And maybe living her life afraid wasn't much better than not having a life to live at all.

Maybe what she *really* owed Charlie was to make the most out of this one precious life she had.

And here, what her clan—her husbands—offered her, maybe it was everything.

She turned to look back in the direction of the house.

Her house.

Their house.

Her heart started hammering a million miles a minute, blood rushing in her ears.

God, could she really do this?

Could she *stay*?

There was still time to go back and slip into bed before anyone knew she'd even gone. She could be theirs for real.

Forever.

Till death them did part.

She took a breath in and for the first time since Charlie died, it was like she could finally fill her lungs completely.

She felt so light inside she thought she might lift right up off the ground.

God, was this what hope felt like?

She couldn't remember the last time she'd felt anything like it.

She smiled, a tear spilling down her cheek as she turned back in the direction of their house.

She was going home.

"—told you what I'd do if it happened again."

Audrey startled at the sound of voices and jerked back from the fence she'd been leaning against.

"I know, but if you'll just listen I can explain."

Wait. Audrey frowned and leaned close to the fence again. She knew that voice. It was Camila.

Didn't Camila live with her clan at the house at the end of the row? This must be her house. Audrey leaned in close and looked through a small crack between the slats at Camila's back yard.

Just in time to see one of her husbands punch her so hard in the stomach she was knocked to the ground.

Audrey's hand slapped over her mouth to stifle her cry of shock.

She wanted to jump the fence and tackle the bastard but Camila held the hand not cradling her stomach up in supplication and the man backed off. Not before throwing a steaming pot onto the grass beside Camila.

Camila flinched and pulled back but some of whatever was in the pot must have gotten on her because she let out another small cry of pain.

And then the man slammed back into the house, leaving Camila weeping in the back yard.

Son of a *bitch*!

Audrey dropped the small backpack and grabbed the top of the fence, pulling herself up and then over.

Camila was so distraught she didn't even notice Audrey running up to her.

"Hey," Audrey whispered.

Camila shrieked and Audrey clapped a hand over her mouth. Camila's eyes were wide with terror before she finally realized it was

Audrey. The moon provided enough light to make out each other's features.

"Audrey, what are you doing here?" Camila asked, then she threw a worried glance in the direction of her house. "You can't be here. You need to go."

Audrey's jaw locked. "Because he beats you? I thought you and Sophia said this was a place where men worship the women in their care."

Camila's head whipped back to Audrey. "They do." Her voice was hard. "Compared to what's out there?" She jerked a hand out wide. "A few bruises are nothing."

"That's bullshit," Audrey said through clenched teeth. Her first impulse was to grab Camila and take her back home. Nix would smash this bastard's face in as soon as he heard.

But then her eyes flipped up to the door Camila's husband had disappeared through.

Because he'd been familiar. Audrey frowned and then her brain finally made the connection. Jeffries. His name was Jeffries.

And he was Nix's second in command at the Security Squadron.

Thinking back, he'd even been there that first day Nix had picked her up in the field. His predatory gaze had been one of the things that had set her running away from Nix's little group in the first place.

Dammit, who was Nix gonna believe? Her and Camila or his trusted second in command.

You, dummy.

Except how would she explain why she'd been out here? I was just taking a stroll behind the neighborhood fence in the middle of the night?

And didn't this prove she'd been right to be skeptical of this place all along. God, for a brief few seconds there, she'd wanted to believe in it all. That Nix and the other guys wanted her. That those vows they made in the church were real. That it all meant something.

But this place wasn't the utopia they tried to pretend it was. She'd only been here three weeks and already the ugly truth was exposing itself.

And Camila was in danger. Her other husbands had to know about the abuse. It wasn't like the bruises wouldn't be apparent on her naked body.

Audrey believed that none of her own husbands would ever hurt her. But that didn't mean that everyone in this town treated their women right. She had proof right in front of her that they didn't.

Audrey held out her hand to Camila. "Come on. I can get you out of here. There's a place where women are safe and free from men. I'll take you there. But we have to go *now*."

Camila's eyes darted fearfully down to the hand Audrey held extended toward her. She kept glancing back and forth between the house and Audrey's outheld hand, clearly waffling on what to do.

"Come on, Camila," Audrey said urgently. "How long have you lived here? And has it ever changed or gotten better."

That got Camila's attention. She focused on Audrey and her bottom lip quivered. She still held one hand against her stomach where Jeffries had hit her. Her eyes flashed and after another moment of hesitation, she gave the smallest nod Audrey had ever seen.

"All right. I'll come with you."

Audrey expelled breath she hadn't even realized she'd been holding.

"Come on. I've got a motorcycle waiting," Audrey said. "And everything else we need." She glanced down at her watch. 11:55. "We have to hurry though. There's a short window when our way out of town will be unguarded."

Camila nodded, a little more confidently this time. "All right. Let me just go get some clothes and I have some bread we can—"

But Audrey was already shaking her head. "It's too late already as it is. Plus, he's inside. No. We go right now."

"I'm in my nightgown," Camila objected. "If we run into men on the road, you think me being in a nightgown isn't going to get us raped and killed? Plus, Jeff was just leaving for work. He'll be gone by now. He's on the midnight to eight a.m. shift. Everyone else is asleep."

Audrey glanced toward the house nervously. But Camila was right. Riding around in that pink lace nightgown would get them killed or captured before they made it out of the damn territory. And Camila was bigger than her—she wouldn't fit in Audrey's clothes.

"Fine, but quick," Audrey said. "Just get dressed and then get back here as quick as possible okay? I've got everything else we'll need."

Camila nodded rapidly, head like one of those old bobble-head dolls. Charlie used to collect them from abandoned cars when he and Uncle Dale went out on raids.

The next second, Camila was hurried back into the house.

Audrey paced for a couple seconds, then jogged to the back of the yard, getting in position to boost Camila up and over the fence. Her heart was racing so fast, she could hear blood rushing in her ears. Even if this went perfectly, they wouldn't have much time to spare.

A fifteen-minute window to get the motorcycle out through the abandoned road was small enough and she'd already wasted time she didn't have. Now with this big deviation, taking Camila with her... they'd just have to move their asses to break the motorcycle out of the workshop in time and—

The back door of Camila's house banged open and Audrey looked up, ready to wave at Camila to get her attention.

But it wasn't Camila.

It was her husband, Jeffries, with two more men flanking him on either side. And they were heading straight for Audrey at a dead run.

She barely had time to pull her gun, click off the safety, and fire.

CHAPTER TWENTY-ONE

NIX

Nix jerked awake, shooting up in bed. At first he thought the loud noise was just a remnant of his nightmare. It was another dream about Roxy being chased down through the woods. While Nix was chained to a tree, impotent to help.

But Clark was up too, and he hurried to the window, jerking the curtain back. "Was that a *gunshot?*"

"Where's Audrey?"

Nix's heart stopped at Mateo's question. Fucking stopped in his chest for the second it took to swivel on the mattress where she'd just been wrapped in his arms.

At least that's where she'd been when they'd all fallen asleep.

Where.

The fuck.

Was.

Audrey?

Nix ripped the sheet back and grabbed around on the dark floor for his jeans.

"Fuck," he yelled, throwing a pair of jeans toward Mateo after sticking one leg through and realizing they were far too small. "Where are my fucking jeans?"

Everyone was talking at once, but someone finally lit a damn candle so they could see what they were doing.

Nix snatched his black jeans off the floor, yanking them on as he stumbled out the door and down the stairs.

The others followed right on his heels. When they got outside, they obviously weren't the only ones who'd heard the shot.

A fucking gunshot.

In the clan family neighborhood.

"Maybe it's not what we thought," Clark said, looking around. "Maybe one of the construction trucks just backfired."

Nix ignored him. That didn't explain where Audrey was. He was gonna get some fucking answers. He was heading in the direction of the Commander's house when he heard an uproar from the end of the street.

Nix started sprinting in that direction.

He was running flat out but within three paces, Mateo flew past him. Fucker could run. Good. The sooner one of them got some answers, the better.

"That way. She went that way," Nix heard Jeffries' woman Camila saying to Mateo. She was standing in a bathrobe on her front lawn, pointing toward the road that led south out of town.

Mateo was asking her something else but Nix went up to her and grabbed her by her shoulders, giving her a shake. "What did she say to you? How long ago did you see her?"

"Get your fucking hands off our wife."

Charles and Leo stepped up beside Camila. Leo shoved Nix back and Charles wrapped Camila close to his chest, an arm around her shoulder.

"Your wife shot Jeffries," Charles said, nostrils flaring in the moonlight. "The crazy bitch is trying to run away from you. So you'll want to step the fuck back."

Nix felt the words like a physical blow to the face. Trying to run away...

WHAT?

"What?" Mateo asked, sounding like the wind had been knocked out of him too.

"It's true," Leo said. "The doctor's in with him now." He squeezed Camila's shoulder. "Tell them, honey. Tell them what you told us."

Camila swallowed, glancing up at Leo and then Charles. She swallowed and looked down at the ground. "I was kissing Jeff goodbye on the front porch. You know, because he has night patrol. We saw Audrey walking by..." Her voice trailed off.

"And then?" Leo prompted.

"And when we tried to ask what she was doing, what was in her backpack," Camila swallowed again, face crumpling, "she pulled out a gun and shot Jeff." The last words came out barely above a whisper.

Nix wanted to grab her again and scream at her that she was lying. He wanted to shake her until she told him the truth. It didn't make any sense. Not his Audrey. Not his *wife*. She wouldn't leave them. Not after yesterday.

"Thank fuck she's a lousy shot," Charles said. "She only winged him in the thigh."

Nix's jaw locked. "You said she went that way?"

He pointed toward the road. And saw that Mateo had again beaten him to the punch and already taken off sprinting.

"She said something about a motorcycle," Camila finished.

Motorcyc—?

Then everything clicked into place. Son of a *bitch*.

He turned back to Charles. "You said Jeffries was heading out on night patrol?"

Charles nodded, eyebrows furrowed in confusion. Nix wasn't going to waste his breath explaining.

He just ran for the stables. It was two blocks away and he didn't let up the entire time. When he burst into the stables, the guards jerked to position and grabbed for their guns.

"Captain," said Henry, the primary guard, lowering his rifle.

"Jeffries's patrol animal," Nix barked. "He should be saddled up and ready. I need him now." When the stable hands didn't start moving fast enough, he yelled, "*NOW* or I'll strip your rank so fast you'll be enjoying communal bathrooms with twenty other men and have to wait a fucking year to get back on the fucking lottery rotation!"

That got results at least. Only moments later, Jeffries's horse was being brought to the front of the stables.

Nix didn't waste a second. He climbed up in the saddle, swung his leg over, and shot out of the stable in the direction of Mateo's workshop.

Within a few minutes he passed up the sprinting Mateo. Maybe stopping to pick Mateo up would have been the team-player thing to do, but Nix was only thinking of getting to Audrey as quickly as possible. And he wanted to confront Audrey on his own terms.

To beg her to tell him it wasn't true.

He tightened his thighs around the horse, urging him faster still. The horse hooves sounded like a drum beat against the asphalt.

Nix squinted, searching the road ahead. It was empty, but just there in the distance, he could make out the silhouette of the engineering workshop against the moonlit sky.

The motorcycle. He was so fucking stupid. Of course she'd seen it. And seen it as her ticket out of there.

Maybe she's not running. You might not have the full story.

But just as he rounded the back of the workshop, he saw a small figure slipping in one of the back loading bays.

Son of a bitch.

She was running.

He gritted his teeth and urged the horse even faster. He didn't bother dismounting when he got to the back of the workshop.

A guard was laid out by the entrance. What the hell had she done to him? Was he dead? Jesus fuck, she'd been conning them all along, pretending to be so sweet and innocent.

The bay door was open, which meant it was tall enough for him to go in, horse and all.

Audrey's shriek of surprise only confirmed it was her. Up till that last moment, some part of him had still been hoping...

A flashlight shot his direction, momentarily blinding him until he urged the horse to the wall where he knew the light panel was. He reached down and flipped the lights.

Every other time he'd been here, he'd marveled at the ridiculous luxury of having light at the touch of a switch, but at the moment, he was only glad that it let him see Audrey in all her deceitful glory.

She had one leg swung over the motorcycle. And in her hand she held a gun. A fucking gun. Aimed right at Nix.

He gave a mirthless laugh. "You gonna shoot me sweetheart. Damn, I guess until death we do part is gonna come sooner rather than later, huh?"

CHAPTER TWENTY-TWO

AUDREY

What was Nix doing here?

The gun shook in her hand. Everything had gotten so screwed sideways. She was trying to salvage this disaster of a night the only way she could think of.

Go back to the original plan. Forget her stupid momentary insanity and do what she'd planned all along. Take the out. Go to Nomansland.

"Get out of the way, Nix." Her voice was strong in spite of the tears pouring down her cheeks. "You have to let me go. It's the only way."

God, she could still feel their hands on her. Camila's men had been running straight at her and she'd squeezed the trigger. She barely realized what she was doing, but then Jeffries screamed and fell sideways.

But his two other thugs kept coming for her. She tried to jump the fence and escape them but she'd barely gotten her hands over the top before they yanked her roughly back to the ground. Jeffries lay in the grass just feet away from her, cursing to the high heavens.

Until he saw she was beside him.

He'd lifted the hand not clutching his bloody thigh to her throat. "I swear I'll make you regret this, little girl. You better run far and fast and pray I never catch you."

He'd let go of her, his face a mask of disgust.

And Audrey had dragged herself to her feet and run. As she passed by the back of the house, she saw Camila standing in the back door, watching silently as she ran past.

But none of it mattered now. Audrey forced her arm steady as Nix stared her down.

"Told ya. I'm not moving. You gotta shoot me."

Damn him.

This town obviously had secrets. Secrets Nix either didn't know or didn't consider important enough to bother with.

Neither option was comforting. She'd been right in the first place. She should have listened to the signs and gotten the fuck out of town. Do not pass go, do not collect one hundred dollars.

She shouldn't have gotten involved with Camila. The woman obviously didn't want her interference. Audrey couldn't be absolutely positive, but she was pretty sure Camila had gone directly inside and informed all her husbands that Audrey was in the back yard.

Bringing her to this inevitable moment.

She raised her gun higher and lifted her second hand to help brace it. "Don't think I won't," she said in the hardest voice she could muster. "Get out of my way. I'm going to Nomansland and there's nothing you or anyone else can do to stop me." She wouldn't shoot him but she had to make him believe she would.

"Oh yeah?" Nix asked, face hard and voice mocking in a way she'd never heard before. "Because from where I'm sitting sweetheart, it looks like we've got ourselves a good old-fashioned Mexican stand-off."

Wait, what?

And then she saw it. Underneath his left arm that was so casually draped over the saddle, he had a long-barreled black handgun in his hand. Pointed at *her*.

She'd seen that particular gun before. Her eyes widened right as he raised it.

"No wait!" She lifted her hand. "Wait, you don't understand—"

Before she could finish her thought, Nix had pulled the trigger.

The last thing she saw before losing consciousness was the silver colored dart sticking out of her chest.

CHAPTER TWENTY-THREE

AUDREY

Audrey woke up confused.

But it only took a few moments of groggy blinking before she remembered where she was and smiled.

She was in her bedroom.

Their marital bedroom.

She rubbed her legs together, smiling in spite of the ache she felt there. She rolled over to get up so she could use the bathroom.

Which was when she was jerked backward and realized she was cuffed to the bed.

"What the—"

And then the rest of the night came flooding in. Her escape. Changing her mind. Almost coming back but then seeing Camila and—

She looked up and realized she wasn't alone.

Nix, Mateo, and Clark stood at the bottom of the bed like sentries, all solemn faced and staring at her like she was an exhibit at a pre-Fall zoo.

"Unhandcuff me," she said, yanking at the cuffs attached to the bedframe by short chains. Her ankles were shackled too. "Look, I can explain everything, if you just—"

"Explain what?" Nix snapped, cutting her off. "Explain how you snuck around the Commander's house on the morning of your own *wedding* so you could steal a pistol from his personal arsenal?" His voice had a cruel, mocking edge to it that Audrey had never heard before.

He leaned both fists on the bottom of the mattress. "Or maybe you mean explain how you played us for weeks pretending to be something you weren't, manipulating each of us to get what you needed. Or do you mean how you whored yourself out last night just so we'd let down our guard and you could finally get your way and escape? Do tell me. Did I miss anything?"

How could he— If he would just let her get a word in edgewise— Audrey felt seconds away from busting into flame she was so furious.

"Don't forget the bit about how she shot the township's Security Squadron's second in command," Clark piped in, arms folded across his chest. "That went over really well with the Commander."

"I guess we should feel lucky not to have all been murdered in our beds after she fucked us," Nix said coldly.

Audrey yanked at her chains, wanting to jump on him and punch and scratch his eyes out for how he was talking to her. "Well I guess you've got it all figured out, don't you? You're Mr. Security expert. *Nothing* gets by you." She let disdain drip from her voice.

As far as she saw it, this was all *their* fault. They were so sure their high and mighty township was so perfect, they missed the monster right in front of their faces. Or should she say, the five monsters? Because there was no way any of Camila's husbands didn't know what was going on between Jeffries and her. Hell, maybe they got in their hits and slaps when they could too.

And Nix, Mr. Self-Righteous himself—did he even check in on the women after they raffled them off? Did anyone?

No. They just took the *men's* word that they were treating the wives *so* well. How many other women were living in hell, imprisoned in these pristine gilded cages?

"Wow," she laughed bitterly. "Well at least your true colors have

come out at last. No more pretending all of this isn't against my will."
She rattled the handcuffs.

"No." Mateo stepped forward, deep furrows in his eyebrows.
"We're protecting you. Audrey, leaving the township is no laughing
matter. I couldn't bear it if something happened to you—"

"Oh, so you're locking me up for my protection," Audrey said,
eyebrows at her hairline. "Well, that makes it *so* much better."

She turned her face away. She couldn't even stand looking at them
anymore.

"It's not like that—" Mateo started but Nix cut him off.

"You want to go get yourself killed?" Nix suddenly shouted, slamming the wooden footboard with the flat of his hand.

"You want to wave a gun around and fucking *shoot* someone, then
you're gonna whine about the fucking consequences? Boo hoo. Poor
you. Safe and sound when there are a thousand women out there being
raped and mutilated and then raped some more until they lose their
fucking minds!"

Audrey jerked back at the vehemence in Nix's voice.

He stormed out of the room without giving any of them a second
glance. The door slammed behind him.

Audrey bit the inside of her cheek hard to keep from crying. And
then she glared at Clark and Mateo. "So? Let 'er rip. Lemme have it.
Tell me what an evil bitch I am."

Clark just sighed and shook his head at her in clear disappointment. "It's been a long night. I'm gonna go get some sleep."

Audrey stared at the wall while he left. She could see out of her
periphery that Mateo was still there.

"What?" Audrey asked. It was harder and harder to keep hold of
her bravado. It was going to crack any second and she couldn't bear
anyone seeing that.

"Just leave," she bit out. "I don't want to see any of you. Don't you
get it? I was trying to run away. To *leave* you. I would have rather
risked *dying* than staying here with you all."

She regretted it the second it came out of her mouth. But she kept
her chin jutted out because otherwise she'd just absolutely fucking lose
it. *Please go, just go*, she begged in her head.

Mateo didn't say anything back for a long, long moment.

She dared a glance his direction, having to blink rapidly to keep the tears back. He was still there. Hadn't moved a muscle.

Finally he did, and she sucked in a breath when he came close to the bed.

"I made vows to you yesterday," he said, voice quiet but clear, "and I meant them." Out of her peripheral vision, she saw him drop to his knees beside the bed. "Vows to love, honor, and protect. I'm sorry I've already failed you."

Audrey's lip trembled so badly that she had to suck it into her mouth and bite down hard. And still, her chest shook with the silent sobs trying to escape.

She wanted to say he didn't do anything wrong. That he hadn't failed or done anything he needed to apologize for. But she didn't dare speak a word because she knew she'd start blubbering. And if she gave into it, she didn't know if she'd ever stop.

"My life is your life," he went on. "I'm bound to you for eternity, and I will do anything to serve you, help you..." He lifted up only far enough to place a kiss on the top of one of her feet and then the other.

"...and love you," he whispered before rising silently and leaving the room.

After that it was impossible not to give in.

She turned on her side and bawled into her pillow to muffle the noise.

How had everything that had been so perfect the night before gone so horribly, horribly wrong?

And where did she go from here?

CHAPTER TWENTY-FOUR

DANNY

"Is she okay?" Danny asked as Mateo came down the stairs last. Danny looked past him, wishing he could get even a glimpse of Audrey. Mateo didn't say anything, he just stomped past him.

Nix wouldn't let Danny or Graham up to see her. He said it would be too much for her having all five of them there when she woke up.

Danny knew Nix didn't think much of him. If he thought of him at all.

Guys like that, they were happy to *use* muscle like him, sure. To send guys like Danny out to the front lines. Just another dumb fuck to slow down the enemy. Or to haul shit around and do the heavy lifting while Nix stayed in his Security Squadron Headquarters thinking up more shit for guys like Danny to go and do.

Guys like Danny weren't supposed to question orders. And usually, he didn't.

He'd certainly heard it enough times growing up. *You're just like your father*, his mamá would always say. *Big, pretty, and dumb as a board.*

So maybe he should just keep quiet and wait to see what the other guys said.

"You can't just keep her locked up like an animal," Mateo said, going right up and getting in Nix's face. Danny had never seen the small man's face so red.

"Like hell I can't," Nix said, toe to toe with Mateo. Even though Nix had a good foot on him, Mateo didn't flinch. "She fucking *shot* my second in command. Do you know what hell I caught from the Commander for that? We're lucky he was in a good mood and willing to listen to Sophia arguing for leniency. But if anything like this happens again, whatever she does, we'll all pay for. An eye for an eye."

"Shit," Clark swore, running a hand through his hair.

"She was scared," Mateo shot back. "All this is new to her. We should have expected she wouldn't just settle in so easil—"

"She betrayed us!" The vein in Nix's neck stood out as he yelled it.

The room went silent. Nix glared them all down. "She's had this planned the whole time. The only time she could have stolen the Commander's gun was yesterday morning when she was supposed to be getting ready for our wedding. Think about it. She fucked us all knowing she was about to leave. Using sex to make us lower our guard. She's nothing but a wh—"

Danny stepped forward and took a swing at Nix's face.

Nix wasn't quick enough to duck and Danny's fist made contact with his jaw, snapping his head to the side. Nix stumbled and almost went down, cussing and grabbing his face.

Danny stood up taller. "Don't talk about our wife like that."

Danny might not be a smart man. But he knew the difference between right and wrong. And it was wrong to disrespect your wife like that.

Nix laughed, wiping his lip and spitting blood on the rug. "What, does that hit a little too close to home, Martinez? You worried your new wife is a little too much like mommy dearest?"

Son of a—

Danny swung again but this time Nix moved out of the way in time.

Bringing his mom into this was a low blow. Danny and his mom joined the township almost from the time it first started. She was one of the lucky ten percent of the female population with the natural immunity to Xterminate. Danny was just fourteen.

But she'd had the choice of whether to join a clan or not because pre-Fall, she'd had her tubes tied after having Danny. She was one of just a few women in the town who elected not to get married but instead to share her favors widely and take numerous lovers.

"Hey," Clark shouted, getting in between them and holding his arms out to keep them separated as they circled one another. "That's enough.

Danny looked around at the rest of the guys. "You're just gonna let him talk about Audrey like this? She's the best thing that's happened to anyone here."

It was true. Because of how his mom had chosen to live, it meant Danny had never had a shot at being a part of a real family. Guys came and went—just like they had all throughout Danny's growing up even before The Fall. Except once they got to the township, it was at a far higher volume.

"And besides," Danny went on, "do we even know why she shot at Jeffries? Maybe she had a good r—"

Nix cut him off with a loud scoff. "Gee, I wonder why." His voice dripped with condescension. "Maybe because she was trying to escape and he was in her way. She didn't snoop around and steal a gun from the Commander's personal armory just for shits and giggles. She knew she might have to shoot her way out of here. And it didn't stop her. What if it had been one of us in her way?"

But Danny kept shaking his head. "That's not fair. We don't even know what she was thinking."

"I agree with the kid," Mateo said.

Danny tried not to wince at the *kid* comment. He really needed to work harder at growing his beard instead of shaving it every day just because he got annoyed with the sandpaper texture.

"She was *thinking* that she could make idiots out of us," Nix growled. "It was all a lie. The marriage was a lie. Last night was a lie."

"Last night was a lie?" Graham asked, rocking back and forth and repetitively flicking a rubber band on his wrist.

He had all kinds of weird little habits like that, but he was a good guy. So fuckin' smart Danny felt even dumber than usual around him. But a good guy.

"Last night *wasn't* a lie," Danny said. He'd never spoken up this much with the guys, but now that he had, he couldn't stop.

"Last night was real. We married Audrey and she married us and it was real. I think we should ask her what happened and why she shot that guy."

Nix's face twisted up in that way it did when he thought Danny had said something stupid. Danny's ears felt hot and his toes curled up in his boots.

"You think we can believe anything that comes out of her mouth?" Nix said. He shook his head. "I know the grey matter between your ears isn't officially a muscle, but maybe you could try exercising it from time to time anyway."

"Hey," Clark said sharply. "Don't be an ass."

"It's his natural state," Mateo muttered, pacing back and forth across the living room. "All I know is I'm going to go get her out of those cuffs right now." He grabbed the key that had been tossed on the mantle and headed for the stairs. Nix hurried to get in his way.

Danny didn't say anything else. He just walked up to stand beside Mateo. Danny crossed his massive arms over his chest and looked down his nose at Nix. He was one of the few people in town who could manage this since Nix was six foot two.

Nix looked at Clark but he didn't find any sympathy there. Clark put his hands up. "I agree with them. You can't keep her locked up like a prisoner."

"Graham?" Nix asked, obviously exasperated.

"Doesn't matter. It's three to two," Danny said. Even he could do that math.

But Graham spoke up anyway. "Trust, love, and respect. You must trust, love, and respect one another. That was what we promised in the church yesterday. Chaining her up isn't any of those things."

Danny smiled at Nix. "Four to one."

So Nix couldn't do anything but fume as Mateo pushed past him and ran up the stairs.

CHAPTER TWENTY-FIVE

AUDREY

The guys were arguing downstairs. Audrey could hear them. She knew they were arguing over her. About what to do with her.

She closed her eyes and thumped her head back against the pillow. Lifted it and thumped it again.

Shit. She'd really stepped in it this time.

Why was she being so stubborn? No matter what was going on with Camila's clan, her men weren't like that. She should go down there and tell them what had really happened.

Nix had just pissed her off so badly, refusing to listen to her when she'd tried to explain and she'd reacted.

You're as stubborn as a donkey, her dad used to tell her when she was a kid. After she kept sassing him—and this after her infamous green beans dinner table standoff—he took her out to a farm so she could spend an afternoon with a real, live donkey.

He said they could leave as soon as she got the donkey to perform a list of tasks, like taking him on a walk through one pasture to another.

No matter how she dug her feet in and yanked on his lead, that donkey just would *not* move.

She got the picture. And yeah, it wasn't her most attractive quality, she got that.

Nix had just made her so *mad*.

She took a deep breath.

But Mateo would listen. And Graham. Probably Danny too. Eventually Nix would have to hear her. And Clark. They were well-respected members of the community. They could help Camila and—

A sudden noise had her lifting her head. And freezing.

Because climbing in her bedroom window were the two men who'd ran at her alongside Jeffries this morning. Two of Camila's other husbands.

Audrey opened her mouth to scream but the one on the left, a pale man with blond hair, lifted a black handgun and pointed it at her. "Squeal and I'll shoot you dead, bitch."

Audrey's breath caught and she looked to the door. Shit. Why had she driven the guys out?

She was so *stupid*. Why'd she think she was safe just because the door was shut? She knew Nix had been lurking outside the night before the wedding, watching in case she ran. The ladder he'd used was probably still out there.

Before she could make up her mind about what was best to do—not that she had many options being handcuffed to the damn bed like she was—the blond and the other man, a big guy with a long, gnarled beard, were leaning over her on the bed.

The blond guy slammed a dirty hand over her mouth.

Right as he did it, she realized she should have screamed anyway. Screamed her head off. They wouldn't have shot her—the noise would have brought her husbands running just like her screaming would have.

The man with the hand on her mouth leaned over her and crushed her down into the bed with his weight. His hand squeezing her face so hard tears burned at the edges of her eyes.

"Jeffries wanted me and Julio here to send you a message. You talk and you're dead. It won't be an easy death either. Jeffries likes playin' with bad girls like you. He'll take it out on you long and slow."

Audrey struggled underneath him while he squeezed her breast, yelling into the hand at her mouth.

The blond laughed and pulled back. "But you be a good girl and we'll forget this little incident ever happened. No one would believe you anyway. It's your word against ours. You be a good little wife to them boys now, ya hear? That's all you gotta do."

"If you scream when I take my hand off your mouth, Julio will slit your throat, ear to ear." Julio slid a giant hunting knife out of a sheath at his waist and Audrey's eyes went wide.

"That's right. Julio just loves sharpenin' that thing." The blond leaned over again, his foul breath hot on her face. "There's no where you can go that we can't get you. Now, you gonna be a good girl?"

Audrey nodded, swallowing down her fury. The guys were downstairs. She just had to get these fuckers out of the room. That was all. She could think again once she was safe.

The pressure on her mouth finally let up and the blond lifted off the bed. Julio was already at the window.

That was when Audrey heard footsteps on the stairs. Her head swung toward the bedroom door. Then back to the blond who'd apparently heard it too.

"Get the fuck outta here," he said, all but shoving Julio out the window. He'd just hitched his leg over and disappeared over the ledge when the bedroom door was shoved open by a heaving Mateo.

"I'm so sorry, Audrey," Mateo said. "We'll never treat you this way again. You're not our prisoner. We never want you to feel like that."

Audrey's eyes shot to the window. She wanted to blurt out what had just happened. Mateo was being sweet. He was always sweet.

Danny, Clark, and Graham followed Mateo into the room, and together they helped him free her from the cuffs and chains. She sat up in bed, rubbing her wrists where the cuffs had chafed.

She glanced at the door and saw Nix out in the hallway, arms over his chest, a disapproving frown on his face.

She looked at the guys helplessly and then back at the window. *It'll just be your word against ours.*

Shit. After what they thought she'd done this morning—well, what she'd *planned* to do before changing her mind at the last moment—there was no way they'd trust anything she said.

And they said they'd kill her.

If she told her husbands, they could stop them... unless they couldn't. Who knew how deep the corruption in this town really went?

So even though it made her nauseous to do it, she ignored all of them, climbed under the sheets and comforter, and pulled them up tight.

And she didn't say a word.

CHAPTER TWENTY-SIX

NIX

"I can't thank you enough for how decent you've been about all this," Nix said to Jeffries as he looked over the duty roster Jeffries had drawn up for the next two weeks. "Especially considering the circumstances."

Nix looked down at Jeffries's leg. He was wearing shorts and his thigh was still wrapped in thick bandages where Audrey had nicked him with the bullet.

Jeffries waved a hand. "You forget, I've got my own little woman at home. I know how difficult they can be. Especially in the beginning. It just takes time, patience, and commitment to making it work."

Jeffries was the last man in the world Nix ever thought he'd be getting romantic advice from. But it turned out Jeffries was a surprisingly good guy. Maybe Nix had misjudged him these past few years. He'd always thought of Jeffries as ruthless and efficient, but maybe marriage had mellowed him.

And if it could do that for a guy like Jeffries, maybe there was still hope for Nix's clan.

"Still," Nix said. "Camila offering to take Audrey on at the candle and soap shop after everything... well, your clan is being more than generous with us."

After a week, the Commander had let Audrey out from under house arrest, but only if one of her husbands was with her at all times. Which was fine by Nix.

If he had his way, he'd never let her out of his sight.

But he still had a job to do, so he had to switch out shifts with the other guys. He was always nervous when he wasn't personally watching her, though. Which was why it was doubly generous of Jeffries to offer to take over more responsibility at the Security Squadron while Nix took time off to look after Audrey.

Jeffries just offered a good-natured smile. "It's a brave new world, right? We're only gonna make it if we all work together. Isn't that what the Commander's always telling us?"

Nix nodded and slapped Jeffries on the back. "I'm gonna go do a perimeter check in, then I'm off to pick up Audrey for the night."

Jeffries chuckled, clapping his shoulder in return. "Good luck, brother."

Nix huffed. "Don't I know it."

The perimeter check only took an hour and a half on horseback. Everything looked good. Guards were awake and alert and the perimeter scouts who regularly rode twenty miles outside town in all directions had all come in on time, no problems reported.

It was just the kind of quiet day Nix liked.

Now, he'd just go pick up Audrey and head home for a nice meal. This morning Clark said he hoped to trade for some extra deer meat, so they might even have real meat in the stew Mateo was heading home early to cook. That'd be a damn treat.

He was smiling as he dropped off Champ at the stables and then made his way over to the candle and soap shop to pick up Audrey.

The door was open but he knocked anyway. "Hello?"

He stepped inside. The front of the shop space was full of displays of all kinds of different candles and soaps. He knew they made everything in the rear of the shop or out in the back parking lot, which was probably where the girls were. And Graham, who was on guard duty this afternoon.

"Audrey? Camila?" he called, heading further into the shop.

But before he'd taken more than a few steps inside, Audrey came running out from the back. She ripped the apron she was wearing off over her head and threw it, knocking a whole display of candles and soaps over.

"Audrey?" Nix asked. "What's going on? What are you—"

But she just pushed past him and hurried out into main street. She didn't stop there either. He followed her, feeling his hackles rise. He felt like a goddamned schoolboy chasing after a girl like this.

It didn't take long for his long strides to outpace her and when he did, he grabbed her elbow. "Stop. What the hell's going on? Did something happen?"

She jerked her arm out of his grasp. Her eyes were bright with fury. "What happened is that I'm tired of being a fucking slave! I knew you were full of bullshit. *We honor and protect our women in this town*," she said in a mocking tone. "Fucking liar. You mean you make them slaves for all your menial labor and then you chain them to the bed. Because we're sex slaves too, aren't we? Just supposed to be available to fuck whenever you get a goddamned hard-on." She spat the words and then spun and continued stomping down the street.

Nix's whole body went hot. Everyone was staring. How dare she make such a fucking scene after all he'd done to overlook her attempted escape?

He'd spent hours—fucking *hours*—begging the Commander to let her out from house arrest. He'd tried to give her the most freedom possible. So she wouldn't feel like she was in *prison* back at the house. Her words.

And after all that, she threw it back in his fucking face?

"Phoenix?" Graham asked, hurrying across main street toward him, looking after Audrey. "Why is she walking away like that? What is she mad about?"

Nix turned on him. "Where the fuck were you? You weren't supposed to let her out of your fucking sight."

Graham's eyes slid away and he pushed his glasses up his nose, then started flicking the rubber band around his wrist. "I— Um, there was — I had to— That is, the—"

"Just fucking get out with it," Nix demanded. He didn't have time for Graham's bullshit right now.

"Security call. They needed me to check the long-range scanners and radar on the computer," Graham finally managed to get out. "I didn't leave her alone. Camila's husband, Julio. He was there. He said he'd watch over the women."

Nix frowned. He'd just come from Security Squadron Headquarters and there hadn't been anything flagged that would warrant checking the long-range scanners. Maybe something came up in the last ten minutes? He'd look into it later. Right now, he had a bigger problem.

"Come on," he growled, taking off at a jog to catch up with Audrey. Last thing he needed now was for her to try to make a run for it again the one moment he didn't have eyes on her.

When they got to the house, though, they found her up in her room.

In bed. Sheets pulled up over her head like she was a little kid.

And she wouldn't say a damn thing. Just pretended like he wasn't even there.

"Real mature, Audrey. When you're finished throwing your tantrum, the grownups will be downstairs," Nix finally yelled, slamming her bedroom door on his way out.

He'd never met anyone more ungrateful in his damn life.

CHAPTER TWENTY-SEVEN

AUDREY

Twenty Minutes Earlier

All week Audrey had been working at the stupid fucking candle and soap shop, forced to put up with Camila and her evil clan guard dogs. Nix said it was such a *generous* offer from their clan after she'd shot Jeffries, she couldn't refuse.

So she came every morning, not saying a single word to Nix as he walked her there. He or one of the other guys stayed with her throughout the day—which was the only thing that made it bearable.

But even then, Audrey could feel the filthy eyes on whichever of Camila's husbands was spending the day with her crawling all over her body the whole time.

At least they couldn't be too disgustingly overt about it when one of Audrey's protectors was in the room.

But Clark always brought work with him and he was usually absorbed in the corner, endlessly scratching away in some ledger or other. And Danny got restless and had to go on quick jogs around the block every half hour.

Then the looks from Camila's husbands became taunts. Filthy language followed by even filthier suggestions of all the things they wanted to do to Audrey.

Camila ignored it, pretending like she couldn't even hear it.

When Audrey glared at her and asked her how she put up with it, Camila just kept on doing what she was doing, ignoring her. Audrey finally jerked the bowl of hot lye and fat Camila was mixing, spilling some on herself and burning her arm in the process.

Bullshit, Audrey said. *They're abusing you.*

But all Camila said was that it was better than what happened to women in the rest of the world. And without another word she'd taken her bowl back from Audrey and continued stirring.

It had been unpleasant, but Audrey could put up with a bad work environment. When the world ended, it was surprising how adaptable you became. So she kept dragging herself out of bed each morning.

Today hadn't been too bad, really. Mixing the hot lye to make the soap totally sucked. Her eyes burned and some of it had splashed up on her arm and burned like hell.

But at least they got to be outside for most of it, and Audrey felt less claustrophobic than when she was in the small front room with Camila and her clanmate.

But they'd finished with the soap and now were stocking shelves.

Okay, so still not bad.

Nix would come in twenty minutes to switch off with Graham and he never did anything else when he was there, just stood with his arms crossed over his chest watching over her. Camila's husband—the big gorilla Julio—wouldn't try anything with him in the room being so observant.

But then Graham got called away.

Twenty minutes before Nix was supposed to show up.

A runner came from the technology office and after talking to him for a few minutes, Graham came and gave her a quick kiss. "I'm sorry, I have to go. There might be a security breach and they need me to check the satellite imagery. But Julio's here and he won't let you out of his sight, right?"

Graham looked at the big man who nodded, a creepy smile crawling across his face.

"No, wait, Graham—" Audrey started, but he was already making a beeline out the front door.

And that's when the *back* door pushed open and Jeffries stepped in.

Fuck his warnings. Audrey bolted and opened her mouth to scream for Graham, but Jeffries was too fast.

His hand was over her mouth before she got more than a quick yelp out. Julio immediately grabbed Audrey, wrenching her arms down and wrapping one arm around her waist to lock them immobile at her sides.

Audrey had looked frantically at Camila, begging her with her eyes to go get help.

But when Camila lowered her gaze and only nodded at Jeffries before slipping out the back door, Audrey's heart sank through the floor. Hundred to one odds, Camila *wasn't* going for help.

"My leg still aches where you shot me, bitch," Jeffries hissed in her ear." I'm gonna have a scar forever. It's time to pay for that. You play the whore for Nix and now you're gonna do it for me."

Jeffries moved his hand from her mouth only long enough for Julio to clap his over it. She screamed in the brief second she'd been able to and prayed, *please, please, let someone have heard her.*

Meanwhile Jeffries unbuttoned her jeans and yanked them down.

"Let's see this pussy that's got Nix so entranced."

Jeffries shoved his finger roughly inside her body.

She screamed into Julio's hand and tried to bite and jerk free from his grasp but it was no use. He had her pinned to tight.

"Aw, I don't see what's so special. Seems like a regular ole' cunt to me. But Phoenix Hale, ooh, he's gotta have the best of *everything*, don't he? Commander gives him the cake appointment. Squadron *Captain*. Meanwhile I'm stuck working graveyard. Even though I'm the one who saved the Commander's life when he was about to get blown to bits on the Louisiana front. But what do I get for that? Squadron fuckin' *Lieutenant*."

Jeffries laughed a dark, ugly laugh, jerking his hand inside her around and making her cry out. With his free hand, he started yanking roughly at his own belt.

"Well real soon, Phoenix fuckin' Hale's gonna learn some life lessons about who's the bigger man. Everything that fucker has is gonna be mine. Startin' with his precious little bitch's cunt. Funniest fucking part? Your word against mine? He wouldn't even believe you."

Audrey could only glare in hatred. He was wrong. So fucking wrong. Because Nix *would* believe her.

In spite of how bad things had been between them, she thought of sitting him down and telling him everything. She imagined him pulling her into his arms and comforting her. Telling her she didn't have to worry anymore. He'd take care of everything.

And he would, too. He'd strangle this rat-faced bastard until he choked on his own tongue. Then he'd break Julio in two and string the blond up by his own guts in the town square.

Imagining the revenge Nix would take on her behalf was enough to have her smiling under Julio's disgusting hand.

One of Jeffries's eyebrows lifted. "Maybe he *would* believe you." He nodded. "He's such a boy scout. He probably would." He grinned an evil fucking grin. "Guess I'd have no choice but to kill him then."

Not before he kills you, Audrey thought with burning hatred.

Jeffries just laughed more. "I can see what you're thinkin', bitch. It's written all over your face. But you think it's just the five of us who wanna live by our own rules and run our clans the way we want? The Commander's clueless as to what's really going on in his little township. We play by his rules right now, sure. But our day's comin'. Soon."

He leaned in and chuckled at her struggles against the continued invasion of his hand "All I have to do is blink sideways and Nix will be called out on a dangerous security mission. Then," both his eyebrows shot up, "*poof*, backup doesn't show when he calls for them. Goodbye Captain Phoenix Hale."

Audrey's breath hitched, furious tears choking her.

"There are protocols in place in case I suddenly disappear, too, so don't think that getting rid of me will take care of your little problem. Like I said," he jerked his hand upwards and she cried out, "we're a *multitude*. Like in the damn Bible. We got men everywhere. In every guild of workers. All over the government. Phoenix Hale is *nothing*."

"Hello?" came a distant call from the front of the shop. Audrey's head jerked up. *Nix*. It was Nix's voice. She felt a rush of hope and terror. He would save her.

But then Jeffries would *kill him*.

Jeffries just laughed again. He finally pulled back from her, removing his hand from her sex. Her whole body shook while he lifted the finger he'd just had inside her and raised it to his lips. "Remember, *shhhh*. Or he dies. And all the rest of them too."

Then Julio let go of her mouth and both of them slipped out through the back door.

Audrey let out a strangled cry and then yanked her pants up, running toward the front of her store as she did her button.

And she didn't stop running except briefly to yell at Nix when he got in her way—something she felt immediately guilty for—until she was all the way home, upstairs in her room.

She scrubbed her vaginal area with soap and water and then double-checked the locks on her window. And then scrubbed herself some more.

She'd wedged several thick dowels between the window and the frame so even if someone did manage to get past the locks, the window would still be jammed closed. She wouldn't be having any more unexpected middle of the night visitors. She checked them and made sure they were secure.

Then she got in bed.

A week later, she still hadn't left it other than for bathroom breaks.

Because she didn't see any way out.

Sooner or later, Jeffries would catch her alone and Nix wouldn't come in at the perfect moment. Jeffries would finish what he started.

And if she said anything to her husbands, she'd be dooming them to a death sentence.

CHAPTER TWENTY-EIGHT

MATEO

"This ain't right, man," Danny said. "She shouldn't be there up in bed like that all the time. She doesn't even talk anymore. Just sleeps and lays there all day."

Mateo agreed but Nix wouldn't hear it. He'd stomped out earlier muttering about spoiled princesses and tantrums.

Mateo thought Graham was with them. He'd been nodding along while Danny and Mateo talked about Audrey, but then all the sudden he just got up from the kitchen table and the next thing they heard was the front door slamming closed behind him.

Clark sighed and looked at his watch. "I need to be getting to work too. We've got the Fort Worth delegation coming in at noon. Speaking of—they'll be wanting an update on how the helicopter's coming along."

Mateo just shrugged it off. What did he care about helicopters or anything else when Audrey was upstairs, obviously miserable and suffering?

"They're representing the President of Texas," Clark said, obviously annoyed. "You can't just shrug off the President."

"I don't care about the stupid President," Mateo growled.

Clark raised his eyebrows and pulled back. "You really have grown a pair lately." Clark stood up. "It's inconvenient timing, though. I don't suppose you could wait until after we've wowed the President with our engineering and technological genius so he continues to see a point in letting us run our little experiment here? You know, the one that allows you to moon over our little wify in peace, under the umbrella of the President's protection?"

Mateo just shrugged again. He'd get back to the engine when he got to it. There were other capable engineers in the workshop. Okay, so Tony and Brett had once mistaken a catalytic converter for an NI turbine, but that was neither here nor there.

In a world like the one they lived in now, there was always some pressing crisis or other. Audrey was a problem that couldn't be put off. She was too important. She was the only thing that mattered.

"Danny, will you go check on the stew?" Mateo asked. "She wouldn't eat breakfast but maybe we can get her to have an early lunch."

Danny nodded, obviously happy to have something to do.

Clark just shook his head at both of them. "I'll be back at sunset."

Mateo went upstairs as Danny headed out back to the firepit.

Mateo knocked on the bedroom door even though Audrey never responded. When he pushed it open, Audrey was laying in the same position he'd left her when he'd gone downstairs to talk to the clan.

She shifted positions occasionally, moving from her side to her back to her stomach to her other side like a roasting chicken. She'd been in bed for a week now.

Her eyes were lackluster. Lifeless.

It was like all week she'd been sinking deeper and deeper.

Mateo had seen it before.

He hadn't been the only one captured and brought to Hells Hollow. He was just one of the few that managed to hold on to his sanity.

The question was, what the hell had happened to Audrey to make her take this turn?

They didn't know anything about her life before Nix had picked her up and brought her into town. She hadn't exactly been in a talkative mood after getting tranqued and kidnapped.

He should have pressed her for answers in the few weeks when everything had been good.

Okay, so they'd only been good because she was secretly planning to escape, but still. They'd bonded, all of them. Mateo refused to believe it was all some elaborate manipulation like Nix seemed determined to.

She'd been scared after the lottery but she'd had a fighting spirit. So what the hell had happened to douse that flame?

"Audrey?"

No response. She didn't even look his way.

"Danny's going to bring up some stew."

Mateo approached the bed and sat down on the edge, reaching for her hand. Right before he could make contact, she snatched it away and pulled her arm underneath the blankets.

It hurt. Mateo couldn't lie. It was far too easy for his old demons to rear their ugly heads.

Of course she doesn't want you touching her. You're a disgusting, nasty, repulsive animal and she's pure and perfect and—

Mateo closed his eyes briefly, swallowing back all his self-recriminations and forcing a smile. "It's a bright, sunny day out. But not too hot. Want me to open the window? We could get a nice fresh breeze blowing—"

"No!" Audrey said, arm shooting back out of the bed in a stop gesture.

She froze as if she was just as startled by the sudden movement as Mateo was. The next second she'd sunk back in bed, her face turned away from Mateo. "I'm not hungry."

Then she made the briefest eye contact. "But don't leave. I mean, if you want." The words were short and stilted and she turned her back to him just as quickly but Mateo froze.

She wanted him to stay.

No, she wanted you *not to leave.*

Not exactly the same thing. He frowned. Was it?

Then he shook his head in frustration with himself. He needed to get over his neuroses.

Something was wrong with Audrey. Very wrong.

"If you're not hungry, then I'm not hungry either." Mateo laid on the floor beside her bed. "In fact, I'm not eating again until you sit up and tell me what's the matter."

For a long time, the ticking of the clock was the only sound in the room.

Then the door opened.

"Who wants stew?" came Danny's overly cheery voice. "Oh." Danny stopped at seeing Mateo laying on the floor. "Um. You tired, man?"

"I'm going on a hunger strike."

"What?" Danny and Audrey said at the same time.

The next moment, Audrey's head appeared over the side of the bed. "You can't just go on a hunger strike against..." She fumbled for words. "Against me being depressed!"

Mateo just nodded solemnly. "I can and I will. You're the most important thing in my life now. You're my wife. And I'll do anything to show you how much your happiness and well-being mean to me."

She let out a huff and threw a hand in the air. "Well, it would make me happy if you got up off the floor. Right now."

"Are you ready to tell us what's wrong?"

Audrey glanced away and then pulled back from Mateo's view. "Nothing's wrong."

Her voice had gone distant again, and not just because Mateo couldn't see her any more.

"Bullshit," Mateo said.

"What?" Audrey's face appeared over the side of the bed again.

"I said bullshit," Mateo repeated. "Something happened. I don't know what, or when, or how. But you're different. And I don't think it's just because you didn't get to run away that night."

Audrey breathed out so hard her nostrils flared. "You're crazy." She pulled back from the edge again and Mateo could hear the sheets ruffling as she settled back under the covers.

He imagined her crossing her arms over her chest and smiled. This at least was the most life he'd seen out of her in six days. He'd take anger over apathy any day.

Unfortunately, that little outburst was the most Mateo got out of Audrey for the entire week.

He stayed on the floor, sometimes sitting, often laying, especially as the week drew on and he grew weaker and weaker without any food. He drank water but that was all.

Even Audrey had started eating. She made sure to do it where Mateo could see her. Sometimes she'd even get out of bed and sit on the couch by the window so he couldn't avoid seeing.

She never said a word.

She just ate.

Extremely.

Slowly.

Mateo had to hope it meant he was finally getting to her. If his hunger strike upset her enough to be constantly trying to tempt him to eat again, then maybe she'd finally break.

She slept off and on throughout the day and night.

Sometimes she talked in her sleep. Sometimes she cried out. Never any words Mateo could make out. But she was so clearly in pain.

It ripped Mateo's heart in two.

Hunger and weakness had a way of making one's priorities star-tlingly clear. The food, yes, obviously he wanted that. He was obsessed thinking about it the first few days. But that passed. Once you accepted the sharp, gnawing pain and gave yourself up to the fact that it wasn't in your control whether you ate again or when, an odd sort of peace and clarity descended.

What Mateo realized?

Audrey was broken.

So was Mateo.

But maybe it was just more obvious with them.

Yesterday Nix had come in and yelled at Audrey. Totally lost his shit. He'd yelled that she was selfish for what she was doing to Mateo.

How she was hurting *Mateo*. How simpler everything had been for *Mateo* before she'd come.

Okay, so maybe it didn't take hunger strike induced clarity to see through Nix's thinly veiled pain.

But Clark and Danny, and Graham—they all had their issues.

Maybe they were all just walking around like broken glass, full of sharp, piercing edges, doomed to stab into each other no matter what they did.

But then Mateo thought of their wedding night.

He thought about the words the Pastor Jonah had said.

Family.

Clan.

Mateo didn't know much about family, never having had one he could remember. But he'd always thought maybe the point of it was that when you felt all jagged and cut up inside, your family could come alongside you and help hold you together.

Like together you'd be stronger. You wouldn't just shatter into a million little pieces when shit came at you. Cause life was a bitch and she came swinging with a sledgehammer.

Life was swinging at his Audrey.

His family.

His wife.

She was fracturing in front of their very eyes and he wasn't giving her the help she needed. He wasn't holding her up.

He sat up and, grabbing the bottom of the bedframe for steadiness, slowly got to his feet.

Shaking his head against the dizziness, he stood as tall as he could. He could feel Audrey's eyes on him but he didn't look back, knowing it would just send her gaze skittering away.

"Audrey, I see your pain," he said, reaching for his belt and unbuckling it. "I see it and I want to take it away. I'll do anything to ease your burden."

He heard her breath catch as he slid his belt free of the last loop.

He was so attuned to her every breath, he felt her stiffen as he stepped closer to the foot of the bed. It pained him that she could think even for a second he meant her any harm. It was only more proof that she needed someone she knew she could trust completely.

"This is for you."

Mateo set the belt on the foot of the bed and then knelt down, head bowed.

CHAPTER TWENTY-NINE

AUDREY

Audrey could only stare at the belt. And then at Mateo down on his knees like he was at church.

But he wasn't at church. He was bowing to *her*.

All week he'd been hurting himself. For her. And now he wanted her to do... what? Hit him with a belt?

"Stop it," she snapped. "I'm not going to—"

"Please."

Audrey stopped at the pleading note in his voice. He looked up at her and his gaze was so open. So frank and sincere. It cut through all the shields she'd been so carefully putting up all week against him and everyone else.

"I don't understand," she said helplessly. She didn't. She didn't understand anything. She didn't understand a world where men like Jeffries thrived and her brother died. She didn't understand how Mateo continued being so kind to her when she'd done nothing to deserve it. She didn't understand why she was alive and so many other women had died. She didn't understand any of it.

"It wouldn't just be for you," he said, eyes darting to the belt. "It helps me too. Sometimes I need the pain so I can..." His head bowed low. "I just need it."

Audrey swallowed. She wanted to tell him he was crazy. She wanted to yell at him to get the hell out.

But even after a week spent sleeping and doing nothing but laying around, she was so *exhausted*. She was tired of fighting.

Mateo was offering what felt like a lifeline.

In the back of her mind, Audrey knew there were a hundred very good reasons she should just turn away and try to go back to sleep.

Instead, she lifted the sheets and dropped her feet to the ground. Her legs felt strange after barely using them all week. Heavy. Like she'd strapped lead weights to her thighs and torso.

The two steps she took to pick up the belt were awkward. It felt even stranger in her hand.

She doubled it up and ran it down her palm. It made a slick *hiss* noise and then a *snap* when she yanked it taut.

A shiver went through Mateo's body and from the briefest glimpse she saw of his face, it didn't look like it was from fear.

He really *did* want this. She'd heard about people who liked that kind of thing but she'd never met one before. At least that she knew of.

Audrey frowned, not sure she could do what he was asking. "So where do I..."

"Anywhere on my back," he said. "We can start with ten and then see where we go from there. If you want."

She moved around so that she was looking down at his back. She lifted the belt, swallowing hard.

Then she shook her head. No, she couldn't—

"Please," Mateo said, like he could read her mind. "Look, I'll even keep my shirt on so it will barely sting."

It seemed like he really did want her to do it. And maybe letting off some steam would be a good idea? God, what'd she have to lose at this point?

So she brought the belt down. It made a light slapping noise along Mateo's upper back.

"Come on," he said. "You can go harder than that."

She sucked in a deep breath and brought down the next blow with a little more force.

"Harder," he said again.

So she went harder. And then harder still.

And somewhere around lash number seven, something happened.

She was back in the woods. Hearing Charlie calling her name. Turning just in time to see that monster bash her beautiful brother's head in with a bat.

Audrey screamed and swung the belt.

Because fast on top of that, she was seeing Camila's body flying to the ground after Jeffries slapped her. And then Jeffries grabbing her in the back of the soap shop.

The burning smell of lye. She'd never forget that smell. Combined with his sour breath. And his hand, oh God, his finger, it was, he was—

"What the—?"

Audrey dropped the belt and blinked in confusion, seeing Danny at the door. His eyes were wide with horror.

Audrey gasped and heaved for breath, feeling like she'd just run five miles.

And then she followed Danny's line of sight.

To where Mateo was lying on the floor, red stripes leeching through his gray shirt all over his back.

"Oh my God! Mateo!" She collapsed to her knees beside him.

What had she done?

CHAPTER THIRTY

MATEO

Heaven was real.

Mateo thought after everything he'd— There was just no way that God would ever let him in, not after—

But he was *here*.

Heavenly beings brushed kisses like butterfly wings all up and down his face and neck.

But then the pain registered. Searing pain all over his back.

So not heaven after all?

He sighed, resigned when the brush of angel lips disappeared.

Hell it was. Was this his eternal punishment, then? To be teased by gentleness and warmth only for it to be immediately pulled away?

Then the lips returned and Mateo sank against the pillow underneath his face, every muscle in his body relaxing against the mattress. The kisses continued down the nape of his neck, over to his left ear and then back around to the right.

"I'm sorry. I'm so sorry. I don't know if you can ever forgive me, but I'm so, so sorry. I just went somewhere in my head and then when I looked up, you were on the floor and— Oh my God, please believe me. I'm so sorry. I never meant to—"

"Audrey?" His voice came out as a croak.

"Mateo!"

He'd never heard her sound so glad or relieved.

Wait. He blinked. So was this a dream, or not? He flexed his fingers and toes and felt his stinging back. Okay. So he was pretty sure he wasn't dead after all. That was something.

But what was Audrey doing apologizing and kissing him?

Dream was the only logical possibility left.

"Let me go get the guys. Nix gave you some pain medication and it knocked you out pretty good."

But when she tried to move away, Mateo grabbed her wrist. "Don't go." He turned his head to look up at her even though it hurt his back.

"Mateo—" Her eyes were wet with unshed tears. "Why didn't you tell me? Who did all this to you?" Feather light fingers traced down his back between the fresh welts.

Any other time, with any other person, he would have shut down.

But this was Audrey. And even if it had gotten fucked sideways, the point of a power exchange was to open up to a person in ways usual communication couldn't.

Audrey was more open than he'd ever seen her since she'd been here and he could either use the opportunity or wimp out and shut it down right here.

But he'd come too far to do that. He wanted to know everything about her and the flipside of that was her knowing everything about him.

"After the bombs fell, I was captured."

He told her about Hell's Hollow. He told her about the cage they kept him in.

He sat up, unable to keep laying out on his stomach while he spoke. Laying on his belly felt too... exposed.

"Mateo, your back—" Audrey tried to object but Mateo just waved her off. He'd been hurt far worse than this in the past. He swung his legs over the side of the bed and sat beside her, careful to keep about a foot of space between them.

"After around eight months, they moved some of us into the barracks," he continued. "I don't know if it was a promotion of sorts— cause we'd survived the longest? Or if they just wanted easier access to our bodies. They shot us full of antivirals—it was still early enough after The Fall that they'd looted every pharmacy in a hundred mile radius."

"If you were smart, you could work the system. If you—" Mateo swallowed hard. "If you catered to a man's particular... perversions, you could become a favorite. It meant better provisions. It meant survival. So I got good at it. Giving them exactly what they liked, exactly the way they liked it."

"Mateo," Audrey tried to break in again but he just shook his head vehemently and went on. He'd make his full confession.

"Others wanted me just like I was. Some liked getting me hard, too. And the things they did... I'd get hard, sometimes even without them asking. And I came."

His chin dropped to his chest as he admitted his ultimate shame. "I *liked* it."

But then Audrey's hand was underneath his chin, jerking his head up.

"Did you want to be there? Did you want to be having sex with those men?"

"No!" God. Was that what she thought of him?

"Exactly," she said, voice hard and eyes intense. "You were there against your will. They were raping you, Mateo. You adapted. You survived. There's no shame in that."

He shook his head. She didn't understand. "Maybe it started that way. But by the end, when Nix and his security team raided the base and freed me, I was so used to it all that I didn't know if I was glad to be rescued or not."

But Audrey was still shaking her head hard. "No. That's bullshit. You were kidnapped. Forced into sexual slavery. And you blaming yourself for how you survived, even for one single second, is total bullshit. You need to stop it. Right now."

Mateo coughed on a huff of air. "Just stop it?" he asked, incredulous.

She nodded decisively. "Just stop it. Right now."

"Oh, just like that?" He threw his hands up. "I'm a fucking disgusting, filthy piece of shit. Every time I touch you my skin crawls because I know how I'm defiling you and you think I can just—"

She suddenly leaned forward, grabbed his face, and kissed him.

It wasn't any sweet little peck, either. It was a full on, tongues involved, hungry, devouring kiss.

Audrey's hands moved around to clutch at the back of his head while his own hands trembled at his side.

Was this really happening? Was she really all but in his lap, kissing him like she wanted him? *Him?* After what he just told her?

But then the next second she pulled away and he heaved for breath. Okay. Now it was over. She remembered where they were. Who they were. She'd get back in bed and he'd lay down at her feet, like things were meant to be and—

But Audrey didn't climb back in bed.

Instead she slid her hands down from his shoulders along his biceps and to his forearms as she dropped from the bed to the floor.

On her knees in front of him.

No, that was wrong. She should never be on her knees.

"Audrey," he shook his head, leaning a hand to urge her back up.

She pushed his hand away and whispered, "Please. Let me."

He swallowed hard and pulled his hand back, breathing hard when she started unbuttoning his jeans. Before he even fully registered what the hell was happening, her petite hands were on his cock.

He froze in astonishment.

Well, most of him froze. His cock was plenty active. Twitching and growing in Audrey's hand as she rubbed her thumb over his tip and then smoothly jacked him up and down.

A shudder of pleasure hit his spine and racked outward through his body. "Oh God," he sputtered.

Her hands on him— It was— He couldn't remember the last time he'd felt—

That was when he saw her lowering her head toward his shaft.

He should stop her. He couldn't let his pure angel put her lips there. Not when so many other foul memories tainted him. He might not be physically diseased, but that didn't mean that—

Her tongue peeked out from between her lips and licked the small slit at the top of his cock and *holy God in heaven*—

Every ounce of air hissed out of his lungs as Audrey grinned up at him. And then that sweet little pink tongue slipped out again and licked up the underside of his cock.

An animal groan he didn't recognize came from his throat and he felt like his damn heart might stop.

If she kept that up, he'd never make it. He'd die right where he sat. He'd spontaneously combust from ecstasy, no doubt about it—

Turned out he didn't have any damn idea what ecstasy was. Because next she sucked the head of his cock into her hot mouth. And she sucked. God did she suck.

"Audrey," he choked, one hand dropping to her fiery hair. He wasn't sure if he meant to push her away or drag her closer.

In the end, he just kept his hand there, feeling her bob down and then suction with a vacuum force as she slowly pulled him out of her mouth like he was a lollipop she was determined to polish off.

Every time she took him in her mouth, she swallowed him deeper, too. God, had she even given a blow job before?

The thought that he might be her first had him swelling so much he almost exploded right there.

It was only the knock at the door that broke the haze of lust long enough for him to swallow and force the coming orgasm back.

Without letting his cock out of her mouth, Audrey turned slightly to look at the door.

"Hope I'm not interrupting," Danny said as he walked into the room. "Dinner's almost r—" He froze, his eyes going wide as saucers at seeing Audrey on her knees with Mateo's cock in her mouth.

"Holy shit," Danny whispered, hand dropping to his dick. Even through his jeans, Mateo could see the outline of his quickly hardening shaft.

Then, Audrey did pull her mouth off Mateo's cock, letting him go with another of those satisfying *pop* noises.

And she proved again why she was such a damn miracle.

She kept one hand on Mateo's cock, stroking him up and down. And with her other hand, she pulled down her pajama pants, underwear and all, and swayed her ass temptingly at Danny.

"You wanna join us?"

"Y-yes ma'am." Danny said, stumbling as he hurried to jerk his boots off and get his pants down.

Audrey's attention went back to Mateo's cock.

That was, until Danny stood awkwardly behind her, pants at his ankles. "Um. What should I do now? Do you want me to get on the bed? Or, I can pick you up and we can—"

Audrey said something around Mateo's cock that he couldn't understand, apparently, neither could Danny.

Audrey shook her head and released Mateo's cock. She finally looked over her shoulder at Danny. "On your knees." A pleading note entered her voice. "Fuck me from behind."

Mateo hardened even more at her crass language. He knew men in the town shared old copies of *Playboy*, *Maxim* and the like. He'd heard stories of theaters in Fort Worth, the new capitol, where, if you paid a load, you could get in to see old pornos. And he had vague memories of watching porn himself back in the day.

But it had always seemed so forced and faked. The couple girls Mateo had been with before The Fall had been mildly enthused but the relationships never lasted long.

He'd had no idea that a woman could like sex, love and crave sex even, like Audrey seemed to.

The next second, Audrey's hot mouth was back on Mateo's cock and all thought was obliterated.

Danny didn't waste any time. In two seconds his pants were off and he was crouched behind Audrey. He dropped his hands to her hips and his eyebrows knit in concentration as his cock bobbed against her ass.

God, that was hot.

Without ever letting up suction on Mateo's cock, Audrey reached down between her legs. When Danny's eyebrows shot to his hairline, Mateo assumed she'd taken him in hand. Was she guiding him inside her?

By the look of absolute freaking ecstasy that took over Danny's face, Mateo would bet so. Danny's fingers grasped at the flesh around her hips and his pelvis thrust forward. Audrey's body jerked and Mateo snapped, "Gentle."

"Oh." Danny's eyes popped open, looking down at Audrey. "Sorry, are you okay?"

Audrey's only response was to hum around Mateo's cock that was halfway down her throat. God in heaven, was she trying to kill him?

"I'd say you're fine," Mateo gasped, clutching at the bedspread.

Danny grinned and pulled his hips back, then thrust in again, though more gently this time. "Holy shit, sex is fucking amazing," he whispered, voice full of awe. His eyes were locked on the spot where his cock disappeared into Audrey.

Mateo laughed. Actually laughed. He'd never imagined feeling this good again in his life. That *sex* could feel this good. Light.

Beyond the blowjob—which was fucking amazing—he couldn't remember the last time he'd felt so carefree. He wanted to stay in bed with Audrey for weeks on end, playing and exploring with her body, laughing with her.

The other guys too. Just having some fun for once in his life. It was a foreign concept but suddenly he wanted it more than anything.

"Well shit, will you look at that?"

Mateo glanced up to see Clark and Graham at the bedroom door, their eyes alternately flicking back and forth between Audrey's mouth on Mateo and Danny at her backside.

Danny grinned and started pumping more energetically. "Shit, you guys see me fucking her pussy? I'm fucking her so." *Thrust.* "Fucking." *Thrust.* "Good." *Thrust.*

Mateo watched in fascination as Danny's mouth dropped open and his forehead scrunched, his whole body going stiff as he clutched Audrey's hips.

Mateo imagined Danny's cum spurting deep inside her and it was enough to set him off too. He tapped Audrey on the head. "Baby, I'm gonna— If you don't want to—"

But she just swallowed him deeper down her throat with more suction than ever.

His whole body lit up as he came so hard that for a moment he felt like a fucking god.

And even when he came back down to earth, he was still riding high. Because there was Audrey, lapping at his cock like she couldn't bear to miss a single drop of his cum.

He ran his fingers through her hair, breathing so hard he felt like he'd just outrun a damn bobcat.

Clark lingered at the door, eyes dark with lust, but Graham strode right in. "Is it my turn now? Can I fuck you, Audrey?"

CHAPTER THIRTY-ONE

GRAHAM

Audrey laughed and Graham worried he'd said something wrong. He was always doing that. Saying the wrong thing. No matter how hard he tried to fit in, he was always missing things. Social cues. Sarcasm. He was really bad at sarcasm.

Why couldn't people just say what they meant?

And what was their obsession with wanting you to 'look them in the eye'? He'd never understand why staring at someone's eyeballs instead of their nose or a little past their shoulder meant you were paying more or less attention to what they were saying.

Didn't they get it? Life was full of a million distractions. A billion ticking, clicking, twitching distractions that would drive him over the edge if he didn't use his little tricks to help cut it all down so he could focus enough to get anything done.

Focus. That was all he was after. A little peace and quiet so he could accomplish his work.

Except lately the distractions were coming from inside his own head.

Thinking about Audrey.

And sex.

And sex with Audrey.

He had a good life here. His mom had died when Xterminate hit, but so had most everybody else's. And he still had his dad. He had a job he liked. A good place to live and food to eat. He was happy.

Well, he *thought* he was, anyway.

Till he met Audrey. And he suddenly realized he hadn't even known what he'd been missing. She was so nice. And funny. And beautiful.

And she was a really good kisser.

Before getting married, he'd always thought the idea of kissing was sorta gross. Swapping saliva with someone seemed entirely unsanitary.

He thought he'd understood about sex, too. He'd known pleasure was involved, but he'd known it on intellectual level. As in: it was necessary for the species to procreate, so, evolutionarily speaking, of course it was pleasurable to encourage that procreation.

But it's main purpose was still functional. To create babies.

And then came the wedding night.

When he'd slipped between Audrey's thighs and his cock sank into her hot, wet pussy, well he thought it might just be enough to make him start believing in God. Because if something could feel *that* good, if pleasure that extreme existed and he hadn't even had a clue about it, who knew what else about the universe he might not know?

He masturbated sometimes, sure. Everyone needed a stress reliever here and there. But it had been nothing—*nothing* like having sex with a real, live woman. With Audrey.

And then she'd tried to run away and everything had gotten bad and confusing between everyone.

Graham didn't like to think about how bad the past several weeks had been. He'd been distracted at work. Not to mention using the bandwidth for things he wasn't supposed to. The Commander would be very mad if he found out. But Graham had been trying to fix things. To make it better.

Now though, it looked like things might be better all on their own.

Audrey was having sex with them again. That meant the bad time was over. She was happy again?

She was certainly smiling as she licked Mateo's cock.

Graham liked it when she smiled. And seeing her lick another man like that made his own cock so hard it almost hurt.

So when she was done with Mateo, he went to her and asked if it was his turn.

But then she laughed and he worried he said the wrong thing. Was that not how it worked? Didn't they take turns? Or was the wedding night special, and normally she just did one or two of them at a time? Were they supposed to have their own assigned days? Was there a calendar somewhere he could sign up?

"Yes," Audrey said, holding on to Mateo's thighs as she stood up, that beautiful smile still on her face. "It's your turn to fuck me now."

She closed the gap between them, going up on her tiptoes. Graham's breath stuttered. Whoa. He thought she was going to kiss him but instead, she moved her mouth to his ear.

"How do you want to fuck me?"

Graham choked and his cock jumped, straining against his khaki slacks. "I— Um, I—"

Audrey laughed, throaty and musical at the same time.

Was she laughing at him?

When she pulled back, he couldn't be sure, but it didn't seem like she was making fun of him.

She reached down and took his hand, drawing him toward the bed.

Sex. Sex was about to happen again.

Graham let go of her hand only long enough to yank his polo shirt off over his head. Then his hands fumbled at the button of his slacks.

"Let me help," Audrey said, looking at him from underneath her eyelashes and biting her bottom lip.

How had he never noticed women's mouths could be so sexually arousing? He could watch her bite that lip for hours. He could study every nuance of the way her lips moved when she gasped and how they felt underneath his when he kissed them and—

"Do you want me to ride you?" Audrey asked, running her thumb along Graham's bottom lip. "Or do you want to be on top? Or do you want to take me from behind like Danny did?"

Graham felt his eyes widen as he envisioned every scenario. It was like being at a buffet. His mom and dad used to take him to a buffet cafeteria restaurant when he was a kid. There were just too many good options. It was impossible to choose. How did he know which would be the best? If he chose the apple pie, what if the pecan was better and he missed out? Or what if he got the macaroni and cheese and it turned out runny when the mashed potatoes would have been amazing.

And now here Audrey was offering him decisions of infinitely more weight. He'd been on top last time because well, that had seemed the easiest for his first time and he hadn't wanted to embarrass himself.

But now—should he be adventurous and try something new? Or stick with what he knew worked? But then he'd never know if the other positions felt even better?

"All right, this is taking too long," Clark said from the doorway, finally walking in. "He's gonna ride you, Princess, because I want to play with your ass."

Graham didn't know if he was relieved or annoyed to have the decision taken away from him. But after another couple seconds, he couldn't say he much cared, because Audrey was helping him get his pants down.

Mateo moved off the bed and Audrey pushed Graham backwards onto the middle of the mattress.

Then she climbed on top of him, smile wide.

She stroked his shaft up and down. It felt so good he couldn't help but close his eyes and sink his head back into the pillow. Cutting out all other visual stimuli helped him focus on the sensation of Audrey's hand.

Why did it feel so different than when he masturbated himself? It didn't make any sense that it should. But it did. Whoa, but it did. It was like the head of his cock became a hundred times more sensitive.

And when Audrey brushed the tip of his shaft against the wet lips of her pussy, Graham couldn't help but groan.

Then her hand grasped low on his shaft and she took him into her body. She was so slick, he slid right in.

The next second, though, she was clasping around him with her muscles. Her body was gripping his cock from the *inside*.

"One," he gasped, eyes flying open so he could see his cock disappearing into her pretty, pink pussy.

He pulled his hips back and then thrust upwards. "Two."

She helped. She rocked her hips back when he pulled out and then forward when he lifted his hips to impale her with his dick.

He was buried so deep his balls mashed up against her ass. And when she moved her hips down, she did this little grind and swivel thing. It was for her clitoris. He'd read all about the clitoris.

As soon as he learned he'd won the lottery, he'd read everything he could about female pleasure. He still didn't think he had a good grasp on it. Sometime he'd need to do an in-depth inspection of her sex. Mateo seemed to understand it really well. Maybe he could show him how it worked.

"Eight," he gasped out as Clark knelt on the bed beside them. While Audrey rode Graham, Clark reached out and grasped her breasts. He didn't squeeze them like Graham would have. No, he just rolled her pink nipples between his thumb and forefinger until they became hard little nubs.

It seemed to Graham like it would hurt but Audrey seemed to like it. She gasped out and dropped a hand between her legs.

Graham tilted his head to watch in fascination as she started rubbing little circles with her middle finger round and round the very top of her slit. Was *that* where the clitoris was?

He frowned and almost lost count for a moment. But he shook himself just in time. "Seventeen."

Still, his breathing grew more labored as her hips began rocking wildly on top of him, her finger never stopping its quest.

And it hit him all over again just like it had the first time—this wasn't a quiet, respectable pairing for the simple purpose of creating offspring.

No, Audrey was hungry to orgasm. If any of their previous encounters were an indication, she liked to orgasm many, many times. She was almost insatiable.

Though, when he was watching her with Mateo and Danny earlier from the doorway, he wasn't sure if she'd come.

But she was going to come now. With his cock fucking her.

"Twenty-eight!"

Whoaaaa. He wasn't sure if he'd make it to sixty. She was so sexy. So, so sexy. He'd masturbated multiple times since he'd first had sex with her. But none of it had even come close to what it felt like having her hot pussy clenching around him. To seeing her face scrunched with need as she chased her orgasm. To feeling her wetness mixed with another man's cum lubricating Graham's way as his cock slid in, and out, and in again.

"Fifty-seven."

Thrust.

"Fifty-eight."

Thrust even harder.

"Fifty-*nine*."

His head was going to fucking explode. But no, *no*, it couldn't be over this quick. He wouldn't let it be over. What if she got mad at them again and this was the last time he got to have sex with her for another month?

"Sixty." He gritted his teeth, thrusting in, pulling out and then thrusting in again. "*One*."

He breathed out in relief even as he felt his balls bursting with the need to come.

But he couldn't come now. Not until he got back to sixty again. "Two. Three."

He squeezed his eyes shut as he started the countdown all over again.

"Lift off him for a sec, baby," Clark said.

Graham was about to protest but Clark quickly continued. "Go reverse cowgirl so he can see me play with your ass while he fucks you."

Audrey made a whining noise, still strumming at her clit as wildly as ever, but when Clark took her by the shoulders and directed her off of Graham's cock, she went.

Clark helped turn her around so that her back and ass were to Graham. His eyes widened. Because while watching her face and breasts and had been great, looking at her sweet, plump ass was just as amazing.

Especially when she rolled her hips back and forth. He watched the place where his cock disappeared inside her, whispering now. "Seven. Eight. Nine."

And then, Graham didn't see where he'd gotten it, but Clark had a small tube in his hand and he squirted a clear gel on the tips of his first two fingers. Graham's eyes flipped between his cock and what Clark was doing.

Too much. It was too much. All happening at once.

He squeezed his eyes shut and focused on his counting.

Even with his eyes shut, the stimulation of his senses was still close to overload. So many sounds. The squelch and slap of Audrey's flesh against his when she dropped down and ground against him. The loud breathing of all four men in the room. Audrey's high-pitched little gasps.

Did that mean she was close to coming? She couldn't come yet, though. Not till they got to sixty again.

What if she didn't understand that?

He almost lost count, worrying about her coming too soon. Sure it would still feel good, but he didn't know if *he* could come then, if it wasn't perfect, if it all went—

Graham's eyes popped back open as he felt himself starting to go soft. No. No no no. He was the one ruining this. Not her. Him and his stupid, screwed up brain.

Audrey paused on top of him, looking over her shoulder.

He averted his gaze, feeling his ears burn.

But Clark apparently didn't notice anything was off because he used Audrey's momentary stillness to pry her ass cheeks apart and dropped his head down. "Been dreaming of eating this little asshole ever since our wedding night."

And Graham's cock went ramrod hard again as he watched Clark's tongue flick out and lick all around Audrey's asshole. He did it from the side, like he intended Graham to be able to see.

And it was just so... *wrong*. So dirty.

Audrey's butt cheeks clenched and her little asshole puckered tight as Clark's tongue continued licking and thrusting.

And, his cock fully hard again, Graham couldn't help but thrust too. He punched his hips upward, eliciting a long whine of pleasure from Audrey. She wiggled her ass against Clark's tongue and he chuckled.

Then he brought one of his lube-coated fingers up to where he'd been licking and probed her little asshole with his forefinger.

Whoa, whoa, was he going to—

Clark's finger popped inside Audrey's ass and she moaned even louder.

Bed springs squeaked as the other guys joined them on the bed. Graham didn't look at them. He kept his eyes locked on Clark's finger sawing in and out of Audrey's tight little ass.

How did it feel? Having both Graham's cock and Clark's fingers in her at the same time? Because Clark had slid in a second finger and then—whoa, dang, *whoa*, no way—a third.

He was stretching Audrey's asshole so good. Graham hadn't even known a woman could be stretched that much. Clark's fingers were far from small or dainty.

But Audrey just took it. She even seemed to like it. A lot, if the way she wiggled and shoved back against Clark's hand was any indication.

Graham thrust upwards as Audrey pushed down and backwards. Graham was balls deep and Clark's fingers were in up to the knuckle.

Then Clark really started working her. There was no rhyme or rhythm to it. He twisted his fingers around and then in and out and then around back and forth some more. Sometimes quick, sometimes slow.

Audrey's cries grew louder and wilder.

She was about to come.

She clenched and ground down on Graham's cock and it was so freaking hot. So good. Whoa, if she kept—

She squeezed his cock even harder. And when she swiveled her hips like that, the tip of his cock dragged along her inner walls.

Her cries reached a crescendo. She'd hit her peak. Her spasming pussy clenched around Graham harder than ever and with a yell of his own, cum shot from his cock deep inside her. He pulled back slightly and then slammed in again, completely emptying his balls.

It was only as he fell backwards on the bed that he remembered he'd totally forgotten all about counting there at the end.

CHAPTER THIRTY-TWO

NIX

When Nix slammed in the house and found the downstairs empty, it only made his black mood darker. One of the Scrapper parties they'd sent out eight days ago still wasn't back. They were due home three days ago.

There was always a chance they'd still make it back.

More likely, though, they were dead. And it was the second party this month not to come home.

He should be out there. He'd never stayed in the township this long. Things were supposed to be stabilizing under President Goddard's government, but in Nix's experience, disappearing resources —as they became more centralized and regulated—just made marginalized people more desperate.

Nix's jaw hardened as he walked into the kitchen. He should be out there with his men. Instead he was stuck with the precious little princess who thought she had it *so* tough here in town with food and shelter and plenty of water to drink.

Nix looked around. Where the hell *was* everybody anyway?

Were they out back at the cookstove trying to make something her highness would deign to eat? Or were they upstairs trying to coax her out of her weeklong tantrum?

A quick glance out the back kitchen door showed no one was out there.

Nix shook his head and went back to the living room to trot up the stairs to the second story.

Which was when he heard them.

And realized exactly what was going on.

He ground his teeth together even as his cock hardened in his jeans. He pushed the door open and saw Audrey riding Graham like he was a goddamned bucking bronco.

With Clark's hand buried up her ass.

Nix got there just in time, too, because she howled as she came. Graham's eyes rolled back in his head like he was gonna fuckin' pass out, Audrey's pussy was so magical.

But it wasn't magical.

It was just a pussy like any other. The fact that it was the only one they had access to had driven them all stupid for a while.

Even him. He'd admit it. He'd gone soft in the head. Thinking all sorts of stupid shit on their wedding night. Forgetting that everybody was only out for themselves. But her running away had shown her true colors and brought him back to his senses.

He was in his right mind again and he saw her for what she was. A user. A smart, manipulative user.

After she realized escape wasn't going to work, she'd done every-thing possible to get them eating out of her hand again. Starting with that sucker, Mateo.

It looked like she'd finally decided it was time to pull the rest of them back in to her little web.

Well, she could try, but he saw through her.

"Clark," Nix snapped as he stomped over to the bed, unbuckling his belt as he went. "Help me lift her up."

Audrey's head swung his direction, her bright blue eyes going wide. *That's right, little girl. It's time to pay the piper.*

Clark stood and, taking Audrey's arms, helped her off the bed. She was naked. Fuck. Nix'd forgotten how perfect her body was. Those full, rounded breasts, her tapered little waist flaring out into that wide, fuckable ass. She followed Clark's lead and got off the bed, eyes on Nix the whole time.

She wasn't the only one.

Mateo climbed off the bed and hurried around, getting right in Nix's face. "Don't you dare give her a hard time."

Nix tried to shove him out of the way but Mateo just kept stubbornly just stepping back in between him and Audrey.

Until she put a hand on Mateo's shoulder. "It's okay, Mateo," she said, her voice soft. Mateo looked over his shoulder and they seemed to communicate something in the gaze.

Nix shook his head in disgust. Fucking wrapped around her little finger.

"You upset her and you'll have me to deal with," Mateo said.

Nix rolled his eyes but then Danny piped up. "Me too."

Graham struggled to a sitting position. "And me."

Nix held his hands up. "As terrifying as three naked men are with their dicks swinging in the wind, I think me and our wife can manage a civil conversation."

"Just a conversation?" Audrey asked, a challenge in her eyes. She glanced down his body to his unbuckled belt. "Seems to me like you came in here with more than talking on your mind."

"Depends." He curled one edge of his mouth up in a smirk as he met her gaze. "You callin' it quits on your dramatics?"

Her eyes flared with fury and Nix's smirk turned to an all-out grin.

"Depends," she said, her voice full of challenge while she cocked her head to one side. "You gonna stop being an asshole?"

Nix's grin dropped off his face. He reached out and slid one hand around the back of her neck. Then he drew her sharply forward and whispered in her ear. "I think you like it when I'm an asshole."

He didn't miss the way her breath hitched at the action. Or the fact that his camouflage security shirt was rubbing against her bared nipples, making them harden.

"I bet you've missed me so much you've had blue balls for weeks," she whispered back, hand snaking between their stomachs and into his pants.

Fuuuuuuuuuuuuuuuuuck. It took everything Nix had not to grind against her hand when she wrapped her firm little fingers around his shaft. Okay, so maybe he'd underestimated or forgotten just how tempting she could be.

But that was fine. They could enjoy each other's bodies. It didn't mean he trusted her or had to give her any more than that.

"I bet you'd just love it if I did." He shoved his pants down his legs and kicked them off. "You love torturing men, don't you? It's what gets you off." Then he took Audrey in his arms and hiked her up. She yelped in surprise but wrapped her legs around his waist.

"Clark," Nix said, nodding over Audrey's shoulder and gesturing him to come closer. A wide grin broke across Clark's face.

"Thought you'd never ask," he said, coming up behind Audrey's back and helping Nix support her weight.

"We're gonna fuck you now," Nix said, staring straight into Audrey's eyes as he held her aloft. "Both of us. You get what that means?"

Audrey gasped and looked behind her at Clark, chest heaving.

"Shh," Clark said, pushing a stray curl behind her ear with one hand. "Just like this baby, but it'll be my cock."

Nix had guessed Clark had been fingering her ass just like earlier and his words confirmed it.

Audrey blinked, eyes wide and eyebrow furrowed. She swallowed hard, then said, "I trust you."

Nix barely bit back his scoff. He had to hand it to her. She had the scared, vulnerable act down cold.

Let's see how good an actress still is with his and Clark's cocks destroying her pussy at the same time.

Nix felt around. She was plenty slick down there, with her own natural wetness combined with Graham's cum. Nix didn't know who else she'd fucked before he'd gotten there.

But he'd be the last and he'd make sure to be the most memorable.

Flexing his biceps, he hefted her body up in his arms just enough to line up his cock with her entrance. Inch by inch, he lowered her down on his cock.

Her eyes shot wide. "I forgot how big—" Her choked whisper broke off as her arms squeezed tight around his neck and she buried her head into his chest.

Nix's cock flexed as soon as he was balls deep and he squeezed her ass. *Shiiiiiit.* For a second he had to close his eyes against how good it felt. He'd forgotten. It had only been three weeks but he'd forgotten. Maybe on purpose.

Because if he'd remembered it felt this fucking good, he would have been joining Mateo on the goddamned floor, begging her to take them back every second of every goddamned day.

He tried to reject the thought as soon as he had it.

No. She was a manipulator. She was—

"I'm gonna come in now too, beautiful." Clark's voice was low and raspy.

Nix lifted Audrey and dropped her, wanting one more moment where she was only his. And then he felt her whole body go tense as Clark stepped closer from behind.

"Relax," Nix whispered. "Shh, it's gonna be okay, honey. Just relax."

What the fuck was coming out of his mouth? But he couldn't stand the thought of her hurting. That was just him being decent. He was a decent guy, that was all.

"I promise, baby," Clark said, dragging his mouth along the back of Audrey's neck, "if you thought what I did earlier felt good, this will blow your fucking mind. Having both of us take you at once, it'll be like nothing you've ever felt before."

Audrey sucked in a deep breath and, looking into Nix's eyes, repeated, "I trust you." Then she frowned slightly before her eyes widened and the softest fucking smile lit her face. Like she'd just had some realization. Her eyes glowed with warmth. "You'll keep me safe. I trust you."

Then suddenly Nix was the one who couldn't breathe, Roxy's voice ringing in his head: *You know why I'm not afraid? Because I'm with you. And you'll never let anything bad happen to me.*

"You're so beautiful, baby," Clark said from behind, dissolving the memory of Roxy's voice. "That's right, keep nice and relaxed like that. Shit. Oh fuck, baby, that's right, let me in. Holy shit. Holy shit, baby, your ass is so tight. Do you have any idea how amazing it feels to fuck this tight little ass?"

Audrey's chest heaved against Nix's and she sounded out of breath when she gasped. "Now you. Move, Nix. Oh God, move so I can feel both of you together."

Aw fuck, she was killing him. Nix was completely back in the moment. Did she have any fucking idea how hot she was? How amazing she was, taking both their cocks and asking for more?

Nix pulled his hips back and then pushed back in again. And holy mother of Christ but he could feel the fullness provided by Clark's cock. It made it feel like she was squeezing around Nix's shaft twice as hard.

"Oh fuck. Aud, you're so—" Nix broke off, not even knowing how to finish the sentence.

Audrey pulled back, her arms still around his neck. And for several long moments, they just fucked, slow and deep, gazes locked.

And he couldn't keep more than two thoughts together in his head.

There were things about her that he... He wasn't supposed to... She was—

Beautiful.

Perfect.

All that mattered.

He leaned in and kissed her hard. She kissed him back just as hungrily, groaning into his mouth and digging her nails into his shoulders when Clark started fucking her so vigorously her body was thrust repetitively into Nix's.

And it was clear by the way she dropped her head back the next moment that she loved it.

Goddamn she was perfect.

She reached one arm out back toward the bed the next second. Her eyes were still squeezed shut in pleasure as she called out, "Danny. Mateo. Graham. I need all of you."

Then put her arm back around Nix's neck, thrusting her pelvis against his as she sought her pleasure.

Within seconds, the other men were surrounding them where they stood in the middle of the room. Mateo reached in to pinch at Audrey's nipples. Graham dropped to a crouch, looking upwards from underneath, no doubt to watch Nix's and Clark's cocks disappearing into Audrey's two holes. Danny pulled Audrey's face slightly to the side so he could kiss her.

In between kisses, she gasped, "Touch yourselves. All of you."

Goddammit, Nix was gonna blow.

The thought of all of them, fucking as one... Plus Audrey's tight pussy and the pressure of Clark's cock—

Just like that, Nix was over the edge.

"Come with me," he shouted to Audrey.

But it was like she'd felt him coming, because her face was already scrunched, her mouth dropped open. Then her entire body spasmed around his cock. Her pussy milked Nix so good, so fucking good he'd thought he'd pass the fuck out.

But he didn't. He stayed on his feet and between him and Clark, who seemed to have come simultaneously with him and Audrey, they kept Audrey in their arms.

"Spread her legs," Nix growled to Clark.

Nix didn't know if Clark knew what he had in mind, but he followed Nix's instruction.

Together, they spun Audrey so that her back was to their chests and, Nix taking one half and Clark the other, they held her up so that her legs were wide open, knees out.

Exposing her pussy that was dripping with Nix's cum. And maybe Clark's too, dripping down from her ass.

"Shoot your cum on our wife's sweet pussy," he ordered the other three men. "Mark her as ours."

The words were barely out of his mouth before Danny's cock was right at the lips of Audrey's pussy. He was artless but enthusiastic as he jerked his cock roughly, quickly shooting ropes of thick cum messily all over her pussy.

"Fuck," Clark muttered. "I'm gonna get hard again and be ready for round two if this keeps up."

Graham was up next. He pushed his glasses up his nose with his eyebrows scrunched in concentration, gaze locked on Audrey's dripping cunt.

He was jerking lazily at his cock like it was almost an afterthought but the closer Nix looked, he realized he was muttering numbers to himself. He rubbed his cock up and down Audrey's slit like a metronome and soon had her shuddering with need.

Graham's concentration seemed to focus even more and he centered his attentions with the head of his cock on her clit, rubbing circles around and then back and forth. It was only when she came with a breathy moan that Graham shot his load on her, soaking her curls with pearly, creamy cum that dripped down to combine with everyone else's.

Feeling her shudder in their arms had Nix completely hard again. His arms were starting to get tired, but he'd hold her for a week if it was possible so they could all just keep fucking and fucking and fucking her.

Mateo stepped up last.

Audrey's head had been dropped back onto Nix's chest after her last orgasm, but she lifted it when Mateo approached.

"Come in me," she whispered. "I haven't felt your cock inside me yet, Mateo. Please."

Mateo swallowed hard and when he looked back up at her, Nix thought the dumb fuck was gonna make some excuse.

Instead, he just repeated Audrey's earlier words. "I trust you."

And then he stepped up to Audrey, his cock standing straight out from his body. Audrey's arms were wrapped around Nix and Clark's neck so she couldn't help put him inside her.

Mateo had to make the choice to guide his own cock into Audrey's cum-slick channel. And finally, he did. Almost immediately, his eyes rolled back like Audrey's pussy was fucking paradise. *Not far off, buddy*, Nix thought.

Mateo didn't make a big affair of it.

He fucked their wife with deep, slow strokes. He dropped a hand between them so that Audrey came in a minute flat.

But that wasn't enough for Mateo. Right after her spasms finished, he was whispering, "That's right. Now give me another one. I know you've got it in you. It's right there. That next peak. You're already so close. Give it to me, sweetheart. It'll feel so good. That's right, just give into it."

And she did. Once. Twice. Three more fucking times.

Her entire body was shaking—Nix didn't know if it was another orgasm or if she was just exhausted with all the ways they'd used her flesh the past few hours—when finally, finally, Mateo pulled her mouth to his, kissing her and thrusting deep before stilling.

When he eventually pulled back, cum poured out of Audrey's pussy like a waterfall onto the floor.

Nix and Clark set her back on her feet. She was wobbly and unsteady. Clark held her up and Nix took her other side. But he couldn't help reaching down and dipping a couple fingers to the lips of her sex, swirling them in all the mixed cum, and then shoving them up inside her pussy.

"You're our wife now," Nix growled, repeating the action, scooping more cum off her leg and pushing it back up into her pussy. "So don't you go fucking forgetting again."

CHAPTER THIRTY-THREE

AUDREY

"Shit," Danny swore, pumping his hips and driving his cock in and out of Audrey. "I'm gonna come."

"Jesus, we just started," Clark shouted in exasperation. "Did you even masturbate earlier like I told you to?"

"Yeah," Danny said, looking helpless. Well, as helpless as a guy with giant muscles and a fat cock could while he pumped into Audrey like a goddamned champ.

Audrey thought he was doing a lovely job fucking her with said cock. In fact, if Danny would just lean a little further down, she bet she could get that last little bit of friction she needed so she could—

"What's the unsexiest thing you can think about?" Clark asked, butting in on her almost-orgasm. "Quick. Unsexiest thing you've ever seen. What's the first thing that comes to mind?"

"I don't know. I can't think... Jesus, she's gripping on me so fucking tight."

Clark turned and glared at Audrey. "You're not helping."

Audrey threw her hands up. "Oh now you're dragging me into this?"

"Trust me, your pussy is half the problem." Clark shot her another look. "I've seen him go a full ten minutes when it's just his own hand."

"We timed him yesterday," Graham piped up helpfully from the couch by the window, watch held up close to his face.

"The sanitation buckets at the barracks!" Danny said suddenly, sounding triumphant.

"Ewwww," Audrey said, covering her ears. "You do realize that the other half of sex is his partner still finding it sexy too?"

"All right, all right," Clark said, waving a hand. "Just keep it to yourself. Picture it in your head, don't say it out loud."

"But now I know he's thinking about buckets of crap," Audrey complained. Come on, there had to be a better way than this to—

"Nope," Danny said, "Now all I can think about is how fuckable her tits are. And damn, that ass. Have you guys seen her ass when she bends over to pick something up? I just wanna stick my dick— *Oh*— Oh shit— I'm—"

Audrey shoved her hand down and rubbed her clit furiously, managing to get herself there right as Danny's face did that adorable thing where his nose scrunched up like he was about to sneeze.

Her orgasm stretched throughout her body like one great, extremely satisfying yawn. It left her pussy humming with that satisfying buzz that she was beginning to get very familiar with.

After two weeks spent almost exclusively in bed—though these two weeks had been decidedly more *active* than the previous one— Audrey was learning the ins and out of her own body as well as those of her five husbands.

They'd spent hours exploring one another. Sometimes in twos, sometimes in threes, one time in a giant sextuplet of tangled limbs and cocks and mouths that, now that she thought about it, Audrey was eager to repeat.

She could describe all of their cum faces in detail and she had to say, life as a wife to five men had so many more upsides than she ever could have imagined.

"He made it five whole minutes that time," Graham said from the couch.

Danny's head sank to Audrey's breasts as he slumped over her. "Sorry, Audrey."

"What?" She propped herself up on her elbows, forcing Danny to look up at her. "Why would you be sorry? Enough of this crap. I don't know how or why these idiots have convinced you coming fast is a bad thing."

He shrugged, not looking up at her. "I just hear the other clan men talking. About how many hours they pleasure their women. And then I can't even—"

"That's bullshit," she cut him off and took his cheeks in her hands, pulling his face up so he'd look at her.

"None of them are in this bed. It's just us." She looked around to include Clark and Graham as well. The other guys were out working but she meant all of them.

"All I care about is us finding our pleasure. And I came." She ran her thumb along Danny's bottom lip and grinned when she felt the shudder go through his body. "Did you come?"

He nodded vigorously and she laughed. "Then job well done."

She wrapped her arms around his neck.

He laughed, his voice both deep and boyish at the same time.

Then his face clouded over.

"What?" She pushed a lock of his thick dark hair off his forehead.

"Nothing." He tried to shake it off, but she could still see something was bothering him.

She grabbed his chin and forced his face back to hers. "Don't give me that. Something's up. What is it?"

He shrugged a little and then laid his head on her breasts. "It's just, the craziest thing happened at work today."

She tilted her head to get a better look at him. "Oh?"

"Yeah." He shook his head, brow scrunching up. "I was on construction crew today. We're fixing up one of the old buildings on the square. The old bank at the corner of Main Street and 2nd."

Audrey nodded.

"Me and this guy, George, happen to be taking our break at the same time out front. I didn't know him real well but ya know, he's cool." The line deepened between his brows. "And then outta nowhere. *BAM*. A load of bricks from the second story falls on top of him."

"Oh my God," Audrey gasped.

"He was standing maybe three feet from me." Danny shook his head.

"Is he okay?"

"I don't know. Me and the other guys pulled the bricks off him and he was breathing, but he didn't look good. His head was bleeding real bad and he was confused. Didn't seem to know where he was and kept blacking out. The med crew came and carted him off. It was the craziest thing."

Audrey blinked and then hugged Danny even tighter. Three feet? Just three feet and that could have been Danny?

What the hell? The world was bad enough with genetically engineered viruses and evil bastards like Jeffries without random piles of bricks falling on people and crushing them.

"I'm so sorry," she whispered. And she just kept clutching him because... well, she couldn't seem to let him go.

"And it just got me to thinking," he said into her hair.

She finally forced herself to draw back so she could look him in the eye.

She nodded for him to go on. Whatever he was trying to say, she could tell it was important to him.

"Well, I know I said it on our wedding night. But I didn't really know what it meant then. I do now, though. All I could think as I was coming home was, what if it had been me standing where George was and I never got to tell you? I love you."

His earnest brown eyes searched hers. "You're perfect, Audrey. You're perfect and I love you."

Audrey's heart melted and broke at the same time. He was so sweet.

"You're the perfect one," she said, leaning up to kiss him. It was partially a stalling tactic because she didn't know what else to say. But it was true, too. Danny *was* wonderful. And so were the other guys, each in their own way.

The past two weeks had been amazing. Just stealing away from the real world and hiding away in their little honeymoon sex haven. For once, Audrey had just let go of worrying about all the things she couldn't control.

Jeffries and his threats.

Losing her brother.

In the back of her mind, she knew insane happiness like this was unsustainable. She couldn't stay hidden away forever. The real world always intruded. Even back at Uncle Dale's.

But maybe if you're careful never to be alone, to always stay close to one or more of your husbands, then Jeffries won't bother you.

Was that possible? Was it a real solution, or was she just lying to herself because she wanted it to be?

She hugged Danny close. She was so happy it hurt.

Was it so wrong to want to hold onto that for a little longer?

She could worry about what happened next later.

Tomorrow maybe.

Or the next day.

CHAPTER THIRTY-FOUR

NIX

When Nix got home from security rounds, it was again to an empty house. He sighed and looked toward the second floor, jogging up the stairs.

He didn't hear voices as he approached Audrey's room and for a brief moment, he hoped it meant Audrey had gotten out of the house today with Danny or Clark.

He pushed the door to the master bedroom open and crossed his arms over his chest at the scene that greeted him.

All three of them were passed out on the bed. Audrey and Clark had at least pulled the sheet over themselves but Danny was naked as the day he was born, ass up.

"You know at some point you'll have to leave the house again." Nix said it so loudly that all three of them startled awake. Audrey sat up, looking sleepy and befuddled as she pushed her hair out of her face. "You can't just stay holed up in here forever. It's not healthy."

She couldn't have been that deeply asleep because she caught up quickly and adopted an obviously insincere smile. "Oh I don't know. I think hermitdom suits me."

Nix frowned dropping his arms and walking into the room. "I'm serious, Audrey. I mean, obviously we hope you'll get pregnant soon and then, yes, you'll spend a lot of time at home, but right now, you barely even leave the *bedroom*."

He gestured down, indicating the rest of the house. "It's starting to worry us."

Audrey's head shot to Danny and Clark.

Danny looked chagrined and Clark held up his hands. "We just want the best for you, love," Clark said.

Audrey pulled her sheet up tighter. "Well don't," she snapped.

Nix sighed. It had been a good two weeks but Audrey had just as much spark and spirit as ever. He remembered missing it when it was gone, but now he found himself wishing there was some middle ground to be found.

Nix held out a hand to Audrey. "Will you take a walk with me?"

Audrey stared at his proffered hand suspiciously.

"Jesus, Aud, I don't bite."

"You sure about that?" She arched an eyebrow, getting off the bed slowly and sensuously.

She was naked. In fact, Nix wondered when she'd last worn clothes. Sometimes she wore panties, but he and the guys had a bad habit of ripping them off her so she'd given up after the first week. "Because this mark right here on my neck says different."

She walked right up to him and extended her neck, pointing out the half-circle discoloration of skin where he'd been nibbling on her the night before.

Her pert little nipples were hard points and Nix had to fight against his natural impulse to grab her and slam her up against the wall.

But after two weeks of sating both his unquenchable appetite and hers, he liked to think he had a little more self-control than that.

"Put some clothes on and meet me downstairs," he growled, spinning to head for the door. "Oh, and Audrey?"

She tilted her head at him.

"Don't keep me waiting."

That got him a glare and a huff that had him chuckling all the way down the stairs. Probably to get him back, Audrey didn't come down for fifteen minutes, even though it looked like she'd only thrown on a pair of jeans she was drowning in—maybe one of the guys'?—and an oversized T-shirt that almost completely hid her beautiful figure.

Aw, she was so adorable when she was being passive-aggressive.

But at the same time, he needed to have a real conversation with her. He took her hand and dragged her out the back door.

"Nix. What are you doing?" She threw an arm over her face to shield herself from the sun's bright rays.

"Getting you some Vitamin D."

The glare she shot him would have made a lesser man quail. Good thing he wasn't a lesser man. Besides, for him and Audrey, this kind of bickering was foreplay.

But again, dropping back into bed with her would only be delaying the inevitable and solving nothing.

"I don't want to do this," Nix said gently. "I don't want to fight." He took her hand in his and for several long moments just reveled in the feel of her skin against his.

"I don't know if I ever apologized," he said quietly. "For being an ass back when you were having such a difficult time. I just..."

Fuck. He was no good at this shit. Talking about feelings and shit. But for Audrey, he'd try. "It's just that, after Roxy—" at the widening of her eyes he hurried to clarify, "—Roxy was my sister."

Her mouth widened even further.

"Roxy was my sister and..." Nix swallowed hard like he was forcing himself to continue.

Audrey laid a hand on his forearm. "You don't have to tell me if you don't want to."

Why did she always do that? Pull back at the last minute. Give him an out. He'd seen her do it with the other guys too. For all that she'd let them into her body, she'd still never opened up to them about her past.

Where was her family? Why was she in the field that day? She was holding things back from them—important things he knew could help them all understand her better.

Sophia said she'd mentioned a brother when she first woke up that day after he'd tranqued her in the woods, but Audrey had never said a thing about him to any of them.

And Nix knew if he was gonna get anywhere with her, he'd have to be the one taking the first step. So he took a deep breath and went on. "After I lost Roxy..." His throat constricted just picturing his sister's sunny smile. She was the happiest, most optimistic person. Even after everything.

And then the image of her right at the end flashed through his head. The memory he could never erase.

His jaw went hard but he kept talking. "She thought I was invincible. That I'd always protect her." His voice went thick with a mixture of fury and self-recrimination he didn't bother hiding. "But I wasn't. And I didn't."

He told her about the militia group that had taken over the resort cabins. And how they captured him and his sister.

"Phoenix. I'm so sorry."

Nix only realized his hand was clenched in a fist when Audrey's warm hand covered his. Still, he couldn't look at her. He heard the tears in her voice and he didn't deserve them. Roxy was the only one who ought to be wept over.

"They raped and brutalized her for hours." He said the words but felt an odd detachment from them as he stared at the breeze ruffling the tree leaves of the big live oak in the center of the back yard.

"And I just sat there." He shook his head. "I just sat there and did nothing."

"Phoenix. You said you were chained up! There was nothing you could do."

He shook his head again. She was wrong. "Eventually I realized that if I just broke my hand, I could get free of the cuffs. So I did. And when the guard next came by to taunt me, I grabbed his gun and shot him in the head."

Finally, he looked at Audrey. "So you see. If only I'd done that hours earlier, I might have been able to save her. But I didn't."

Audrey's chin trembled and she rubbed the heel of her palm against her chest. "What happened to her? Was she dead by the time you got to her?"

Nix's stomach went hard as a stone and his throat was so thick, he could barely get the word out: "No."

"She wasn't?" He heard the confusion in her tone and he shook his head the smallest bit.

"No." He stared at the dancing leaves and turned his face up to the sun. It was warm but not too hot yet. Not like it would get at the end of summer. The breeze made it feel even more comfortable.

"Roxy would have loved this place," he murmured, closing his eyes and feeling the breeze slide across his skin.

Audrey didn't ask anything else but he could feel the questions bubbling up inside her. And he'd gone this far. He might as well finish it. He kept his eyes squeezed shut, though.

"It was late at night by this point. Lots of men came running when they heard the gunshot. But I'd spent three years in Afghanistan and I knew my way around an AR15. I took out half the camp on my way to get to Roxy. I think they thought they were under attack. They didn't realize it was just one guy, picking up more guns as I went."

"Anyway, eventually I got to Roxy."

Nix opened his eyes, but only to look at the wide-open sky.

"She was covered in blood. Head to toe. They had her tied to a post and she was just hanging there, limp. I thought for sure she was dead. But then I felt for a pulse. And when I called her name, she lifted her head and looked at me."

He didn't know how to describe what had been in her eyes. It wasn't his Roxy. But it *was* at the same time.

That was the worst part. If he could have just said his sister was already gone, that would have been one thing. But no, he saw a glimmer of his sweet little sister—but it was like her trust in him and the basic goodness in the world had been betrayed in the deepest way possible.

"I cut her free." His voice shook. "When she collapsed into my arms, I thought it was because she didn't have the strength to stand. And maybe she didn't."

He lifted his hands to his head. "Maybe she saved up every last ounce of energy she had so she could grab my gun and shoot herself in the head with it."

Audrey gasped in horror and Nix just kept clutching his head like if he pressed hard enough, he could get rid of the memories.

But no, he wouldn't betray Roxy again. He deserved to remember in excruciating detail how he'd failed her.

"You couldn't have known—" Audrey started but Nix cut her off.

"What the fuck did I think was going to happen after she went through all that? I should have seen it in her eyes. Fuck that, I *did* see it. The hopelessness. But I didn't understand— I just couldn't—"

He turned away from Audrey, walking several steps away before stopping to catch a breath. His chest was so tight his lungs felt like they couldn't expand right.

He'd seen the fucking resort on his map. Why didn't he take them west that day instead of south? He was so fucking *stupid* and it had cost his sister her life. After putting her through the worst hell he could imagine.

He'd closed his eyes again so he startled when he felt Audrey's arms close around his middle, hugging him from behind. Just like Roxy used to.

It was the last straw.

He broke.

He sank to his knees and Audrey went with him, moving around to clutch his head to her chest, whispering soft words he couldn't even make out.

He kept gasping for breath.

Why couldn't he get a fucking breath?

"Shhhh." Audrey ran her fingers through his hair and rocked him. "Shhhh."

It was only then that he realized he was blubbering like a baby.

"But Roxy," he sputtered, hiccupping and gasping for breaths between choking sobs.

"I'm so sorry." Audrey held him tighter to her. "This world has taken so much. I'm so, so sorry."

He buried his face against her, not wanting her to see him breaking the fuck down. Goddammit, this wasn't what he'd meant to do at all when he brought her down to talk. He'd just meant to tell her his sister died. Not all... this shit.

He took several deep, gulping breaths. *For fuck's sake, get yourself under control.* He clenched his jaw and forced himself to breathe more regularly.

Finally when he felt it was safe, he pulled away from Audrey and ran his hands roughly down his face.

Then he pressed his forehead to hers. "I may never know who put my name in for the lotto that night. But I'll never be able to repay them even if I spent the rest of my life trying. You mean everything and that scares the shit out of me. I'm sorry I was such an ass about it."

He pulled back and took her small hands in his. Christ she was beautiful. Strong and fragile at the same time. Her fiery red hair caught and reflected the sunlight. His fire angel. Full of piss and vinegar and passion and hard and soft.

Slowly, so slowly, she leaned in and pressed her lips to his. The kiss started gentle but quickly escalated. As things always seemed to do between them.

Not even a minute later, she was climbing into his lap and straddling him.

"Talk is cheap," she whispered with a devilish glint to her eye. "You wanna apologize? Show me how sorry you are."

Nix grinned and then, in one smooth motion, grabbed her, lifted her, and then had her on her back on the grass, his body poised over hers.

"Your wish is my command."

CHAPTER THIRTY-FIVE

AUDREY

Audrey held Graham's hand as he walked her to 'work', just like he or one of the clan had every day for the past two weeks. Yes, she'd ventured back out into the world.

She decided she could either let fear make a prisoner of her, or she could trust her clan to protect her.

Almost daily she had the argument with herself about whether or not to just tell them about the threats Jeffries had made. Surely, if she told them while they were all together, and then they went as one to the Commander, then...

We're a multitude, Jeffries had said. *We got men everywhere. In every guild of workers. All over the government.*

At the time she thought he'd just been talking about Jacob's Well Township. But what if he meant on a larger scale? Like, was there some revolutionary anti-President Goddard movement brewing or something?

Or was Jeffries just lying out his ass? Maybe it was just him and Camila's four other husbands who were the rotten apples.

But if he was telling the truth...

Then saying anything could get Nix killed. Or Clark or Graham or Mateo or Danny.

And ultimately, that was enough to end every argument. It was simply a risk she wasn't willing to take.

So she stayed quiet.

And stuck like glue to whichever husband was shadowing her for the day. Sometimes she joined them at their work, sometimes they came with her.

Today she was heading to the Food Pantry working with Sophia.

Graham rubbed his thumb in circular patterns over her palm as they walked. Audrey smiled, knowing he was secretly counting the number of strokes. She loved all his little quirks. The new things she discovered about him and the other guys every day.

Maybe eventually some of their habits would get on her nerves. But right now, she loved the sense of discovery she felt whenever they spent time together.

She loved watching them get to know each other too. Some of them knew each other before the lottery, others just in the most cursory way. But now they were getting to know one another *intimately*.

Because it wasn't like she was in five separate marriages—no, it was just one big marriage. They were bound to each other as much as they were to her. She grinned to herself as she and Graham turned onto main street. Some of them took to clan life better than others.

Clark was always yelling at someone or other while Mateo often got stuck in the role of peacemaker. She loved watching Mateo come out of his shell to calmly arbitrate disputes between a hotheaded Danny and a furious Clark or Nix.

Graham needed routine and he'd had a hard time moving into the new house, with everything changing. But she loved how he'd really put in the effort to build new routines around his new clan.

She loved the way—

And then she paused, realizing the thread going through all her thoughts.

She *loved*.

She almost tripped over her feet at the revelation. Graham caught her, his eyes flipping up to hers for the briefest half second before he focused back on the pavement.

Then they kept on down the road.

But Audrey felt like she was walking a few feet above the street.

She loved them.

All of them.

When Danny said he loved her that day, she hadn't known what to say back. Plus, he'd probably just said it because of the sex. Constant orgasms would do that to a guy, wouldn't it? Sex was powerful. It made you feel things strongly. Maybe more strongly than you would ordinarily feel.

And it wasn't like they'd eased up on the sex much. Well, okay, they weren't doing the marathon twenty-four hour sex anymore, with Audrey sleeping in between the guys' work shifts.

Still, though, most nights she and at least three—and sometimes all five if they were all there at once—got their release. But equally and sometimes even more satisfying were the long minutes afterwards when the guys would hold her close.

It was hot sometimes, being surrounded by all that male body heat. But when Mateo ran his hands through her damp hair and Nix scattered kisses down her back while Clark played lazily with her still-buzzing cum-soaked pussy... God, it was like nothing else in the world.

She hadn't known goodness or satisfaction like that could still exist in the world today.

But she didn't just love them for what they could give her. She loved them for themselves.

She was married and she was in love with her husbands.

The realization had her smiling all morning while she and Sophia doled out morning porridge to the townsmen who depended on the daily communal food assistance.

With a town population of over five-thousand and more applications to settle here every day, it took a veritable army of staff to feed them.

And while Audrey couldn't say the food was exactly... a tempting feast, so to speak, she'd learned from Sophia all week long about how everything they served was carefully thought out.

Sophia took her on a tour her first official day volunteering, in between meals. "This is where the magic happens," Sophia said, clapping her hands as she took Audrey around back of the Pantry.

"You see the John Deere tractor out there?" She pointed out the back window of the Pantry's kitchen.

Audrey looked and then nodded. The tractor looked out of place in the small open space of the parking lot between the back of the Pantry and the cooking lean-to.

Since everything had to be cooked over an open flame, it was decided early on that it should be cooked separate from the Pantry building. Eventually a barn-like structure had been erected, with open walls for ventilation so the cooks didn't spontaneously combust during the heat of the Texas summers. Guards stood at posts all around, protecting the town's second most valuable resource after its water—the food.

"I could have kissed Finn when he and his Scrapper team brought this baby back." Sophia beamed at the tractor.

"I don't get it," Audrey said. The thing didn't look especially large or fancy. "Does it help you harvest the corn or something?"

"Oh no, better than that," Sophia said. "It's a John Deere Grinder-Mixer. Back in the old days I guess they used it to grind up meal for hogs? Anyway, till they brought that, we were stuck trying to grind the corn and wheat into flour with these ridiculous hand-made mills. If you don't get the meal fine enough, it gives you horrible gas and diarrhea."

Audrey nodded soberly. Chronic diarrhea could kill you in today's world. If you couldn't manage to keep weight, your chances for survival dropped considerately.

"So we all had to spend hours of back-breaking work just to get the meal fine enough. Until that beauty arrived. It can grind nine tons of wheat, barley, or cornmeal per hour."

"Holy crap," Audrey said, looking at the machine with new respect.

"Exactly," Sophia said with a wide grin.

They prepared different kinds of food for the men. Two meals a day were served. The first was at ten a.m. and it was usually a corn and bean mash—or rather, *porridge* as they called it, to make it sound more palatable.

The second meal was usually bread and soup made of whatever vegetables they'd farmed or managed to trade for that week plus, every other day, tiny amounts of meat.

"Everything a body needs, right boys?" Sophia smiled as two, big burly men brought in the huge pots of soup to serve the second meal.

"You got it, Miss Sophia," said one of the men, his eyes lingering on Sophia.

He was young, maybe just a couple years older than Sophia, and over the last couple weeks, Audrey noticed he seemed to get Pantry duty a lot more often than any of the other security guards.

Audrey nudged Sophia in the shoulder. "Hey. What's his name?" She pointed to the guy in question.

Sophia looked up from the trays she was arranging and glanced over her shoulder. "Who? Oh, you mean Griff?"

"That's his name?"

Sophia shrugged—a little too nonchalantly, Audrey thought.

"I think he *liiiiiiiiikes* you," Audrey teased.

Sophia's cheeks went pink. "He does not," she whispered, eyes glancing furtively over her shoulder again to where Griff was slicing bread.

"Hmm. Do guards usually stick around to help you guys cut the bread?"

A small frown curved Sophia's mouth. "Well, no." She glanced at Griff again. He looked up at the same time and when he saw Sophia looking his way he smiled and gave a small wave.

Sophia whipped her head back around, cheeks fully red.

"He likes you," Audrey sing-songed.

"Stop it," Sophia snapped. "He does not."

Audrey felt her eyebrows go up. "All right, all right. Touchy much?"

Sophia huffed out a loud breath through her nose. Then she turned to Audrey, looking genuinely upset. "You of anyone should know better. That's not how it works around here. When I turn twenty, I'll have a lottery. It wouldn't be fair otherwise."

Audrey put down the clean forks she'd been piling into a serving bin. "Sophia, I'm sorry for teasing you. But you do realize how screwed up what you just said is, right?"

Sophia's mouth pursed into a hard line. Then she turned away from Audrey. "You just don't understand."

Audrey let out a disbelieving noise. "I don't *understand*? Are you kidding me?"

She followed Sophia as she went out to get more clean trays from the wash station by the well out back. Graham followed them at a distance.

"Yes, you don't understand," Sophia said, eyes flashing when Audrey caught up with her. "You just show up here, not having any idea of how things work. You get five amazing husbands. And all you can do is complain about how we do things."

Aw damn, this girl was looking for a fight.

"I got lucky," Audrey said. "But you have no idea who you'll be paired with in the lottery." Audrey thought of Camila and shuddered. "Besides, haven't you ever had a crush on someone? Or thought about what it would be like to get to know someone and then fall in love?"

"Of course I dream about falling in love," Sophia said, throwing up her hands. "And I will. With my *husbands* after we're married. Arranged marriages are what people have done throughout history. And they were perfectly happy."

Audrey didn't know about that. And with Sophia being the daughter of the Commander, if Jeffries wasn't lying and they had accomplices throughout the township... what if one of those men was drawn as a husband for Sophia?

And what if... could they have any influence in the lottery itself? *Could* someone fix a lottery? Who had access to the lotto before it was placed out there on stage for the Commander to pull names?

She couldn't remember the night of her own lottery. Everything had been so crazy. Had the Commander himself pulled the names out of the box or was it someone else? But... how come *all* of Camila's five husbands just happened to be working together? That was suspicious. Really suspicious. Or did Jeffries recruit them after they all won the lottery?

It was so much to consider that it made her head hurt.

Because if they *could* influence the lottery, then... well that meant that by not saying something, Audrey could be dooming Sophia to a marriage like Camila's.

Audrey's stomach clenched. It was bad enough she felt guilty every day for not telling her clan. Now would she have to worry for every woman who had a lottery?

"I'll just take these out back," she mumbled, grabbing a stack of trays.

"I can take those," Graham said when she got halfway back to the building. He was already grabbing them out of her arms so there was nothing much to do except pull the door open for him.

"Thanks," Audrey said, glancing up at the sky. The sun was starting to drop close to the horizon. "It's almost time for dinner."

Graham nodded. "Nix should be here any minute to relieve me."

"Did I hear my name?" Nix asked, grabbing Audrey and dipping her back, giving her a deep kiss.

She gasped and laughed, smacking his shoulder. "I'm at work. Let me up."

"Not till you kiss me hello, wife." Nix grinned at her and her heart did a squishy melt thing. God she loved this man.

She rolled her eyes but landed a quick peck on his lips.

"A real kiss," he growled.

And then he took her lips in a demanding kiss that had all her worries from moments ago disappearing.

By the time he finally pulled back and helped her up to her feet again, her sex was buzzing and she was so turned on she wanted to pull Nix and Graham into the small supply closet for a quickie.

Nix must have seen the lust in her eyes because he swatted her ass and said, "Patience is a virtue. And there's a line of hungry men outside waiting to get fed."

"Fine," she sighed dramatically. And saw Sophia watching them with a longing expression on her face.

"See," Sophia said as they lined up to serve men their daily soup and bread. "That's what I want. What you have with your clan."

Audrey looked at Sophia. She was so young. But she wasn't a kid. She'd grown up in this world the same as Audrey had. Audrey reached over and quickly squeezed her hand. "I want that for you, too. More than anything."

Sophia flashed her a smile. But Audrey still felt the weight of all her secrets more acutely than ever.

————

The Food Pantry was set up so that they fed the waiting men through a large open window at the front of the building. Each man got a small tray, a bowl of sprouted oat and cornmeal mash or soup and bread, depending on what meal it was.

Since it was the afternoon meal, it was soup and bread. It was late in the day, almost sunset, and a jazz band had set up in the town square right outside. It had been a warm early summer day, but not too hot.

People were out all around the square. Listening to the band. Chatting and laughing. Eating. Sharing gossip. Kids ran around shrieking and giggling. Some people were even dancing, a handful of women in the crowd laughing and partnering indiscriminately with lots of men.

Audrey couldn't help smiling at the peaceful, idyllic scene. Three months ago, she wouldn't have believed that a place like this could exist. But here it was. Somewhere out of time. Sure life here wasn't exactly like it had been before The Fall—nowhere ever could be—but it was still a place that would make anyone hopeful for a real future.

About halfway through serving the meal, a man wearing the same fatigues Nix always did showed up. Audrey was ladling soup into a row of bowls and watched out of the corner of her eye as Nix and the man had a tense conversation.

Finally Nix gave a decisive nod and then turned and came over to Audrey. He had to shout to be heard above the blaring trumpets. "There's a situation at Squadron command. I have to go."

Without even thinking about it, Audrey's hand shot out to grasp his forearm. He couldn't go. She was only safe when she was with him. Or another of her clan.

"Can you get Graham or Clark?" she asked, searching his eyes. "Or Danny or Mateo?"

His mouth was a hard line as he shook his head. "No time. But this is Wayne." He clapped the man in dark fatigues on the back. "He's a good man. He'll take care of you."

Audrey's eyes flicked over to Wayne. He nodded reassuringly at her.

Audrey looked back to Nix and leaned in. "Are you *sure?*"

Nix frowned and Audrey realized how odd it would be if she insisted she didn't feel safe without him. It would only bring up more questions she couldn't answer without endangering his life.

He seemed to trust Wayne. That would have to be enough for now.

"Okay," Audrey forced a smile and reached up to kiss Nix on his cheek. "Be safe."

She continued serving the meal, Wayne taking up residence in Nix's place in the corner.

It's just like having Nix there, she tried to console herself.

Okay, so, no, it wasn't.

But she'd be fine. She'd get through her shift and then head back to the house. Danny and Mateo would be home just after sunset, right about the same time she and Sophia had finished handing things over to the dishwashers and locking up.

Close to the last half hour, when the end of the line was actually visible, Sophia had just pulled the lid off a fresh soup pot when she came up and yelled in Audrey's ear, "Hey, can you go back to the supply closet to get some more salt? We're almost out."

She gestured with her head toward the shaker they kept at the serving window. Men were theoretically allowed only three shakes, but Sophia and Audrey were usually more generous. Yes, they needed salt for making jerky and a number of other activities, but salt was one of the few supplies they were never short on.

Audrey nodded as she finished ladling soup into a short, leathery-faced man's bowl. She headed toward the back, but only after making sure Wayne was right on her heels.

It was dark in the back of the building since night was falling outside. The quiet was nice after the loud music of the past hour, though. Maybe next time she'd request the band set up a *little* further away from the Food Pantry.

She stumbled when she ran into a box she hadn't seen on the shadowy floor. She should have brought a candle with her. Oh well.

There was just enough light not to run into most things at least, though the closet would probably be pitch black. The bucket of salt was right inside the door on the left though. There were several there, all stacked up. She could just grab one and bring it out so she could fill up the—

A hand clapped over her mouth from behind. She was yanked backwards against a hard body.

She screeched and struggled, but whoever it was, a man obviously, had too firm a grip.

Wayne! Where was Wayne?

Could he see her? Had his eyes not adjusted to the dim light yet?

She looked frantically left and right but couldn't see him. Where the *hell* was he?

"Looks like we're going to finally have that alone time, cunt."

Jeffries. Of course.

A shudder of revulsion rocked Audrey's body.

Stupid. So fucking *stupid* to think she could avoid ending up right back in this position.

Then again, she'd run through what had happened in the candle shop that day a thousand times. And a thousand times, she'd thought through what she would have done different.

Jeffries was so fucking unimaginative, he'd attacked in exactly the same way.

He wasn't the only one who could take advantage of the element of surprise. She couldn't waste a second, though.

She angled her body slightly to the side, pulled her elbow forward, and then jammed it backwards as hard as she could into his kidneys.

He gasped in pain but still managed to keep hold of her.

Okay, then Plan B.

She went completely limp and lifted her arms all the way up, slipping down like an eel out from underneath his grasp.

Then she scrambled forward, crawling and then stumbling to her feet and trying to run. She'd barely gone two feet before Jeffries grabbed her arm and swung her around.

Her arm. He'd grabbed her arm.

She knew what to do when someone grabbed her like this.

The thousands of drills she'd run with Charlie and Uncle Dale back in the bunker were so ingrained, it was muscle memory to lock his hand in the crevasse of her elbow.

And then to strike the back of his elbow with the flat of her palm.

The snap of his bone breaking was only drowned out by Jeffries's roar of pain.

Audrey sprinted back toward the front of the shop when a wall suddenly appeared in front of her.

She was about to attack again when she realized it was Wayne.

"Oh thank God," she said, breathing out in relief. "He just attacked m—"

Wayne gripped her shoulders in a crushing hold. "You tell anyone a single word and we kill one of your husbands. You think that pile of bricks just *happened* to fall on that friend of your idiot husband? The guy who died in the hospital later that day? Your husband was standing in that exact spot where the bricks fell just five minutes earlier."

Audrey couldn't help a small cry of anguish.

Nix trusted this man.

Just like he trusts Jeffries.

"Get your fucking hands off me," she growled.

"Keep your mouth *shut* or Danny won't be an innocent bystander next time," Wayne said coolly.

"You're gonna pay, you fucking bitch," Jeffries snarled from the ground behind her. "And when I get my hands on you again, you're gonna give me exactly what I want."

Audrey jerked away from Wayne and he let her go. She bolted for the front of the building.

The music that had seemed so jovial earlier now sounded like a screaming cacophony. There were too many people in the square. Too many strangers. Too many potential accomplices who could be working with Jeffries.

She could barely hear Sophia calling after her, the trumpets and saxophone were blaring so loudly. And Audrey didn't stop or slow down to explain her sudden departure.

Because she'd just realized a horrible, horrible truth.

There was only ever one solution to the threat Jeffries and his thugs posed.

And next to losing her family, it would be the hardest thing she'd ever had to do.

CHAPTER THIRTY-SIX

CLARK

Two Weeks Later

"You want to do WHAT?" Clark shouted, shoving his chair backwards as he got to his feet. "No. Absolutely fucking not. Nix. Tell her."

But Nix just sat calm as could be on the living room sofa, eyes on Audrey. "Let's hear what she has to say."

What the fuck?

"Look," Audrey said, leaning forward and clasping her hands over her knees. "I'm not running away. I'm trusting you. All of you. I'm coming to you and asking for your help."

Clark couldn't believe what he was hearing.

She wanted to leave.

Everything had been going so great. She'd been happy. Really happy. At least he thought so.

Then, a couple weeks ago, she started withdrawing again. It wasn't like the first time, though. She didn't lay around in bed all the time. No, she kept on going out. Volunteering. Staying active.

But she started locking the door to the master bedroom at night.

Locking all of them out.

At first he just thought she was having her monthly. But then even at meals, she barely spoke. Not even to Mateo, and that guy had the patience of a saint. He'd sit with her for hours, neither of them saying a word.

Nix said to give her time. That women had moody spells.

So fine. Clark had been waiting.

But then she came downstairs today, sat them all down to talk, and announced that she wanted to leave them and go to Nomansland.

Fucking bullshit.

Audrey shook her head and looked down into her lap. "I just..." She took a deep breath and looked back up at them. "I can't stay here anymore. I thought for a second..."

But then she shook her head decisively. "But I just can't. I know the coastal colony exists. If you can just help me get there—"

Clark couldn't listen to this for another second.

"Are you fucking insane?" he shouted, shooting up off the couch across from where she sat on a chair by the fireplace. "You could be pregnant with our son or daughter already."

Her mouth dropped open for a second but then she said confidently, "I'm not."

"And how can you be so sure?" Clark asked, all but getting up in her face. "You could be carrying our son or daughter in there," he gestured toward her stomach.

"I'm not," she bit out.

"How do you know?" Clark objected.

"I just had my period, okay?" She threw her hands up.

Clark swallowed and he could see some of the other guys reacting just as hard to the news. She wasn't pregnant. He didn't even have the brain space to process that at the moment or why he was so disappointed.

He shook his head again. "It doesn't matter. Nomansland is a fairytale."

He looked at the rest of the guys.

And saw Nix and Graham exchange a look. A significant fucking look.

"What?" Clark demanded. "What the hell was that look?"

Graham looked to Nix. Who sighed and then nodded.

"Nomansland is real," Graham said.

They could have heard a pin drop.

"What?" Clark said at the same time as Mateo and Danny. Audrey just nodded.

"Tell them," Nix said, his voice toneless.

"After Audrey ran away... *tried* to run away. I looked into it. Searched the dark web. It was like she said. There's a video of a woman. You have to be a woman if you want to contact her. But then she'll supposedly send you a set of coordinates. You meet. If you're legitimate, her team will take you back with them to Nomansland."

"How the fuck could you keep this from us?" Clark's blood was so hot he felt like he was going to erupt.

"I didn't think it was..." Graham swallowed, looking at Audrey, "—applicable information anymore."

"But Audrey," Mateo asked, brow furrowed in pain, "Why? I thought you were happy here with us."

"Why?" She blinked, like she couldn't understand the question. "How can you even ask me that?" She looked around at all of them. "I've always wanted to leave. From the very first moment I was dragged unconscious into this town. You thought that had changed?"

Silence.

She looked at each of them, one by one, and shook her head with a dark, disbelieving laugh.

"I never wanted this. But no one gave me a choice, did they?" She stood up so quickly, her hair flew out around her.

"None of you gave me a say in any of it. So fine. I tried to make the best of it. I tried to..." She swallowed hard and looked toward the window. "...*forget*." The word was a raspy whisper.

Clark hated the pain in her voice, but she wasn't being fair. "We never made you do *anything* you didn't want to. We didn't force—"

Her eyes flashed. "What else was I going to do? It was made very clear to me. I had three months to consummate this *marriage*. I decided to make it on my terms."

Clark took a step back. Was she trying to say that— Did she think they'd— The whole reason he'd settled in this town was because they *didn't* force women. And now she was—

"I made the best of a bad situation," she said, her voice shaking. "But I never had a choice. Several of you have told me you love me." Her whole body was trembling now and every instinct in Clark's body screamed at him to pull her into his arms.

Even as the words coming out of her mouth were knives in his chest.

"But how could I ever love you back when I was never given a choice in any of it?" Her words were an anguished cry. "How could this," she waved her hands at the space between herself and them, "ever be *love?*"

Yes," she swallowed hard, nodding, "you made my prison bearable for a little while." Her jaw clenched and her eyes went hard. "But that's *all* this will ever be." She waved at the house. The town.

Then, she put the final nail in the coffin.

"And that's all this marriage ever was. A prison. And you're the prison guards. Who occasionally like to fuck the inmate."

Mateo flinched. He wasn't the only one.

Danny was outright crying.

Nix clenched his jaw so hard he was probably about to crack a tooth.

And Clark?

He was only ever in this for the sex. He'd just wanted to fuck with a clean conscience. He'd certainly never told Audrey he loved her.

So why the hell did his chest feel squeezed in a vice so tight it seemed like he'd never pull in another full breath again?

Danny stepped forward, looking around at all of them. "I know I'm not as smart as all y'all." He swiped at his cheek and dripping nose. "But I say loving someone means giving them the freedom to stay with you or not. What we did was wrong. She should have the choice."

He swallowed and then coughed, like he was barely holding his shit together. "Even if it means she chooses leaving us."

Mateo was shaking his head but Nix took a deep breath and stepped forward to stand by Danny. "If it's safe and it's what you want, we'll get you there."

What? What the fuck?

"Audrey," Clark said, her name barely coming out as more than a whisper. He shook his head. He'd never begged for anything in his life before, but he was begging now. "Please. Don't go."

When she turned her face away from him, the heart he never knew he had shattered into a thousand tiny pieces.

And her next words ground whatever was left into dust. "We leave as soon as possible."

CHAPTER THIRTY-SEVEN

AUDREY

Just a little longer. Just a little longer and then you won't have to see the hurt in their eyes anymore. God, she'd never forget the look on Clark's face that night. Like she'd *destroyed* him.

He'd gone out after that and three days later, he'd only come back with bloodshot eyes and skin so sickly looking she wondered if he'd been on a three-day bender. As Assistant Trade Secretary, he was one of the few people who could get his hands on enough booze to do so.

The last three days had been among the worst of her life. Comparable with the days after losing Dad and Charlie.

Except this time she didn't make herself numb. She let herself feel all of it. And she relished every last moment in each man's company, even if she couldn't show it.

She had to keep up the act, the façade that she wanted nothing more than to be rid of them and this place.

You're saving their lives, she whispered to herself a million times a day.

She refused, she *refused*, to get someone else she loved killed. Much less five someones.

Still, it didn't make it any easier when Danny sidled close to her, his eyes a mix of confusion, hurt, and love. Or Mateo with his determination to predict and provide for her every whim. She couldn't count the cups of tea and soup and pieces of bread he'd brought her the past few days. Somehow, last night, he even managed to produce a bowl of chocolate pudding for her.

He must be stealing from the kitchen supplies and she wanted to chastise him for it, knowing he could get in serious trouble for doing so. She didn't, though, because she knew it was his way of showing love when she was denying him every other avenue.

Graham had been holed up with his computer. He'd arranged the face-to-face interview for her and the Nomansland rep. Suffice to say the woman was shocked to see Audrey three months later after she no-showed the first time.

"These stories rarely have happy endings," the woman, Mara, said, an exhausted knowing in her eyes. "It's good to see this one will."

Audrey nodded, barely able to manage a smile as her mind screamed, *This is not a happy ending. It's a tragedy.*

New coordinates were set. Audrey was to meet a woman named Jade, who Mara briefly introduced on screen so they'd be able to verify each other's identification at the meet.

She only gave Graham a perfunctory thank you and then left.

No one else will get hurt because of me.

Nix made it the most difficult out of all of them.

Not because he got mad or yelled or had any of the hundred reactions she would have expected of him. He was quiet and calm, going about all the tasks that needed doing before they left.

Closing up the house. They'd be going back to their quarters they had before she'd come. Without her, they would no longer be a clan. Talk about driving a knife through her chest.

Nix was also working closer with Mateo to get the helicopter prepped.

Yep, the *helicopter*.

Mateo had officially gotten permission from the Commander to take it out on its maiden voyage.

The trip that would have taken her and Charlie weeks on foot would only take a little over an hour and a half by helicopter.

But Nix. She didn't understand why he was acting the way he was. How was he staying so calm? Nothing in her relationship with him would explain his current behavior.

She constantly felt like she was walking on eggshells every time she was around him. She kept waiting for it. Where was the eruption? The screaming? The accusations?

It was midmorning and Nix was helping her put together a backpack of stuff to take with her.

Totally silently. He hadn't said a word for the last fifteen minutes.

She couldn't take it anymore. She slammed the backpack down on the bed and swung around to face him. "Okay, what's the deal? Where's the shouting? Why aren't you calling me a selfish bitch for hurting everyone?"

She expected to see the usual spark that lit in his eye when she challenged him like this. And it's not that it wasn't there—it was. His nostrils flared and his eyes went dark. But it was like— He didn't seem angry. She blinked in confusion. He just looked like he did when he was about to grab her and ravage her.

Her breath caught in her chest. Yes. Oh God, yes. One last time. Or maybe a thousand last times.

She felt her bottom lip start to tremble and she bit down on it hard. She wrapped her arms around herself, forcing herself not to reach out for him.

Still, his eyes were locked on hers, and he seemed about two point three seconds away from pulling her into his arms and grabbing her leg to lift it up and around his hip like he'd done so many times—

"Guys!" Clark's shout came from downstairs as the front door slammed closed. Both Audrey and Nix jerked to look toward the door as Clark continued calling out, "Nix. Audrey. Time to go. *Right now!*"

"Shit," Nix swore, running a hand through his hair. Then he was a whir of action, throwing a few more pairs of underwear and socks into

Audrey's backpack, zipping it, and pulling it over one shoulder. "Let's go, babe. It's time."

Audrey frowned in confusion as Nix put a hand at the small of her back and ushered her toward the door. "I thought I wasn't leaving till tomorr—"

Clark met them in the hallway and gestured them impatiently toward the stairs. "Chop chop. We don't have all day." He looked down at his watch. "Literally. We have about an hour until the Commander gets back, so we gotta get gone."

Audrey let herself be hurried down the stairs but she was still so confused. "I don't get what the rush is. Does the Commander need the helicopter for something later?"

Nix and Clark exchanged a look.

Audrey let out a huff. "What aren't you telling me?"

"We might never have *exactly* provided the Commander the opportunity to acquiesce to our requisition request," Clark said as he took over for Nix, steering her toward the back door.

"What?"

"Just speak plain English," Nix growled. "We never asked if we could take it."

Audrey gasped, swinging Nix's direction as Clark pushed the back door open.

"What are you talking about?" Audrey cried. "I thought you asked him if we could take it."

"More like you assumed we asked."

"But," Audrey sputtered.

"No buts," Clark said.

"I don't know," Nix smirked. "She might need a boost over the fence. I'm happy to provide any and all derriere support."

Why wouldn't they be serious? "So we're going to steal the helicopter?" she asked, still trying to figure out what the hell was going on. "But I've heard you talking."

She looked at Clark. "You said President Goddard himself was interested in the helicopter restoration. Wouldn't stealing it be..." she threw her hands up in exasperation, "I don't know, treason or something?"

"Not stealing. Borrowing," Clark said, arranging his knee and putting his hands on it as a base to boost Audrey over the fence. "We're *borrowing* it. Now. Up."

When she didn't move fast enough, Nix grabbed her leg, almost knocking her off balance, and lifted her foot into Clark's waiting hands.

Before she could say anything else, they were boosting her up and there was nothing to do except grasp the top of the fence and swing her leg over.

"Careful," Nix hissed when she grunted in pain, scraping her arm on the rough wood at the top of the fence slats.

She rolled her eyes and managed to lower herself over the other side far more gracefully than the last time she'd attempted this.

Which was when it struck her. This was a total déjà vu moment. Except now Nix and Clark were on her side. The other guys too. To pull off *borrowing* the helicopter, it would no doubt take all five of them.

"Where are the others?" she asked as soon as Clark and Nix cleared the fence.

"Mateo and Danny will meet us there. Graham won't be able to make it. We'll need him as our ground support in the tech command center."

Audrey blinked, barely able to take everything in. Were they saying that she wouldn't get to see Graham. As in, ever again? That their last interaction, which she could barely even remember—maybe she'd passed him the salt at dinner last night?—was it? The last thing she'd ever say to him was, 'sure, here you go'? The last time she'd touch him was their fingers brushing over a fucking salt shaker?

Her stomach swooped so violently she was sure she was going to throw up.

Oh God.

This was real.

She was actually leaving them.

After today, she'd never see any of them again.

But they'd be alive. They wouldn't be like Dad and Charlie. Killed and probably left to rot for carrion.

Anyway, there was no time to think about it right now because Nix had grabbed her hand and was pulling her forward into a run along the back fence line of the neighborhood. She could tell he was intentionally going slow for her but she could still barely keep up.

Eventually they made their way to the end of the neighborhood fencing. At the back of Camila and Jeffries's house.

Audrey swallowed down the bile that even being there brought up. If it wasn't for that evil bastard, she could have—

She breathed out and cut the thought off before she could even finish it. No. There was no use in 'what ifs.' They wouldn't do her any good. There was only what was.

"We didn't want to take the main road to announce we were heading to the shop, but just pretend we're taking a walk in case anyone happens to be going by and looks this direction," Nix murmured, his hand tightening around hers as he pulled her into the open field heading for the woods at the other side of the small clearing. "Look normal."

Audrey nodded and tried to adopt as normal an expression as she could. Difficult when she felt about three seconds from meltdown, her mind shouting really useful things at her like: *This could be the last time you'll ever hold Nix's hand. This is the last time you'll ever see Clark's face.*

Only Nix and Mateo would be going with her on the helicopter to take her to the rendezvous point. There were only three seats so they were all that would fit.

Which meant in about ten minutes, she'd have to say goodbye to Clark and Danny forever. And only a short while longer with Nix and Mateo and then—

Clark took one of her arms while they strolled across the field while Nix held her other hand. And for a second, Audrey managed to shut her brain off.

If these were her last moments with them, she didn't want to ruin them with her freaking out and grief about what was coming next. There'd be plenty time for that later, she had no doubt.

But right now, for one more minute, five more minutes, they were there on either side of her, their bodies warm and reassuring. Her husbands. Her family. Her clan.

And no matter the fact that she was being ripped away from them and had to hurt them to do it, they would always be her family in her heart. She'd hold them there no matter what came next. She'd love them for the rest of her life.

The field wasn't small, but it felt like they were across it in seconds. And then they started running again, through the woods just out of sight of the road.

Nix crept up to the road when they came close to the workshop. After looking left and right, he gestured for Clark and Audrey to hurry forward. They crossed the road quickly and then Nix ordered them to act normal again as they walked around to the back of the old grocery building to the loading dock.

Danny was waiting outside, chatting and laughing with a couple of guys on smoke break. He was obviously on alert though, because the second they appeared at the edge of the once parking lot, he straightened up.

He clapped the guy he was talking to on the back and then headed in their direction.

"Took you long enough," he said when he got to them. His eyes softened when they fell on Audrey, though. "Hey beautiful." He reached out a hand and took hers. His eyebrows furrowed. "Are you sure you want to do this? You don't have to go. I want you to stay. We all want you to stay. We lov—

Audrey snatched her hand back. "I'm going."

Danny swallowed and Audrey hated the way his entire body reacted to her words, like she'd slapped him. He tried to play it off with a smile, but it was so obviously forced, Audrey wanted to run away and curl up in a ball somewhere.

Instead she straightened her spine. "Mateo's inside?"

Danny shook his head. "The helicopter's around the corner. This way." He turned abruptly to lead the way and Audrey wondered if it was because he didn't want her to see the tears he was fighting back. Her chest clenched but she forced her feet to move forward. *Just a little more. Just a little longer.*

Audrey thought she'd been prepared for the helicopter. But when they rounded the corner and it came into view, she couldn't help her eyes widening. And her head tilting to the side.

Because... um.

"Are you sure that thing actually flies?" she whispered.

It was ancient. Like ancient, ancient. This thing probably first flew when black and white TVs were all the rage.

There was barely anything to it. Just a huge bubble window around the front of it that covered a bench seat with three harness seatbelts. No back seat. No... anything else.

She took another few steps forward hoping that maybe it would seem more substantial up close but nope. That was it.

Literally right behind the back wall of the seats was the big engine she'd seen in the shop. Then there were the rotating blades on top, landing skids on bottom, and two running boards along the side she assumed were for medical litters for transporting the wounded and... that was pretty much it.

"I've witnessed it go up in the air and come back down again if that's what you're asking," Clark said with a clip to his voice.

Um. Wow. "You're really crappy at this whole reassurance thing," she muttered.

"You can see it's a rust bucket." Clark turned on her. His face was dark and he waved a hand toward the helicopter behind him. "There's no way in hell you should go up in that thing. I literally saw Mateo duct taping over a hole where it had rusted through the floorboard. Don't do this."

Audrey stared at the ground, jaw hard. Was she going to have to go through this song and dance with each of them?

"Nix, do you think it's safe?"

She didn't look up at him but she felt his body stiffen beside her. For a second, he didn't say anything and she wondered if he would. Was this his breaking point? Was he going to lose it on her now?

But then he just said, "Mateo would never risk your life. If he says it's safe, it's safe."

Then he started striding toward the helicopter. Audrey took a deep breath and followed him.

As they rounded the helicopter, she finally saw Mateo. He was holding a gas can, filling up the tank while that annoying guy she'd met the first time she was here, his manager or superior or whatever, stood over him yelling.

"What do you think you're doing? I told you it doesn't need to be gassed up until President Goddard visits next week. Are you such a stupid piece of shit you can't understand the words *next week*? Should I put it in your people's language? *No bien*," he said in a terribly exaggerated Hispanic accent. "Gassing up now is *no bien*, understand dumbass?"

"For fuck's sake," Nix muttered darkly.

"Did he really just call him a dumbass when he didn't even know he was mixing up French and Spanish?" Clark said. "Seriously, who the fuck doesn't know *bueno*?"

Mateo didn't move a muscle. He just upended the canister more steeply to continue pouring the gas.

"Hey, fuck-head, did you not hear me?" The man grabbed Mateo's shoulder so hard the gas canister flew out of his hands and fell to the pavement where gas started pouring out, *glug, glug, glug*.

"Look what you did, you fucking moron! Pick it up. And that's coming out of your pay. Sure as shit, I'm docking you—"

Mateo slowly bent over and righted the can of gas, then stood back up.

Audrey had spent the day with Mateo a few times at the shop. And every time it was like he shrank several inches. His shoulders dropped and curved slightly inward. His head dropped, face always down. And he stayed in that position unless he was working with one of the other mechanics, helping them to solve some problem or other.

And at first, that was the posture he stayed in as his boss kept haranguing him. "What a stupid, worthless, piece of shit. Can't even do one thing right. Plus what's that under the tarp on the left medical litter? Did you put the test dummy on there already, too? What a fucking idiot. It's just gonna get stolen if you leave it out here. You shouldn't have even been working on such a sensitive project in the first place. What would President Goddard think if he came and saw this kind of incompetence? You're officially off the team. I guess I'll have to be the one to show him our newest contribution to the country—"

"Enough of this assfuck," Nix growled, starting forward.

But in that same moment, Mateo stood up.

Like, *really* stood up.

Right before her eyes, he seemed to gain a foot. His shoulders went back, his chin tipped up, and his chest went out. It turned out, at his full height, he was actually *taller* than his asshole boss. *Ha.*

Asshole boss—she couldn't remember his name—seemed to realize it at the same time. But he just seemed annoyed by the fact.

He started shaking his finger in Mateo's face and kept on yelling and insulting him. "And what's that on the—"

Which was when Mateo reared back and punched him. Hard too, from the way the guy staggered backward and then fell on his ass.

"Now," Mateo yelled.

Audrey wanted to cheer for Mateo but suddenly Clark and Nix were rushing her forward. Mateo was already climbing in the pilot's side and moments later, the blades started whirring overhead.

Which did not go unnoticed.

Even as Nix hurried her up and helped her into the center of the bench seat beside Mateo, she saw men pouring out of the workshop. As well as a couple guards.

Ever since she'd broken in that night to steal the motorcycle and tranqued the guard, they'd set more security on the place. And they came out now with their guns drawn.

"Oh my God," Audrey whispered.

It was going to happen again.

They were going to get killed because of her after all.

"S-stop," she whispered but her voice barely made any noise, or if it did, it was lost in the roar of the chopper blades picking up speed. "Surrender." Panic spiked through her chest. She swung her head in Nix's direction.

"We have to surrender," she shouted, trying to be heard. "Put your hands up. Don't let them shoot."

She demonstrated by putting her hands up, but Nix only used that as an opportunity to pull the harness down over her head and start buckling it.

"No," she tried to grab his hands. "They'll shoot you!" she shouted but he just shook his head.

"They won't shoot the chopper," he shouted in her ear.

Was that supposed to be comforting? She looked out the front windshield at where Clark stood just barely out of the circumference of the whirring helicopter blades. At least he had the sense to have his hands up. Wind from the blades whipped at his face and clothes. The guards approached him, heads moving back and forth between him and the helicopter.

So they didn't see Danny when he snuck up behind the one who'd lagged slightly further back than the others.

Audrey jumped and her hand shot to her mouth when Danny grabbed the guy from behind. In a single fluid motion, he yanked the semi-automatic out of his hand and slammed him over the back of the head with the butt of the gun.

"Holy shit," Audrey exclaimed.

Nix only turned to look as Danny did a similar move to disarm the second guard. The helicopter blades were so loud, the other guards didn't hear a thing.

As Danny snuck up on the third guy, though, the man swung around, rifle in firing position at his shoulder. But Danny had picked up one of the other guard's guns and before the man could get a shot off, Danny fired a round into his knee.

Audrey didn't hear Nix's whistle but she saw his lips form the little circle.

Then Mateo was smacking at Nix's chest and gesturing to his harness. Nix nodded and pulled it down over his head.

Moments after he clicked it in place, Mateo pulled up on a long lever to the left of his seat, gripped a controller extending from the dash in front of him, and pumped at the pedals with his feet.

He was pulling and shifting and stomping them in a complicated pattern and suddenly they lifted off the ground.

Audrey shrieked and grabbed for her harness at the jerky movement. The left side pulled sharply up before Mateo compensated and righted it.

They made it up about ten or fifteen feet. And then nosedived for the ground. Audrey screamed.

Oh God, *oh God*, they were all gonna *die*.

"Charlie," she whispered, eyes squeezing shut. But then her eyes shot open again as the helicopter swung upwards, sending her stomach through the floor.

She looked over at Nix, who was already staring straight at her. She moved her white-knuckled grip from her harness to grab his hand.

She registered the surprise on his face. But she didn't care that she was breaking character. She couldn't pretend to be a bitch right now.

If they died in the next few seconds, what the hell would any of the rest of it matter? She held onto Nix like he was her lifeline.

And he was. He had been almost since she'd gotten to the township, if she was honest.

Okay, at first he'd scared the shit out of her. She felt like laughing hysterically as the chopper took another dramatic swing, this time to the left. She stared out the window at the ground that was probably thirty feet below them now.

But soon, almost within that first week, she'd known Nix would keep her safe no matter how crazy he drove her.

He intertwined his fingers with hers and moved his other hand to cover it as well. Lending her his strength.

God, she loved him so much. She loved him. She loved all of them. She loved them so much.

Her stomach felt scooped out as the helicopter wobbled back and forth crazily several more times.

Mateo was pulling back on the central control so hard his arm shook.

But then finally, finally, everything smoothed out.

They started moving forward and suddenly it was like the rough take off had never even happened. They were gliding through the sky smooth as a bird in flight.

Audrey coughed out several shocked gasping laughs, then looked at

Nix and grinned. He gripped her hand even harder, bringing it to his lips for a kiss.

For a second their gazes locked, both of them caught up in the joy of being alive and having escaped and...

The smile died on her face.

And now she still had to go through with her plan.

She turned her face away from Nix.

But even though she knew it was stupid and sent the wrong message, she couldn't bring herself to let go of his hand.

CHAPTER THIRTY-EIGHT

NIX

Audrey held his hand for the entire two-hour ride. She shifted several times and they'd had to readjust their hold, but she always let him take it again.

He didn't let himself think about what would happen when the chopper landed. He didn't let himself think about the fact that for the last two weeks, she'd been acting so strange and withdrawn he could barely sleep at night but for worrying about her.

He didn't let himself think about anything except memorizing the warm strength of her hand in his and the feel of her small body against his side on the bench seat.

They couldn't talk on the ride. It was too loud. Once upon a time there might have been headphones and microphones, but those were long gone.

So Nix held onto Audrey and snuck glances at her every chance he got.

And the two hour ride was over far too fast.

No, not yet, it can't be over yet, Nix thought when Mateo looked at the GPS device Graham had lent them and started to descend.

But they were dropping out of the sky toward an open field.

No doubt the heads of everyone they'd passed the last two hours had leapt to the sky but this particular spot was fairly uninhabited. Graham had double-checked satellite feed this morning and there had been minimal human activity and no encampments or known settlements nearby.

Wherever Nomansland was, it wasn't in a thirty-mile radius of the rendezvous location. There was just farmland all around. Galveston and Texas City were the nearest big cities, about forty miles east. The coast was fifteen to twenty minutes south. About sixty miles southeast was the Demilitarized Zone between Texas and Mexico where a tentative peace was holding after almost a decade of fighting. They'd flown over Houston just a little before sunset. It was still just a huge crater from where the bomb had hit.

Still, Nix lifted his leg and pulled both guns he had holstered at his ankles. *Better safe than sorry* had long been his mantra, especially for this mission.

Well, along with, *it's better to ask forgiveness than permission.* They'd never actually asked the Commander if they could use the chopper. Only because Nix knew he'd say *hell no.*

It was always better to avoid disobeying a direct order when possible. As for the hell he and the guys would catch when they got home? Well, they'd face that when the time came.

All that mattered right now was Audrey.

Audrey.

Her face was white as a sheet, gaze locked with Nix's as the ground grew closer and closer. She was so fuckin' beautiful. She was perfect. She was everything.

And he didn't understand. The way she'd clung to him for the ride. Even how she was looking at him now. Like she was going to a funeral. Not claiming her freedom, like she said she wanted.

Her hand had to be cramping from how hard she'd been holding his for the whole ride but she squeezed even harder as they came in for the landing.

Graham and Mateo had mapped out a landing area in an old abandoned Walmart parking lot right by the park where the Nomansland rep had arranged to meet.

Audrey squeezed her eyes shut and kept them closed the whole five minutes it took for Mateo to bring them down and, with more than a few bumps, land the copter.

Nix didn't have it in him to breathe out in relief though.

Because landing meant that Audrey was going to leave them.

Or maybe she wouldn't. Maybe this terrifying ride—and facing possible death—had made her rethink her priorities. She'd wanted a choice. Well now she had one. And maybe she'd realized she could choose them of her own free will and it would change everything—

But then she snatched her hand out of Nix's and immediately reached to release the straps of her harness.

It was a knife to Nix's guts.

He was bleeding from the goddamned inside out.

You knew this was a mistake from the beginning. It's your fault for not marching right up to the Commander the second your name was drawn and not setting him straight. There was a reason you didn't get involved.

It was the same voice that had been shouting at him ever since Audrey told them she was leaving.

Audrey pushed the harness over her head and then, when Nix didn't move fast enough for her, she climbed over his lap, grabbed the side of the helicopter, and climbed down.

She looked wobbly as hell. Fuck, she was gonna faceplant if she wasn't careful.

Nix jerked at his own harness. Goddamned fucking buckles. He ripped at the restraints, trying to get free, his stomach lurching with every unsteady step Audrey took.

She stopped with her hands on her knees, looking like she was about to throw up.

Nix finally got the damned buckle undone and he launched himself down to her side. "Are you okay?" he asked, putting a hand to the small of her back. "Babe, you okay?"

Not that she could hear him with the roar of the rotor blades still whirring but she nodded anyway, pressing a hand to her forehead and standing up.

When she stumbled to the side slightly, Nix immediately steadied her.

And reached the conclusion he had every other time that stupid voice spoke up.

He took her arm and pulled her further away from the copter.

"Earlier, you asked me why I hadn't exploded." He had to speak loudly, but the helicopter was getting quieter and quieter every moment and Audrey seemed to be able to hear him. "Why I wasn't yelling and screaming."

Audrey nodded uncertainly.

Time to put it all on the table. He had to try one last time.

"I told you about my sister, Roxy."

Another hesitant nod.

"After she died, I just cut off." Nix slashed his hand down. "Detached. Nobody and nothing was getting in here again."

He thumped his chest. "Nothing was worth that kind of pain. Nothing. So I did my job. Fought in the war. Risked my life sometimes. Played it safe others. It didn't matter to me. Nothing did. That was the point. I spent the last eight years making sure nothing mattered."

He took a step closer to her. "Until you."

He saw her heavy swallow and the tremble to her bottom lip. Was he getting through to her? Fuck knew he wasn't a praying man, but he'd say a thousand Hail Marys every day the rest of his life if she could just *hear* him.

"I tried at first. I thought I could keep you at arm's length. I could do my job—protect you—without it getting beyond that. Without getting too close."

He was the one swallowing now. "Without falling in love with you. But I was wrong. Jesus fuck was I wrong."

She started shaking her head back and forth but he'd started and he was going to finish.

"The reason I haven't screamed and yelled this week is because I finally realized the reason I was so scared of loving anyone wasn't just because of how much it hurt when I lost Roxy. It's of how absolutely *terrified* I've been of ever letting anyone down like I did her. She loved me. Trusted me to keep her safe. And then she died in the most horrific way possible because I failed her."

"Nix, don't," Audrey said, mouth working as she looked away, blinking rapidly and obviously fighting back tears.

"Letting you go do this is my worst fucking fear," he bit out. "Falling in love with you was one thing. I thought, fine. I just won't let her out of my sight. I'll just guard her twenty-four hours a day. Not that I knew I was doing it because I loved you at first."

He barked out a rough laugh. "Or maybe I'm just an ass and I liked how pissed off it used to make you."

He caught her wobbly smile even though she tried to mask it a second later, still blinking furiously and refusing to look his way.

"But this week I finally realized this is what love is. It's not something I can control like my command squadron. I'm not even sure it's something I ever had a choice in. And even if I did. You're worth it. You're worth the pain. You're worth the fucking years of agony ahead of me if you walk away from me right now. You're worth risking everything for. Because I love you."

He reached a hand toward her cheek and she jerked violently backwards.

Finally, finally she looked at him.

She was breathing so hard her nostrils were flaring in and out and there was a sheen of tears over her eyes that she seemed determined not to let fall.

She shook her head, chin trembling harder than ever. "I'm going to be late."

And then she turned and fled in the direction of the park.

CHAPTER THIRTY-NINE

AUDREY

Audrey was still swiping at her eyes and heaving for breath when she rounded the corner of the overgrown path and a voice said, "You're late."

The woman who stepped out of the trees was thin, stern-faced, and empty of all humor as she looked Audrey up and down. Her dark brown hair was cropped close to her head and she had an automatic rifle in her arms, held in such a way that it was clear she knew how to use it.

"Sorry," Audrey said. Her voice came out low and scratchy. God, everything Nix had said—it was like he was intentionally trying to make sure her heart was shredded through a meatgrinder. Opening up like that. God.

But then she pictured Danny. Crushed under a pile of bricks. And she'd turned and all but ran.

"You get here okay?" the woman asked brusquely. "Any problems?"

Audrey clenched her jaw to keep her emotions in check. She forced her back ramrod straight. "Nothing insurmountable. It's Jade, isn't it?"

The woman nodded, then looked this way and that like she was expecting an ambush from either side. Audrey could only imagine how dangerous this kind of work could be.

"You alone?"

Audrey nodded. "That was the deal, right?"

Jade glared her way. "Yeah, well not everyone sticks to deals they make these days, do they?"

Audrey jumped slightly at her harsh tone but then she nodded again. She got it. The woman was on edge. Anyone would be knowing they might be walking into a trap or ambush. Meeting someone like this blind was a huge risk to both of them, no matter how they'd tried to vet each other beforehand.

So Audrey wasn't surprised when the woman waved to her quickly. "Let's go. I for one don't want to be around when some raping bastard happens to take a walk in the park."

When she turned and started deeper into the woods, Audrey hurried to follow on her heels. It was good though. Trying to keep up with G.I. Jane took up all her energy and focus.

Which meant she couldn't obsess about Nix. Or Clark. Or Mateo. Or Graham and Danny.

Or not.

Because with each step she took, each of their faces rose like ghosts in her mind.

Which was all they'd ever be to her now—ghosts, like Dad and Charlie.

Except for one key difference, she reminded herself. *They'll be alive.*

After about another ten minutes of hard hiking, Audrey's breath caught at seeing a small motorbike. Jade strode toward it, turning and handing the single helmet from the handlebars to Audrey.

"Oh no, you should—"

"Take it," Jade demanded, so Audrey shut her mouth and did as she was told.

Her hands trembled as she strapped it underneath her chin. And it wasn't at the prospect of getting on the motorbike behind this strange woman she didn't know.

She looked behind her. She hadn't heard the roar of the helicopter taking off again. How long would they wait?

"Come on," the woman growled. "We're sitting ducks out here."

Don't think, just go. You can think tomorrow.

Jade got on the motorcycle, and Audrey swung one leg over, sitting behind her and wrapping her arms around the muscular woman's waist.

"Lean when I lean," Jade said.

And then they were speeding off through the woods. If there was a path, Audrey couldn't see it.

But Jade seemed to know exactly where she was going. She rode confidently, speeding around trees and after a while, Audrey realized there *was* a sort of trail. But it was so overgrown it was insane that Jade was going the speed she was.

Audrey clung to Jade for dear life and tried her best to lean when Jade did.

The ride seemed to take a thousand years but was probably more like thirty or forty-five minutes. All Audrey knew was that when they finally stopped, she felt like barfing from the terror of the ride. Which, after the helicopter trip, was saying something.

They came out of the forest onto a road and Audrey barely had time to breathe a sigh of relief before she realized that Jade treated asphalt as an excuse to drive at even more insane, breakneck speeds.

If she weren't strapped to the back of her, Audrey would admire the woman's balls. As it was, she wanted off this rollercoaster, thank you very damn much.

But eventually, eventually, it came to an end. Audrey had been smelling the sea strongly ever since they'd come out of the woods, so she wasn't surprised when Jade pulled them onto a street leading right out to the docks.

"Where are you taking me?" Audrey tried to ask.

But Jade either didn't hear or thought it was useless to try speaking with all the noise because she just shook her head.

It was only when the motorcycle finally came to a full stop on a dock beside a small speedboat that it all really sank in. Another woman sat behind the driver's seat and she waved to Jade.

It was only midday and in the distance, Audrey could see an island. "Is that Galveston island?"

"No, Galveston Island's over there." Jade pointed a little further to the right. "Nomansland is on Pelican Island, the little one to the left. Over there. It's pretty small but there was a Marine Biology branch of A&M University there. All the buildings are still in good condition and there's plenty of space."

Audrey put a hand over her eyes to try to see better but couldn't make out much than a few taller buildings.

Then she looked all around them. She felt extremely exposed. Jade had brought them to an out-of-the-way shipping dock and there wasn't anyone else around.

"But don't you have trouble with men from Galveston?" Audrey and Charlie had studied maps of the coast and there was a long string of islands that ran alongside the coast here. How on earth had Nomansland remained a secret if it was so exposed?

"Drea, that's our founder, did it smart. She had a hell of an armament when she started and she set up treaties with other like-minded cities that helped protect us."

"What do you trade? How do you make your money?"

Jade huffed out in annoyance. "Look, we can explain everything when we get there. Sitting ducks, remember?" She gestured around them, then down at the boat.

Audrey nodded. She climbed off the bike and walked on wobbly legs down the dock. Jade stowed the bike behind a huge, rusting shipping container, then hurried back.

She reached out for Audrey's hand to help her down to the boat.

But Audrey hesitated, looking behind her.

What were the chances Nix and Mateo were still waiting for her?

Stupid.

They would have taken off by now. Talk about sitting ducks. A helicopter would be a target for anyone with half a brain. Everyone in twenty miles who heard them pass overhead had probably headed there to investigate and see if they couldn't get their hands on the thing.

No, she *hoped* they'd taken off. They could be almost halfway back home by now—

She froze.

Home.

A place she'd never be able to go again.

She bit down on her lip hard.

You're saving their lives. That was worth anything. Any sacrifice. Certainly worth the price of her happiness.

She was about to reach for Jade's hand when the worst two words in the English language slipped into her mind, though:

What if...?

Because what if she was doing the wrong thing?

God, hadn't Jeffries proved to her over and over again how dangerous he could be? What if by running instead of warning Nix and the rest of the clan, she was just helping Jeffries and his friends set the rest of the town up for something awful? Because the way Jeffries talked, he and his accomplices didn't have benign intentions.

What would happen to Nix once they decided they all were tired of waiting?

Jeffries said he had spies everywhere. And maybe that was true—in town at least. It was why she felt she couldn't tell the guys. Anyone could overhear, or if they tried to go to the Commander, anyone in his offices or government could be connected and it could get back to Jeffries—

But she wasn't in town right now.

If she could get back to Nix and Clark, she could tell them everything and they could make a plan. Together.

The thought of anything happening to them because of her had just paralyzed her.

She'd been too afraid to even *try*.

But what if when Jeffries and his men enacted whatever it was they were planning, Nix and her clan got hurt anyway? Did she think Nix would just stand idly by while Jeffries tried to overthrow the town?

And while their clan might have officially dissolved once she left, she knew her men. The bonds they'd formed wouldn't just disappear.

They'd fight together.

Oh God, why was she just realizing all of this *now*?

"I have to go back." At first the words were just a whisper, eyes frozen on the horizon. But then she grabbed Jade's arm and whipped her around to look at her. "You have to take me back. This is a mistake."

"What?" Jade asked incredulously. "But isn't this what you wanted? What every woman alive wants these days?"

Three months ago, that might have been true. For a girl who'd lost everything and needed a new family to start over? Sure.

But Audrey already had that.

Why the hell wasn't she fighting for it? Because she was scared?

Charlie's face flashed in front of her.

Then Dad's.

She'd been so scared of anyone else she loved dying for her.

But Nix had been scared too. So terrified that what happened to his sister would happen to her. He had pushed people away the same way she was doing now. But he'd let her in. Let himself love her.

And then, more importantly, he'd faced his worst fear of all and let her go.

But her?

She'd been running scared. All she could see was her fear. She'd choked on it from the very moment Jeffries first threatened them. It was all consuming, all she could see.

She'd let fear drive away everything she loved.

And in the end, they were still in danger anyway. And all because she hadn't had the courage to open her dumb, stupid mouth.

"I have to go back!" she said louder, taking several steps away from the boat. One hand flew to her forehead. Oh God. How was she gonna get back to Jacob's Well?

Jade might take her back to the rendezvous spot, but if the helicopter had taken off, which of course it had, then she was fucked. So beyond fucked.

No.

She'd get back to them. Somehow, she'd get back. She'd warn them about Jeffries without him finding out about them. And together, they'd take down that motherfucker and his cronies once and for all.

Jade made another impatient noise. Then she spoke under her breath. "Enough with this bullshit."

Which was when Audrey felt the prick in the back of her neck.

Even as she tried to spin around in shock, her legs gave way underneath her and she slumped to the ground.

CHAPTER FORTY

AUDREY

It was the second time in the last few months that Audrey had woken up in an unfamiliar place.

She was much quicker to jerk to attention this time around, though. Even though she felt groggy and woozy.

She put a hand to her swimming head as she looked around.

It was a tiny, dark room, maybe the size of a closet. A single fat candle on a shelf illuminated the small area.

But Audrey's attention was immediately drawn to the beaten and bloody woman hanging by chains on the opposite wall.

"Are you alright?" Audrey asked, getting to her feet and taking two steps toward the woman—which was about all the space there was in the closet.

The woman's head suddenly jerked up. One eye was barely a slit, it was so bruised and swollen. She was dressed in rags and her shoulder-length hair could have been blond or dark brown—it was so dirty and matted Audrey couldn't tell.

"You think you can break me?" the woman suddenly shouted at the top of her lungs toward the door. She wrenched against her chains. "You stupid fuckers!"

Then she let out a hysterical laugh, shaking her head. "They think they're so funny. Always throwing the fresh meat in with me. All the women I was trying to 'save.'" She made air quotes with her fingers even though her hands were in shackles. "So I can watch them break. Day after day. Woman after woman. But I don't break. Do you hear that, you motherfuckers?! *I don't break!*"

Um. Audrey thought that might be up for debate.

But enough of that.

Whoever *they* were, they must not have thought Audrey was much of a threat because they'd only handcuffed her. Just her hands, too. Not even her feet. They hadn't even stripped her down either.

Their mistake.

She immediately reached down to her shoe and pulled out the pin she kept shoved in the worn sole. "How long have I been out?" she asked crazy lady.

But crazy lady was suddenly sitting up and at attention as Audrey fiddled with her handcuff lock, especially when a few seconds later, Audrey got it to click free.

"Hour, hour fifteen, tops." She suddenly looked very alert. "Where'd you learn to do that?"

"My brother taught me. Where are we?"

"Pelican island. This used to be the old—"

"A&M Marine Biology Department," Audrey finished for her. "I heard." She made a sour face. "I mean where on the island are we? And what the hell is going on? I thought this place was supposed to be a sanctuary for women?"

This time it was the other woman's face who soured. "I'll explain everything. While you get your ass over here with that lock pick."

Audrey nodded, shaking off the cuffs and hurrying over to the woman. "I'm Audrey, by the way."

"Drea." She held her manacled hands to Audrey but Audrey paused.

"Like the Drea who founded Nomansland, *Drea?*"

Drea's mouth became a hard line. "The one and only. Long story short, they took over about eleven months ago. After my tenth escape attempt, they stopped putting me in rooms with windows. Hence, this beautiful supply closet."

"Who's *they*?" Audrey asked, fiddling with the lock on Drea's first manacle. The lock was larger than she was used to, so it took a little more work figuring out how to hit the tumblers with the pin but eventually she got it.

Drea yanked the pin out of Audrey's hand and started working on her other wrist manacle. "Pig-faced bastards. Spineless sacks of shit. You know, *men*." The lock popped open and she immediately leaned down to her ankles.

"Okay, so we just get the door and then—" Audrey said but Drea was already shaking her head.

"They put chains on it from the outside, too. Can't just pop the lock."

At Audrey's exasperated gasp, Drea just held a hand up. "Look, let's just say I was very determined to escape and they're very determined to keep me here. I know, I know, why not just kill me? Trust me."

Her face darkened even further, though Audrey wouldn't have thought that was possible. "They're plenty of people here who would be more than happy to see that happen. There's just a larger number to whom I'm worth more alive than dead. But my buyers have apparently requested that I be made more 'compliant' first. Either that or they're just trying to drive me fucking nuts."

"Ahh, there," she said, rubbing her raw and damaged ankles after she got them free. Slowly, she got to her feet. She was wearing rags, almost literally. Her shirt, if you could call it that, was a foul brown color and it looked like the stitches were barely holding together. Her pants were little better. Maybe they'd once been yoga pants or pajamas or something, because the cotton was worn so thin you could see the outline of her body through them.

Audrey couldn't imagine what the woman had been through in the last eleven months. And she didn't particularly want to. Because that might lead to thinking about what could happen to *her* if they didn't get the hell out of here.

"How close were you to making it out on your last escape attempt?

Do you know where they keep the boats? Are the keys in them or do we need to—"

"Shhhh," Drea suddenly hissed, her whole body going alert. Then she waved at Audrey to be still. "The guard's coming. Hands behind your back. Against the wall."

Audrey followed Drea's instructions and then Drea leaned forward and blew out the candle.

The next second, the chains outside the door rattled.

Holy crap, already? What was she supposed to do? Should she try to grab the guy? Would he have a gun? How were they going to—

The door opened and light poured in the tiny space.

"How's my favorite bitch to—"

Drea ran straight at the big, pot-bellied guy, letting out a banshee-like war cry.

Even though the guy had to have almost eighty pounds on her, she tackled him backwards to the ground.

She didn't waste any time, either. She grabbed his head by his ears, lifted it, and then smashed it into the ground—once, then again. And again. And again.

By the time she was done, bits of brain were scattered on the floor and the front of Drea's shirt was covered in blood.

Holy shit.

For a second, Audrey was frozen.

Fucking move.

It was like she heard Nix's voice shouting at her in her head.

She listened, scrambling forward. She did a quick check, but it didn't look like the guard had a weapon, so she pulled at Drea's arm. Drea still had hold of the guy's head, looking like she was going to continue hulk smashing it.

"You got him. He's dead. Come on." When Drea still didn't move, Audrey yanked harder on her arm. "*Come on.*"

Finally Drea crawled backwards and stood up, slipping in the guy's blood and almost falling. Audrey helped her up.

"Where do we go now?" Audrey asked.

For a second, Drea looked around them, seeming dazed.

"Hey." Audrey snapped in front of her face a few times. "Get it together. I need you to tell me which way to go."

Drea blinked and nodded, taking a deep breath. "Okay. Okay." She looked around them. "We're in the southern hallway of the old student center. When we get to the end, we can head down the stairs and get the other girls out. Then we'll—"

Her words were cut off by the sound of boots in the hallway. Oh crap, they were about to have more company. Drea obviously heard it too because she'd finally seemed to get with the program. She was sprinting toward the end of the hallway, Audrey on her heels.

Audrey could clearly see the door marked *Stairs* directly in front of them. Almost there.

But right as she was reaching for the handle, it jerked open from the other side.

To the faces of fifteen to twenty soldiers, all waiting with guns raised.

Audrey's hands immediately went up.

But it was like Drea just went crazy. The guards poured out of the stairwell, surrounding them, and Drea started kicking and swinging and snarling curses at all of them. "You'll have to kill me this time, you sons of bitches! Just try and lay a fucking hand on me!"

Two soldiers grabbed Audrey from behind, yanking her arms so roughly behind her back she thought they might have dislocated one of her shoulders. She yelped in pain and could only watch on in horror as the others converged on Drea.

She got a couple good hits in but there were simply too many of them. It wasn't long before her arms were wrenched behind her back too. They forced her down on her knees, and from the other end of the hallway, a tall, muscular man dressed all in black approached.

He clapped as he came. "Quite a performance this time, my dear. As always, you never cease to entertain."

He walked right up to Drea and then grabbed her chin between his forefinger and thumb. "So much fire and it never goes out, does it?" His tone was a mix of mockery and grudging admiration. Who the hell was this guy?

Drea yanked away from his touch and then spit on him.

The man threw back his head and laughed. The soldiers, still with their weapons against their shoulders, looked at each other uneasily.

Then the laughter abruptly stopped and the man swung out with a vicious punch, slamming Drea's frail body into the floor.

Audrey screamed and jerked against the soldiers who held her back.

Which brought the man's attention to her. He turned her way and tilted his head. "And who do we have here? Who's little Drea's new playmate?"

He approached with the slyness of a snake and Audrey immediately went cold. This guy was a fucking sociopath.

"She hasn't made an escape attempt in over three months. I thought I might have finally beat her into submission. So good to know she was just waiting for another little accomplice. She's always had such a soft spot for strays."

He traced his forefinger down Audrey's cheek. She trembled with revulsion. She wanted to be bold like Drea and spit in his face but she wasn't sure the act of defiance was worth the inevitable blow that would follow.

Turned out, she should have gone for it, because the next second, the man grabbed her by the back of the hair and then started dragging her forward.

By her hair.

Fuuuuuuuuuuck!

She howled in pain, reaching up and trying to bat his hands away. But he just kept pulling her inexorably forward.

Ow. Oh God.

Oh it hurt so bad. If she could just get to her feet. Even her knees. Anything to take the pressure off her scalp.

But whenever she got close to catching her balance, he only yanked harder.

She screamed again. How had her hair not all ripped out by the roots by now?

What would they do to her? She wasn't naïve. She'd always known what would happen if she ended up captured and in a place like this. Exactly what had happened to Mateo. And Nix's sister. Would it get to the point where they'd eventually brutalize her so much that she'd lose her mind and prefer blowing her brains out to continuing to take another breath?

At least Nix would never know.

There was the tiniest bit of comfort in that at least.

Didn't mean she didn't continue screaming and fighting like a wild animal to get free of the psychotic bastard's grasp.

Drea shouted behind her but the man just kept dragging her away by her hair. Tears poured from her eyes and her throat was already raw from screaming.

Oh God oh God. Please. Please.

She didn't know what she was praying for but it was all she could think.

Please, just please, pl—

BOOM!

An explosion rocked the building.

CHAPTER FORTY-ONE

NIX

Thirty Minutes Earlier

"She's not coming back," Mateo said, staring after where Audrey went.

"Let's give her an hour," Nix said, eyes fixed the same direction. They'd both been staring at the same patch of trees for forty-five minutes now.

"She's not coming back." Mateo reached out and put a hand on Nix's shoulder but Nix jerked away.

"We stay the full hour."

Mateo nodded, holding his hands up. "No argument from me."

The satellite phone rang. It wasn't the first time. Nix had picked up about ten minutes after Audrey left. Apparently the Commander had called almost as soon as they'd taken off but they couldn't hear him because of the noise.

Suffice to say, the Commander was less than pleased with their *borrowing* his helicopter. Nix informed him they'd bring it back in a few hours but, not surprisingly, that did little to pacify him.

Meanwhile he'd been standing here with Mateo staring at the trees, thinking every shifting branch was Audrey returning through the woods. Coming back to them.

It never was.

He'd felt like simultaneously throwing up and beating the shit out of something or someone the second she'd disappeared out of his sight.

But he hadn't run after her with the dart gun—which yes, he'd brought along with him. And he hadn't started beating the shit out of Mateo—because how the fuck could he let her go? He was her husband too. Why hadn't the bastard made some grand gesture right at the end to convince her to stay?

Anyway, in the end, nothing worked. Not him opening up and finally telling her all his personal feelings. Admitting for the first time out loud that he loved her.

It hadn't mattered.

She'd still left.

So if the Commander was calling back to bitch at him some more, he could go fuck himself.

"What?" Nix snapped after flipping the sat phone open.

"Nix? Where's Audrey? You have to stop Audrey!"

Nix's whole body went rigid at Graham's frantic voice.

"What the fuck are you talking about?"

Mateo responded to his tone, swinging his way. *What?* he mouthed, but Nix just shook his head, turning away so he could focus on what Graham was saying.

"I kept thinking about it. The GPS chip we put in the pudding we fed Audrey so we could track her. What if someone else did the same thing? Anyone could track the location just like we are."

"So I went deeper in the web. Deeper than deep. I pretended to be a member of this elite club and posed as a buyer—"

"Enough," Nix shouted. "What the fuck did you find out? Where's Audrey?"

"Nomansland used to be real. A colony for women. But about a year ago, it was attacked and taken over by the Black Skulls MC who are major allies with—"

"Travis," Nix filled in, spitting the name and looking in the direction Audrey had walked almost an hour ago. Nix went cold. Absolutely fucking ice cold.

"Activate her GPS."

"Already did."

"So where the fuck is she?"

"Pelican island. It's not far from where you are."

Graham gave him the coordinates and he repeated them to Mateo, both of them jogging toward the chopper.

Mateo pulled out his GPS device and punched in the coordinates on the screen.

"I'll call you again when we have her," Nix said, then hung up the sat phone.

While Mateo finished with preflight prep, Nix jumped back down from the chopper down to the medical litter on the left.

Nix pulled back the tarp. It wasn't a crash test dummy under there. It was a small arsenal.

He undid the straps and grabbed several machine guns and swung them over his back.

And then he leaned over and hefted up the shoulder rocket launcher.

When he hauled it inside the chopper, Mateo just gave him one glance and shook his head. "The Commander is gonna be so pissed."

Nix strapped himself in as Mateo fiddled with the instruments. "He'll get over it."

Anything would be worth it. Anything. As long as he got Audrey back safe and sound. Then, for a second he couldn't breathe.

Because what if, yet again, he was too late to save the one person he loved most in the world?

CHAPTER FORTY-TWO

AUDREY

The explosion knocked the bastard holding Audrey off his feet. Audrey didn't know what the hell was going on, but she knew he'd finally let her go.

She stumbled to her feet, grabbing for the wall. The candles in the wall sconces had gotten knocked loose and at least one of them had fallen and started a small fire.

Whoosh.

Make that a *big* fire.

The nearby curtains caught flame and it suddenly lit up like a damn Christmas tree. Then the gunfire started.

Audrey swung around to look back at the group of soldiers, scooting back to the wall as she did so. Who the hell was shooting gun right after—

Oh.

It was Drea.

She must have gotten one of their machine guns during the confusion of the bomb blast and *damn* was she taking her revenge.

The man who'd been dragging Audrey by her hair bolted the opposite direction down the hall the way he'd come, disappearing into the smoke now billowing down the hallway.

Audrey wanted to call out to Drea but she didn't dare distract her. She had a gun, yeah, but so did the men surrounding her.

That was a fact that seemed lost on them, however. They either dropped where they stood or fled toward the stairwell. Where the hell had they found these guys? Cowards R Us?

Whatever, at least they were catching a break. Audrey ran toward Drea to—well, she didn't know what the hell she'd do once she got to her. But they were getting the hell out of here, that was for sure.

Drea ran out of ammo right as one of the last few soldiers seemed to get his shit together. He raised his gun directly at Drea's head.

Audrey tackled him from behind just before he could shoot.

Drea only froze for a second before attacking one of the other few still-standing soldiers. The third decided to go the way of his colleagues and ran away.

Thank God because Audrey wasn't sure how many more acts of heroism she had in her today.

She did manage to snatch the machine gun the soldier she'd tackled had dropped before he could.

"Drea," she shouted, passing off the gun to the more experienced marksman.

Just in time too, because the next second, another figure appeared in the stairwell door.

But then Audrey's mouth dropped open.

She knew those tall, muscular shoulders. She'd memorized the shape of them, spent hours kissing up and down them.

"Ni—" she started to say, but just then, Drea jerked the machine gun up, ready to shoot.

"No!" Audrey threw herself in front of Nix. "This is my husband."

Drea's eyes narrowed in suspicion and she didn't drop her gun.

"Drea," Audrey shouted, grabbing the tip of the gun and shoving it down.

"We gotta go," Nix shouted. "Our little distraction's only gonna last so long. Mateo's waiting with the chopper."

Audrey nodded. "Come on." She waved to Drea.

"Not without the rest of the women," Drea said stubbornly. "I'm not leaving without the others."

"Sorry, lady," Nix said impatiently, eyes flicking up and down the hallway. "We've only got space for one more body. You'll be riding on a med bay litter as it is."

Drea stood up straighter, nodding rigidly. "Okay. Then one of the girls should go in my place. Elena. She's been cracking under all the abuse. She won't last much longer. They're holding her downstairs. We just need to get past Tillerman's office, it's just a little further down and to the right. Come on, I can show you."

"No time," Nix said.

Drea's face went hard. "You'll make time or I'll—"

Nix rolled his eyes. Audrey barely realized what he was doing before he'd grabbed something from behind his back and then—

"Oh my God," Audrey groaned. Drea went limp and started falling. He'd tranqued her. Audrey rushed forward to grab her before she hit the ground but Nix was already there. He hefted Drea up and over his shoulder.

Then he turned to Audrey. "Let's get the hell out of here, baby."

She nodded and they ran.

CHAPTER FORTY-THREE

MATEO

"That motherfucking son of a bitch!" Nix roared, storming away from Audrey on the small abandoned airfield where they'd landed after getting away from the Black Skulls compound.

Audrey had just explained why she'd *really* left. They'd been heading back to the township but she'd started yelling in his ear that they had to stop somewhere. That she had to talk to them. She'd been frantic. Panicked.

Graham had gone over several potential landing sites with Mateo, just in case they ran into any trouble along the way. Secluded areas away from settlements.

Heart in his throat, Mateo had stopped at the nearest one and as soon as the rotor blades slowed down enough to be able to hear one another, Audrey started talking. It all just poured out.

About her planned escape.

About how she was going to turn back because she'd decided to stay.

About seeing Jeffries slap his wife.

And then about his blackmailing her by threatening their lives.

"I'm gonna fucking kill him," Nix said, veins popping out in his neck and forehead. "I'll rip his dick off and shove it down his goddamned throat!"

But Mateo was more concerned with what Audrey hadn't said.

"What was he blackmailing you to do?" Mateo asked. "It wasn't just to keep quiet about Camila, was it?"

The sinking feeling in the pit of his stomach only got worse when Audrey looked away and wouldn't meet his gaze.

Oh God, no. No, please, not that.

"Audrey." He grabbed her hand, his voice full of anguish. "Tell me he didn't—"

"No," she said quickly, shaking her head. There was still a shadow in her eyes, though. "But he wanted to. He cornered me a couple times."

"Wait, what are you talking about?" Nix asked, coming back over to them from where he'd been pacing. "What did he want?"

Mateo's jaw went so hard he thought he might crack a tooth. "He wanted sex."

If Mateo thought Nix had been angry earlier, it was nothing to the pure fury that took over his entire countenance now.

"Tell. Me. He. Didn't. Put. A. Hand. On. You." Every word seemed a struggle to get out through Nix's clenched teeth.

Audrey looked away. "He never got what he wanted. I never slept with him. It's why I had to leave."

Nix breathed out a sigh of relief but Mateo just shook his head.

Again, it was all in what she wasn't saying.

"But he did touch you." The words were dragged from Mateo's throat. Not his Audrey. Why God? Someone like him, he understood. But Audrey? How could God let that monster get his hands on her?

And how could he have failed her so deeply?

He'd known something was wrong. When she'd gone to bed for weeks at a time. He'd *known*.

Audrey's silence was answer enough.

"Why didn't you tell us?" Nix shouted.

Audrey flinched and Mateo stepped in front of her, right in Nix's face. "Don't you dare yell at her. Do you have any idea what hell she's been through? What she's carried all alone because we fucking failed her? Us. You and me." He stabbed Nix in the chest with a finger.

For another second, Nix stayed just as furious. He looked about three seconds from ripping Mateo's head off, actually. But then he looked over Mateo's shoulder and his whole body seemed to collapse in on itself.

"That day. That day you ran out of the candle shop so upset..." Nix's features knit in horror at the realization. "Was that when...?"

Audrey's face was still averted, but neither of them missed her tiny nod.

Nix gasped like he'd just been socked in the stomach. "And I yelled the most horrible things at you in the street." He took a stumbling step back. "And for the next two weeks. I called you *selfish*. Jesus fucking Christ, Audrey. How did you— How could you— You took me back after that?"

He shook his head in anguished astonishment. "You went through that all alone and then I was a monster to you and you still—"

"No," Audrey finally raised her face, shaking her head vehemently and stepping forward to clasp both of Nix's hands. "No, don't say that. Never say that. You're not the monster. He is."

Nix shook his head. "But I still don't understand. Why didn't you *tell* us? We could have—"

Audrey's eyebrows scrunched up. "That's why I had to talk to you. Remember what happened to Danny's coworker? That pile of bricks was meant for Danny. It was a warning. It's not just Jeffries and his small clan. He says the people he works with work in every level in the township. That they're everywhere. That's why I realized I had to come back. I was going to but then that bitch knocked me out."

She glanced down. "I was so afraid of being the one to get you killed," she looked up again, eyes flashing, "but it's bigger than just me. Jeffries and his men are planning something. Something big."

Mateo frowned. "Are you sure? Audrey, he could have been just on his own and saying all that to intimidate you and manipulate you into doing what he—"

But Audrey shook her head, looking frustrated. "It's real. Like one day when I was serving in the food kitchens, this totally random guard turned out to be on his side. You'd left me with him, Nix, because he's one of the men you trust, but then he—"

"Who?" Nix demanded, fury quickly taking over his features again.

Audrey waved a hand. "I don't remember his name. I could point him out in a crowd, though. But that's not the point. The point is, I don't think he was lying. He couldn't help boasting about it because he's so jealous of you, Nix. Of everything you have. It's like he's in a constant competition with you and—"

Nix scoffed. "I barely know the guy."

"It doesn't matter," Audrey cut him off. "He's decided to measure himself against you. Everything you have, he wants. When he talked about you, it was like, I don't know..."

Her lips pursed. "Let's just say when he threatened your life, I felt like it was very real. And I had no power to do anything about it or protect you other than by leaving. If I took away his leverage, then maybe he wouldn't hurt you. But that was naïve and me letting my fear drive me. He's got it out for you."

"I'm gonna *kill* that motherfucker."

Audrey breathed out in frustration. "You can't just go in guns blazing. Aren't you listening? He's connected. We don't know how deep and—"

"You never wanted to leave us," Mateo whispered. All the ramifications of everything she'd said were finally sinking in. "You don't hate us because we forced you to—"

Audrey's brow crumpled. "Oh God, no. I'm so sorry I had to hurt you and say that." Her lip trembled. "I was just trying to protect you. I couldn't have another person die because of me."

"What?" Mateo and Nix reached out for her at the same time as tears started coursing down her face.

And that's when she told them about her brother. And how he'd been killed in front of her eyes the day that Nix had found her.

"*Baby*." Nix pulled her into his chest and Mateo immediately stepped up and wrapped his arms around her waist from behind. Together they cocooned her while she cried silently.

She'd held so much back from them. Kept so much bottled up inside, determined to be strong so she could protect them.

Didn't she know the only meaning in their life came from keeping her safe? From loving her?

"My beautiful, beautiful girl," Nix whispered.

Together they comforted her.

Together they loved her.

And then, together, they made a plan.

CHAPTER FORTY-FOUR

NIX

The noise of the chopper blades roared in Nix's ears as they approached town. Every muscle in Nix's body was taut. He'd only felt such murderous rage once before in his life.

That had resulted in an entire camp of dead mercenary rapist motherfuckers.

But no. He had to stick to the plan.

Before they'd taken off heading home, Nix had opened the sat phone and dialed Graham.

"Do you have her?" Graham asked, picking up before it even finished ringing once.

"We have her," Nix confirmed. "Let me speak to the Commander."

There was a brief silence.

Then the Commander came on the phone. "Here," he said brusquely. "Tell me you're bringing my helo back. Right now."

"We captured one of Black Skull's men." Nix looked at Audrey as he said the next part. "Have Jeffries ready with the interrogation crew in the town square. We're coming home."

That was an hour and a half ago.

No matter how much Nix comforted himself with the reality of Audrey's warm, alive body next to him, fuck. The hour of living without her after she first left them, and then the even more hellish half hour thinking the worst when Graham told them the truth about Nomansland, followed by the tortuous revelations of what she'd been living through with that cunt-faced double-crossing—

Nix squeezed the hand not holding Audrey's into a fist.

Focus.

He couldn't let his rage rule him.

Not right now.

Stick to the plan.

The sun was setting as they flew in over town. It was bizarre to see the little town he'd made his home from this vantage point. There was Mateo's workshop, and the snaking line of the river.

And the town square, growing larger and larger as the chopper descended.

A huge crowd was gathered on the streets all along the courtyard lawn that made up the middle of the square.

Their makeshift landing pad.

Here we go.

Audrey squeezed his hand and he looked at her. He gave her what he hoped was a reassuring smile. The way her brow furrowed, he wondered if it had come off as more of a grimace.

That was fine. He'd have plenty of time to comfort her later.

If the Commander didn't throw him in the stocks for stealing the helicopter, that was. And if their plan went off without a hitch.

No more time for overthinking it, though. He gave Audrey's hand a quick kiss as Mateo landed the helicopter. He'd gotten more and more smooth with each landing. Nix only wanted to throw up for about thirty seconds as opposed to the five full minutes of their previous landings.

Which was good, because he needed all his faculties to focus on the security team approaching the helicopter in a tight ring, machine guns drawn.

It was Nix's best team. He'd trained the men himself.

They were all crack shots.

Jeffries was at the lead, gesturing the men in tighter with his arm not in a sling.

Nix barely clamped down his killing rage.

Keep a fucking lid on it.

He unbuckled himself and raised his hands in a surrender gesture, as did Mateo. Mateo stayed with Audrey strapped in the chopper, though, as Nix climbed down.

He walked around to the front of the chopper as the Commander approached at a tight clip across the lawn.

Jeffries joined him and together they walked up to Nix.

The chopper blades were whirring slower and slower every second, allowing other sound to penetrate.

"You got your spectacle," the Commander said, face grim. "I don't know what you expect to gain by doing this in the middle of town, though. It's not going to make things go any easier for you."

Nix ignored the Commander. He only had eyes for Jeffries.

The chopper blades were winding down even more, now just a low whine. A glance behind him showed his men grabbing Mateo out of the helicopter and forcing him facedown to the ground.

It was now or never.

Nix turned to the townspeople and shouted at the top of his lungs. "Jeffries and his clan have been abusing their wife. Audrey saw him punch her and knock her to the ground."

Gasps and chatter immediately broke out all around the square.

"Arrest this thief," Jeffries yelled, motioning to the security team. "Use all necessary force."

"Then he tried to rape my wife!" Nix shouted even louder, glaring at Jeffries with every ounce of hatred he felt. "He blackmailed her with threats against my life until she felt her only choice was to flee. He didn't break his arm in tactical training. Audrey broke it when he fucking *attacked* her."

"Arrest this man!" Jeffries screamed, obviously trying to drown out Nix's voice. "He stole our helicopter. And high value items from the armory. You can't believe a thing he says."

"He's violated this town's most sacred duty," Nix continued. "To protect our women!"

Nix wasn't looking at Jeffries anymore. No, he had his eyes on his security team. They were looking back and forth amongst themselves, and then to the Commander.

Nix followed their gaze.

But he couldn't read the look on the Commander's stoic face. It all depended on his reaction, Nix knew that. Yes, his words would resonate in the town no matter what the Commander decided, but Nix and Mateo's immediate fate was in his hands.

And, considering what Audrey had told them about Jeffries's connections, if the Commander didn't take their side now, it could be fatal.

No doubt Jeffries would *accidently* take things a little too far during Nix's 'interrogation.' Nix could almost hear the excuses now. *He must have had a weak heart. We followed protocol. These things just happen sometimes.*

"Is this true?" the Commander asked Jeffries.

Jeffries sputtered. "How can you ask me that? He's the criminal here. He's the one who stole the—"

"Is it true?" the Commander's voice was steely.

"Of course it's not true!"

But some commotion at the east edge of the lawn had everyone looking and pointing.

Nix and the Commander both looked to see what was going on. And saw the crowd separating in a circle around a trembling Camila.

"Good," Jeffries said. "We can clear this up once and for all. Camila, *come.*"

Nix's teeth grated. The fucker used the same tone of voice you would when ordering a dog around.

"Commander, we have no idea how long he's been abusing her," Nix said under his breath. "Audrey said he's got her so far under his thumb she's terrified of stepping out of line. She'll say whatever he tells her to."

"Shut up," Jeffries snapped. Then, when Camila was close enough,

"Camila, tell them he's lying. I've never hit you in my life and I never would. The clan and I cherish you. *Tell them.*"

Oh come on. The Commander had to hear how blatantly Jeffries was manipulating her. All but threatening her, right in front of th—

"It's true," Camila said.

Jeffries smiled smugly, looking out at the square.

But then Camila continued. "What Audrey's husband said is true. The men of my clan beat me." Then she lifted her shirt, revealing green and yellow bruises all over her stomach and ribs. "They're just careful not to leave marks where anyone will see."

"You lying whore!" Jeffries shouted. He lunged for Camila but the Commander locked his arm around Jeffries's throat from behind and then slammed him backwards to the ground with so much force he was left gasping like a fish out of water.

The security force quickly moved in and grabbed him, yanking his arms behind his back.

Jeffries was the one with murderous rage in his eyes now. His voice was only a rasping gasp as he lunged against the guard's hold toward Nix. "And *you.* You think you're so much better than me. You're nothing. You're a *fucking* puppet. I had you led around by your dick for months and you didn't even know it. Just dropped your name in that stupid fucking lotto and you were so busy with her cunt I had free reign of the whole fucking squadron."

Nix felt his eyes widen. *Jeffries* was the one who'd put his name in the lottery?

"You think this is over?" Jeffries asked. "This isn't over. Your time's coming. It's coming for *all* of you!"

He spit in Nix's and the Commander's direction and one of the guards smacked him over the back of the head with the butt of his rifle, knocking him unconscious.

"Get him out of here," the Commander ordered, looking around at the crowd, many of whom were heading toward them and shouting angrily. Now the security force had turned and was holding the crowd back. "Jesus Christ, they'll rip him apart."

"As much as I'd like that," Nix said grudgingly, "we need to know what he knows. Audrey says he's not alone. He's part of a network of dissidents."

Nix turned and looked at the Commander more closely. "You don't look surprised."

The Commander's jaw firmed. "I've had my suspicions. But I couldn't name names." He clapped Nix on the back. "I'm glad you've got your wife back. You can have the night with her but I'll need you back in the Squadron Command center at 0600 tomorrow morning."

"Yes, sir." Nix nodded. Well, looked like he wasn't losing his job after all.

The Commander turned to head after the guards dragging Jeffries away when Nix stopped him. "Sir, there's another matter."

"What?" the Commander looked impatient. No doubt he wanted to get into interrogation with Jeffries as soon as possible.

But this couldn't wait. Nix gestured him over to the helicopter and around to the left medical litter where Drea was strapped, still unconscious.

"Jesus Christ!" the Commander exclaimed at seeing her. "You didn't think to mention this earlier?" He lifted a short-wave radio from his belt. "Medical team to town square. I repeat, med team to town square, stat. We have a new female, condition unknown."

"Relax, I just gave her a sedative."

The Commander rubbed his temple. "Don't tell me you tranqued this one too."

"Okay, I won't tell you."

The Commander glared at him. "You're lucky you're good at your job, Hale. That's all I can say."

Then he got to work unstrapping the woman. Audrey climbed down from the helicopter and Nix pulled her into his arms.

"You did it," she smiled at him, her eyes watery. "I never should have doubted you." He leaned down and kissed her.

"*We* did it. Now let's go home."

Audrey looked over at Drea anxiously. "I don't know. Maybe I should stay with her."

"Don't worry. Sophia will take care of her."

Audrey's smile tilted lopsided. "Oh, I'm sure those two will get along famously."

Mateo walked toward them, dusting himself off and stretching his neck. "Good to know you train your men so vigorously." He lifted a hand to massage the back of his neck. "I'll be feeling that takedown for a week."

"Oh, poor baby," Nix said.

Audrey was more compassionate, naturally.

She pulled out of Nix's arms and went to give Mateo a hug. She squeezed him for a good long time. A little too long, if you asked Nix.

But when she pulled back, the gleam in her eye was for both of them. "How about we go pick up the other guys from the Security Squadron Headquarters and then head home?"

She grinned seductively, first at Mateo, then at Nix. "I promise I'll massage all your aches and pains till you feel *allllll* better?"

Mateo grabbed her hand and started dragging her across the lawn in the direction of the headquarters and Nix hurried to follow, taking her other hand. "Aw, do we *have* to go pick up the other guys?"

Audrey's musical laugh was the most beautiful, perfect thing Nix had ever heard in his life.

CHAPTER FORTY-FIVE

AUDREY

Audrey hadn't meant to be a tease. But as soon as they all got home and ate some bread and soup, she was almost falling asleep at the table.

The guys took her up to bed all right, but just to tuck her in.

"Get some rest, beautiful," Clark said, kissing her on the forehead, his eyes so soft it made her want to cry.

They were all being so gentle and loving. Having all these big, tough men treating her like she was their tender, precious treasure. Not like she was a vase about to break. She saw the difference now.

And she never in her life could have imagined a love so big.

"Don't leave," she grabbed Clark's hand when he tried to pull away after tucking her in. The others were at the door. "You've all got to be tired, too. Please. I don't think I can bear to be away from any of you." Not after everything she'd been through the past few weeks. Thinking she'd lost them forever. Part of her wasn't sure this wasn't all a dream and she wouldn't wake up handcuffed in that terrible closet on the island.

Graham, Mateo, and Clark climbed on the bed with her and she immediately started laughing as the four of them tried to position themselves in a way where they'd all fit. It was a familiar problem.

"We need a bigger bed," Graham observed.

"No shit," Clark said.

"So let's do it," Nix said. "Come on, Danny."

Audrey laughed. What, where they going to go out and magically find some huge bed at nine o' clock at night?

But a few minutes later, they were coming back in with the twin mattresses from one of the other rooms. Audrey smiled, drowsing with her head on Clark's chest, Mateo playing with her hair, while Nix and Mateo reassembled the frame and put the bed back together.

Then they pushed it right up against the side of the king-sized bed. Graham moved onto the new bed and reached out to run a hand down Audrey's thigh, like he had to make sure he still had access to her. "This will do."

"But there's still no room for us," Danny complained.

"There's more space on the other side," Mateo said.

Nix nodded and gestured Danny to follow him. A few minutes later and they came in with *another* twin mattress set.

Audrey could barely keep her eyes open. She fell asleep somewhere in between Nix swearing at Danny for dropping the wooden frame on his foot and the mattress toppling over from where Nix had leaned it against the wall, almost knocking over the candle and catching the whole place on fire.

All the guys started shouting at each other, but Audrey just fell asleep with a smile on her face.

———

She had no idea what time it was when she woke up. Sometime in the middle of the night. Maybe just before dawn?

The big candle on the bureau was about three fourths of the way burned down.

Audrey looked around her. All five guys were sprawled out on the new giant bed they'd created.

Her heart expanded so wide she felt sure it would burst.

Clark and Mateo were on either side of her and she tried to snuggle back up to them and go to sleep again.

And tried.

And tried.

Thing was... all she could think about were the five big, beautiful men in bed with her. The men who'd saved her, in more ways than one. She'd been so afraid for so long.

And she hadn't realized it until today—maybe not until right this minute even—but part of her determination that no one else would die for her was the underlying belief that, well, she just wasn't worth it.

She wasn't worth loving. Not when it cost so much.

But what the guys had shown her, time and time again, was that it wasn't up to her. That wasn't how love worked. Love—real love—was boundless. It couldn't be held back or contained or put into a nice, little tidy box. She couldn't control the way they loved her.

Her only job was to accept their love.

To open her arms and embrace the way they cherished her.

And to give them back all the love she had and more.

She licked her lips, her legs shifting restlessly. Speaking of opening her arms and receiving love... Her body was positively *aching* to take in and squeeze around all that sweet, sweet love.

She bit her bottom lip and stroked down Clark's arm.

To his stomach.

Lower.

His cock woke up before he did.

He started growing in her hand and then shifting his hips back and forth. She grinned and climbed down the bed, trying to be careful not to jostle him.

She wanted to wake him in a far more spectacular fashion.

He shifted a lot in his sleep, so the sheets were already down around his waist. She pulled his cock out through the slit in his underwear and lowered her head.

She loved the salty musk of how cocks smelled and tasted. It was so... manly. Her sex clenched as her tongue extended and she licked just the tip up and down over the little slit of Clark's dick. It twitched and grew longer. She had to fight back her giggle.

Next she laid the flat of her tongue on the mushroom head and swirled it all around, back and forth.

Clark's body shifted and he let out a small groan.

He was going to wake up any second and she wanted it to be to her swallowing down his cock. Oh, and she couldn't forget the visual aspect.

She quickly pulled her shirt off over her head. The cool night air felt amazing against her breasts and in another second, she had her panties off too and tossed to the floor.

Then she bent back over Clark's cock and sucked him in her mouth, grabbing the bottom of his shaft with her hand. She bobbed up and down, increasing her suction every time.

Clark groaned even louder, rolling so that he was fully on his back. Audrey glanced up his body, expecting him to be looking down at her. But he still looked fast asleep.

All right, now this was starting to get insulting.

She sucked even harder, bobbing so deep he hit the back of her throat. She took a deep breath and then swallowed him a little. His hips jerked upwards and his cock grew even longer. She moved her hand up and down his shaft where her mouth couldn't reach. God, he must be nine inches long. Ten even.

She rubbed him more vigorously in concert with her suction, adopting a rhythm that had his hips moving with her.

"Holy shit!"

Clark's sudden shout had her almost jerking off his cock but his hand that shot to her head kept her in place.

She felt movement all around her as the others shifted awake but she kept her focus on Clark. She gripped his shaft even more firmly and with her other hand, started playing with his balls.

"*Christ*." His voice sounded raw. His hand on her head was tentative, caressing, like he couldn't believe what was happening was real and he had to keep checking it was really her.

She'd never felt more powerful or beautiful.

"Audrey!" he shouted, his hips pumping in and out two more times before his cum erupted down her throat in several great spurts.

She swallowed it all eagerly, sucking and licking and stroking and trying to make him feel as cherished as they'd all made her.

He'd raised up on his elbows he came and his stomach heaved as he flopped backwards onto the pillows. "Christ."

Audrey pulled off his still mostly hard cock with a little *pop*, grinning so wide she thought her face might split.

When she looked around, all five pairs of eyes were wide and focused straight on her.

She was still perched on her hands and knees over Clark's cock, so she wiggled her ass back and forth.

"Who wants to take my pussy first tonight?"

Danny was closest and he started reaching for her hips but Graham suddenly surged forward and pushed him out of the way. "Me."

Graham flipped her on her back and shoved his boxers down in the same motion. Then he lifted her left leg and, without any fanfare, he pushed inside her.

His face was strained with pleasure, but it was also something else. He dropped an elbow by her head and reached his hand toward her, gripping the back of her neck and burying his fingers in her hair.

Then he dropped his face down to hers, forehead to forehead. His rough breaths sawed in and out of his chests.

And he fucked her.

God, how he fucked her.

With wildness and abandon and an intensity she'd never felt from him before.

There was no counting.

No measured, orderly finesse.

He just *took* her.

Her pleasure rose up sudden and sharp. When he moved and slanted his mouth over hers, she devoured his lips hungrily.

His hips were jerky and artless as he punched forward, back, forwards again. His cock reaching deliciously deep inside her.

"I was so scared—" he whispered harshly between kisses. "When I found out those terrible men had you. I wanted to die."

Oh Graham. The hell he must have gone through, waiting to hear back from Nix and Mateo. Not able to do anything about the situation. How helpless he must have felt.

She kissed him even more furiously, meeting his thrusts with her own, grinding her clitoris against his pelvis each time.

"I'm sorry. I'm so sorry," she whispered. And then there were no more words, only the higher and higher pitched gasps as her pleasure bloomed.

Oh God, oh God, it was coming.

She clutched his body to hers as it hit. *Make him whole*, she prayed as the light split her body from her core and exploded outwards.

She clenched on him and with two more pumps, Graham was growling and shoving so deep inside her she couldn't help but howl in pleasure.

She didn't stop holding him, even when both their pleasure had passed. He clasped her just as tightly. She realized then it would take time to heal the wounds she'd inflicted.

Yes, she'd had her reasons, but it didn't mean the hurt was any less. And she'd happily spend the rest of her life making it up to these beautiful men.

"I love you, Graham," she murmured in his ear, stroking through his hair with her fingers. "I love you so much."

His head shot up at this, eyes wide. For a long second, he made eye contact with her before his eyes drifted to the side and then shut. He swallowed hard and she could see he was barely holding back some intense emotion.

"I love you so much," she repeated, putting her whole heart behind the words. She'd make sure to say it all day every day. Not just to Graham. To all of them.

Graham nodded and when he breathed out, it was like he was exorcising a ghost. "I love you, too," he whispered.

They kissed one more time.

And then, as if he knew he'd been monopolizing her, he shifted off of her, but he didn't let go of her hand.

She looked to Clark. "I love you, Clark." She'd never said it to him before either. To any of them. Not another day would go by without her telling them, though. Each and every one.

He nodded, his face suddenly full of feeling. "I—" he broke off. "Me too." His eyes dropped.

"You love yourself?" Nix said with a smirk. "Tell us something we don't know."

Clark glared daggers Nix's way. "No smartass, I love Audrey." He looked shocked the second the words came out of his mouth, but then he looked at her, blinking several times. "It's true. I— I love you."

She smiled and crawled over to kiss him. She started to pull back but he clutched the back of her head, extending the kiss.

She laughed into his mouth but kissed him back.

"I love you too, Audrey," Danny said enthusiastically. "You know I do."

Clark finally let her go and she turned with a wide grin for Danny. "I know you do. You were the one with the courage to say it first." She laughed. "It scared the crap out of me at the time."

"Oh," Danny frowned. "Sorry."

"No." Audrey climbed over Clark's prone form to him. "Never apologize or take it back. It meant so much to me, even if I didn't think I could accept it at the time. I love you, too. I'm sorry it's taken me this long to say it."

The grin that took over Danny's face was so bright the whites of his teeth rivaled the candlelight.

Audrey laughed and threw her arms around his neck. "I love you!" she shouted. "I love Danny Hale!"

"I love Audrey Hale!" he yelled back just as exuberantly, lifting her in his arms and swinging her back and forth.

She giggle-screeched but soon her giggles were cut off by his mouth. He kissed her deep and it wasn't long before his cock was bobbing against her pussy. She reached down and directed him inside her.

He growled low, grabbing her ass and settling her down on his lap as he sat back on his heels.

"Ohhhhhhhh," she groaned. The angle was soooooooo good. Why hadn't she ever tried this position before?

Danny guided her by her ass up and down on his cock. She threw her head back, breasts in his face and rode him. He pulled her nipple into his mouth and sucked hard.

Thirty seconds passed.

Then a minute.

Then two.

And Danny just kept pumping calmly in and out, not seeming like he was having any trouble keeping himself in control.

"You're doing it," Audrey gasped as her pleasure rose again.

When she looked down at him, he let go of her nipple and met her gaze. And for once, all the easy-goingness was gone from his face. He looked at her with the intensity reminiscent of Graham's. "I just think about what it was like when I thought we'd lost you. And suddenly it's the easiest thing in the world to hold back. Because being back inside you. Audrey, I never thought I'd have this again. I'm never going to take a second of it for granted. And I always want every moment with you to last an eternity."

Audrey's heart did that thing where it felt so full she thought it was gonna explode again. Too much. Seriously, this was all too much. How could one woman contain all this love? All this happiness? It was fundamentally unfair to the rest of the universe.

But she would never be so ungrateful so as to sabotage the love these men wanted to lavish on her again. Her job was to accept. To accept and to love them back with her whole heart. She kissed Danny deep and they made love.

And made love.

And made love.

Audrey didn't know how long it was later when she felt her third orgasm of the night cresting—twenty minutes? Thirty?

"I'm coming," she whimpered restlessly, moving more quickly over Danny's cock. "Come with me."

"Not yet," he murmured. "Just a little longer."

"Now," she said.

"Just a little longer."

"*Now*," she demanded, clenching her sex on his cock with all her might. "You give me your cum right this second, Danny Hale. I want to feel your seed so deep up inside my core I'll feel it heating me for a week. I want to feel that giant, gorgeous cock of yours thrust and pulse and absolutely just lose your—"

Danny roared and shoved in as deep as he could go, several quick jabs and then she felt it, the quick rush of his release, which tipped her over the edge as well.

"Fucking finally," Nix said. "Mateo, get the lube."

Audrey only had a chance to give Danny one last brief peck before Nix was dragging her off him and pulling her onto the side bed.

He laid back and she straddled him, laughing at his urgency as he slung her leg over his hip Then he paused. "Shit, babe. You've been fucking for almost an hour now. We can take a break and let you catch your br—"

"Are you gonna get your cock in me or am I gonna have to start finger-fucking myself?" she asked with a lifted eyebrow.

Just like she knew it would, her dirty talk made Nix's eyes darken so they were almost black. He smacked her ass, making her yelp and then giggle.

Nix entered her with one deep stroke. She'd been readied by the other three guys, but Nix's girth was always a bit of a surprise. A very, very pleasant one.

She cried out as his huge cock stretched her wide and hit that spot so deep up inside her that only he and Clark seemed to be able to hit.

Oh God, she wasn't gonna last long. It seemed contradictory, but the more times she came a night, the more she was *able* to come. Like priming a pump. There was a sweet spot where the orgasms would get truly, insanely, blow the top of her head off explosive, sometimes around number four or five, before going back to just being regularly fan-fucking-tastic.

But she had a feeling she was just ramping up to the pop her head off kind. Tonight was that kind of night.

"Lube up and stretch her ass," Nix growled. Audrey's eyes widened but her sex only clenched harder around Nix's huge cock.

"Oh she likes that idea," Nix grinned, squeezing her hips with his hands and dragging her back and forth over him.

It was true. She did. She hadn't done it since that first time with

Clark and Nix, and she had to say, she'd been curious to try it again now that she was a little more sexually experienced.

Mateo teased at the rosette of her puckered asshole for long minutes, driving her crazy, before finally inserting one finger.

She thrashed on Nix as he worked a second finger in. And eventually a third.

By the time Mateo lined himself up behind her and his cock itself pushed through her tight ring of muscle, she felt completely feverish with need.

Having Nix and Mateo inside her at the same time— Oh, oh—

"Oh God—" she screamed. "Please. More! Give me more. I want your everything. Don't hold back. Please God, don't hold back."

So they didn't. Nix especially just let absolutely go, rutting in her like an animal, lighting up that spot inside her with. Every. Single. Thrust.

Her orgasm burst on her so suddenly she screamed and clawed at the skin of Nix's shoulders.

He fucked her even harder, his cock feeling impossibly huge and tight with her ass so full of Mateo's cock, both of them working in tandem.

"I love you!" she shouted. To Nix. To Mateo. To every man in that room. "I love you so fucking much!"

She reached out to the left and Graham took her hand, Danny covering both of theirs with his. With her right, she reached out blindly into the empty room. Clark must have known exactly what she needed because he hurried off the bed and around, dropping to his knees and clutching her free hand in his.

Six as one.

Bound in marriage.

In pleasure.

In love.

Forever.

EPILOGUE

CHARLIE

Charlie blinked blearily at the sunlight coming through the window where it wasn't boarded up. The sun was setting. Another day gone.

He looked at the wall where he'd just finished scratching a line into the cinderblock with a small rock he'd found on the ground, briefly glancing up at all the similar hash marks.

Three months. It had been over three months since he'd woken up in this very room—covered in his own blood, with a headache so bad he'd been convinced he was gonna die.

He had no idea where he was. A tiny office in a really old building, he thought. Cream-colored painted cinderblock walls. It had an institutional feel. Maybe a hospital?

There was a thick wooden door with a tiny rectangular plexiglass window, but all it showed was the end of a dark alcove, so no clues there. Through the limited view out the window, he could only see the plumbing of another building.

When he'd first woken up, part of him had wanted to just give up and die. Because no matter how many times he shouted questions at the guards who occasionally delivered food and water, no one would tell him anything about his sister Audrey.

Had those bastards killed her right there by the spring where they'd knocked him out? Or did she manage to run away after all?

In the end, he'd fought for consciousness and clung to life as hard as he could. Because what if she was here? What if these mother-fuckers had her too? What if they were—

He cut that line of thought off just like he did every time it sprang up. He'd go fucking insane if he let himself go there.

Voices sounded in the hallway and he scrambled to his feet. Well, as much as he could with the handcuffs and connected ankle fetters. He shuffled hunchbacked toward the door and the small plexiglass window.

And saw *her*.

He thought she was a mirage the first time she came and pushed his tray of moldy bread and sour mush through the skinny two-inch rectangular hole that had been sawed in the door.

She was tiny with long blond hair, wearing a faded white dress. Like some sort of angelic apparition.

But then she got closer and he saw that no, she was a flesh and bone woman. Because surely an angel wouldn't be walking with a limp and have a black eye and a split lip.

She refused to approach with the tray until he backed up to the opposite wall. Then she slid it through and ran away as fast as she could.

Charlie couldn't even be mad that the tasteless bowl of mush spilled all over the floor. If he were her, he wouldn't voluntarily get within three feet of a man either.

He hadn't spent the last eight years hiding Audrey away from the world for nothing. Which was when it hit him—*Audrey*. If Audrey was here, this woman might know her.

It was all he could think about. So the next time the woman came, he ran for the door and started firing questions. "Do you know a girl named Audrey? She would have been brought here the same time I was. Two months ago."

The woman was so startled by his voice she'd dropped his tray and fled.

"Wait!" he'd shouted after her. "Audrey. Do you know her? She's my sister. Please!"

But all he heard was the sound of rapidly fleeing footsteps. And then nothing.

She didn't come back for three days.

It wasn't unusual to go that long between meals. They gave him a gallon of water once or—if he was lucky—sometimes twice a week. But meals were hit or miss.

Still, the next time he heard light footsteps approaching, he backed away to the farthest wall and raised his hands in surrender.

He didn't dare say a word. If Audrey *was* here, this girl could be the key to getting information about her and he wasn't going to fuck it up again.

She was cautious as she approached. Hesitant.

He waited as patiently as he could manage.

She shoved the tray through the hole, sending the bowl splattering again, and then ran away.

As much as it killed him, he did the same thing the next three times she came.

And on the fourth, he said in his calmest, gentlest voice, "I won't hurt you."

She startled so much she almost dropped the tray again.

But she didn't make a run for it.

Considering that a win, he continued, still not moving from the wall and keeping his hands up and visible. "My name's Charlie."

He didn't push any further than that.

She didn't say a word. Just shoved his tray through and skittered away.

But the next time, he started talking about Audrey. "I have a sister about your age. Her name's Audrey. She drove me crazy growing up. Little sisters, you know? Always coming in my room and bothering me and my friends when we were playing video games. Trying to tag along when I'd go to the mall." He shook his head. "Jesus, it feels like a million years ago."

The woman hadn't bolted. The tray was paused halfway through the slot.

Charlie didn't move an inch but he kept talking.

"Dad and I couldn't believe how lucky we were when all the girls and women in town got sick but she stayed healthy. It was like a miracle." Charlie huffed out a sad laugh. And then, when the woman still didn't leave, he told her about what happened with his dad and the mob that came to the front door, and how he escaped with Audrey out back.

"She's dead now?"

Her voice was so soft at first Charlie thought he might have imagined it.

He sat up straighter and she flinched backwards, tray clattering against the slot as she yanked it back.

"Sorry, sorry," Charlie said, chains rattling as he lifted his cuffed hands again and put his back flush with the wall. "I didn't mean to scare you. I— I don't know where she is. She was with me when—"

He swallowed, looking down. "The men from here, they attacked us when we were getting water." He lifted his eyes to hers where she watched him warily through the plexiglass. "I thought if they brought me here, then maybe they brought her too."

Her eyes dropped and Charlie's heartbeat sped up. What did that mean?

"Is she here? Do you know her?"

Her eyes flicked back up to his. "A lot of girls come through here."

Nausea hit Charlie fast and hard. She was confirming his worst fears. No, his worst fear was that Audrey was dead. But what this woman was describing was a close second.

It was an open secret that girls were trafficked all over the territories. The president had officially outlawed it, but there was a reason Charlie chose to stay with Audrey in an underground bunker for almost a decade.

Law and order were so far from a reality yet, it was fucking laughable. The Wild West looked like a picnic compared to the New Republic of Texas, and the New Republic was actually way better than most places in the former US.

Charlie bit his cheek against the million questions he wanted to ask. *Don't press it. She's just opening up. Push too hard and she could bolt again.*

But then those big doe eyes of hers came back to him. "I could maybe... ask around."

"Yeah?" The word came out half-strangled. Was she really just— Just offering like that when he'd— "Cause that would be— It'd be fuckin— Sorry, I just, it would mean everything—"

"I'm not promising anything," she said sharply. Then, as if she'd just remembered the tray in her hands, she gestured down to it with her eyes. "Here. Take this."

And, though she watched him warily, she stood still as he approached. He came slow, careful. She was skittish as a deer. When he got close enough to take the tray, he saw her hand was shaking.

And for the first time since she'd shown up, he thought about her. *Really* thought about her, and not just in relation to the info she might be able to get him on Audrey.

What was life here like for her? She said girls came through. But not her? She obviously had some sort of position here. Maid? Servant? Slave?

While her split lip was healing, she had a fresh bruise on her cheek. "Who hurts you?"

Her eyes shot up to his through the glass and he realized too late how harsh the question had come out.

He didn't apologize, though. Or look away. For a second, neither did she.

In spite of the bruise and her too pale skin, she was undeniably beautiful. So, so fucking beautiful. She had huge, translucent green eyes that looked far too sad for the rest of her angelic face.

What the fuck had happened to this girl to bring her here?

"I have to go," she whispered. "If I can find anything out about your sister, I will."

And then she was gone.

She didn't come back for a week. The longest goddamned week of Charlie's life. And when she did, she didn't have any news about Audrey.

"It doesn't mean she's not here, though," Shay whispered.

Shay.

That was her name. Like the sound of a sigh.

"Travis Territory is big and there are several processing facilities."

All thoughts of beautiful names and sighs fled at that. Charlie's blood went ice cold.

Processing.

Facilities.

For.

Women.

Even though he hadn't eaten in a week he wasn't sure he was gonna be able to get down the food on the tray Shay brought.

"But I'll keep asking around," she rushed to add, obviously seeing her words upset him.

One of the guards who came through sometimes walked by then so she yanked back and scurried away.

And it continued like that for weeks. Quick, stolen conversations broken up by long, endless days of nothing.

But during the moments she was there, Jesus, it was more than a lifeline. Charlie lived for the sound of her soft footsteps on the tile outside his door.

Though she didn't yet have any information on Audrey, Shay filled in so many gaps. He was being held in Travis Territory. To the southeast of what used to be Austin, Travis Territory centered around a township where a good-sized river sprang up from the Edwards Aquifer. Before The Fall, Charlie had even visited the place. You used to be able to take glass-bottomed boat tours on the river and watch the springs bubbling up from the source waters.

And now it was home to one of the most powerful and corrupt governors in the country. Arnold Travis.

The building where Charlie was being held used to be a faculty office in the English building of the old college campus.

The one thing Shay wouldn't talk about, though?

Herself.

Anytime Charlie asked anything about her, she clammed up and scurried off. So he learned not to. Because every second talking to her through the door was like being able to breathe after days starved for oxygen.

Thinking of their brief moments together helped get him through the hard days.

And there were plenty of hard days.

Because as much as he tried to hold out hope, in his darkest moments, it was too easy to believe the worst about Audrey. They'd been in the middle of fucking nowhere when they'd gotten ambushed. Even if Travis's men didn't get her, what were her chances out there all alone in the world?

She wasn't even safe on her own *uncle's* fucking property.

Some days, if not for Shay, it would have been too easy to give into the dark thoughts. Take this week for instance.

Audrey's twenty-third birthday was coming up in a couple weeks and he couldn't get this one memory out of his head. Audrey'd been maybe six and it was before The Fall. Before Xterminate, before any of it.

He was eight and playing with his friends in the backyard. He'd already told her to go away but instead she just went over to the swing set and started swinging, staring longingly at him and his buddies where they were playing armies by the back fence.

Little sisters were so *annoying*, he remembered thinking.

He'd been climbing a tree when all the sudden she started up an unholy wailing. Just looking for attention, like always. He shook his head and ignored her, climbing higher.

But she just kept crying, louder and louder until she was screaming bloody murder. He kept waiting for Dad to come out of the garage and take care of it, but he must have had that stupid old rock music he liked playing. And Dad *had* made him promise to look out for his sister for the afternoon.

So with a huff, he climbed down from the tree and went over to the swing set, face flaming in embarrassment at having his friends see him have to deal with his sister who was such a freaking *baby*. She was six but here she was wailing her head off like a two-year-old.

She was even laying on the ground by the swing set, like she'd thrown herself on the ground to throw a full out tantrum.

"Come on, Audrey," he muttered as soon as he got close. She just wailed even louder. He rolled his eyes and knelt down on the ground beside her. Her face was cherry red and fat tears ran down her cheeks.

"Audrey, stop crying." He hated it when she cried. It was loud and well... he just didn't like it. "Come on, sit up." He held out a hand and hiccupping, she took it. He put his other hand to the back of her head and helped her sit up.

"All right. You're okay now. Calm down. It's okay."

And then he pulled his hand away from the back of her head.

It was covered in blood.

Like, *covered.*

Blood dripped off his fingers, even.

Charlie's stomach cramped just at the memory. He'd been playing with his friends, having *fun,* and she'd been lying there, seriously hurt. Crying—no, *screaming* for him—and he'd just ignored it, for what? Five minutes?

The sound of those screams kept him awake at night. Filling the silence of his office prison.

Look out for your sister.

His Dad had made him promise the same thing he had so long ago when the bad times came. *No matter what happens to me, look out for your sister.* And Charlie had sworn, *sworn,* both to his dad and to himself, that he would never fail her again like he had that day in the backyard.

But he had. And ten thousand times worse.

Because whatever she was going through right now, wherever she was, wouldn't be solved by a trip to the emergency room and twelve stitches to the back of the head.

And he was stuck in this fifteen-by-ten-foot room, fucking *useless.* She was out there, with God knew what happening to her, screaming and screaming for his help and he couldn't get to her—

"Let *go* of me. This is for the prisoner!"

Shay.

Charlie jerked to attention and ran to the door, ankle fetters yanking taut and tripping him halfway there. He hit his knees hard but then stumbled back to his feet and scrambled to the door.

It was almost dark out now but there was a single candle burning in the hallway of the alcove. Charlie got to the window just in time to see the big, bald guard who sometimes patrolled yank the tray of food out of Shay's hand and then backhand her.

"No!" Charlie roared, pounding the door with his fist. "Shay!"

Her body was knocked to the ground where she lay crumpled like a ragdoll. "Shay!"

The bald bastard nudged her with his big, booted toe, then chuckled and walked off, tray in hand.

Charlie was about to pound at the door again but fisted his hands and bit back his curse. Because goddammit, he didn't want to do anything to bring the guard back.

Yet again, he was fucking useless. Another woman he cared about was laying out there hurt and he was here, just feet away, and he couldn't do a goddamned *thing* to help her.

As soon as the guard's footsteps were gone, he dropped to his knees to look through the tray slot.

"Shay. Shay! Can you hear me? Are you okay?"

But she just laid there.

Fucking lifeless.

Fuck. *FUCK.*

Charlie grabbed at his hair, wanting to yank it out by the roots and—

But then he heard a noise.

The smallest groan.

"Shay!" He smashed his face to the hole in the wall and thank God. She was moving. He shoved his fingers through the small slot. "Shay, Jesus, are you okay?"

What the fuck, obviously she's not okay.

"Sorry, that's stupid. Can you sit up?"

She rolled over and dragged her body farther into the little alcove where the office was, out of the path of the main hallway.

When she finally sat up, he expected tears. He expected a bitter grimace. He even expected to see blood.

And she did have a fresh split lip, blood trickling down from the corner of her mouth.

But what he didn't expect?

For her to be fucking smiling.

She was grinning. Huge.

"Shay?" Charlie asked uncertainly. "Are you feeling okay? He hit you pretty hard."

When a small giggle escaped her lips, Charlie really started getting worried. But then she hopped to her feet.

And when she came near, there was a light in her eyes he'd never seen before.

"Shay, what's going—"

"I know where Audrey is."

Charlie coughed in shock, hand going to the plexiglass. "Where? Is she okay? Who has h—"

"Back up." Shay gestured impatiently for him to move back.

He frowned, totally fucking bewildered.

"Back *up*."

He took a couple steps away from the door.

That's when her grin got even wider, though he wouldn't have thought that was possible. And, with one quick glance back toward the hallway, she produced a keyring, holding it up briefly so he could see through the plexiglass.

Holy sh—

He didn't even have time to finish the thought before he heard the click of the lock turning. Then the door pushed open.

He could only stare in shock as Shay slipped inside. Her dark head was bowed as she flipped through keys on the keyring. Then she reached for his hands.

"Shay," he gasped. "How did you—"

She didn't look up from unlocking the shackles around his wrists. "I stole them off Carl when he was grabbing for the tray. I'd scrounged up some butter for your bread and made sure to pass by him. I knew he wouldn't be able to resist."

"But he *hit* you."

Shay just shrugged it off as if it was nothing. She got his wrists free and then dropped to his feet. The sight of her, crouched down at his feet, was just too much.

"Shay, Shay, stop."

Charlie leaned down and put his hands on hers, taking the keys.

Those endless green eyes of hers flashed. "I know where Audrey is. And I'll tell you. Better yet, I'll take you there." Then her face went flinty with determination. "As long as you help me get the hell out of here."

He felt his eyebrows shoot to his hairline. This woman was full of surprises. But everything she was saying was music to his fucking ears.

"You've got a deal." He'd protect her. Yes, they'd only recently met, but he was *not* going to let her down.

In another half minute, he had the shackles off his feet. The chains dropped to the floor and he stood fully upright for the first time in three months.

Then he reached out a hand to Shay.

"Let's go."

———

Continue reading to enjoy an extended preview of Theirs to Pleasure, the next book in the Marriage Raffle Series

(Chapter 1 is the epilogue you just read 😊 So we're just starting at chapter 2)

CHAPTER 2

CHARLIE

"Get your hands off me," Charlie roared as the giant with the scar down his face wrestled his arms painfully behind his back and shoved him forward. After all they'd done to get here to Jacob's Well? "Shay! Shay, are you okay?"

They'd escaped Travisville and traveled all night on a stolen four-wheeler to get here—not to mention walking the last two miles when the four-wheeler ran out of gas—and now these motherfuckers were going to treat them like *this*?

Charlie strained to look over his shoulder at Shay. Another soldier in dark fatigues led Shay forward with a hand at the small of her back. How dare the bastard fucking touch her?

"It's okay, Charlie," Shay said, hurrying up to his side. "Trust me. Everything's going to be okay."

How the hell could she say that? They were met with hostility almost the second they'd arrived at the Central Texas South border five minutes ago.

Charlie asked about his sister and one of the guards radioed it in on a walkie talkie.

Then, *bam*, next thing Charlie knew, he was eating dirt with a knee in his back and his arms wrenched behind him. Bastard had him zip tied in thirty seconds.

If only Charlie weren't so damn weak from three months in that prison... He'd tried to work out back in the cell when he had the energy so if he ever had the chance at escape, he'd be strong enough to make the most of it, but still. Some days he was living on what had to be maybe eight hundred calories a day if that and others they didn't bring him any food at all.

How the hell was he supposed to protect Shay if he couldn't hold his own against some prepubescent guard with more muscles than brain cells? But that was how it went, wasn't it? When it counted, he always failed at protecting the people he cared about.

Then he had to endure the humiliating experience of being thrown on the guard's horse to be taken into town with a black bag over his head. At least before everything went dark, he'd seen the other guard helped Shay on his horse in a decently respectful manner. But relying on the chivalry of a stranger in a strange town was not what Charlie had in mind when he'd vowed to protect Shay.

There was nothing to do other than stew furiously about it while he was jostled ruthlessly up and down on the back of the horse for the ride into town, though. Finally they stopped in front of a building that turned out to be some kind of security headquarters.

That was where this dickhead with the face scar had taken over.

When Charlie demanded to see his sister, the guy totally lost his shit. He shoved Charlie up against the wall by his throat.

It was only Shay's screaming that stopped the crazy bastard from choking him to death. Then another man stepped up and said the Commander should decide what to do with them. So the scarred guy —*Nix*, Charlie heard someone call him—let go of Charlie's throat only long enough to start marching him across the street and town square into what looked to be an old courthouse.

People in the street all stopped to stare.

As soon as they got in the building, a man's voice echoed off the granite walls. "—the rules apply to every woman who enters the township."

"What if I said I was a lesbian?" an angry woman's voice challenged.

There was a pause. Then, "Are you?"

Another long pause. "Yes. Yes, I *am*. So no matter how long you give me to *acclimate*," the word came out acidic, "to the idea as you call it, it would still be rape. No matter what."

What in the holyo fuck was going on in this place? Even the huge oaf dragging him around had paused in the corridor outside the door as the shouting continued.

Charlie's eyes shot to Shay. Some woman in there was talking about being raped. Coming here had been a bad idea. He never should have risked it. He was so blinded with excitement about seeing his sister again and Shay had been convinced it would be a safe place. But they were obviously so, so wrong.

"You're being impossible."

"Me?" the woman sounded absolutely enraged. "I was the commander of a sovereign territory and you brought me here against my will. Now you try to impose your *barbaric* polygamic practices on me, and *I'm* impossible? This is all bullshit nonsense anyway. What we need to be discussing is organizing a rescue mission to go back for the rest of the women still being held at Nomansland—"

Charlie's whole body jolted. They knew about Nomansland?

"I told you, I've put the request in to President Goddard multiple times. But he doesn't feel it's a priority at this time considering our limited resources—"

"Not a *priority*?" the woman all but roared.

"We'll be out here all fucking day if we wait for these two to stop," Nix said, rolling his eyes and knocking. Without waiting for a response, he pushed the door slightly open and said loudly, "Bad time?"

He slid it open wider, revealing a woman with long blonde dreadlocks standing toe to toe with a tall, distinguished looking man who was dressed in similar military fatigues as the guards.

"I was just leaving," the woman said, still glaring at the man for another long second before turning on her toe with a grand flip of her rope-like hair.

She stormed past them, only pausing when she noticed Shay. "Oh. Hi. This bastard gives you any trouble," her eyes flicked back toward the man by the big oak desk, "you come find me."

"Drea," the man said sharply, but the blonde just squeezed Shay's arm and then left without a backward glance.

The man by the table sighed heavily and waved them in. "What is it now?"

He stood up straighter when Shay moved out from behind Nix, though. "Oh. Hello. I'm Commander Wolford."

He smiled and walked toward Shay like there was nothing at all unusual in the world.

"Don't you fuckin' touch her," Charlie snarled, yanking to get away from the big ape who had a tighter hold on him than ever.

The Commander leveled a glare over Charlie's shoulder, presumably at Nix. "Who is this? What's he done?"

"He's a stranger. He showed up at the border today asking about Audrey. Claiming he was her brother." He jerked one of Charlie's arms up and back in a way that almost had his bone snapping. "Her *dead* brother. The only fucker who'd even know her name and to say he was her brother would be her fucking cousin, who tried to—"

Charlie jerked his head around to look at Nix, his eyes wide. "She's here?" Jesus, it was true. She was really here. He hadn't let himself really believe it. But the only way Nix could have known any of what he'd just said was if Audrey was really here.

"I *am* her brother," Charlie said. "That day by the spring when we were attacked. I was hit over the head and the last thing I saw was those bastards going for her. Is she okay?" The man had relaxed his grip on Charlie but his face was impassive. "Just tell me if she's okay," Charlie demanded.

"She's fine," the Commander said from behind him.

Charlie swung around. "I'll believe it when I see it. Where is she? Take me to her. Now."

"You're in no position to be making demands," came the growl from behind him.

"Oh yeah?" Charlie challenged. He was tired of this bastard's attitude. "And who the hell are you to even get a say in it?"

"I'm the Security Squadron Captain. And her husband."

Her... *what?*

"You son of a bitch," Charlie yelled and launched himself at the larger man even though his hands were still zip tied behind his back.

He hit a solid wall of muscle and all but bounced off. Motherf— As soon as he got his strength back, he'd—

"Nix," the Commander snapped. "Enough. Go get Audrey. You know how happy she'll be to see her brother's alive."

"*If* he's her brother." Nix glared at Charlie.

"Well the quickest way to find out would be to go get Audrey, wouldn't it?"

Nix's mouth went tight but he finally sent a sharp nod in the Commander's direction. He didn't leave before directing a harsh, "Watch him," to the other guard, though.

"What the hell is going on here?" Charlie moved further into the room toward the Commander. "That woman when we came in. She was talking about polygamy and rape and now I find out my sister has a *husband* after only three months."

The Commander let out a heavy sigh and put a hand to his temple. "We live in a new world. Things couldn't go on as they were or—"

"Look," Shay said, cutting in and stepping between the Commander and Charlie, eyes on Charlie. "I probably should have clued you in to a few things before we got here. Then again, we were escaping Travis Territory on a four-wheeler and didn't exactly stop for snacks or to chat along the way, so..." she lifted her shoulders in a help-less little shrug.

"What?" Charlie took a step toward Shay. "What aren't you telling me?"

"Charlie! Oh my God!"

Charlie whipped around. Audrey. The relief of seeing her safe and healthy made him stagger a step backward. She came running toward him, a huge, disbelieving grin stretched across her face.

She flung herself at him, wrapping her arms around him. "How? You were dead! The blood. There was so much blood!"

Then she pulled back, face stricken. "Oh my God. You weren't dead and I just *left* you there. Oh God, Charlie. How can you ever— Oh my God, why are your arms tied behind your back. Nix, cut him loose. He's my brother!"

Nix did as she said and Charlie didn't even take a swing at him, that's how relieved he was to see his sister again. He pulled her back into his arms, shuddering with relief.

"Hush." He pulled her back into his arms. *Jesus*. After all this time, she was safe. She was here and she was safe. He hadn't failed her completely. She was alive. Unless he was dreaming. Oh God don't let this be a dream.

"Are you real?" she whispered and he laughed.

"I was just wondering the same thing."

She giggled against his chest and it was the most wonderful sound he'd ever heard in his life.

He pulled back just so he could get another look at her. It had only been three months but she seemed so changed. She wasn't as skinny for one. Her cheeks were rounded out. And her hair looked... softer, or something.

And well, she was smiling. Like she couldn't stop. And Charlie didn't think it was an act for the other people in the room. Audrey never could act for shit. She'd done a play when she was in Jr. High and it was so painful he felt the audience cringing around him during her speaking parts.

But that was part of what made Audrey Audrey.

"Jesus, where are my manners?" Charlie ran a hand through his hair. "Audrey, this is Shay. She helped me escape and get here." He ushered Shay forward.

Shay held out her hand but Audrey threw her arms around her just like she had Charlie. "Thank you, thank you, thank you, *thank you*. You've won a devotee for life."

"So the border patrol agents said you claimed to have come from Travis Territory. That you were detained there against your wishes?" the Commander broke in.

Charlie nodded absentmindedly, still too focused on his sister.

"Yes," Shay answered, and Charlie realized the Commander had been speaking to her all along.

"And I always heard talk about this place," she continued. "No one watches what they say in front of the help. So I knew you treated your women well here. And I don't have a problem with the lottery system. I just want a place where I can finally be safe."

The Commander's face softened but Charlie could only look back and forth between them in confusion. What in the holy fuck were they talking about? "Lottery? What is she talking about?"

"Charlie, calm down," Audrey said, putting a hand on his forearm. "Just give them a second to explain. It sounds bad at first, I know it does, but it can actually turn out really—"

Why were they all suddenly acting like a bomb was about to detonate?

"What. Is. She. Talking. About?"

"It's a lottery to see who I'll marry," Shay said calmly.

Charlie all but choked, sure at first he'd misheard her.

But then she went on. "There aren't enough women to go around anymore. Everybody knows that. So Central Texas South Territory came up with a solution. Each woman marries five men. The only way for it to be fair is to have a lott—"

"No fucking way." Charlie's head whipped around to his sister. "Aud. Tell me you didn't."

Audrey's face was screwed up in that way she did when she used to come home with a bad report card she knew would disappoint her parents. Fuckin' hell.

"Look, Char, it sounds worse than it is. Once you get to know the guys themselves, you'll understand. They have protections in place. Not just anyone can enter the lotto."

"You don't believe that," Charlie scoffed. "You're a shit liar. Why are you protecting them, Aud? Are they holding you here against your will? Cause I'll—"

"No," Audrey breathed out loudly in frustration. "Okay, look, I still have some reservations about the whole thing. My husbands treat me like a queen but there was one case of abuse discovered recently."

Charlie's jaw tightened and all he wanted to do was grab Shay and Audrey, steal one of the trucks he'd seen outside, and get the hell *out* of here.

"But we've cracked down on the vetting process since then," the Commander broke in. "It's more rigorous than ever. Any man raises a hand against a woman, he loses the hand and then is exiled."

"Oh yeah? Did that happen to whoever abused that woman?"

The Commander's gaze stayed rock steady. "Yes, it did. To four of the husbands. Unfortunately, the crowd got to the fifth before we could. Jacob's Well does not tolerate mistreatment of women."

"No, you just treat them like objects to raffle off with no say in the matter. They're human beings," Charlie said incredulously. He couldn't believe he was having to explain this fucking concept. "They have the right to choose how they live their lives. Who they live their lives with. You can't just—"

"You think *you* can solve all the world's problems?" the Commander cut him off, obviously out of patience. "You want to restore law and order in the midst of anarchy?" He held out a hand. "Go right ahead. Be my guest. This is the best we can do in imperfect circumstances.

But your own sister has found happiness here. And so have a lot of other people."

"This is what I want," Shay said, stepping forward again. "But I've seen enough in my life not to just take some stranger's word for it, okay? So let's wait a little bit before we pass judgement. Take a look around. Meet everyone."

Charlie nodded. Good. So she'd call a stop to this nonsense as soon as she saw for herself how insane—

"I want protection I trust. Which is why I'll only agree to a lottery if it's for four husbands," her eyes flicked his way, "with Charlie as the fifth."

Wait.

WHAT?

CHAPTER 3

SHAY

Shay clocked the exits as she followed Sophia, the Commander's eighteen-year-old daughter, to the room where Shay was supposed to sleep for the night. In the Commander's own house.

"Oh my gosh, I'm just *so* excited you're here," Sophia said, clapping in excitement. "We haven't had a new girl in ages. Well," she rolled her eyes. "There was Drea, but she barely counts."

Drea. The name was familiar. Oh right, she was the woman they'd overheard arguing with the Commander when they'd been first brought into the courthouse.

"I don't think that woman would understand the concept of fun if it walked up and bit her in the—" Sophia broke off, eyes going wide like she'd just realized what she was saying. "Oh, um. Anyway." She laughed and held out a hand, gesturing at the room. "*Ta da.*"

Shay glanced around. Wow. That was a lot of... pink. Sort of like a bottle of Pepto-Bismol had thrown up all over it.

They were on the second story. A quick glance showed the window wasn't barred. After Sophia left, Shay would check if there was a trellis or drain pipe she could climb down if need be. If the last eight years had taught her anything, it was to always have an escape route ready. "Nice place."

Sophia laughed. "It's atrocious. You don't have to pretend. The style of my eight-year-old princess-loving self is going to haunt me forever, seems like. But it's a waste of resources to repaint and redecorate when so many other homes need *actual* repair so..." she held out her arms, eyebrows scrunched, "welcome to my pink palace...?"

Shay pulled her lips up at the side in what she hoped passed for a smile. That looked natural, right? She hadn't been around... well, *people*... in a long time.

And this girl was a little *too* bubbly and friendly. In Travisville, they had girls like her to greet any new female arrivals who were brought in. *Welcome, welcome. You're finally safe. Travisville is a wonderful place to make your new home!*

Then—after the girls were fed and back in good health—came the bait and switch. They were sold off to the highest bidder, often after six months of 'training' at the processing center.

Jacob's Well wasn't supposed to be that kind of place.

Then again, neither was Travisville. Officially, at least. Slavery was illegal in the new Republic of Texas, but that had never stopped anyone in Travisville. Especially Colonel Travis himself, who had a reputation as the best flesh trader in Texas. Among certain circles at least.

Then again, it was from the higher ups in Travisville that she'd overheard the rumors about Jacob's Well. And since the monsters there didn't like the Commander here—and that was putting it mildly —that only said good things for him. Colonel Travis himself and the Commander were enemies. Apparently it was personal, too, though she'd never heard the whole story.

But Colonel Travis's temper was legendary and he didn't make a secret of his animosity for Jacob's Well's Commander.

And the enemy of my enemy is my friend, right?

She wasn't the naïve girl she'd once been, though. She didn't trust anyone in this township farther than she could throw them.

Which, considering how large the border guards and that huge scarred man, Nix, had been, wasn't very far at all.

So how come all she wanted right now was to run downstairs and throw herself in Charlie's arms?

You don't know that he's any better than anyone else in Travisville was. Not really. Bringing him a few meals here and there didn't mean she *knew* him.

Yeah, they'd been helping each other... but escaping had been in his own interest. It wasn't about her at all. They'd used each other. Plain and simple.

Still, even as she thought it, it felt wrong.

She'd decided a long time ago that the only thing she could ever trust from another person was that they'd always be looking out for their own self-interest.

But Charlie... if he was just looking out for himself, then why did he object so much to the marriage thing? It was the perfect opportunity if he wanted to fuck her.

Then again, he *had* been trying to get her to leave Jacob's Well almost as soon as they'd gotten there. Maybe he wanted her all to himself and didn't like the idea of sharing?

Again, the thought felt wrong though.

Maybe it was the way he'd followed her directions so unquestioningly as they'd snuck off the old college campus where he'd been kept prisoner in Travisville. She was so used to Jason grabbing her elbow and jerking her back if she took even a step ahead of him on the rare occasions when they walked anywhere together.

Stay at my back, bitch. Who do you think you are? Bitches walk at their master's heels.

But Charlie had just waited patiently for each whispered direction as she led him down to the river. It had been a new moon last night, so there'd barely been any ambient light. Just the little bit from the few buildings powered by solar panels whose batteries had been charging all day.

When Charlie took her arm, Shay had almost jumped out of her skin. But his touch had been gentle. He was reaching for her so *she* could lead *him*.

She couldn't remember the last time someone had touched her without it being—

A knock came at the door and then Audrey peeked her head in. "Hey guys."

"Hey hon." Sophia's face brightened, which Shay would have said was impossible just a minute before. Shay'd never met anyone so damn... *smiley*. And she had been in a sorority back in college before The Fall, so that was saying something.

"You and Charlie been reconnecting?" Sophia asked.

Audrey nodded with a wobbly grin and a sheen of tears coating her eyes. "I just can't believe he's really here. That he didn't— That he's—"

"Oh honey." Sophia jumped up from where she'd been perched on the edge of the bed and hurried over to her friend, wrapping her up in a hug.

Shay felt awkward and out of place watching the affection between the two friends. Everything since breaking Charlie out of his cell had felt a little like a movie—like she was outside her body watching all these things happen without really being part of any of it.

If she closed her eyes, she'd wake up in the little broom closet where she slept. It would be another day of arduous and never-ending routine.

Cooking. Cleaning. And waiting—always waiting in case *he* felt in the mood to call for her. Jason liked her to be at his beck and call, any time of day or night. Sometimes for himself, sometimes to entertain friends...

But God, she was being such a fucking princess about the whole thing. She'd had it so much easier than most women in Travisville. She'd never seen the inside of the Women's Processing Center. She hadn't been sold off to some stranger as a sex slave.

Back in the beginning, when she was just a stupid, stupid girl, she'd even given herself to Jason willingly. He'd been handsome, charismatic...

So who could she blame except herself for everything that followed?

She was too old to have been that naïve—nineteen when the bombs were dropped. That was old enough to have recognized Jason for the psychopath he was.

The strong will always take advantage of the weak.

It was one of the most basic facts of life. But she'd been stubbornly walking around like a romantic little fool. She might as well have painted a target on her back announcing: Stupid and Desperate: Please Take Advantage Of.

Love will conquer all, she had told herself in the beginning. And later, she thought, *my love can change him*. It was far too late when she realized that he'd never change and finally understood that fighting back was futile.

But she'd helped Charlie escape. She was here, in Jacob's Well, wasn't she? She'd really done it. Those weren't things a weak person did.

Maybe, just maybe, she could wrestle back some control over her own life. One way or another, this was a new chapter. It all depended on what she made of the opportunity.

"And you," Audrey said. Shay looked up to see Charlie's sister coming toward her, arms outstretched. "Oh my God, I can never thank you enough."

Before Shay could really register what was happening, Audrey had her wrapped in a hug so tight Shay had a hard time breathing. "Charlie told me how brave you were. How you risked everything to get him out of there." She squeezed even tighter for a moment before pulling back and looking Shay in the eye. Tears spilled down Audrey's cheeks, but her smile was so wide and full of gratitude, Shay immediately wanted to jerk away.

These people didn't know her. If they did, they wouldn't like what they saw. She wasn't a good person.

But that was fine, she'd made her peace with the fact a long time ago. She did what she needed to do in order to get by and to take care of what needed taking care of. Freeing Charlie had just been a means to an end, not something she'd done out of the kindness of her heart.

"It was nothing," she mumbled, pulling back.

But Audrey just scoffed. "You gave my brother back to me from the dead! That's not nothing."

"Yeah, well." Shay tried for a smile and lifted a hand to the back of her neck, grabbing her hair and twisting it into a loose bun before securing it with a hair band Sophia lent her. "No big deal."

"She's modest, Audrey, leave her be," Sophia said. "Besides, the real question is who's gonna be chosen in her lottery. I saw Daddy leaving about twenty minutes ago. They could be drawing the names right this moment." She clapped excitedly. "Who do you think would be a good match for her?" she asked Audrey. "You've been here long enough to get a feel for the town."

But Audrey just laughed and held her hands up in surrender. "I leave that to the town gamblers and the romantics. All right, I've got to head out. Nix gets grumpy when he doesn't have a warm body to snuggle up to at night."

"Swoon," Sophia said with a longing little sigh, holding her hands to her chest. "I want a Nix."

Audrey laughed. "Hands off. He's all mine."

Sophia rolled her eyes. "I don't want *your* Nix. I want *a* Nix. Someone strong and manly and capable like him." She made a little squee noise and hopped up and down. "Just four months away from my nineteenth birthday now. I can barely sleep some nights I'm so excited!"

Audrey just shook her head good naturedly and dropped a kiss to Sophia's forehead. "Take care, sweetie." She looked to Shay, her gaze warm. "So good to meet you. I'm sure we'll see a lot of each other." Her smile broadened. "A little birdie told me we're about to be sisters-in-law, after all."

Shay nodded, again attempting what she hoped came off as a natural smile. She'd just gotten away from one controlling man. And here she was, marrying five more.

But it was all part of the plan.

And it *wouldn't* be the same. Not at all. She wasn't the naïve girl she'd been eight years ago when Jason first walked into town. She'd learned the lessons that had been beaten into her and she'd learned them well.

She'd be the strong one now.

And she could give them her body, that was nothing. She'd given it a hundred times before. The difference was, this time it was *her* doing the giving, not Jason. And that was everything.

Plus, in return she'd gain everything she'd ever wanted. *Family*. It was the only thing worth fighting for in this shitastic world. She was done with being alone. Nobody could survive alone, not for long.

"So," Sophia said after Audrey left, pulling out a big binder and a purple glitter pen. "Let's make a list of potentials and then we can put down pros and cons for each of them."

When Shay just kept standing there, Sophia waved her forward again as she settled in on the bed, back against the plush pink headboard. "Come on, silly."

Sophia's forehead scrunched in concentration. "All right. There's Sebastian, he's the town's chief engineer." She glanced up at Shay and smiled, one eyebrow lifting. "He's handsome. And smart. That's two in the pros column already for him. And, let me think. Oh! Ryder. He's the blacksmith, and just between you and me," she leaned in, "I've daydreamed about those huge muscles of his more than once."

Shay shook her head and laughed. See, she could pull off being a normal girl. No problem.

"Oh my God," Sophia said, pulling back. "I can't believe I forgot about Diego! He supervises all Central Texas South's construction crews. He's tall, has the most gorgeous black hair, and—"

As Sophia went on, scribbling names and attributes about man after man, Shay could only think about one. Charlie. If Audrey and her husband, Nix, had finally left, did that mean Charlie was downstairs all alone?

Was he thinking about her? Or was he just happy to be reunited with his sister? She knew she'd taken him by surprise demanding that he be one of her husbands.

That had *not* been in the plan.

You don't really *know him*, she reminded herself for the umpteenth time. *He's no more trustworthy than any other man.*

But he'd seemed so concerned about her, staying close the whole time they snuck from the college down to the river. He'd helped her down the river bank and gestured her to get in the river first, holding out a thick branch to make sure she didn't get swept away too quickly. Even as they floated the few miles down river, he'd make sure to always stay within a few feet of her. And when they reached the small damn that marked the border of Travisville? Without a word, he'd been the one to sneak onto the river bank and take out the guard there, securing them the four-wheeler they'd ridden all the way to Central Texas South's border, right at Jacob's Well.

He hadn't minded the fact that she'd climbed on and taken the controls.

She'd been relying on a map she'd overseen, along with her memories of the area from long ago. Shay had lived in Travisville for almost a decade, and she knew it like the back of her hand. Back before The Fall, she used to drive all over the hill country in the area because she loved the views.

But Charlie hadn't known that. He'd just climbed on the four-wheeler behind her and wrapped his strong, steady arms around her waist in complete trust.

Maybe it was that he reminded her of how she used to be. A thousand years ago... And it made her want to smack him and shout, "Wake up!" before the world crushed him.

She shook her head and looked toward the window. It was still dark out. What time was it? Ten or eleven at night?

"I think I'm going to try to get some sleep," she said, cutting Sophia off mid-sentence as she listed another guy.

"Oh of course, I'm sorry. You must be exhausted and here I am rattling on." Sophia immediately hopped off the bed. "I just get so carried away. Like I said, we don't get a new girl very often." She paused, tilted her head to the side, and grinned at Shay. "I'm just *so* happy you're here."

Shay shrank a little under Sophia's intense consideration. "Yeah. Um. Me too..."

Sophia grinned even wider and Shay's face hurt just looking at her but then Sophia was bouncing over and throwing her arms around her. Shay went immediately stiff but Sophia just kept on squeezing.

Finally Sophia pulled back, laughing. "Sorry, I'm a hugger. Dad's always trying to remind me of a little thing called *personal space* but I usually only remember after I've violated it."

"No, it's fine," Shay said, voice as stiff as her spine.

"Oh good," Sophia said. "Because you know how sometimes you

just have so much happiness and excitement pent up in you and it just has to come out somehow?"

Shay could only stare at the girl and blink. "Um..."

But Sophia just laughed again and pulled her into another hug. It was much quicker, though. Thankfully.

"Sleep tight," Sophia said as she pulled back. "Don't let the bedbugs bite. And just think, tomorrow you'll get to meet your new husbands. So exciting!"

And on that ecstatic utterance, Sophia flounced out of the room.

Leaving Shay feeling a little shell-shocked. While she'd prepared herself for a lot of different scenarios on this little adventure, she could genuinely say that Sophia Wolford was something she'd never expected.

Shay thought she'd feel relieved to be alone. It was the first moment of solitude she'd had since before she'd broken Charlie out. But instead, the room felt... too quiet.

She glanced at the door Sophia had exited through and immediately hurried over, trying the knob. It turned easily and when she pulled on the door, it gave with no problem.

So she wasn't locked in. Okay. Good. Her hammering heartbeat slowed, but only marginally. She went back to the bed and changed into the sleep clothes Sophia had laid out for her—an oversized shirt and some short girly boxers with hearts on them.

After changing, she sat on the bed, back against the headboard, eyes darting around at every little sound.

Sophia said her father was out conducting the lottery right now. What if Shay's new *husbands* decided they didn't want to wait for tomorrow and came for her in the middle of the night?

Yes, she was committed to seeing this through—but only on *her* terms.

When had any man she'd ever known been willing to let her have anything on her terms, though? Never. Not in recent memory.

Except for one.

So before she fully realized what she was doing, she was bolting for the door and down the stairs.

Charlie might be naïve but he was strong. Even after losing weight from not having a normal diet, she'd seen him working out in his cell regularly. He'd taken out that guard at the dam like it was nothing. And she'd felt it when he'd wrapped his arms around her on the four-wheeler.

And in a world where she didn't trust anyone, for some reason, she trusted that he genuinely wanted to protect her.

Foolish probably.

Even after all these years, maybe she hadn't learned her lesson after all.

CHAPTER 4

CHARLIE

10 MINUTES EARLIER

"So, you just, what?" Nix asked Charlie, eyes hard. "Up and walked out of Travis's camp? Just like that?"

Charlie's jaw was so rigid, he was sure he was about to crack a damn tooth. Reconnecting with Audrey had been more than he could have ever dreamed of.

Except.

Except for the fact that her damn *husband* had been breathing down their necks the whole time. Charlie had only had a few minutes alone with his sister when they first got to the Commander's house. Nix and the Commander were stopped outside by another soldier in fatigues to discuss something. Charlie dragged Audrey into the house and asked in a rush, "Aud, tell me the truth. Are they holding you against your will? Because I swear, I can get you out. We'll find a w—"

"What?" She'd sounded flabbergasted. "Charlie, no. I love my life here. I love my husbands."

Husbands. Fucking *plural*. Charlie flinched when she'd said it but she just kept repeating that once he got to know her husbands, he'd understand.

Well, he'd spent all evening with the son of a bitch currently sitting across the living room from him, Nix, and he was no less tempted to murder him. The whole time Audrey sat on the couch opposite Charlie, the fucker had kept a hand on her knee, rubbing circles with his thumb. And every time his thumb traveled in that little looping path, Charlie fantasized ways of killing him. He could use the fire poker. Or there was that carving knife he'd seen in the kitchen. Really there were all sorts of things he could use as a weapon. A man could get inventive with enough motive and Charlie, he was motivated.

"Seems awful convenient to me, you just showing up out of the blue like this."

Charlie shot up out of the armchair where he'd been sitting. "You got something you wanna say, just say it."

Nix stood up too and took a step toward him. "I'm saying your story sounds like bullshit. I know Arnold Travis and no way you just walked out of the center of his encampment."

"I never said I was in the center." Charlie's eyes narrowed. "What the fuck do *you* know that you're not saying?"

Nix scoffed like Charlie was an idiot. "I'm the Captain of the Security Squadron. It's my business to know about the layout of our chief rival's town."

"Oh yeah? Just like it was your business to fuck my sister and brainwash her into thinking she's happy here?"

"You better watch your mouth." Nix jabbed a finger his direction, "before I shut it permanently."

"Aw, what's wrong? I'm not a vulnerable, impressionable young girl, so you can't mind-fuck me, is that it?"

"You son of a—"

Right as Nix started toward Charlie, Audrey came bounding down the stairs. "Hey guys, I'm ready to—" She paused on the last step, eyes shooting back and forth from Nix to Charlie. "What's going on? Is something wrong?"

Nix's face, which had been hard with menace only moments ago, turned suddenly soft as he looked at Audrey. "No problem, babe. Your brother and I were just getting to know each other better."

Audrey's head swung Charlie's way, like she was looking for confirmation. Charlie could see by the hope in her eyes that she wanted what Nix had said to be true. And if he was going to help her, he needed her to trust him. He couldn't alienate her right out of the gate. It would take time to see what sort of conditioning they'd done to her so he could figure out how to *undo* it.

"Yep. He used to be a big Cowboys fan. Just like Dad." Charlie slapped Nix on the shoulder a little harder than was strictly necessary. "Say, Nix," Charlie looked over at him, "how old did you say you were again?"

"I didn't," Nix growled.

"Oh good," Audrey said, either missing the tension between them or choosing to ignore it. She pulled both of them into a group hug. "Now my family is complete," she breathed out happily, eyes closed in contentment.

Charlie and Nix just glared at each other over her head.

Then Nix put an arm over Audrey's shoulder. "Bedtime, wife." And he all but dragged her toward the door.

"Oh," Audrey said, and then giggled and swatted at his hand when he pinched her ass. Right there in front of Charlie. Fucking bastard.

"See you tomorrow, Charlie," Audrey called over her shoulder. Then she was gone, the door shutting behind her with a resounding *slam*.

Charlie dug his hands into his hair and pulled, leaning over to growl in frustration through clenched teeth. This was so goddamned infuriating. To be so close to his sister and then for her to be acting like, like...

He shook his head. He couldn't believe this was how he found her after all these months. Was he glad that she was healthy? Of course he was. But while she might be in great physical condition, her mental faculties were another story entirely.

What in the holy fuck had they *done* to her? Okay, so she had seemed normal enough all evening. Over dinner, she'd laughed and joked just like she was... well, the old Audrey.

But she couldn't be. She'd been married off to *five*... Jesus, he couldn't even wrap his head around it. And they thought they were gonna do the same thing to Shay? Over his dead fucking body.

His eyes went to the stairs. The house was quiet. He had no idea what time it was. It had been dark for hours. The Commander had gone out a while ago and who knew when he'd be back. Could Charlie sneak up there, grab Audrey, and get out, or were there soldiers on guard outside the house watching in case they tried to do just that?

I know it all seems weird and too good to be true, but it's real. Audrey's words from earlier came back to him. At which point he'd looked at her like she was crazy. One woman having to marry five guys was not his idea of 'too good to be true.' The fact that she was even saying that shit was worrisome. Then she went on, *I'm not saying it's perfect here or some kind of utopia, but these are good people.*

Yeah, well, he'd feel better with a knife strapped to his belt just the same. He slipped into the kitchen and looked through the knifes in the block on the counter. The butcher's knife might be a little bit overkill, but he grabbed it anyway, along with several smaller steak knives. He stowed the butcher's knife underneath the couch cushion and then made up the couch with the sheets and blankets Sophia had brought down earlier.

One knife he put under his pillow, the other underneath the couch, still easily accessible. Only then did he turn out the lights. He'd scope out the situation in the backyard in a few hours. If it was all clear, then he'd go get Shay. The bastards had shoved a black bag over his head on the way in to town, but they obviously had horses, and those shouldn't be that hard to find—

A noise had him sitting up straight and reaching for the knife under his pillow.

Until he saw the feminine figure coming down the stairs by the light of a single candle still burning on the mantle.

A feminine figure wearing only what looked like a long t-shirt.

Charlie gulped.

"Shay?" he whispered. When she didn't answer, for a second, he was horrified that it was the Commander's daughter coming to, like, seduce him or something.

But then Shay's soft voice came through the darkness. "It's me."

He relaxed but only for a moment. "You ready to get out of here? I haven't had a chance to scout the grounds yet, but if you just give me a second, I can check the yard and see if—"

"Shh," Shay said, coming and sitting down on the couch beside him. "Lay down." Tentatively, she extended a hand and touched his shoulder. Then she ran it down to his elbow. "I just..." she trailed off, pulling her hand back like she'd suddenly been burned. "It's stupid but..."

"What? What is it? Did something happen up there? I swear, Shay, I'll—"

"No, no, nothing like that."

Then she grabbed his hand and after another second, tentatively toyed with his fingers. Charlie's skin felt electric everywhere her skin touched his. And not just because she was a beautiful woman... or because of all the years it had been since touching a woman was even a possibility.

Touch from Shay seemed like a privilege. Every time she touched Charlie, he got the feeling it was a big step for her somehow. There was always a hesitancy to it, like she was proving something to herself or pushing a boundary.

So he kept his own hand slack, not wanting her to pull back like a skittish deer.

"I just didn't like being up there alone," she whispered it like she was confessing a personal failing. "I mean, I spent plenty of time alone in Travisville. But now that I'm here, it's different. I don't know how to explain." Her head twisted as she looked back and forth from the front door to the doorway that led to the kitchen."

Charlie was close enough to her that he felt the small shudder go through her body. She dropped her face. In the darkness he couldn't make out her features but he could imagine the distress on her lovely face.

"Do you think I could... I don't know. Maybe sleep with you down here tonight?"

"Oh." Charlie swallowed. The truth? Her being so close already had him fighting a stiffy. Which made him the world's biggest douchebag. Especially because as soon as she'd sat down in just that t-shirt, her long legs on display in the light of a sputtering candle on the mantle, he'd had the overwhelming thought: *she said she'll marry you. Which means you might get to have sex with her sometime soon.*

"Shay." He shook his head, shifting so he could sit up—but her hand shot back to his forearm to stop him. Her grip was so forceful it took him by surprise. This time when she looked at him, the angle was just right that her eyes caught and reflected the candlelight.

And he could see the fear there. Real, terrible fear. "Please. Can't we just lie here together tonight? Leave everything else till the morning?"

Her looking so afraid had taken care of his hard on at least. But it ripped his chest open to know terrible things had probably happened to her to put that fear there.

"Yes." He shook his head and laid back down, opening his arms. "Yes, of course. Whatever you need."

As she laid down, head in the crook of his arm and back against his chest, he vowed, "Always. Whatever you need, I'll always be here for you."

This was one vow he swore he would never break.

Charlie and Shay's book, Theirs to Pleasure, is AVAILABLE NOW

Want to read an EXCLUSIVE, FREE 45 page novelette, Their Honeymoon, about Audrey and her Clan's honeymoon that is available only to my newsletter subscribers, along with news about upcoming releases, sales, exclusive giveaways, and more?

Get *Their Honeymoon* by visiting
BookHip.com/QHCQDM

Have you missed any of the books in the
Marriage Raffle Series?

MARRIAGE RAFFLE SERIES
Theirs to Protect
Theirs to Pleasure
Their Bride
Theirs to Defy
Theirs to Ransom

ALSO BY STASIA BLACK

MARRIAGE RAFFLE SERIES

Theirs to Protect

Theirs to Pleasure

Their Bride

Theirs to Defy

Theirs to Ransom

BREAK SO SOFT SERIES

Cut So Deep

Break So Soft

Hurt So Good

STUD RANCH STANDALONE SERIES

The Virgin and the Beast: a Beauty and the Beast Tale (prequel)

Hunter: a Snow White Romance

The Virgin Next Door: a Ménage Romance

ACKNOWLEDGMENTS

Aimee Bowyer, beta reader extraordinaire! Thanks for saving my buns on this with the proofreading and your general fabulous feedback as always. You're encouragement meant an extra lot on this one because the story meant so much to me. Love that you connected with it as much as I did. HUGS!

Emily E— So great to have you on board as a beta. Omg, you're save on the wedding vows, I'm still slapping myself in the forehead for that one. Like, it's my big teaser now for the book, her saying, 'I do.' Fairly important, lol. Thanks so much for your enthusiasm for the book and coming on board :)

Melissa Pascoe—the more time we spend together, the more I rely on you. You are amazing, fantabulous, can't-live-without! Thank you so much for keeping my schedule straight and helping things stay hopping. *mwah*

Bobby and the crew in the master class at Butterfly Promotions, meeting ya'll has been a game changer. I bow down.

And thanks as always to super hubby. Love you forever.

ABOUT THE AUTHOR

STASIA BLACK grew up in Texas, recently spent a freezing five-year stint in Minnesota, and now is happily planted in sunny California, which she will never, ever leave.

She loves writing, reading, listening to podcasts, and has recently taken up biking after a twenty-year sabbatical (and has the bumps and bruises to prove it). She lives with her own personal cheerleader, aka, her handsome husband, and their teenage son. Wow. Typing that makes her feel old. And writing about herself in the third person makes her feel a little like a nutjob, but ahem! Where were we?

Stasia's drawn to romantic stories that don't take the easy way out. She wants to see beneath people's veneer and poke into their dark places, their twisted motives, and their deepest desires. Basically, she wants to create characters that make readers alternately laugh, cry ugly tears, want to toss their kindles across the room, and then declare they have a new FBB (forever book boyfriend).

Join Stasia's Facebook Group for Readers for access to deleted scenes, to chat with me and other fans and also get access to exclusive giveaways:
https://www.facebook.com/groups/StasiasBabes/

Printed in Great Britain
by Amazon

29153315R00209